A TIME FOR LOVING

The fire glowed a soft red, lighting the room in a roselike glow. As Shelby slowly stood up, her filmy nightgown revealed the shadowed form beneath it.

Brad could feel his heart begin to pound with a fierce beat. Shelby had always been breathtakingly beautiful to him, but this sight was beyond anything he had experienced before.

Shelby stood very still. He had to come to her. He had to. There was no other way he would believe.

Slowly, Brad walked across the room. He stopped so close that she had to look up at him. He put his hand against her cheek.

But Shelby could not surrender to this, not before Brad knew and believed how she felt. . . . and shared the very force she felt within her now, urging her into his arms.

She rested one hand against his chest. "I love you, Brad Cole, and if you have believed in anything in your life, believe in that. If you can't . . ." She inhaled a ragged breath. "Then please . . . don't touch me. Please don't just pretend."

"There's no room to pretend anymore," he whispered. "Shelby Vale, I want you more than I've wanted anything in my life."

She closed her eyes and waited for his kiss . . .

Sylvie F. Sommerfield

Song of the Heart

PINNACLE BOOKS
Windsor Publishing Corp.

PINNACLE BOOKS
WINDSOR PUBLISHING CORP.

*This book is dedicated to Taylor,
the brightest addition to my life.*

PINNACLE BOOKS are published by

Windsor Publishing Corp.
850 Third Avenue
New York, NY 10022

First Printing: March, 1995

Printed in the United States of America

Prologue

Charleston, 1870

Charleston Harbor gleamed silver in the early-morning light. The sun also caught the rainbowlike reflections through the lead glass doors and windows of the Stapleton mansion.

Within the study the mood was not as bright as the sunlight. Winter Stapleton glared at her stepmother and repeated with great anger the words she had just heard.

"You mean if I don't marry Carl James you would deliberately wreck Father's business?"

"My, you are always so blunt, Winter," Anne Stapleton said coolly. "I did not threaten you *or* your father. I simply said, if you didn't marry into the James wealth, I might be forced to withdraw my financial support from Joseph's affairs."

"That would ruin him, and you know it. His reverses have only been few. Give him some time. He will recoup any losses he's suffered and then you can do as you please."

"I'm afraid I don't choose to wait. I've already answered for you. You will marry Carl James within a few months. We don't want to rush, or people will think it unseemly. The engagement party will be held within the next two weeks."

"And if I don't?"

Anne Stapleton shrugged her shoulders and smiled enigmatically. "The choice is yours."

"My father will never stand for this. Once he knows how I feel he'll never permit the wedding."

"I don't doubt that for a minute. Joseph has always been too sentimental when it comes to you. But you won't tell him." Anne pursed her lips in pretend thoughtfulness. "Unless you have no regard for him at all. You see," her crystal-blue eyes pierced Winter with a cold look, "Your father is in a . . . temporary financial dilemma. He has overreached himself, and I," she smiled with a shrug, "am the only one with the capability to help. And I shall . . . if the circumstances are right. Of course, if I don't his situation will be very difficult time for a long, long time. Perhaps even permanently."

"If my father has no money, or he loses what he has, you'll lose, too."

"Hardly, my dear. I have planned for just such a contingency. Believe me, it will be your father who pays."

Anne walked toward the door, then paused and turned again to face Winter. "And I do believe it's time to tell your would-be lover, Gregg Phillips, that you'll not be seeing him again." She laughed at Winter's attempt to control the contempt and helpless anger she felt, and the defeat she couldn't hide. "You thought I didn't know that you had begun to think seriously about him? It's one of the reasons I'm insisting on this marriage. Because if you continue to see him, your father's disgrace will be the payment." Anne laughed. "My dear, I know every move you make. You'd best begin to plan what you will wear to your engagement party."

She opened the door and left, leaving Winter alone with her cheeks flushed with rage and her fury held in check by sheer determination. She knew she must choose her beloved father's life or her own. She looked up at the portrait that hung above Joseph's desk of a slender beauty with hair like corn silk, and eyes the color of spring violets. "Oh, Mother," she implored, "how I wish you were here. Father has not been the same since you died, and now this woman owns his very soul. What am I to do?"

She sighed resignedly. She knew what she had to do. Her father had suffered much in the past few years. First his shipping business had had severe losses, then her mother had died in a terrible accident that left him in a state of deep mourning. A mourning deep enough to make him vulnerable to an evil woman like Anne Marks, who, within a year, became her stepmother.

No, she could not let her father suffer any more than he already had.

She had deliberately kept her mind from tall and handsome, Gregg, who swore he loved her more than life. She would meet him one more time . . . to tell him she couldn't see him again, and of her coming wedding. With a bitter sigh, she left the study to find a sanctuary in her room to shed her tears alone.

The engagement party two weeks later turned into the affair of the season, and everyone gazed in awe at the huge emerald that weighted Winter's slender hand.

Gregg Phillips watched in angry frustration as the woman he loved to desperation danced by on the arm of the man she was now promised to marry. He was so frustrated he did not realize that Joseph Stapleton was standing beside him until he spoke.

"This indeed appears to be quite a mystery for both of us, Gregg." Gregg turned to look at Joseph's puzzled face as he watched his daughter. Even Gregg could see that he had aged a great deal in the past two years. Heavy worry lines surrounded the blue eyes.

"I don't understand." Gregg was desperate. "She just wouldn't listen to reason. Winter is as honest as the day is long. But one day she says she loves me, and the next that she's going to marry him. She doesn't understand men like him. She knows nothing of his reputation." Gregg's voice broke against his anguish.

"No, she doesn't, but *I* do. Maybe," Joseph said thoughtfully, "we can find the answer to this situation," he smiled grimly at Gregg, "before it's too late to put a stop to it." Gregg looked at him with a glow of hope in his eyes. "Come into my study, away from this . . . farce."

That night, Winter sat in her bedroom. Her mood was one of utter desolation. She was not aware that her door had opened and closed quietly. Joseph stood just inside the door and watched his daughter. For a moment he could envision the wife he had loved and lost, and with heartwrenching determination he assured himself he was not going to lose his daughter as well.

He could feel her despair. There was no doubt in his mind that some force was bending her to a will not her own. The thought left a bitter taste in his mouth and anger in his heart.

"Winter," he said gently.

As she spun about to face him, a quick smile lit her eyes. "Father, I didn't hear you come in."

"I can see you didn't. Your mind was a million miles away."

"Oh, just daydreaming." She tried to sound nonchalant, but he could see that she had been crying.

"Winter, I want to talk to you."

"Of course." She led him to a comfortable couch. "We have not had much time to talk lately. How are things with your business, Father?"

"The truth is, very bad at the moment. But there is a light at the end of the tunnel. The James family is so pleased about the coming wedding that, after it is a fait accompli they plan to invest a substantial sum."

That her eyes escaped his gaze was enough to tell

him that he'd struck the right point. The point he'd suspected.

"Winter," he said as he reached to take her hand. "What I just told you was not so. I just needed to confirm a suspicion I had."

"A suspicion?"

"Is this marriage happening against your will?"

"Against my will?"

"Stop repeating what I say while you look for an answer. Somehow, you are being forced into this wedding. I'm not the only one who believes this. Gregg Phillips does as well, and it's not only breaking his heart, I think it's breaking yours, too." He held her hand between his. "Winter, you must tell me the truth. I will not have you destroy the rest of your life. I love you, child."

"Oh, Father," Winter sobbed. She threw herself into his arms and he held her against him until her tears ceased.

"Now," he said gently, "tell me what this is all about."

Haltingly, Winter explained. When she finished, Joseph's face was grim. "Well, she is right about one thing . . . but she is damn wrong about the other. I am in temporary financial straits, but I will not sacrifice you to pay for it. The worst of it is that within two months I will have the money it takes to be solvent once more, but within that two months she could destroy everything I've built."

"What can we do?"

"The one thing we *can't* do is let her succeed with this plan, and we cannot let her know that *I* know what she has been up to. There's got to be a way to forestall the wedding and not make her suspicious until it's too late. We have to have time."

"I'll do whatever is necessary."

"For a while you must go along with the situation," he instructed. "Can you manage that?"

"Of course."

"I don't know yet what we can do to protect both of us, but whatever it is, it might take a great deal of courage on your part."

"Father, you know I would give my life for you."

"I know, as I would for you. But I don't want you to give your life for me. I want you to live it. Now," he said with feigned gruffness, "get some rest."

He left the room, but neither he nor Winter got much sleep at all that night, or for the following few nights.

A week later, Anne invited a few guests for dinner. Joseph had made sure Gregg was among them. Carl, of course, was present, and wearing a smug, self-satisfied smile that annoyed both Gregg and Joseph.

They gathered in the formal living room to enjoy drinks before dinner and to wait for Winter who was late coming down.

When the wait seemed interminably long, Anne sent a maid to find out what had delayed her. The woman returned with a pale face and carrying a note in her trembling hand.

Anne snatched it from her and read it with narrowed eyes.

"Well, it looks as if our Winter's run away. The note says she's going far enough that no one will ever find her. That she cannot stand to live here and face the future any longer."

Carl gave a muttered curse, and when Anne looked at him, she could read the malicious anger in his eyes. She didn't trust him not to say something foolish that might upset her plans. She gave an almost imperceptible shake of her head and watched him struggle for control. But she knew Carl James would not keep that control for too long.

Anne turned glaring and suspicious eyes toward Gregg, but his face had gone pale and his eyes had filled with a combination of worry and fear. Then her gaze went to Joseph, who also seemed frightened.

"We'll find her," Joseph declared. "She cannot have gone far."

"What can I do to help?" Gregg asked at once.

"You can check every friend of hers you might know. Scour the city. I'll contact all of our relatives. She must be traveling by public transportation. Don't worry. We'll find her."

The search culminated two days later when evidence proved that a woman matching Winter Stapleton's description had bought a train ticket to St. Louis.

"Joseph," Anne said, as if she were truly worried, "perhaps you should hire someone. Someone more qualified to find Winter. A detective or some such person. We have no idea what grim conditions she might be facing even as we speak."

"You're right, Anne. I'll send the most qualified person money can buy. We'll find my daughter. I promise you we'll find her."

Chapter 1

St. Louis, Missouri

Brad Cole wanted a drink. He wanted a drink so bad that he had to grit his teeth and mutter a curse. He'd done everything possible to save his ranch, and every effort seemed to be in vain. He had tried the bank in North Platte, but had been turned down. Then he had gone further afield to Lincoln, only to meet the same negative results. Then he'd thought of an old friend in St. Louis and had grasped for his last straw—Morgan Little. He'd gone to Morgan—had come close to begging for the loan he needed—who had placed his request before his board of directors, but the result had been the same.

Now, to get a message from Morgan was a monumental surprise. He crossed the street slowly and paused at the door of the bank for a minute, then stepped inside. Immediately, he became aware of the subtle glances of the women and the more overt looks of the men.

At thirty-three he had an aura of confidence and strength about him always that drew attention. His smoke-gray eyes could chill to the bone or warm to the core. His hair was black and thick and in need of a cut. His leather jacket was smoothed over broad shoulders, his lean, long legs encased in jeans that hugged narrow hips. On his feet were worn black boots. His six-foot-three frame was muscular and carried no excess fat.

He lit the cigar clinched between strong white teeth that flashed against the deep tan of his face.

Walking slowly across the lobby, he saw Morgan Little rise from behind his desk and smile. It was a good sign, he thought hopefully. He extended his hand to Morgan, and Morgan shook it enthusiastically.

"I'm glad you decided to stay in St. Louis a few more days, Brad. I just got a message from a friend who might have the answer to your problem."

"A friend? From here?"

"No, in Charleston."

"Charleston? What does Charleston have to do with my situation?"

"Not your *situation,* but definitely with *you.* Sit down, Brad. I have a lot to explain."

Brad took the proffered chair with a puzzled frown. He wasn't enjoying the cigar any longer, so he placed it in the ashtray. The puzzle didn't last for long.

"How long would it take you to get to Memphis?" Morgan asked.

"Memphis? A couple of days by boat, I suppose. Why should I be going there?"

"When you were a Ranger, my friend, you had a reputation for finding and bringing in any man you went after."

"But I'm not a Ranger any longer. I'm a rancher. A rancher who needs to take care of his own problems."

"I know. But . . . Look, I can't make the loan, I've told you that."

"Then get to the point, Morgan. Why did you ask me here?" Brad's brow grew together in a dark frown.

"I know how you can make the money you need."

"Who do I have to shoot?" Brad grinned wryly.

"Very funny," Morgan laughed. "You don't have to shoot anyone. You have to find someone."

"How does this connect to Charleston?"

"The missing person is from Charleston. The parents would meet you halfway . . . in Memphis. They would pay you, and give you all the information you need. Knowing you, it should only take you a matter of a week or two to find this missing person." He bent a bit toward Brad, "And it would solve your problem . . . without interest."

"Morgan," Brad laughed as well, "you keep saying 'missing person,' as if it's some kind of secret. Just who is this and what's he done?"

"To tell you the truth, Brad, I've said all I'm permitted to say. I only know the job would not be difficult for you. A couple of weeks and all your problems would be over. What do you have to lose?"

"Why would these 'parents' want to meet me half-way?"

"To keep from wasting time. I understand that this person was last known to have bought a ticket to St. Louis."

"I see." It sounded easy to Brad all right. Maybe a bit too easy. For some reason it made him slightly edgy. Still, he had a lot to lose and a great deal to gain.

"Brad . . . a couple of weeks," Morgan coaxed. "Bring your man back, collect the money you so desperately need, and be back at your ranch in no time."

"Who are these people?"

"The name is Stapleton, and if we wire them they will be on their way to meet you."

"They agreed to the money I need?"

"And more."

"More?"

"You need five thousand dollars." Morgan sat back in his chair and smiled broadly. "You meet them and agree to do the job . . . and the price will double that."

"Double!"

"Yes. You'll not have a money problem again."

"All right . . . all right. Wire your friends. I'll catch the first boat out."

"I don't think you'll regret this. It's going to be an easy and profitable little excursion. I'll be here for you to thank when you get back."

Brad rose and again extended his hand. "Thanks,

Morgan, but it would have been much simpler if you'd just have loaned me the money."

"If it had been up to me I would have in a minute. But it *wasn't* up to me. Your ranch is your heart. I know that. That's why I grabbed this opportunity when it came."

"So send your wire . . . and thank you."

Brad wished he had Morgan's confidence. But as Morgan said, his ranch was his life and he had no intention of losing it. He thought of the years he had spent as a Ranger. The men he'd brought in . . . and the ones he'd been forced to leave behind. He thought of the money he had hoarded, one coin at a time, of the mud and the rain and the heat he'd faced. He thought of the small, snug house he'd built with his own hands and of the friends who'd worked with him, of the hours of blood and sweat that had been poured into it. No, he couldn't lose it now, and if not losing it meant chasing this runaway across the country and dragging him back, then that's what would be done.

As Brad climbed the hotel stairs he was prepared to face these wealthy Stapletons. On the boat to Memphis he'd tried to envision what they would be like. Probably snobs, whose only son had run off with a sweet young thing and scandalized the family.

He knocked on the door and was admitted by a distinguished-looking man.

"Mr. Stapleton?"

"Yes. Are you Mr. Cole?"

"I am."

"Come in, please."

Brad's attention went at once to the woman seated in a chair by the window. She regarded him coolly and with appraising eyes. He thought he'd looked down a gun barrel into eyes like that.

"This is my wife, Anne. Anne, my dear, this is Mr. Cole."

"How do you do, Mr. Cole." Anne rose. "Mr. Little has explained why your services are necessary, I presume."

"Yes." Brad wasn't too sure he liked this woman. "But I'm afraid he couldn't supply me with the name and details about the man you want me to find."

"We chose to have it that way," Joseph said.

"I'm afraid, Mr. Stapleton, that I can't find a man if I don't know what he looks like or where he's likely to go."

"First, let's take care of the transaction. The price was five thousand now and five when you succeed."

"That's been agreed on."

"Good," Joseph said. He took an envelope from his pocket and handed it to Brad, who put it in his pocket. "Aren't you going to count it?"

"I don't think I have to do that. If we don't at least start out trusting each other we may as well forget it." He half smiled. "Now, can we get down to some of those details?"

"Yes," Joseph said quietly. "To begin with, the person you are looking for isn't a man. It's a woman. My daughter."

"A woman!"

"Yes, Mr. Cole. And it is very important that you find her. *Very* important. She's my only child . . . and my only heir."

"Maybe," Brad said softly, "she ran away with a man."

"No," Anne said quickly.

"No?"

"The only man she could have—or would have— run away with has been with us . . . helping us during the entire search. If she is not with him, then she's alone."

"Then this job ought to be simple. Is she young and pretty?"

"Yes," Joseph replied, puzzled. "What difference does a thing like that make?"

"A pretty girl? West of St. Louis?" Brad chuckled. "Will be as easy to follow as a buffalo in a china shop."

"That's encouraging, Mr. Cole," Anne answered stiffly. "Can you give us a reasonable idea of how long this will take?"

"There's a time limit?"

"Two months. We have to have her back in two months . . . for her wedding."

"I see."

"No, Mr. Cole, you don't see. Winter is a bit on the selfish and spoiled side," Anne said.

"Anne! That's not so," Joseph protested.

"Then why would she allow an engagement party, accept a ring, set the wedding date, and then run away. She needs discipline."

"That's really none of my business," Brad cut her

off, "Mr. Stapleton, is your daughter under age? I mean, is it a legal affair?"

"My daughter won't be twenty-one until August. Since this is May . . . yes, she's still under age. Bring her back." His eyes held Brad's. "Bring her back safely."

"I'll do that."

"If you'll step over to that window with me I'll show you a picture of Winter. You can carry it along. That way there will be no mistake."

Joseph took a four-by-five picture from his pocket.

The girl who looked back at Brad surprised him with her beauty.

"The picture doesn't do her justice, but at least you'll be able to recognize her," Joseph said.

"This is fine. A girl who looks like this, I should have her back within two weeks. She's too beautiful to be hard to find."

"Well," Brad said, "I guess I'd better go. The sooner I get moving the sooner we'll get back." He put the picture in his pocket. "Will you be here or—"

"We'll be in Charleston." Joseph said firmly. "Here is my card with my address on it. When you find my daughter, please bring her back to me. She is a fine and beautiful girl, Mr. Cole. I don't want her hurt by anything or anyone."

"Don't worry, I'll guard her with my life. We'll be at your home within the two months."

"I'll hold you to that, Mr. Cole," Anne said. "The balance of your money will be waiting for you."

"Can you give me any idea of where she might be headed?"

"I haven't a clue," Joseph said. "We have a distant relative in Colorado, but I doubt very much if Winter would go there. She is a very clever girl, too clever to go right where she thinks someone might look."

"I'll start in St. Louis. Like I said, I doubt if she'll be too hard to follow."

Brad felt quite satisfied. He had not exaggerated. Winter Stapleton was a very beautiful woman, and she was traveling alone. He had a feeling he'd have her home in even less time than he'd imagined.

He was even more satisfied three days later in St. Louis. He'd learned a wagon train had left for the gold fields of California five days before. He also found the store in which Winter Stapleton had bought serviceable traveling clothes and some equipment. He didn't doubt her location, and within hours was on the trail.

On their journey back to Charleston, Brad Cole was the topic of Anne and Joseph's conversation.

"What's your opinion of Mr. Cole?" Anne asked her husband.

"Morgan Little gathered all the information I needed when I decided to contact him. After what Morgan told me, I think Cole's just the man to find Winter. Morgan's known him a long time."

"But what did he tell you about him? After all, you are trusting your daughter to his care for a great deal of time, and most of that time will be spent alone."

"What do I know about him?" Joseph said thoughtfully. "He was born and raised down near

Philadelphia. When he was about twelve, his father bought a small ranch out West somewhere. He was a city man who didn't understand the danger of Indians. There was an uprising and his parents were killed and the ranch destroyed. He was only about nineteen then and thought he could rebuild and run the ranch himself. For a while he seemed to be doing all right. Then a band of white renegades came through. Nearly killed him. Robbed him of everything he had and burnt what they couldn't take. He was mad, but smart. He decided to get them but to get them legally. He joined the United States Rangers."

"He got them?"

"Oh, he got them all right. One at a time he got every one of them. He became a real hero. Then he got into a tangle and was shot up pretty bad. I guess he lost his taste for hunting men and not having anything for himself, so he took every dime he ever managed to save and sank it into a ranch out near the Nebraska border in a little town called Mesa Hills. Works himself real hard from all reports, but he suffered some financial setbacks lately. That's the only reason I was lucky enough to get him."

"How did you know about him?"

"I didn't, really. But when I found Winter had gotten a ticket to St. Louis, I called in Morgan Little, asked him to find me the best man possible to trace Winter, find her, and bring her back, just like I said I would. Morgan has a fine reputation. He says we could not find a better or more trustworthy man. So

I wired him to ask Mr. Cole. When he agreed," Joseph shrugged, "you know the rest."

"Well, I hope he succeeds as well this time as he has in the past. I believe our little Winter is dashing into more dangerous territory than she realized."

"Winter is a strong and resilient girl. I have a feeling Mr. Cole has his job cut out for him."

"You have encouraged her to be so obstinate. She is badly in need of guidance. I hope marriage to a strong man will cure her of these fancies."

"I agree, Anne. For the first time in a long while, I believe you are right. Winter would do well to marry the right man."

"And Carl James is just the right man to put an end to her childish and stubborn ways and turn her into a woman who knows a woman's proper place."

"As you do," Joseph replied.

Anne's eyes snapped toward him, but there was no sign on his face that the words meant anything other than great admiration.

Gregg was waiting impatiently for their arrival. He stood on the train platform, hat in hand and a tense look on his face. His classically Scandinavian handsomeness spoke of Viking ancestors, with eyes as blue as a cloudless summer day and hair a golden blond. He had a wide, easily smiling mouth which ordinarily lit his eyes and drew responsive smiles. Under usual circumstances he had an easygoing and fun-loving nature. But this was an unusual situation and his worry deepened the blue of his eyes and created furrows on his brow.

He was scared for Winter, and would have gone so far as to give her up just to know she was safe.

"Have you had any word . . . any sign at all of Winter?"

"No, Gregg," Joseph said. "You must be calm."

"Calm! How can I be calm when I'm certain Winter is in very grave danger?"

"I do not see, Mr. Phillips," Anne said coolly, "where it is your business . . . or your right to involve yourself in this."

"My only right is that I care a great deal about what happens to Winter. I feel this is somehow partly my fault."

"As it truly is," Anne said. "I imagine you should be blaming yourself. But I think your involvement is unwelcome."

"Anne!" Joseph spoke her name with a touch of anger. "Gregg cannot stop worrying about someone he cares about just because she is promised to another man. It is simply a human emotion."

"I have enough . . . *We* have enough problems to contend with. We'll keep you informed if we learn anything, Mr. Phillips. In the meantime . . ."

"In the meantime I shall not bother you. I am going to my parents' home in Savannah. I would appreciate it if you would let me know there what progress is reported. Until you do, I shall stay out from under foot."

"Frankly, I find those the most considerate words you've said since the whole sordid affair began."

Now that Anne was to be rid of Gregg, she became more conciliatory. "Rest assured," she smiled, "that we will let you know when Winter is back . . . and the wedding is to take place."

"I'm going to stay away, Mrs. Stapleton," Gregg said. "But you are being unfair to Winter and to me. I do love her and—"

"If you loved Winter, you would not want to interfere in what is best for her. The James family has everything. Did you ever consider what you would be doing to her? You have very little to offer."

"I know," Gregg said miserably, "and that is the only reason I'm going. I'll concede to your wishes for what is best for Winter. But I must know that she has been found, and that she is safe. Only then can I leave her life completely."

"I see," Anne nodded. "Then we will surely let you know."

"Thank you, Mrs. Stapleton." He bowed slightly. "Mr. Stapleton." He extended his hand to Joseph. "Thank you, sir, for being so understanding. I shall await any word from you."

"And you shall have it, my boy."

"Thank you, sir." Gregg sighed heavily and turned to walk away.

"Insolent interferer," Anne muttered.

"The man can't be blamed for loving someone."

"Well, he'll just have to choose another someone. It is ridiculous to consider letting Winter marry so far beneath her station, and to a man who has so little."

"Well, that seems to be taken care of, Anne. Gregg has, for all intents and purposes, taken himself from

our lives. By the way, where is the very worried pro-
spective bridegroom?"

Anne's flushed face revealed her annoyance. "I
told him I would let him know what news we had.
He's a very busy man and can hardly take time off to
meet us here."

"No, of course not," Joseph agreed.

When the Stapletons arrived home, they had
hardly become settled when visitors were announced.

"Mr. Jeffrey Brenner and his sister, Mrs. Stapleton. I told them you had only just returned from the
station."

"It's all right, Roberts," Anne said. "Show them
in, please."

Moments later Diane Brenner breezed into the
room, followed by her brother, Jeffrey.

Jeffrey Brenner at forty-one was a dashing
charmer who knew his own abilities well. Though his
hair was flecked with salt and pepper, his face was
unlined and tanned, and his body was kept in perfect
shape. Jeffrey had long ago let his moral conscience
give way before other priorities, namely ambition
and greed. His sharp green eyes could recognize an
opportunity at any distance.

Jeffrey's sister, Diane, was cut from the same bolt
of cloth. Ten years younger than her brother she was
just as aggressively charming . . . and just as much of
an opportunist.

"Anne, my dear," Diane said in a syrupy voice.
"And, Joseph. How terrible this must be for you

both. Have you had any word . . . any word at all?"

"No, nothing," Joseph replied. He liked neither of the Brenners. "We are taking every possible step."

Jeffrey inquired as to the meaning of Joseph's words.

"We do know that Winter bought a train ticket from here to St. Louis," Anne elucidated. "But of course we also know she did not stay there. A friend of Joseph's wired that there is no sign of her. Where she could have gone is beyond me. Anyway, we have hired someone who Joseph assures me is one of the best men in the Territory to find her and bring her home. There will be no doubt," Anne smiled, "that you'll both dance at Winter and Carl's wedding two months from now."

"What a relief to know that all will go well," Jeffrey said quietly. His eyes met Anne's for a minute. "I'm very happy for you."

"Thank you," Anne replied.

If Joseph or Diane noticed the look that passed between Jeffrey and Anne, neither made any motion to reveal it.

"Then you will still come to my dinner party next week?" Diane questioned.

"Whether there is news or not by that time, Joseph and I will come. It will do us very little good to sit in this house and dwell on the matter. If there is any word at all, it could be brought to us there as well as here."

"I'm really in no mood for a party until I know that my daughter is safe," Joseph said. He sipped a whiskey and appraised his two visitors. "Her safety is much more important to me than frivolity."

"Really, Joseph," Anne protested, "there is no need to be rude to our friends just because we are suffering a trial at the moment. After all, we have done all that is humanly possible to do. We can do little more than wait, and I refuse to barricade myself in this house until we hear something. It might be days . . . weeks."

"I'll consider it," Joseph said reluctantly. "Now, if you all will excuse me, I have some very important business to finish. I'll be in my study, Anne. Jeffrey . . . Diane . . ."

"Good day, Joseph," Jeffrey replied.

Diane was the first to speak when Joseph was out of sight.

"Joseph seems a bit put out."

"It's that careless daughter of his," Anne said angrily. "If I didn't need this marriage for my own means right now I would pray that spoiled child would be caught by a band of marauding Indians and done away with."

"My, my," Jeffrey chuckled, "you have let that little chit get under your skin. Don't worry, Anne, I'm sure she'll be found and properly tied up in a neat little package for dear Carl to unwrap."

"I should like to see Carl wipe that arrogant pride from her."

Jeffrey chuckled again. "Don't worry, I have a feeling once he gets his hands on her, he'll take care of that streak of stubborn pride. He'll have her eating out of his hand once he teaches her what love, honor, and *obey* really means."

"Well, plan on me being at your dinner party anyway, Diane. I'm not going to let her spoil my fun."

"I've already seen to it. Now I must run along. I'm quite certain," she smiled knowingly, "that you two won't mind being alone for a while."

As Anne closed the door of the drawing room, Jeffrey smiled and set down his glass of whiskey. Then he extended his hand to her. In a moment she was in his arms and returning his kiss with a passion and fury that would have surprised her husband had he known . . .

Joseph had gone into his study to have some time alone to think.

He poured another glass of whiskey and stood by the large window that looked out over the garden. He turned for a minute and looked up at the portrait of his deceased wife, then raised his glass in a silent toast.

As he drank a small door on the opposite side of the room opened to admit a small, elderly man.

"Walters," Joseph smiled. "Come in, man, come in. I've been very anxious to see you."

"I thought you might be, sir." Walters crossed the room to stand close to Joseph. "You have shared a toast, I believe," he said as he motioned toward the portrait. "I should like to think our beloved Martha is watching over her daughter in some way."

"I hope as you. But we must accomplish more on a more mortal plane. You've seen to all of my instructions?"

"Yes. I accompanied her to St. Louis and made some of the arrangements myself, except for the purchase of new clothing. That I am not too accomplished at, so I let her have whatever she needed."

"She is on her way then?"

"She is that, sir."

"You made sure she had plenty of money?"

"Absolutely. I would not want to see her need for anything."

"And you sent our friends Dobbs & Jasper on the wagon train to protect her should she need help."

"I have, sir. She'll be well taken care of. Miss Winter Stapleton is on her way toward California, and she will continue on that path until you say it is safe for her to return."

"I need to send her a wire. There has been a slight change in our plans."

"A change?"

"You know that my . . . Anne insisted I hire a man to find her?"

"Yes, but I thought—"

"I realized only after I spoke to him just how good he is at his job. She must be warned to expect him."

"You are right. There is a telegraph in the first town the wagon train will stop. I shall send her a wire."

"Very good."

"Sir, if he is important . . . I mean, if her watchdogs are not enough . . ."

"I told you. Warn her that she is only to delay her journey home . . . slow him down as much as she possibly can. Two months, Walters, that's all we need. Then she will not have to worry about Anne's plans any longer. She must gain enough distance so that the time spent to bring her back exceeds the time we need to tie up this business deal I'm working on. Once it is completed none of us need worry about any kind of pressure."

"She knows that, sir. She is a quick-witted girl. She'll provide whatever delays are necessary, no matter how accomplished the man."

"She has won your heart as well as so many others," Joseph smiled.

"That she has. I shall try to keep as close a contact as I can. One way or the other we'll protect her."

"Now, Walters," Joseph smiled, "as the old Romans would say, let the games begin."

"And, sir, if I may toast you, may the best man—and the best woman—win."

They drank together, and Walters left at once to make sure the telegram was sent. Pleased with the way the situation was working out and assured that the wire would arrive in plenty of time, he went to his own home to enjoy an evening meal with his wife.

Many miles away, providence was creating a much different circumstance. The telegraph operator in the town of Kansas City sat listening carefully and jotting down the message that was coming in.

Once the message was ended, he tore off the piece of paper and called his assistant, Farley Deets, to deliver it.

The ten wagons had been camped on the outskirts

of town shaded by a stand of trees and near a small stream where the group had been refreshing their water supplies.

As fast as Farley could move, without losing his air of self-importance, he walked down the board sidewalk toward the encampment.

By the time he reached the edge of the city he paused, stopped short in his tracks by the sight before him. Where the wagons had been was now only a deserted stand of trees with a small stream running through it.

Once he'd gotten his shock under control, he turned around and made his way back to the first shop he could find. He opened the door and stuck his head inside. "Mrs. Magruder," he called. The wagons down by the stream . . . they aren't there anymore."

"No, they been gone about three, four days. I thought you'd a known that," Essie Magruder laughed, "bein' as how you know most of the business of every other soul in town." Her laughter was filled with amusement.

"No need for impertinence, Mrs. Magruder," Deets smiled back. " 'Pears nobody took a notion to tell me. Now I've got a genuine problem. I have a wire here for that nice young girl that was traveling with them. How do you suppose I'm going to deliver it now?"

"Don't rightly know. Maybe you could find someone to ride out to catch up with them."

"Maybe . . . maybe. I'll have to check around town

and see if anybody's going that way. Good day, Mrs. Magruder."

Deets went straight to the sheriff's office. Sheriff Tate knew the coming and goings of nearly every citizen in his town.

"Well, Deets," Tate grinned, "looks to me like you're in luck."

"How so?"

"There was a gent in here just an hour ago looking for that same girl. If he's going on to find her, maybe he could just carry your wire to her. There sure ain't no other towns they're stopping at until they reach St. Joseph."

"Whereabouts can I find this gent Sheriff?"

"I think he was headed for a bath and a shave. Looks to me he's been traveling hard since he left St. Louis."

"I'll go see if I can catch up to him. It would sure be fine if he'd see to delivering this. After all, that girl might just feel real good about getting this here message."

"I suppose. But you better go along. He seemed in a right smart hurry. When he gets himself cleaned up I have a feeling he'll be on his way."

Deets started at once toward the hotel, where he asked about the visitor and got both his name and the fact that he'd appropriated the only bathtub in the place and had been soaking in it for the better part of a half hour.

"You don't suppose I could go in and ask him a favor, do you? This message is important. I don't like my messages to go undelivered if I can help it."

"No, I suppose you don't. I must say you're good at your job. This gent may be tough, but he doesn't appear mean."

"Okay, well, I'll take my chances and go ask him if he'd mind doing me a favor."

Deets knocked on Brad's door with a determination. Brad was his hope of keeping his record intact, and he didn't plan on taking no for an answer if he could help it.

"Yeah!" The voice that came through the door sounded quite like a man who was relaxing after a long, dusty ride and was not prepared to be tampered with.

"Sir . . . it's real important that I talk to you for just a minute."

When permission came, he went inside . . . and came out ten minutes later more than satisfied. His job was done, the message would be delivered.

Brad had decided to stop only because he wanted to make sure he was on track, and the need for a bath and shave could be tended to at the same time.

Now he was saddled up and ready to ride, with no doubt left in his mind that he was on the right trail. He had a telegraph wire in his pocket assuring him of that.

Winter and her companions were two or two and a half days ahead of him, but he didn't worry. He could travel a whole lot faster than they could. He'd catch up. After all, Miss Stapleton had no place else to go.

He smiled to himself as he mounted and rode from town. This was going to prove his easiest job ever.

In a couple of days he would reach the wagons and within another two weeks he would be depositing the wayward Winter Stapleton in the laps of her parents.

He took the wire from his pocket and smiled as he tore it in very small pieces and let it flutter in the breeze. Someone had seen fit to try to warn the elusive Miss Stapleton. He was curious as to why, but it really didn't matter. The warning was never going to reach its destination.

Chapter 2

Brad rode at a slow, mile-eating pace. That night he camped very late, and before he slept he looked again at the face of Winter Stapleton. In the firelight she seemed to look directly at him. Even though the picture had no color in it, he knew from what he had been told that her hair was the soft yellow of ripe cornsilk and the eyes were a velvet violet.

He was fascinated with the seemingly delicate-looking creature and could not stop wondering why she had run away. They would travel together for a few weeks. Maybe he would find some of his answers then.

Even when he slept he dreamt jagged dreams that were only vague shadows in the morning.

He rose long before dawn, self-confidence filling him as he ate breakfast. Everything was very simple. It was one thing to follow a man who was wise in the way of outwitting and outrunning, and prepared to fight when caught, but this sweet-faced young woman would be easy. She would cause him not one whit of a problem.

Finished with breakfast, he broke camp and saddled his horse. By the end of the next day he should come across the wagons. Confident, he rode easily, stopping only at midday to eat a quick lunch.

Two days later, the sun hovered close to the horizon when he crested the last hill and looked down at the wagon train that was already drawing into a circle, a caution against an Indian attack—and preparing to make camp for the evening.

They had traveled well, putting a lot of distance between them and Kansas City. They were outside of St. Joseph, and in another couple of days they would have crossed the Missouri and been well on their way toward Lincoln.

He kicked his horse into motion and rode down toward the wagons. He wanted to cause no problems with these people, so he'd tread warily. But as soon as he knew for certain she was there, he'd find a way to take her and go.

He hailed the guard as he rode closer and was welcomed inside the circle of wagons. He was greeted by three very calm and very intimidating men.

"Evening, gentlemen. Who is the leader of this group?"

"I am, sir. My name is Augustus Main." The older of the three stepped forward. "And who might you be?"

"My name is Brad Cole and I've traveled almost two days to catch up with you."

"Step down and join us for supper."

"Thanks," Brad said as he dismounted. He studied the area about him carefully, but there was no sign of anyone who looked like Winter Stapleton.

His horse was led away by a young man and he was brought to the central fire and offered a plate of hearty beef stew.

"Where are you going, friend?" Augustus asked.

"Actually, this is about as far as I'm going."

"Oh?" Augustus was puzzled now.

"I'm looking for someone I believe is here in your camp." He withdrew the picture and handed it to Augustus. "Her name is Winter Stapleton, and it is very important for me to talk to her."

"Ah . . . yes."

"Then she is here?" Brad smiled. This was just as easy as he'd thought it would be.

"No, sir, I'm afraid she's not."

For a minute Brad just paused and looked at him, not quite sure if what he was hearing was the truth or not.

"I don't understand. She left St. Louis with you over a week ago."

"Yes, sir, that she did. Pretty young thing. Traveling with two of the strangest characters I've ever met. One a big man, built like the side of a barn, and the other a tall, thin man you'd think a strong breeze could blow over."

She had people to protect her, Brad thought. His estimation of her went up a notch.

"So she was traveling with two men. Did they leave the train alone . . . just three of them?"

"Yes they did."

Brad was growing exasperated at having to draw all the information from Augustus piece by piece. He inhaled deeply. It was already getting too late to move on tonight.

"They didn't leave on foot," he prodded. "So just how did she . . . they leave?"

"Traveling show."

"What?"

"Traveling show. You know, actors and singers and such. They was heading up toward Lincoln. I guess they're going to go on to Fort Kearney."

A traveling show was not all that rare in these parts, but what really aggravated Brad was that she had a jump on him again. He just didn't know how much of one.

"How long have they been gone?"

"Let me see now." Augustus seemed to be concentrating very carefully. "Way I can figure it, she's been on her way . . . little over five days now."

Five days! Damn. She had been pretty sure someone would be on her trail and had dodged him neater than anyone had ever done. Respect and anger brushed shoulder to shoulder in his mind.

"Mind if I bunk here tonight? I'll be gone by morning."

"Not a bit. Make yourself at home."

"You said they went north?"

"Yep. On their way to California they were, but had a few shows on the way. I think Bennet was the first place the show was to play in."

"How fast is she traveling?"

"Well, that wagon is lighter than ours, and since

there's only three of them, they could be making pretty good time."

"Great," Brad muttered. "You don't know where they plan to stop after they pass Bennet do you?"

"No, come to think of it, I don't."

"Thanks anyhow. And thanks for supper, I've become pretty sick of my cooking."

"You're welcome, friend." Brad became aware that Augustus was studying him carefully. "You related to that girl, maybe?"

"No, no relation."

"She was only with us for a short spell, but she seems a real nice girl. My wife and daughter took to her. You ain't after makin' her any trouble, are you?"

"No. She's a runaway and her parents are real worried about her. They want me to bring her back home before she runs into any serious harm."

"I see," Augustus replied. It was a minute or two before he smiled, and Brad felt as if he'd been judged somehow. "Well, you feel pretty much like those two fellows who are traveling with her then. Real protective they was. I'd step right careful if I was you, 'cause if that girl don't want to go home with you, I have a feeling those two could be pretty hard to handle."

"I'll be careful."

"You best do that because those two ain't of a mind to let that girl get hurt . . . in no way."

"Augustus," Brad held his eyes with his own, "I have no intention of hurting her. You and I both know a Charleston-raised girl won't stand much of a chance out here. She belongs in her own home, among her own kind."

"Women is hard to read," Augustus grinned. "There ain't no tellin 'em what's best for 'em. Good luck . . . but I think you got your hands full."

Augustus walked away and Brad could have sworn he was laughing.

His horse had been unsaddled and cared for by a boy of about twelve, and his belongings were under one of the wagons where he would sleep. He thanked the boy and flipped him a coin, watching his eyes widen in surprise.

"Jeez, mister, a whole dollar!"

"I'm tired and I appreciate the help."

"If Pa says I was to do it, then I would a done it for nuthin'."

"Augustus is your pa?"

"Yes, sir. I'm Tad."

"Well, Tad, if you feel I been cheated, why don't you make up for it?"

"How?"

"By telling me a few things I need to know."

"Like what?"

"Well, let me see. You had some newcomers traveling with your train for a while."

"Yeah." Tad's eyes brightened. Obviously, Winter Stapleton had made more than one conquest.

"A very pretty lady."

"Uh huh. She was real pretty and she was nice, too. She was helpin' me with my numbers."

"Did she have friends?"

"Whew, boy, did she. I ain't never seen a man as

big as Jasper. I seen him bend a horseshoe like it was nuthin' . . . with his bare hands. I ain't lyin', honest."

"I believe you." Brad chuckled. He began to wonder if this Jasper wasn't going to pose a real obstacle.

"And what about the other man who was with him?"

"You mean Mr. Dobbs?"

"Yes, Mr. Dobbs."

"Well, Mr. Dobbs . . . he was real smart like. He was always saying funny things by somebody . . ." Tad paused thoughtfully. "Shake Pear . . . or something like that."

"Shakespeare?" Brad offered.

"Yeah. Who was he anyhow? He sure did talk funny. I ain't never met a man who talked like Mr. Dobbs said he did."

"That's because Shakespeare has been dead for a long time."

"That sure is crazy, walkin' around talking like a dead man. Yeah, Mr. Dobbs sure was funny."

"But you liked him?"

"Yeah, I guess. He gave me a couple of books and said I should read more."

"You ought to listen. Thanks, Tad. I've gotten my dollar's worth."

Tad's pleased smile was enough to convince Brad that he too, felt it had been a fair exchange.

Settled for the night, Brad tossed in his blanket roll under the wagon, using his saddle for a pillow. He folded his hands behind his head and contemplated the fascinating puzzle of Winter Stapleton.

She had surrounded herself with a unique group,

and they must have been assured that someone would be coming after them. His curiosity about her was steadily growing.

She was going to prove more of a problem than he had planned on. Still, his confidence was intact. He would find a way to get her out of the clutches of her two bodyguards, it would just take a bit of thinking. Satisfied that time was still on his side and the problem had not gotten beyond his control, he rolled over and went to sleep.

The sun was not up and only a band of grayish white on the horizon heralded the coming day when the rattle of harnesses and subdued voices told Brad the camp was stirring.

The smell of bacon frying cause him to realize quickly that he was ravenous.

By the time he'd cleaned himself up and shaved, the entire group was gathering for breakfast. As he approached the fire, a stocky woman, her hair pulled back in a severe bun and brown eyes that sparkled with humor, smiled at him.

"Good morning. You rode in late last night. From the size of you I'd say you're in need of a good meal. My name is Hettie."

"Good morning, Hettie, I'm Brad Cole, and I sure am hungry. That bacon smells like heaven."

"How many eggs? Six, seven?"

"Three will do," Brad replied with a laugh as he lifted the heavy coffee pot and poured a tin cup full.

"Shucks. My boy, Tad, can eat that many. You a light eater or just shy?"

"Neither, just traveling quick. Augustus is your husband?" He added the question to change the subject.

"Sure is. Heading for California we are. Augustus tells me you're looking for that girl that spent a bit of time with us."

"Yes, I am."

" 'Pears to me a young man ought to have more interesting things to do than follow an innocent young girl across the country and draggin' her back to where she don't want to be."

"Her parents are worried sick about her," he said defensively. "They want her back home."

"Why did she run from parents who loved her so much? Did it ever occur to you that she might have her reasons?"

"Maybe. Maybe I'll ask her when I see her."

"You going to ask first, or just drag her back?"

Now his own pride was being challenged and, worse, he began to have a glimmer of doubt.

"I'll ask her."

"Good."

"Then I'll take her back."

"You're a stubborn cuss," Hettie chuckled as she handed him his plate. She studied him carefully. "But I don't think you're as hard as you try and look. You ask her and then you do something a man always tries real hard not to do."

"What's that?"

"Listen."

Before Brad could comment someone called out to Hettie, and soon they were surrounded by hungry people. Brad went to gather his gear and saddle his horse.

He said good-byes to Augustus, Tad, and Hettie and rode away, aware of Hettie's smile.

He'd moved hard this time, stopping only to rest his horse occasionally and eat. He intended to travel long into the night. The moon was three-quarters full and so he could see well enough to narrow the distance between him and Bennet.

He knew Bennet well. They were in his territory now and he knew every ridge and valley. Still, it took him over two days of such hard travel to reach the small town.

When he finally rode in he was dusty, hungry, tired, and in desperate need of a hot bath. He'd not bothered to shave during his journey, and a dark stubble was rapidly growing into a short beard.

But he felt as if he had closed the distance very effectively. With luck, Winter Stapleton was still in Bennet. Sometime in the next few hours he meant to come face-to-face with her.

It was still early evening and the town seemed very alive. Raucous music came from a number of saloons and people filled the streets.

He rode past a tall white frame building, then suddenly reined in his horse and sat looking at it. Bennet Music Hall, the sign read. On an instinct, Brad rode down the alley next to the building and came around the back. He smiled a satisfied smile. He'd made it in time. There was a wagon, with a canvas cover, painted in brilliant colors. Knights Traveling Players. They were here and they were performing.

He rode around front and looked at the billboard nailed to the wall. Tonight at eight-thirty was the final performance before they moved on. Brad was pleased with his luck. He would have to follow Winter Stapleton no longer.

Eight-thirty gave him more than two hours. He headed for the hotel. He would get a room for at least long enough to clean up and change . . . then he meant to watch the performance before he faced Winter Stapleton. If some deep part of his mind chided him for taking all this time with his grooming, he pushed it to the back of his mind.

He shaved carefully and bathed, washing his thick black hair and wishing he'd had a haircut. He came downstairs at seven-thirty and walked across the street to a restaurant and ordered a large meal.

At a quarter after eight he headed for the music hall where people were already gathering. He bought his ticket and waited for the doors to open. Leaning one broad shoulder against the wall of the building, he listened to the talk swirling about him.

" . . . She's the prettiest gal . . . That voice must be like what an angel sounds like . . ."

It was obvious Winter Stapleton had made quite an impression on the town already.

The doors opened, and he moved with the crowd. He found a good seat affording a perfect view of the stage. In several steps he could be up there if he wanted to.

The heavy curtains were still closed, and the footlights were just being lit, causing the deep wine curtains to dance with shadows.

Always a patient man, Brad was a bit surprised to find impatience forming a hard knot in the pit of his stomach.

Then the curtains parted and a tall, thin man waited in seeming modesty until the applause died.

"Ladies, and gentlemen." His voice was professionally resonant yet mellow and carried well to the back of the theater. "Welcome to the last performance of the Knight Traveling Players. It has been their pleasure to entertain you for the past two evenings. Tomorrow they leave for Lincoln, but for tonight we hope again to bring a little pleasure to your lives. To begin the evening's entertainment Mr. Robert Dobbs will regale you with a soliloquy from Shakespeare's *Romeo and Juliet*. Ladies and gentlemen . . . Mr. Robert Dobbs."

Again it was quite obvious from the sound of the applause that the people of Bennet thought well of Mr. Dobbs's performance.

Though the first man was thin, Robert Dobbs looked, just as Brad had heard, as if a good stiff wind would blow him away. But when he spoke Brad could actually feel his voice to the toes of his boots. The voice had a timbre and strength that caught him up at once, and the excellence in his poise and gesture held the audience rapt. Brad would have sworn you could have heard the proverbial pin drop, as the poetic words of Shakespeare tumbled mellifluously and passionately from Dobbs's lips.

When he finished the soliloquy the applause was resounding. Brad was surprised at his reaction to the reading. He had really enjoyed it.

When Mr. Dobbs disappeared backstage, the master of ceremonies reappeared. Again he held up his hand and waited for the audience to become silent.

"And now, ladies and gentlemen, you have a treat for which I know you have all been waiting. For the past two nights you have cheered our lovely nightingale's performance. Tonight she gifts us with three songs from her repertoire. Together let us enjoy . . . Miss Shelby Vale."

Brad wasn't exactly startled at the name. After all, it was clever to travel under an assumed name. But he was startled when all the lights in the theater went out. Obviously the rest of the crowd expected it, for there was no rustling about. In fact, there was a breathless, expectant silence.

Suddenly a beam of light was directed downward, making a circle of light on the darkened stage.

He never expected the vision that seemed to appear magically from the depths of the shadows. When she appeared in the circle of light, there was an audible sound throughout the hall, almost like a collective sigh.

Between one breath and the next Brad was struck a blow that rocked him. Not, since the age of sixteen had he considered himself a novice with women. He'd had many beautiful women walk through his life. But never had he had one affect him as deeply as this one. He felt that the breath he had just sucked in so deeply was stuck in the center of his chest. He could feel his pulses pick up a heavy, throbbing beat.

She stood in the mellow gold glow of the hidden source of light. Her hair, unbound, fell around her shoulders and hung nearly to her waist in a thick mass of waves and wayward curls. It was like a shimmering sea of golden wheat. She wore a gown of deep green that made her ivory skin gleam in the light.

"Good Lord," Brad breathed softly as every sense, every nerve in his body reacted.

From the darkness somewhere behind her the soft strum of guitars filled the quiet room. Then she began to sing, and her voice sent tendrils of seductive sound to surround each person. To Brad it was as if she were singing just to him.

> " 'True love is only for the heart
>   That's not afraid of breaking
> For true love can sometimes be
>   The hardest pain of all.
> Fate lets you meet, and kiss, and touch
>   And fills your life with treasures
> Only to snatch it from your grip
>   And leave the taste of ashes
> But true love, in time, will stand
>   Above the pain that fate inflicts
> For true love shields the heart with iron
>   And breaks uncertain fate.
> When love is proven by adversity
>   And stands the test of time

When passion gives way to deeper truth
Then, true love survives.' "

When the last note of the love song died away, the
crowd was on its feet, filling the room with thunderous applause. Brad rose with them, lifted from his
feet by the magnetism of this woman and her music.

When the applause was finally brought under control, a chair was provided, and a guitar handed to her
from the darkness. She sat and lightly strummed it.
Then there was again no other sound but the blending of the guitar and the golden voice of the woman
who sang.

The applause was even more enthusiastic than the
first time. Then, the crowd was silenced again and she
began the third song.

The magic continued with a rare beauty that was
almost painful. But when she ceased to sing and rose
to her feet, the crowd knew the magic was not only
over but that it might never come their way again.

This time the applause would not be halted. Flowers were tossed onto the stage accompanied by coins
of all denominations from dollars to hundred-dollar
gold pieces.

The light on the stage went out and an instant later
the footlights were being lit again. Only this time the
stage was empty.

Brad rose. Despite her musical talent, or how she
had made him feel, he had a job to do. His whole life
and future depended on his success.

He made his way backstage, and amid all the hustle and bustle, he eased around until he found Shelby Vale's dressing room.

He knocked, but there was no answer. Alarmed that there might be an outer door to the room, he turned the knob and swung the door open a few inches. Enough to look around it and into the room.

She was seated before a large mirror, immobile, and caught in some kind of mystic daydream. For a minute he was reluctant to shatter it.

Again he had to stir himself to more control and less admiration for a lady who was both unpredictable and out of his reach.

He pushed the door open wider, at the same time knocking again. She spun around with a smile, but the smile faded as she realized he was no one she knew.

"Hello, Miss Winter Stapleton," Brad said quietly.

He had to give her credit for control. She never blinked an eye.

"I'm afraid, sir, you've made some kind of mistake. My name is Shelby Vale."

"This is no time for games. I know who you are, and I've traveled quite a distance to bring you back."

"Back? Really, sir, you must forgive me. But I do think you're a bit addled. Whoever you're looking for, it isn't me. As I said, my name is Shelby Vale, and I don't even know your Winter Stapleton. If you'll excuse me, I have to prepare to leave."

Brad reached his hand into his pocket and withdrew the picture he'd carried for so long. "Is this you?"

"Quite obviously it is. Anyone can see that. Where did you get it?"

"Your father gave it to me when he hired me to bring you home. Now . . . anytime you're ready."

"You mean," she laughed, "that you walk in here off the street and wave a picture of me and you expect me to leave with you."

"Something like that."

"My father has been dead for two years," she said firmly, "and I am not Winter Stapleton . . . I am Shelby Vale. *And,*" her eyes met his directly, "I'm not going anywhere with you . . . now, or ever."

"Look, Miss Stapleton. I'm taking you home one way or the other. Either willingly," he grinned, though his eyes held no humor, "or tied up and flung over my saddle. That's up to you.

"My, we are arrogant, aren't we?"

"No . . . just certain."

"Umm, well, your certainty doesn't mean too much to me because I'm not going with you either way."

"No?"

"No. First I'll scream my head off, and I don't think the citizens of this town will take kindly to you . . . flinging me over your saddle. Mr. . . . ?"

"Cole, Brad Cole."

"Well, Mr. Cole, please go away, and I'll do my best to forget you ever made such a fool of yourself."

He reached out and grasped her arm, bringing her close to him. Although he watched her eyes widen in surprise, he saw no fear. But he instantly became completely aware of her in a way that shocked him.

The scent of her perfume, he admitted, could lead any man astray.

"There are ways and ways, Miss Stapleton. I'll have you out of this town before the citizens can blink. Don't doubt that. Now, why don't you just save us a whole lot of trouble."

"My name, Mr. Cole, is Shelby Vale," she said coldly, "and I'll thank you to take your hand off me. I will make you one promise. I'm not going anywhere with you at any time."

"You're going back to Charleston with me."

"Charleston! I wouldn't walk across the street with you. But . . . Charleston!" She laughed. "You walk into my room uninvited and suggest, a bit aggressively, I might add, that I'm going to cross half the country with you. Let me repeat one more time before you leave. I'm not the unlucky lady you're after. *I am Shelby Vale.*"

He expected her refusal, but he also expected more honesty. Both of them knew she was lying. If nothing else, he wanted her to admit who she was . . . he'd take care of the rest later.

He released her arm, only to grip her shoulders. He was about to speak when the world seemed to turn topsy-turvy. He was gripped from the back by a hand that felt to him to be the size of a ham, lifted from his feet, and deposited none too lightly in a heap on the opposite side of the room.

When he could gather himself, he sat up and looked toward his attacker. Winter stood beside the largest human being he had ever seen. Beside him she

SONG OF THE HEART

looked like a child . . . a very pleased and amused child.

"I think, Mr. Cole," she said, "that you had best decide to leave . . . now. I should hate Jasper to break something . . . valuable."

Brad got to his feet and walked back to both of them, being very careful not to get within arm's reach of the bear of a man.

Jasper must have stood six feet six inches and weighed close to three hundred pounds. Remembering what the boy Tad had said, he didn't doubt for a minute this man could bend a horseshoe with his bare hands. It wouldn't have surprised him to find out he ate nails for breakfast, either.

"Your bodyguard, I presume," Brad said.

"This is still very wild country, Mr. Cole," she smiled. "One does not know what emergencies might arise. Would you like Jasper to escort you to the door?"

"No, thank you just the same." He looked into her eyes and smiled. "It seems to me you have more reason to have a bodyguard than just a pretty face. I have a job to do, and I intend to do it." He watched her face as he spoke and was again fascinated that he saw no sign of fear. He started toward the door, hoping that this mountain of a man didn't intend to stop him.

"Mr. Cole?"

"Yes?" He turned to face her again.

"My name is Shelby Vale. Remember that. If you are searching for someone . . . search somewhere else."

"Maybe I'll do that."

When he'd left the room, the two remaining occupants looked at each other.

"Do you think we've seen the last of him?" Shelby half whispered.

"No," Jasper said, "he didn't appear to me to be the kind of man to give up easily."

"There's no way he believed me. He took me by surprise. We were followed much sooner than I expected. Tell Dobbs to hurry and get ready. It's time we get to the wagon and leave this place. We need to put some distance between us and that very stubborn gentleman."

"I'll tell him. We'll have the wagons ready in less than an hour."

"I'll gather a few of my things and meet you out back. Hurry, Jasper."

When the big man left the room, she moved swiftly. Taking a satchel, she stuffed clothes and scattered objects in it, then scurried to the alley behind the theater where the wagons sat in the dark. She tossed the satchel inside. The two men, soon joined her, and they headed the wagon away from the town.

They drove the balance of the night, then found a stand of trees in which to rest the horses.

Only then did the three take the time to talk together.

"I was waiting for him . . . or one like him," she said. "But I didn't expect someone so persevering. We'll just have to stay one step ahead of him."

"I could muss him up a bit so he wouldn't be following us for a while," Jasper suggested.

"No. We don't want to hurt anybody. Let's rest here during the day and travel by night. And we won't go to Lincoln as we planned. Instead, we'll go to Milford. We'll keep control and just outsmart him."

The two men were silent. It was their job to protect her, and they had orders to do whatever she deemed necessary. So they complied, though neither was too sure.

"You two get some sleep," she instructed. "I'll wake you when it's time to go. If you're going to drive all night you need rest."

"What about you?" Dobbs questioned.

"I can sleep in the back of the wagon as we ride. Don't worry. We're perfectly safe here. He's probably way past us by now."

Reluctantly they did as she said, finding a comfortable place in the back of the wagon.

She spent the balance of the day considering her situation and the plans she had made. They still seemed good and she wouldn't have to deviate from them. She rested during the heat of the day and then began to prepare an evening meal. The sunset drew her attention for a while, then as the sky began to grow darker, she put more wood on the fire. She would have to awaken Jasper and Dobbs soon, but since the stew wasn't quite done, she decided a short walk would make her feel less restless.

Putting a cloak about her shoulders and the hood of it over her head to camouflage her light skin and hair, she sat on a broken log to think.

She had to be careful and she knew it. She had

looked into his eyes and had known at once he was
dangerous. Dangerous to her plans because he was
efficient and clever.

She was reasonably certain she wouldn't be caught
up with so quickly. She had let her guard drop at the
theater and let Mr. Cole too close. She vowed something like that would never happen again.

The night air was still warm, so she decided to walk
within the shadows of the trees to stretch her legs.

She rose from the log and walked several feet away
from the wagons.

The night sounds were as soothing as the warmth
of the breeze had been, and they lulled her senses. She
didn't hear the soft rustle from behind her until it was
just a second too late.

A hard arm came about her and his hand covered
her mouth.

"So we meet again, Miss Stapleton. But this time,"
his voice was a warm chuckle in her ear, "on my
terms."

Chapter 3

He watched the fury dance in her eyes, but with the handkerchief tied about her mouth and her hands tied before her to the pommel of the saddle, she could do little else than glare. He had a reasonably good idea of the verbal abuse he'd take if he untied the gag, so he didn't.

He'd been cautious as he'd taken her. He'd deliberately brought another horse and had trailed her party with an experienced eye. When he found them he'd tied the horses some distance away and moved in slowly.

Now she was riding behind him, broiling with a helpless anger.

She'd watched him carefully destroy any sign of their passage to make anyone who tried to follow them unable to trace their trail.

By the time dawn began to break they were nearing the small town he'd chosen. It was a town Winter had not even known the existence of, and one she was miserably certain Jasper and Dobbs would not never consider.

They sat just within the shadows of some trees that bordered the town. As he reached over and finally pulled the gag from her mouth, she fairly sputtered her fury.

"How dare you! Do you believe I won't scream my head off? I'll have you arrested! I'll see you hang for this!"

"I should have left the gag on," he said with amusement.

"You are making a very costly mistake."

"I don't think so."

"What can I do to get through that thick head of yours that I'm not Winter Stapleton?"

"You can't do anything. When your father gave me this picture he begged me to bring his daughter home. I think your conscience ought to be a bit shriveled. Your parents are suffering and I'm going to see that you get put right back in their laps."

"Just how much are you being paid for this little farce?" she sneered. "What price does the big, brave bounty hunter put on bringing in one girl—the *wrong* girl, I might add."

"The conditions are not your affair. You could have gone home in much more comfort. You chose this path, not me." He looked at her and smiled the same aggravating smile that made her grit her teeth and shake with the desire to throttle him.

"I will not go back to Charleston with you."

Again he laughed softly. "Don't bet on it."

"I promise you," she replied in a level voice, "you

will never get me back to Charleston, but if by chance you do, you'll be the one to regret it."

"Well, right now we have to find a nice, safe place to rest a while, and I have to pick up some more supplies."

"In town?" she asked hopefully.

"Miss Stapleton," he chided in a teasing voice.

"I wish you'd stop calling me that. My name is Shelby Vale."

"You're damn obstinate."

"Shelby Vale," she insisted.

"You want to play it that way, all right. I'll call you Shelby . . . but Winter Stapleton is going home. And now I plan to find us a room."

He saw a flicker of fear in her eyes for the first time and knew what she was thinking.

"Don't get ideas in your head. I don't molest wayward little girls. You need to go home and grow up first." He was pleased when he saw the fear turn to anger again. Anger he could handle, but her being afraid of him annoyed him.

Before she could speak again, he replaced the gag and carefully put the hood over her head to shadow her face. Then he rode toward the back of town, down the back streets that were deserted, and stopped behind the only hotel in town. He tied their horses and lifted her down, carrying her like a well-protected child, with her cloak so tight she could not move or turn her head. He carried her into the lobby where one very sleepy clerk was waiting impatiently for a change of shifts.

"I'm in a hurry," Brad snapped at the clerk. "I

need a room quickly, my wife is sick. I can sign the register as soon as I put her to bed."

The clerk didn't care who came and went as long as they paid when they left, and he handed Brad a key. The former Ranger was going up the steps before the clerk thought to even look at the woman in his arms.

Inside the room she uttered a muffled scream as Brad dumped her unceremoniously on the bed. He removed her cloak and untied her hands. She tried to move, but he quickly put a stop to that.

"I'm sorry to say I don't trust you for a minute. You'll stay gagged. And, what's more, I'm tying you to the bed until I get back. I'm going to get some food and supplies. You might as well rest. Get some sleep if you can. We'll be out of here after nightfall."

He rose and left the room, quite aware that she had not made a sound but that her eyes—those wide violet eyes—had followed him accusingly.

He moved around carefully, studying the town, making sure there was no sign of the show wagon. Satisfied, he went to the closest store, which was just opening its doors. There he bought enough supplies for the two of them to travel to St. Louis. He'd figure the logistics for the rest of the trip when he got there.

He took the horses to a livery, where he instructed the stable hand to feed and brush them well. Then he stacked the supplies with the livery man, telling him he'd be back to pack the horses later in the afternoon.

He smiled a greeting at her sitting bound in the hotel room and was rewarded by a malevolent glare that could have burnt him to a cinder. He sat beside her.

"I know by now you must be a bit 'uncomfortable.' You need some freedom and privacy. I'm going to untie you and go out and lock the door. Don't do anything foolish." He held her eyes with his, "You understand?"

She nodded vigorously and he untied her hands. Quickly, she snatched the gag from her mouth.

"You may have gotten us this far, but there are a lot of miles between here and Charleston."

"I know," he chuckled, "but this will be the last town before St. Louis. There will be no more opportunities to come in contact with anyone."

"As you said before," she smiled for the first time, "don't bet on it."

"I'll be right outside. Give a couple of knocks on the door when you're finished."

Once the door closed behind him, she rose from the bed and tried to renew the circulation in her arms and legs.

She tested the door, all the while knowing he hadn't forgotten to lock it. Then she walked back and sat on the edge of the bed to consider her plans. After a while she smiled.

It was almost a half hour before she rapped softly on the door and again heard the lock click.

Brad noticed the change in her demeanor at once. It was as if she had taken the time to consider her position and knew she could do nothing to change it.

By the time he closed the door behind him she was again seated on the bed. Her head was bowed so that the curtain of pale blond hair partially covered her face. She suddenly looked very helpless and vulnerable.

"I know you must be tired, since we traveled all night. You have to be hungry as well," he said. "I'm going down to get us something to eat. We'll stay here at least until after dinnertime. Then we have to get started. I think you need something to wear besides that gown."

She didn't answer, and he took a few steps toward her. His approach brought her head up. He was caught totally unprepared for round eyes filled with misery and tears. It struck him like a fist in the stomach.

"Look," he tried to explain, feeling more guilty by the minute. "You're under age, and you're not equipped to handle life out here. You can only get badly hurt. Don't you understand you belong at home with the parents who obviously love you?"

"You don't understand." Her voice was tremulous and the crystal tears escaped to trace down her cheeks. "I did not run away from my parents. I'm not the woman you are looking for. You have separated me from my friends, tied me up, and forced me here. Can you blame me for being afraid?" Her voice caught on a sob and again her head bowed.

Hettie's words came to him, to try listening to her. But they were followed by Anne Stapleton's voice calling her selfish and spoiled. This, added to the instinctive feeling he'd gotten when he met Mrs. Stapleton, was enough to tangle his mind. He was touched by confusion and she knew it. She looked up at him again and tried to smile.

"I am tired, and I am hungry. If you take me to the restaurant and to get some clothes. I . . . I promise I won't try to get away. I do need to get some sleep if I'm going to be fit to travel."

His common sense at once shrieked denial, but he was caught up in other senses as well and common sense took a battering.

"How good is your word, Miss Stapleton?"

"My name . . ."

"I know, I know. Shelby. All right, Shelby, how good is your word?"

"As good as yours. While we eat, while we shop for my clothes . . . until we come back here, I promise I won't try to get away."

His gaze met her eyes steadily and just as steadily she returned it.

"All right," he agreed, ignoring the little voice in the back of his mind that called him a fool.

She stood immediately and brushed the tears from her cheeks. She was surprised when he crossed the distance between them and caught her chin in his hand, lifting her face to meet his.

"Don't play games. Get it through your head that I'll do whatever I have to do and you might find out you've bitten off more than you can chew."

"I need to eat. And if I'm going to travel the way you say, I need more serviceable clothes. I'm not going to try and get away."

"All right. Come on."

He was cautious, waiting for her to make some

aggressive move, to scream, cry, try to run. But she did none of these. She walked demurely beside him to the restaurant where they ate a silent meal. Then they went to the closest store where he purchased a riding skirt, boots, and a shirt and jacket for her. At the last minute he added a wide-brimmed hat.

When they crossed to the hotel again he felt reasonably good about the situation, priding himself on the fact that he'd made himself clear. He would have no more trouble with her.

Once inside the hotel room he told her to get some more sleep, that they would have a late-afternoon meal and be on their way.

"What about you?" she asked softly.

"I've gone without sleep too many times to count. It doesn't bother me much. Besides, I have to see to the pack horse."

"Oh, and, *Shelby,*" he smiled, "this window faces the livery. That's where I'll be. If you should decide to try something, don't. I can't miss it from there."

Her smile matched his. "Don't worry."

"Just so you understand."

He left the room, locking the door behind him. This time she didn't have to test it, nor did she want to. She needed some sleep and this was not the right moment to do anything. With another soft smile playing about her lips, she curled up on the bed. Some minutes later she drifted off into a surprisingly relaxed, contented sleep.

* * *

Brad had been careful to keep the hotel window in sight, expecting to see her climbing out at any time. He packed the horse carefully, taking extra time to make sure there was enough of everything so that they could travel without entering another town.

He took the chance and crossed the street to the saloon, where he had two drinks and bought a bottle of whiskey to carry along. He had a feeling traveling with Miss Winter Stapleton was not going to be easy.

He slid the picture out of his pocket and looked at it. As her father had said, it didn't do her justice. He'd felt inexplicably drawn to the picture, now but the real person was an even more potent force. He would have to be very careful. This sweet, rich, spoiled, and very innocent beauty could be hazardous to his state of mind. He couldn't dream dreams that were impossible. He'd had his dreams before, and it didn't pay to lean on them too hard. They had a way of breaking

When he finally crossed back to the hotel, he realized that an hour or two of sleep would do him good as well.

He entered the room quietly. She was sound asleep, breathing deeply.

He stood over her for a minute, taking the picture to hold in the recess of his mind without even realizing it.

Her lips, slightly parted, were soft inviting. Her hair, spread against the pillow, forced him to fight the urge to lace his fingers through it. *God,* he thought, *what the hell am I doing?* He had felt the tightening in his loins and the heat of desire touch his blood. This would never do. He forced himself under control. He dragged a nearby chair close, sat down and propped his feet on the bottom of the bed. After a while he dozed.

It was midafternoon when he awoke to the surprising knowledge that she, too, was awake and lying there watching him.

She had awakened some minutes before and for a brief moment contemplated trying to slip out of the bed unnoticed. But her good sense prevailed. He had the key to the door and she was quite certain he was too quick and much too strong for her to grab it and get away. No . . . she would wait.

She watched him considering what she would think if she had met him outside of this situation. That he was a very handsome, exciting, and interesting man there was no doubt, and he seemed intelligent . . . perhaps too intelligent. She would have to be very, very careful to play her part well.

When she saw him stir, she smiled, and when his smoke-gray eyes settled on her, she suddenly caught her breath. It was as if he had reached out and strummed her senses.

"I believe you said you wanted to leave by midafternoon."

He let his feet drop to the floor and stood up, stretching to relax his tight muscles, quite unaware of her admiring glance.

"You'd better change your clothes. I suppose you don't want to leave that dress behind."

"I don't think it matters. It was only a stage costume anyway."

"Speaking of the stage," he said. "I was at your last performance. You have a beautiful voice."

"Thank you."

"You must have had quite a bit of training."

"Yes. My parents were very understanding and generous."

"And you cause them all this grief?"

"I don't think you'll understand. But this situation is not causing my parents grief."

"No, I can't understand. I met them and they're very worried about you."

She shook her head and breathed an annoyed sigh.

"I'll go out in the hall while you change." He was surprised when he could no longer resist touching her hair. It felt like strands of satin, as he thought it would. "You'd best do something with your hair. It needs to be bound up."

She smiled at him, reached down and tore a small strip from her petticoat. Then with both hands, grasping her hair she swiftly braided it into a long, thick braid and tied the end. "There," she said. "How's that?"

"Fine," he replied, quite reluctant to tell her that he would much rather have seen it remain down. "I'll wait." He walked to the door, unaware of the glow in her eyes and the satisfied smile on her lips.

She changed her clothes quickly and tossed the dress on the bed. Then she rapped on the door. When he came back in, he was grim and silent. He couldn't say to her that he thought she looked remarkably beautiful . . . But she was just as satisfied with the look in his eyes.

"Ready?"

"Yes."

"No tricks. I want to get out of here without hurting anyone. The only thing you can do is cause someone else a problem."

"I have no intention of causing anyone else a problem," she replied. *Except you* was a thought she kept to herself.

When they rode out of town, he breathed a sigh of relief. It would be an easy trip from here on.

They rode until the sun was just beginning to touch the horizon. There had been no complaints from her, which surprised Brad.

"Down by that stream is a good place to camp for tonight. Are you tired?" he asked.

"A little. I learned to ride as a child, but this has been more than I'm used to."

"By the time you get to St. Louis, you'll be able to ride all day if you need to."

She smiled, but didn't reply. St. Louis was not her planned destination.

While he took care of the horses, she gathered some wood for the fire. With each casual move and defenseless action she watched his own defenses lower.

"Hungry?" he questioned.

"No, not really."

"Me, either. You might as well relax. We'll be up and riding by dawn."

He spread his blanket down and tossed his saddle

nearby to use as a pillow. She carried her blanket to the opposite side of the fire. He smiled to himself, realizing she wanted to keep as much distance between them as she possibly could.

But her motives were not the ones he'd suspected. She knew the effects of light and darkness, and she knew she made a more interesting view across a low-burning fire than if she were sitting beside him. He could not help but look at her, and she wanted his full attention.

"Do you like the theater?" she asked softly.

"Haven't had that much time to attend them. I did see Langford when she performed, and Booth once."

"You've been a very busy man. What do you do with yourself when you're not bounty hunting?"

"This is not bounty hunting," he said. But she heard, with pleasure, the annoyance in his voice.

"Oh? What would you call it, taking money to drag someone to an unwelcome fate?"

How could he explain to her that he would never have done such a thing if his ranch—all he had in life—had not been in danger.

"It was necessary," he said bluntly. "I think you'd better get some sleep."

"All right . . . Good night, Mr. Cole. Sweet dreams."

He remained silent. As she spoke she turned slightly from him, as if dismissing him from her mind. She began to hum softly to herself at the same time that she loosened her hair and ran her fingers through it. She took a brush from her saddlebag and began to work it through her hair. Then she began to sing softly, her voice barely touching the breeze, but audible enough to draw his attention.

He had leaned back against his saddle and drawn his hat down low over his brow, but he could still see her, even if he appeared not to. And she was too good a performer not to sense when she had the attention of her audience.

In the end, Brad, refused to be spellbound by the lovely vision across from him. As she was sure he would do, he sat up and turned his side to the fire and fought a battle to get to sleep.

She was satisfied. There would be no questions and answers, no prodding into her past and she would be saved any revealing words she might have uttered.

She had slept well all midmorning and early afternoon and was not a bit tired. This was good, for she didn't plan on getting any sleep . . . not right now.

She lay awake, listening to his even breathing until she was sure he was deep in sleep.

Slowly, she eased herself up until she was standing, all the time keeping one eye on him. He showed no sign of moving.

She bent to gather up her blanket, rolling it neatly into a bundle to tie behind her saddle. Then she took hold of the saddle, easing it up very slowly so the metal pieces would not make any noise.

She had just turned and taken a step toward where the horses were tied when his amused voice came to her.

"Don't even think about it." He said the words with a laugh in his voice and without even turning to look at her.

She spun around and glared at his broad back. Then she tossed the saddle down and again spread her blanket.

"Good girl." He still had not looked at her. "I'm a light sleeper. Got used to it when I was a Ranger and there were those trying to kill me." He turned now to look at her. "If you're planning on slipping away, don't. You won't get fifty feet from this camp."

She rolled in her blanket and turned her back to him, and was rewarded by his soft laugh. She was so angry, it took her awhile to fall asleep.

True to his word, it was hardly light when he sat up and began to get ready for the day. He looked across the now-dead fire and saw that she, too, was awake.

"Good morning." He smiled at her and received nothing but a cold look. "I'll make a fire and start some breakfast. Are you hungry?" Again he received no answer. He stood and went into the dark shadows of the trees and returned a few minutes later with several pieces of wood.

She stood as he approached and he watched her warily. Then she started for the privacy of the brush.

"You have five minutes," he said firmly, "then I'll come after you."

"You are a cold-hearted beast," she snapped.

"Five minutes" was his only reply.

She walked a good distance away and relieved herself, then walked to the small creek that bubbled in a thin silver ribbon nearby. She washed her hands and face and ran her fingers through her hair to untangle it before she braided it again. Then she walked back to the camp. He was placing wood on the beginnings of a fire and she stopped to watch him. As she walked slowly toward him, he glanced back to see her.

"I'll have a fire started in a jiffy. Get into the packs and dig out the pot and the coffee." She walked a few steps closer. "I'm not the best of cooks but we can have something warm. Unless *you* want to cook?" She grew closer, bent and lifted one of the logs in her hand. It really was sturdy and solid. Before she really had a chance to consider the means fate had put in her path, she raised the log above her head and brought it down with full force. There was a solid thud and he fell sideways and lay still.

Unsure of how long he would remain in this condition and knowing it would most likely take too much time to saddle her horse, she ran to his saddle and took the rope he carried.

Swiftly she tied his hands behind his back and fastened his ankles firmly together. It took every ounce of strength to turn him over. She had to make sure he wasn't seriously hurt.

He seemed to be breathing all right and even groaned once as he struggled to regain consciousness. She went to her horse, put the bridle on and led it back to where her saddle and blanket lay. By that time he was stirring.

As the mist of blackness parted before his eyes, Brad felt the sharp pain in his head. At the same time he realized he was immobile.

She was standing a short distance from him, laying the blanket across her horse's back. As she bent to lift the saddle, she saw he was conscious. Their eyes met, she smiled and continued to lift the saddle and swing it up on the horse's back.

"You'd better run fast, because you're not going to get far. That I promise you." He snarled the words, angry because he'd been sloppy and careless. No man had ever gotten the better of him, and now a woman had made a fool of him. It didn't sit well. Then she promptly made it worse and rubbed salt into the wound. She walked to him, kneeling beside him and smiling.

"I've tried to explain to you, Mr. Cole, but you are very hard headed, no pun intended, despite what you did to that piece of wood. I am not Winter Stapleton, and I'm definitely not going to Charleston with you. Now please don't take this personally, but I've really got plans of my own . . . and they don't include you." To his complete shock and even deeper consternation, she bent and brushed a light kiss on his lips. "I'm going to leave a knife right here beside you. In a couple of hours you should be free . . . and I'll be far enough away that it won't do you any good to follow. Good-bye, Mr. Cole. Better luck next time." Her laugh was soft and it scraped his nerves like sandpaper.

"Next time is right, princess. The next time I'll be a little more careful. I won't turn my back on you." His smile was nearly vicious.

"Does the money mean that much to you?"

"You wouldn't understand it, but it's no longer only money. Now it's a matter of principle."

"Princ—" she began, then her laughter sounded

again. "Don't tell me. You're the Ranger who always got his man? Too bad. Not this time."

She rose, dropped the knife several feet from him, and walked to her horse and mounted. She waved jauntily at him and rode away. The curses he uttered would have made a drunken sailor blush. He struggled to get himself into a position to grab the knife and begin to cut himself free.

Her figuring had been right. It was a little over two hours by the time he'd gotten completely free, gotten the pack horse ready and his horse saddled.

He wanted to rush after her, but he had to stop using his anger and start using his head.

He stood still for a minute, concentrating on possibilities.

"Where," he muttered. "Where?" He paced, forming a picture of the possible places she would go. Then suddenly he stopped pacing and smiled. He mounted his horse and rode very slowly from camp.

She rode easily, stopping now and then to try to obliterate her trail, as she had seen him do. When she found a small stream she rode up it to keep her tracks from being followed.

After an hour she left the water. She knew exactly where she was going and why. She'd known when she left him what she had to do and where she had to go. Born and raised in a self-sufficient family, she had learned to be hardy and efficient. She'd learned to ride well, to hunt and trap. She had camped out and cooked over an open fire. She also learned how to use the sun and the stars to get where she wanted to go.

She knew she wouldn't have trouble finding the trail. Hadn't she, Jasper, and Dobbs talked it over so often? Hadn't they made a number of alternative plans? They were waiting, and she knew where.

The town of Rockville was so small that few visited it, or even rode through it. It lay in a direction she was sure Brad would not consider. They had agreed on several key towns so that if they were ever separated they would have a good chance of meeting again.

She was right. She recognized the wagon parked near the edge of town, and smiled. When she rode up to it, it seemed deserted, but a second later Jasper appeared from behind, rifle in hand and Dobbs close by.

"You're all right?" Jasper questioned at once, his eyes scanning her as if looking for the slightest bruise.

"Yes, Jasper, I am."

"We were very upset to find you gone," Dobbs said. "Jasper tried to track you, but the gentleman seems to be quite adept at hiding his tracks."

"He most certainly is," she agreed, then went on to explain how he had taken her and where they had gone. To their amusement, she explained how she had gotten away.

"I hope his headache lasts for a week," Jasper growled.

"Well, it won't, Jasper, and we have a job to do. I have a feeling he won't be that far behind and I want to put as much distance between me and Charleston as I can. I want to make his job as difficult as possible, and I want it to take as long as possible."

"You think he'll catch up with us?" Dobbs asked.

"I don't underestimate his ability or his determination. He has something at stake, but I don't know what it is. I wish I did. It's given him a lot of interest in succeeding in bringing me back. Leave it to *her* to hire such an efficient man."

"What do you suggest we do now?" Dobbs' smiled. "Jasper and I are at your service, my lady."

"Then," her smile sparkled, "let's go on to our next engagement. Only this time, we keep our eyes open."

"If I get my hands on him again," Jasper said, "I might just have to muss him up."

"Oh, Jasper, he doesn't want to hurt me. He wants to do his job. And we," she laughed, "are going to make sure he doesn't."

The wagon left the town, using no well-traveled paths. For two days they rode and they watched. She was surprised when there was no sign of Brad.

Traveling slowly gave her time to think, and it surprised her where her thoughts wandered. She remembered acutely the taste and feel of his firm mouth when she had taunted him with a kiss and wondered, much against her will, how it would be if he had returned the kiss.

They came into the town of Champion just after dusk and found a quiet, shadowed alley in which to put the wagon.

It was Dobbs's job to arrange for the night's entertainment, and Shelby was prepared to sing again. She would stay a day or two ahead of Brad, and by the time he found out where she was and got there, they would be gone.

When the stage was darkened and Dobbs's own particular lighting invention was creating the golden spot in the center of the stage, she stepped into it with confidence.

Dressed in a gown of black lace she sang of moonlit nights and lovers, and even she knew that she had never sang better. She could hear the appreciative applause from the audience when her song was done.

Because she stood in the light and all the theater to her was a dark pool, she did not see the tall form at the back of the hall. She was not aware of his rapt attention and appreciation, both of her beauty and her music.

She was also not aware of the glint of promised revenge in his smoky gray eyes . . . nor the other emotions that held him immobile.

By the time the lights came up and Dobbs was again in midperformance, the tall form had vanished.

In the back of the theater Jasper hovered so close to her that Shelby felt stifled. He'd done so since the day she'd returned. She knew it was out of concern for her, but sometimes she wondered if she couldn't have done better without her two guardians.

It was late when Dobbs was finished and the three of them went to a small restaurant and had a late supper. Then they returned to the wagon. Jasper and

Dobbs decided she would be safer close to them than in a hotel room alone.

She was tired, so with the two men outside, she climbed into the wagon, undressed and went to sleep.

Chapter 4

The next morning all three awoke early. Even though Dobbs and Jasper assured her there was no sign of their shadow, still the feeling of tense foreboding followed her.

"We have to leave here as soon as possible."

"I'll keep a close watch on you," Jasper said. "But I don't think he has a clue as to our whereabouts."

"There's no doubt he'll be on our trail, though." She was sure of it. "I just need to put some more distance between us and Charleston before he gets here. If we could get past Denver and start for California, we just might suceed. If Brad Cole does catch us then, it won't matter . . . or we can just go home."

The two men regarded her closely. She had found a place in their hearts. They wanted her safe.

"Once you're gone two months, we can go back on our own," Dobbs stated thoughtfully. "If we can continue to dodge this man, you can return without his help when the time comes. I resent his thinking he can just grab you and drag you back like some kind of criminal. Besides, how can you trust him? He might have other motives in mind."

"I really don't think he's thinking of anything else. He had more than one opportunity to take advantage of me and he didn't. It looks like we have an honorable man with stubborn determination on our hands."

"The really dangerous kind," Dobbs said thoughtfully. "The type to follow you to the ends of the earth."

"I don't doubt that for a minute. But if we're clever we can stay one jump ahead of him. After that much time passes it won't matter. It will be too late when he does get me back."

"One step ahead of him," Jasper replied. "If he's on our trail now, we won't be able to play all those engagements you planned. If he's as clever as you say, he only has to use the telegraph to find out where the show is playing and be there . . . maybe even before we are. It's time we started some real serious planning."

"No," she said thoughtfully, "I think it's time we split up temporarily."

"Split up!" Dobbs said. "No way in the world are we going to let you go off alone anywhere."

"I didn't exactly mean that."

"Well, what *did* you mean?"

"We need to confuse him a bit."

"How?" Jasper's frown warned her the explanation had better be good.

"After tonight's performance we are going to do a quick exchange."

"What for what?" Jasper questioned quickly.

"Me, for . . . someone else."

"Who else?"

"Jasper, you and Dobbs can scout around. Go over to that . . . house at the edge of town. There has to be one girl there who wants to move on."

"A brothel! How . . ." Dobbs was quite amazed that she knew anything about such a place, and a bit embarrassed that she was so very sure he and Jasper did.

"Come on, Dobbs, there's one in every town on earth. Trust me that you'll find a girl who's anxious to leave. When it's dark and the show is over, you need only bundle her up and leave town. Leave right down Main Street so no one can miss it. She can wear one of my bonnets and one of my dresses. If she's careful no one will see her face."

"And you?" Jasper scowled, ready to protest.

"I have riding clothes. You, dear Jasper, will make sure there's a horse out back of the theater, I'll go on while you lead him another way. By the time he finds out it's not me, he'll be on my trail, which will be quite cold by then."

"I don't like it," Dobbs said at once. "It leaves you at risk and alone. No, I don't like it."

"Do you have a better idea?"

"Yes, I think I do."

"Then tell me."

"Time is what you need. So . . . we'll find a girl and leave town like you say. But you'll stay here. We can lead him on a merry chase before he knows it's not you. After a week of twisting him around, Jasper can slip away and come back for you. It will eat up the days you need and you can be safe right here."

"Hmmm," she said thoughtfully. "That's not really a bad idea."

"Of course it's not," Dobbs chuckled. "If it's time you want, then it's time you'll get."

"What about our next engagement?"

"That's still a week away. I'll wire them and explain we have been detained but that we'll be along as soon as possible."

"I don't like leaving you alone. If anyone back East finds out, there'll be hell to pay. And if anything happens to you, I don't want to face Mr. Stapleton," Jasper argued.

"Jasper, in the first place, the man following me does not mean me any harm. In the second place, it's that show wagon he'll follow. I'll be perfectly safe here. Once the time has lapsed I don't care if he finds me or not, the race will be over. Then, we only have to board a train and go back home where both of you can relax."

"I still don't like it. I got a good look at him and I don't think he's anybody's fool. What happens if he doesn't fall for this?"

"How could he possibly not? He'll come into town after you leave and everyone will tell him we've moved on. Why should he even think I haven't moved on with you?"

She could see that Jasper was less than happy about the plan, but he just couldn't think of anything to say that would stop her.

"I'll take a walk over to Belle's place," Dobbs said.

"By tonight, after the show, I'll have someone to take your place."

"Thanks, Dobbs. Jasper, don't be put out with me. I'm sure this will work, I'll be safe in a hotel room for a while. I'm really not afraid of him."

"Sometimes," Jasper said cautiously, "you're much too brave. If this works, in a little over a week we'll be back for you. I don't like it, but I guess I can't stop it."

"I do have one suggestion," Dobbs said. "I'm going to find you a companion who can get food for you, or anything else you might need. It's best you don't go out on the street."

"You're right. I wouldn't want him to see me when he does pass through. The hotel room will be in someone else's name, I suppose?"

"Absolutely. That's the first thing he'll check on."

"Then you two go along and set this plan in motion. I'm going to check on my costumes. I want tonight's performance to be one of my best. This is my last day of freedom for a week, so I plan to do something with it."

"You be careful," Dobbs cautioned.

"I will. He can't be around yet. He had no idea where we were going, and since we changed even the plans we had, it will take him a couple of days to find out where we are. I need some taste of freedom to last the week of imprisonment."

"It sounds terrible when you say it that way," Jasper said. The whole idea was clearly unsettling him.

"I'll be fine, Jasper, really I will, and I'll be very

careful. Once you two leave I won't budge out of that hotel room. I promise. But until tonight's performance, I still have my freedom. Let me enjoy it. Now, hurry along."

Dobbs, and a still very reluctant Jasper, left the wagons to set the plans in motion.

She really enjoyed going through the costumes for the night's performance, so she took her time and chose carefully. The costume was a deep burgundy with a tight-laced waist and a very full skirt that made her look delicate and slim. She chose brilliant glittery artificial rubies and diamonds for her accessories so that they would dance in the glow of Dobbs's light.

She planned on wearing her hair in a very severe manner tonight to finish off the illusion of an elusive and elegant lady. She always had to choose her music as carefully as the costumes she wore. It was this blend that created the illusion and made it whole.

Satisfied with her choices, she realized she was very hungry. Washing and dressing quickly, she made her way to the closest restaurant. Dobbs and Jacob found her there a half hour later doing justice to a dish of bacon and eggs.

"Well, it's all arranged," Dobbs announced. "I had a nice long talk with Belle, the . . . ah . . . owner of the establishment. She's got a girl that just fits the bill. Blonde and young. If we're careful she should pass for you. In the meantime, there's a young lady who has already gone to the hotel and gotten a room in her name. Here's the key. Her name is Charlotte and she'll be in and out to see that you get everything you need and keep up appearances. Make sure you lock yourself in."

"I could handle this gent once and for all," Jasper said. "I could put a stop to him chasing you."

"We don't want anyone hurt, Jasper," she said, but deep inside, after her short bout with Brad, she had her doubts. The first time they met, Jasper had the advantage of surprise. The next time might be different. "He won't be in town that long. We'll watch closely. When he comes and finds out we've gone, he'll be on your trail at once. No one is going to bother me."

Both men nodded, but both were still fighting the thought that they might be making a very big mistake.

At one time Belle Devilin had been a flame-haired beauty. Life had not always been generous to her, but she had always retained a steady outlook. Born Constance Bradly, she had run away from a lecherous stepfather when she was a well-developed fourteen. From then on she played the game of life with whatever cards fate decided to give her.

Known for her ability to outdrink and outgamble any man alive and for the fact that she carried a derringer in one garter and a slim-bladed knife in the other, and was deadly with both. She also had the reputation of a woman of straight forward honesty with a heart as big as Texas.

Her slanted green eyes danced with humor as she

gazed at the man who sat comfortably in a chair close by, his feet propped on a stool.

"If I didn't know you as well as I do, I'd have my doubts about you. What are you really up to, Brad?"

"I'm not up to anything except doing a job and doing it well."

"Job? I thought you quit the Rangers and was just working your ranch?"

"I had."

"Then why are you chasing after this girl? She caught your fancy?"

"Hardly. She's a spoiled little rich girl. Not for me."

"Then let her get what she deserves."

"I can't. Spoiled and rich she is, but she's an innocent, too. She doesn't know what she's getting into out here. Besides, I've been hired to see she gets safely back to her parents."

"Fanny and I saw her perform the other night. She's some girl, and in a place like mine she could make a fortune."

"Forget it, Belle," Brad said with a dark scowl, "she's going home."

"My, my," she grinned tauntingly, "we are a bit touchy, aren't we?"

"Don't get clever. I've no designs on the lady except to see she gets safely back into her parents' lap, and that I collect."

"Collect?" she replied with one raised eyebrow.

"Don't look like that. I told you it was a necessity. Look . . . I stand a chance of losing everything. I need the money her family is paying me. Nobody's getting hurt."

"Well then, what do you say we just have her snatched, and tonight you can bundle her up and carry her home."

"Won't work. I tried that. Those two bodyguards of hers are quick and smart."

"You scared?" Belle laughed at the ridiculousness of this statement.

"Have you seen the size of Jasper?" Brad laughed in response. "Besides, I don't want to cross their paths if I don't have to. I don't really want to hurt either of them. It's better we let them think they're pulling something off. When they're gone with your girl in tow, I'll just move in and take her off your hands."

"I've known you a lot of years, Brad. This isn't your kind of game. How far do you think they'll go before they realize you're not on their trail? From what you tell me, they're a pretty clever group. They'll be back here in no time."

"A day or two head start is all I need. They won't stand a chance of trailing me after that."

"And what about this girl? She doesn't sound easy to handle. She got away from you once."

"Once," Brad said with a wry grin. "You don't think I'm going to trust her enough to let that happen again?"

"I hope you're doing the right thing."

"What's that supposed to mean?"

"Remember, I've gotten this story from two sides. This Dobbs talks about a whole different situation."

"What's his story?"

"He says the girl's running away from a forced marriage."

"Forced marriage," Brad scoffed. "Probably a man her family knows she'd be better off with."

"Being a man yourself, maybe you wouldn't understand. But marrying someone you don't love would be a terrible thing. Maybe she's just scared."

"Scared! Come on, Belle. She's not scared of anything or anybody. Traveling out here, looking like she does, takes a lot of courage."

"She's beautiful . . . isn't she?" Belle's question sounded almost like a casual afterthought.

"Beautiful is hardly the word," Brad fell into her trap neatly. "She's . . ." Catching the glimpse of humor in her eyes, he paused. "All right, so she's beautiful. That has nothing to do with the situation. I have more important problems to solve. She's going home, and I'm going to get my ranch back on its feet if it kills me."

"Sorry. I know how much the place means to you. I didn't mean to make it sound unimportant. But you were always a man to see both sides of a fight, so I kind of figured you'd understand. Marrying a man you don't want is a kind of hell . . . one that lasts a lifetime." Belle rose and walked to the door. "I'll let you know when they leave."

"I'm . . . I'm going over to the theater tonight anyway. Thought I'd take in the performance. Just to help me keep it in mind that she's a damn good actress who knows how to use everything she's got."

"Oh, yes. Of course," she smiled as she opened the door.

"Belle," Brad's voice was exasperated, "don't read any more into this. It's just curiosity."

"Why, Brad . . . I wouldn't doubt that for a minute." If he wasn't mistaken he thought he heard very soft laughter as she left, closing the door behind her.

He remained seated considering his plans. Almost absently he took the picture from his pocket and gazed at it.

"Everything ready, Jasper?"

"Yes," Jasper replied. "After the performance you go backstage. The switch will be made. I'm sure he's going to trace everything right from here. Once we've gone Charlotte will meet you at the hotel. For God's sake, be careful."

"I will. Please don't worry so." She smiled with much more confidence than she actually felt. "Now I'd better get ready. Once we put this into motion there'll no time to play with." She went to Jasper and put her hand on his arm, standing on tiptoe to kiss his cheek. "You've been wonderful, Jasper, and I'm grateful. Before long this will all be over, and we can all stop running and settle back into a normal life."

"I hope you're right. This all sounds good, but I'm not too sure that man is going to rise to the bait so easily. I'll be watching. I'll backtrack and check the trail after a couple of days. If he isn't following us we'll skedaddle right back here."

"I don't expect anything to go wrong, but if it should, I'll find some way to leave word."

"Don't worry. Word or not, I'll find him. If he touches you . . . this time I won't be so gentle with him. He needs a hard knock or two to get the message," Jasper grumbled as he left the dressing room.

Less than half hour later she stood before her full-length mirror and examined herself carefully. She was pleased with what she saw. All her costumes were designed carefully to take advantage of her own coloring and the unique lighting.

She had twisted her hair into a chignon at the nape of her neck. She was satisfied, and she was ready.

Moving carefully among the clutter of props and the people, she made her way to the wings, where she stood and watched the last of Dobbs's Shakespearean performance. She admired his talent very much, and was mesmerized as completely as the audience.

To the sound of hearty applause Dobbs joined her in the wings. He smiled, wiping the perspiration from his brow.

"They're a fine crowd tonight, and you, my dear, are enough to enchant them."

"And you are a flatterer."

"Everything's ready. The lights should go out soon. This is a farewell performance, so go on and show them your extraordinary talent."

"Dobbs . . ."

"I know, my dear. But this is only a temporary good-bye. We'll be back to collect you and take you safely home. In the meantime, relax with the idea that we'll lead him a merry chase. There," he said as the theater darkened about them, "that's your cue. Now don't worry your pretty head about anything, except giving your finest performance."

As the mellow gold circle of light appeared on the stage, she hugged Dobbs fiercely and whispered, "I really appreciate this, Dobbs. Take good care of yourself." Then she was gone with a whisper of silk.

The sound of applause reached him as he watched her step into the circle of light.

"God be with you, child," Dobbs whispered as he walked back to his dressing room where the girl he had hired to play the part was waiting. Now it was only a matter of a quick exchange in the silence of the darkened theater when the music ended and the stage was empty.

Brad stood immobile, fighting not to recognize the emotion that held him as the mellow light touched the stage. Then she stepped into the circle, and despite his effort at control, he could feel his pulses pick up a beat and senses heighten.

If anything, she seemed even more beautiful than the first time he'd seen her perform. When she began to sing, he, as all the others, was held spellbound. Her voice was warm as it wove a story of unrequited and tragic love.

If this was all the control he had at a distance, how was he going to get her all the way back to Charleston without seriously damaging what little control he had left? He fought to retrieve and hold on to his anger. The anger he had felt when she'd knocked him out and then rode away laughing. He remembered her taunting kiss, and his anger grew. He needed it to wipe out the taste and scent of her in that one brief moment.

He slowly built his barriers until control was once more in his grasp. He wouldn't allow her to ever get the upper hand again.

Still, secluded in the darkness, he allowed himself to enjoy the magic she could weave.

When the lights went out, Brad made his way out of the theater at once and found a place where he could watch the little charade the three of them had planned.

He smiled when he saw them leave the theater and deposit their baggage in the back of the wagon. When Jasper and Dobbs slowly guided the wagon out of town, Brad felt more than satisfied. Before dawn, when he knew from experience that a person's guard was at its lowest . . . then he would move. This time Winter Stapleton would not slip from his grasp.

The burgundy-colored dress was hung in the closet along with her riding clothes. She sat in her chemise and sipped from a cup of hot tea while she slowly loosened the pins from her hair. Once she brushed it till it glowed, she carefully gathered the mass into a thick braid.

She would be spending several days imprisoned in this hotel room, and had tried to make herself as comfortable as possible. The girl who was to be her liaison had not made an appearance yet, so she left the door unlocked until she was ready to go to sleep, just in case Charlotte came. She would make sure it was locked carefully once Charlotte was settled.

Outside, the street was quieting for the night. Except for the faint sounds of revelry from the saloons, the town seemed to be nearly deserted.

Through her open window a faint breeze billowed the curtains. She suddenly wished fervently that Dobbs had at least left her a couple of books to read. It was going to prove to be a trial of boredom. This made her think of the necessity that had created the situation, and the man behind it.

She smiled to herself. It was not the first time she thought that under any other circumstances meeting Brad Cole might have been very interesting. He certainly was handsome, and when he wasn't obnoxiously overbearing he could be quite interesting.

Maybe, she mused, when all of this was over she would have to look up one Mister Brad Cole and apologize for so much inconvenience.

Setting the cup aside, she rose from the bed and walked to the lamp, which she turned down to burn very low. Then she went to the window and drew the curtain aside.

It certainly was a beautiful night. The sky was so dark that the stars glittered like diamonds against black velvet. The breeze carried a scent she didn't recognize but did enjoy.

She sighed and let the curtain fall back into place, then turned and walked back to the bed. She didn't look forward to a tediously long night. Already she longed for the freedom to take a walk.

Since that was not possible, she'd propped the pillows up behind her, her mind drifting to past times. After a while she was caught up in the pleasant memories.

Her thoughts made her smile, especially when she considered Brad's displeasure as he searched one town after another for her. But this pleasant thought, that led to even more comfort, betrayed her. She drifted into unwanted sleep.

Brad was annoyed at his own impatience. He'd stood in the shadows of the street below and watched her when she appeared at the window. He saw the lamp dim until the room was almost dark. He had to give her enough time to fall asleep. He went to the saloon and had a couple of drinks. Then he checked his equipment for the tenth time.

He waited, ignoring his imagination that was doing its best to prod his senses. He would not be her victim. Not now . . . not ever.

He had a key to the hotel room in his pocket, which he'd gotten from Charlotte. It was not long before morning, the moon low in the night sky. The perfect time to move. He crossed the still-darkened street and entered the hotel.

The night clerk dozed behind the desk. He'd never had the occasion to check in a guest after midnight, so he usually caught up on lost sleep.

Brad moved silently across the lobby and up the

stairs. When he paused outside her door, he reached for the knob at the same time he reached in his pocket for the key. But the knob turned and the door gave slightly. Good God, he thought, she'd actually left the door unlocked. Her innocence of the dangers around her spurred his anger and his determination. This naive little girl had to be gotten home before she ran across a danger she was not prepared for.

Like a silent ghost he slipped inside and closed the door soundlessly behind him.

She slept soundly, obviously secure that he was nowhere in her vicinity. He smiled as he looked down at her, then silently he moved around the room, gathering her riding clothes and boots.

When he had set them by the bed, he sat down slowly and gently on the edge of the bed so that he still wouldn't disturb her sleep.

He knew when he awakened her the battle would begin. But he resisted rousing her at once. She looked so . . . vulnerable and defenseless. If his conscience gave a twinge, he tried his best to ignore it. His actions would cause no harm to anybody. In fact, he justified, it would really be the best thing for her in the long run.

She drifted in a mist-filled dream. First, she was walking in a strange place, a place semidark and filled with shadows. She didn't know where she was going, only that there was an urgency to go on. She realized then that there was a presence, a shadowy form, but she felt no fear of it. Instead, she felt a warmth, and knew without speaking or hearing any words that this presence was a protector, not a threat.

Then dark forms seemed to detach themselves from the shadows. Frightening forms that stirred fear. But the protector hovered near, assuring her that she was safe, that it would let no harm come to her. It spoke, but she could hear only a vague whisper.

"Sleeping beauty, it's time to wake up."

At the same time she heard the voice she felt a weight, as if it were pressing her down. Slowly, she tried to fight off sleep and the uncomfortable pressure.

Brad had bent forward so that some of the weight of his body would hold her down once she awoke.

"Come on, sleeping beauty," he repeated softly, "it's time to wake up."

She struggled slightly against the pressure, and Brad watched as she slowly came awake. Her eyes fluttered open, confused and heavy with sleep.

When her violet eyes met gray ones, for a minute the shock stunned her to silence. But his large hand covered her mouth firmly before she could make a sound.

He grinned, and she could have shrieked her fury.

"Hello there, princess. You really didn't think I was going to give up that easily, did you? We have a little debt to settle."

She wriggled desperately trying to free herself, but he was so much bigger, and she didn't delude herself that she could successfully get out of his grasp. She lay still and let her eyes express her emotions.

He nodded. "Good girl. Fighting isn't going to do much good. I hate to do it, but I'm afraid I have to gag you and tie you up again. I'm pretty certain you aren't going to go along without any trouble."

Furiously, she shook her head negatively, her gaze promising him revenge if she got free.

"I thought not," Brad sighed in pretend regret. "That's why I came prepared." First, very efficiently he gagged her, using his weight to hold her. Then he tied her hands and ankles. Only then did he stand erect and look down at her.

"I hate to do it this way, but I discovered, to my momentary embarrassment, that you are very clever, very quick, and you can't be trusted for a minute. I learned a long time ago not to make the same mistakes twice."

He took a blanket, quite aware that her gaze was following his every move. He put her clothes and the toiletries from her dresser in the blanket, and rolled it into a neat bundle.

He took the second blanket and came back to her. "It's a bit cold outside, and since you aren't exactly dressed for travel, this will have to do." As easily as one might handle a child, he wrapped her cocoonlike in the blanket.

He watched her eyes grow calm and even become touched by amusement.

"You don't think I'm going to get you out of here like this do you?"

She shook her head, her eyes defiant.

"Well, I am. Don't doubt it for a minute."

Without another word, he bent and lifted her from the bed. Hefting her over his shoulder, he heard her groan of fury and felt her begin to struggle again. She gave a muffled squeal of protest when he slapped her sharply on the bottom.

"You'd best be quiet," he warned. But amusement danced in his eyes.

She remained quiet, but he could almost hear the wheels of her mind spinning. He had an idea she was planning some form of revenge already.

Getting to the stable seemed so easy for him. To her it was frustrating. Then to find he had a wagon ready only added to it. When he unceremoniously dumped her in the back; she lay fuming. Vows of murder and mayhem filled her mind.

The wagon lurched forward, and in a short while they had left the town behind.

She had no idea of how long, how far, or even in what direction they traveled. She only knew it seemed to her like hours before the wagon came to a halt in a stand of trees so dense she could no longer look up and see the stars.

She lay still, hearing him move around. *Just like an arrogant man,* she thought angrily. *He's taking care of the horses first, then he'll condescend to take care of me.*

When he finally came for her, he lifted her from the wagon and stood her on her feet.

He unwrapped and untied her, and her first move was to snatch the gag from her mouth.

"You're never going to get away with this!"

"Of course I am," he chuckled in the face of her anger.

"I've been betrayed."

"You mean Belle? She's an old friend of mine.

When I told her what the story was, she understood that a girl like you belongs at home."

"I'm not going back to Charleston with you!"

"You've said that before. Can't you think of something more original? You're going back. You could just be smart and make the best of it. But, rest assured, I'm a lot wiser than to believe any of your acts again. This time I'm not playing games."

Their eyes met and held for a long tense moment. But wisdom soon took over for her. There would be a time and a place. Now was not it.

"I have enough supplies in the wagon to get us to St. Louis. From there we'll wire your family. Right now you'd better get some rest. I have some food to hold you over until we make camp tonight. We'll be traveling in an hour."

He walked away from her and began to gather foodstuffs from their supplies. After a moment she dressed. Then she gathered all her control, and with a half smile on her lips, walked over to join him.

He looked at her with surprise, but it was surprise tinged with wariness. She knew she needed her wits. As he had said, he would never fall for the same trick twice. No, she had to think of something, as he had also said . . . original.

Chapter 5

Jasper, Dobbs, and Louise Martin rode the slow-moving wagon hoping to give Brad enough time and enough trail to follow them. Louise had kept herself within the confines of the wagon, except for the display of her presence to the townsfolk who watched their departure.

But the farther they went, the more morose and silent Jasper became.

"You're still fretting about this situation," Dobbs said to him, more statement than question.

"Yeah."

"Why?"

"Damned if I know," Jasper shrugged.

"How can he believe anything other than what everyone tells him? She left with the wagons. He should be on our trail by nightfall."

"I guess."

"You still don't accept it, though. Why?"

"I just don't think he's foxed this easy. I moved

around a bit and I checked with the sheriff. This Brad Cole is an ex-Ranger."

"So?"

"With a damn good reputation."

"So?" Dobbs repeated.

"So I think he's sharp enough to think as fast as we do . . . maybe faster. He might look for something like this and be one jump ahead of us."

"Look, she was going to go off by herself. This was the best idea. You knew we couldn't let her drift around on her own."

"She should have just let me deal with him. I wouldn't really have hurt him, just—"

"Mussed him up a bit," Dobbs finished. "I know. Look, Jasper, let's just give this plan a chance. If it doesn't work," he shrugged, "maybe you *will* have to stop him for a while."

"Shoulda done it the first time when I had the chance. That night in her dressing room."

"You sure are a stubborn, one-track-minded man."

"So's he. I'd say that's how he lived so long as a Ranger."

Reasonably certain that he was not going to be able to ease Jasper's discomfort, Dobbs informed the big man that he was going to try to sleep for a while.

Jasper acknowledged his words with a brief nod and Dobbs climbed in to the back of the wagon. As the moon rose higher, Jasper's mood grew blacker. He'd always regarded his deepest feelings about people, even at first meetings, to be something he could depend on. His first impression of Brad Cole as he had watched him talking to Shelby had been of a strong, determined, and very capable man.

At one time in his life, he himself had been pursued by Rangers, and he knew their abilities. Dobbs and Shelby were too sure of themselves, and that often bred disaster. Overconfidence, when dealing with a man like Cole, could be more than dangerous.

He thought of Shelby. There was no doubt in his mind the girl had more than her share of beauty and courage. But this combination could also prove her undoing.

More than admiring her pretty face and her talent, Jasper truly liked Shelby. In a way she reminded him of the sister he had not seen for so many years. Not in looks, but in some indefinable way that couldn't be put into words.

As the horses plodded on, Jasper morosely held the reins while he let his mind remain on Shelby and the fact that she was alone.

When dawn came, Jasper pulled the wagon off the rough, rutted road and drew it to a halt in the shadows of a stand of trees. By the time he had climbed down, Dobbs was looking out from between the canvas flaps.

"The horses are tired," Jasper explained. "They need to be fed and watered. I'm hungry, too, and I'll bet Louise could use some food."

"I'll wake her up. You're right. We should have a bite to eat and rest the horses. But we can't waste too much time."

The stillness of the wagon had brought Louise

awake on her own, and she soon joined Jasper and Dobbs to eat a spare, quickly prepared meal.

The day was bright and beginning to warm beneath a cloudless sky. When the horses were rested to the satisfaction of a still-reluctant Jasper, they were again on their way.

But the longer they traveled, the more Dobbs could feel the anxiety building in Jasper. Even Louise's happy chatter did not brighten his mood.

They stopped again at midday, and Dobbs finally reached the end of his patience.

"Jasper, for heaven's sake. If you're going to get lower by the hour, you might as well do something about it."

"Such as?"

"Take one of the horses and ride back to town and assure yourself that she's safe. Then maybe we can get on with our plan."

Jasper smiled for the first time. "I can be there and back before morning. I won't let anyone spot me. Maybe I can find out just how close he might be."

"Anything," Dobbs said dryly, "to ease your mind. For God's sake, watch yourself. We didn't set this plan up for you to spoil it."

"I'll be real careful. I've been around his kind before. If he's close, he'll never know I am."

Dobbs eyed Jasper speculatively. There was a lot about the man he called friend that he didn't know. Still, there was no doubt in his mind Jasper was that rare thing: a real friend. He never intended to ask any question Jasper might not want to answer. In this territory a man's past was his own.

Dobbs and Louise settled themselves to wait, while Jasper took one of the horses and rode back toward town. He took his own path, keeping away from the road, and was very careful that no one saw him.

It was sundown when he reached the edge of the town but still too light for him to take the chance of approaching it without being seen.

He waited until it was dark enough that he could move around cautiously, then concealed his horse in a stand of trees and made his way on foot to the hotel.

For a man of his size he moved with a surprising agility as he used a tree and a back-porch roof to gain entrance.

He walked down the hall to the room Shelby was supposed to have remained in, and knocked lightly. It would have been impossible to tell who was more surprised—Jasper, or the man who opened the door.

Jasper was too intimidating a presence for the man to get belligerent. Besides, he wore a wicked-looking gun.

"Yes, sir, can I help you? Were you looking for someone?"

"Yeah. What are you doing in this room?"

"I . . . I'm staying here. I paid for it."

"When?"

"This morning."

Jasper was puzzled and alarmed, and his expression did a great deal to alarm the occupant as well. In fact, it scared him to death.

"Look, if there's a problem, just ask the desk clerk. He'll tell you. This is my room."

Jasper had no intention of asking the desk clerk, but there were a couple of other people who, he thought angrily, better have some pretty good answers.

"No, it's all right. I'm sorry. Maybe I have the wrong room. I'll check."

The occupant breathed a soundless sigh of relief and closed the door. But Jasper didn't go to the desk clerk. Instead, he left the hotel the same way he had entered it.

Jasper stood in the dark alley behind the hotel and considered what had just been revealed. He also considered exactly what he could do about it. Once he'd made a decision he set about putting it in action with grim determination matched by a slow-building anger.

Charlotte Webster sat on the edge of a comfortable chair in Belle's office and watched her intently.

"I sure hope those two don't get too wild if they find out that girl's gone. It's you and me they're going to come looking for."

"Stop worrying, Char. It will be a while by the time they get back here. We have our stories straight. After all, we just couldn't tie her to the bed. Obviously, she wanted to leave. So she left without telling us. It's not our fault. You went over to her room and found her gone. You can't be blamed for that."

"She'll be all right? I mean . . ."

"Brad would never hurt her. I told you what he said. He's never lied to me. That girl needs to be back home." She turned to look at Charlotte. "You and I both know how hard it is out here with no one to help. She'll be gobbled up and her loving parents will never see her again. This is the best way. We can trust Brad."

"Yeah," Charlotte said. "It's sure no place for a girl like her to be."

"We'd better get on down to work. We're not going to make any money sitting up here." They both rose, then Belle spoke again. "Char. Thank you. I owe you one."

"Don't thank me, Belle. If you balance this against all *I* owe *you,* I'm still pretty deep in debt to you. You know if you ever need anything, you only have to ask. I'd be on the street or worse if you hadn't picked this stray kitten up."

"Well, c'mon, kitten. Let's get to work."

Belle was just a step or two ahead of Charlotte as they walked to the door. But when she opened the door, both gasped in shock at the imposing bulk of Jasper filling the doorway.

"Where is she?" Jasper's voice came like the growl of a grizzly, and struck just about the same amount of fear. Charlotte stood in wide-eyed terror. This man could break her in two without raising a sweat.

"I said, where is she?" he repeated. He stepped into the room and closed the door behind him. The two women backed away from him. Belle was the first one to recover.

"Jasper, you scared the hell out of us. What are you doing back here so soon?"

"I came back looking for Shelby, and she's gone. Now, suppose you two stop pussyfooting around and tell me what's going on. She better not be hurt . . . and that Ranger had better not have found out her whereabouts."

Belle, retained her calm. But Charlotte's courage melted like wax in the sun from the cold threat in Jasper's voice. He saw her face go pale, and even though she clenched her fists, he could see her hands were shaking. She was scared . . . and he knew it.

"I think you two better explain to me just what happened."

"We don't know," Belle said quickly.

"You don't know!" Jasper's eyes flicked to Charlotte. "You were supposed to stay with her. You're the one who should know." He took another step toward Charlotte, who nearly fainted in fear.

"I don't! I don't know! I only know I went over there after the place closed and she wasn't there. I don't know where she went. All her things were gone, too. Like . . . she changed her mind and just took off."

"She's too smart to do that." Jasper's growl made Charlotte utter a soft moan of terror.

"Jasper, let her alone," Belle pleaded. "She doesn't know anything else. She went over to the hotel when she got done working. It was about two or three in the morning. Shelby was gone, and she'd taken all her things. We had no idea where you were, so there was nothing much we could do about it. The girl must have come up with an idea of her own and just left."

Jasper's heart skipped a beat. He sensed they weren't telling the exact truth, just as he realized there was little he could do about it unless he got physical with them, and that he couldn't do. He'd never raised a hand to a woman in his life and he wouldn't start now much as he would have liked to shake the truth from Charlotte.

"Belle, this is serious. I've got to know when and how she left here. Was she with anyone?"

"There's nobody that can tell you that unless the night clerk at the hotel saw her leave. I'm sorry, Jasper. We . . . we did what we were supposed to do."

"Damn," Jasper muttered. He'd never felt such a combination of anger and helplessness in his life. He was a good tracker, and could most likely have tracked a snake over rocks. But the deep respect he had for the ability of U.S. Rangers was not unfounded. The adeptness he had for tracking was a match for how adept they were at concealing tracks.

He had to get to Dobbs at once. Dobbs would be able to devise the right plan.

Still, this did not dissolve the anger he felt at Belle and Charlotte. He looked coldly at them both.

"I'm gonna get word to Dobbs. We'll be back here. You explain to him how you couldn't keep track of one girl. We've got to find her or there's going to be a lot of trouble. You two," he added accusingly before he turned to leave, "don't have any idea what you've done."

He left, and the two women exchanged uncertain

looks. They began to wonder what the real truth was
. . . and what they really were responsible for.

Dobbs amused Louise with quotations from the
works of Shakespeare, followed by thorough explanation of the meaning behind them. Louise was fascinated. But all the while he was nagged by a subtle
and undefined worry.

Jasper had good instincts. Besides, he was a man to
be counted on not to get out of control. Was his
worry about leaving Shelby behind justified? Had
they just made their first mistake?

As the day wore on, he became more tense, and by
nightfall he was wishing for Jasper's quick return,
though logic told him it would be impossible for his
friend to get back before it was nearing day.

Even after midnight, and when Louise was comfortably asleep again in the wagon, he could not rest.
He sat by the low-burning fire and considered their
alternatives if it proved that Jasper had been right all
along.

He allowed his mind to consider any situation that
could possibly have arisen. If he were Brad Cole
. . . if he were Brad Cole . . . Knowing the breed of
man as he did and knowing of Jasper's unrest made
his nerves even more jangled.

By three in the morning, he was still unable to
sleep, and still as tense as a drum. Then he heard the
sound of an approaching horse.

He stood slowly as Jasper rode into the camp,
dismounted and came to stand beside him.

"Jasper?"

"She's gone."

"Gone! Gone where?"

"I don't know. There's no sign of her."

"But Belle . . . Charlotte?"

"They don't know where she is, either . . . or so they say."

"So they say. You don't believe them?"

"No."

"Why? What do they have to gain?"

"I don't know. But I'm damn sure she just didn't up and walk away on her own."

"You think he figured out our little game?"

"I told you, Dobbs. He's not the kind you can fool so easy. Somehow he anticipated what we were going to do a minute before we did it."

"All right, Jasper. We can't just stand here and talk about it. Hitch the wagon back up. We're going to lose a day or so, but we have to go back and start tracking him from there."

Within an hour they were on their way back to town at a much more rapid pace than when they had left it.

Dobbs knew there was little sense in trying to question Belle and Charlotte any further. There was no time to dally. If they were going to pick up the trail, they'd have to start as fast as they could.

* * *

Brad watched Shelby closely, prepared for any move she might make, and letting her know with every glance and every action that he didn't trust her for a second.

They ate a rapid, and as far as she was concerned, hardly edible meal, and before she had time to get too comfortable he told her they were ready to move.

"Why such a rush? I'm bruised and sore from that wagon ride. Can't I rest a bit longer?"

"Don't be clever," he grinned. "If you're thinking to slow me down until your friends get here you're wasting your time."

"I'm tired!"

"Too bad. When you get back home you'll have a nice soft bed to rest up in. Until then we'll move and move fast."

"I should have let Jasper have a go at you that first night. It would have saved us both a lot of problems."

"Both?" His grin was getting aggravating.

"Mr. Cole," she said sweetly, "you haven't begun to have trouble yet. Why don't you just let me go? You're never going to get me back to Charleston."

"Such confidence." This time he laughed and came to stand close to her. "You might prove to be a spoiled pain in the neck, *Miss Stapleton,* but I assure you, you will be right beside me when we get to Charleston."

"We have a long, long trip ahead of us." This time her laugh was soft. "I hope you keep looking back over your shoulder. You just don't know Jasper and Dobbs the way I do. They won't be as far behind you as you think." She pushed past him and climbed up on the wagon.

Brad sighed and got up beside her. He wondered where the idea had gone that this job was going to be easy.

They traveled in silence. He'd tried to break the barrier a couple of times, but she made it clear further conversation was out of the question.

Cautious to keep one eye on her, he made camp that night. There was no doubt in his mind that he'd have to eventually tie her up, just to be able to get a good night's sleep. But somehow the idea annoyed him.

They sat across the fire from each other in the same strained silence.

"You didn't eat much."

"You're not the best cook in the world," she replied. "What was that we just ate anyway, rattlesnake?"

"You know," he frowned at the annoying words, "on the stage you're an angel. Too bad it doesn't carry over after you leave it."

"Under better circumstances it does. One has to consider the company one is in."

"My problem," he retorted, "is trying to figure out why your parents are chasing you across the country to bring you back to get married? I would think they'd have pity on the man and let him know when he's well off."

"I should have known some bounty hunter

wouldn't have any idea of how to be a gentleman."

"What made you decide to join up with a traveling show when you ran away?"

She looked at him closely, then pushed her dish aside. "My parents gave me years of music lessons. I like to sing. It gives me pleasure."

"Your parents were good to you. But you didn't consider them when you ran. Your father was really upset. His last words were for me to see that nothing happened to you . . . to protect you."

Shelby was well aware of what she had to do. Even though she didn't want to deceive him, she had to keep the doubt alive in his mind. She had to make him believe he had to finish the job, at the same time she struggled to reach his understanding.

"Then protect me," she said softly as she bent slightly toward him. "Protect me from having to go back and face a marriage to a man who is, at best, a scoundrel who would bed any woman if there was enough money in it for him."

For a second he was caught in the same magnetic power as he'd been when he'd first seen her on stage. And for that same brief second he felt a stirring within him that had very little to do with protection.

"I can't see those worried parents forcing you to marry a man like that," he said defensively.

"They told you, didn't they, that—"

"That you were to be brought home for your wedding."

"Yes."

He rose and walked a few paces away and stood with his back to her, out of range of those eyes and that tenuous thing she possessed that could wrap itself around him and stop him from thinking logically.

He could hear the slight movement. He was aware she had taken a few steps around the fire and stood a short distance from him.

It was then the realization came to him that quite possibly, and most likely, he was taking part in one of the best performances she had ever given. He smiled and turned to face her. She was only a couple of feet from him . . . but his guard, and his memory, were in full swing.

"I still think you'd better get some sleep. We're going to get a real early start in the morning."

"Why don't you try listening to reason?"

"You know, I have to give you credit. You're one of the best actresses I've ever seen. But if I 'listen to reason,' as you put it, tomorrow I'll be regretting it while I'll still be able to hear you laughing. Why don't *you* listen to reason and come along peacefully?"

"My, what a brave soul you are. I go along peacefully to my execution and you walk away with a profit."

"Execution," he laughed. "It can't be that bad?"

"I'm not going back to Charleston," she said firmly as the beginnings of real anger began to dance in her eyes.

"Oh yes you are. There's too much at stake to— Never mind. You're going back. Once my job is finished you can argue your way out of that wedding with your parents."

"I'm just warning you," she smiled.

"No cooperation, huh?"

"Not a minute."

"Well, I wasn't going to do this. But I see I don't have much choice."

He took the few steps that lay between them and had her in a firm hold before she realized what he was doing. She struggled against him, afraid for the first time that his intentions might be more than she'd bargained on.

But when he reached for a rope that still lay across his saddle she nearly shrieked.

"You're not going to tie me up!"

"I sure am. I'm not going to stay awake all night keeping one eye on you." Despite her furious struggle, he bound her wrists and ankles. Then he lifted her and placed her gently on her blanket. To compound the situation he attached the end of the rope to the wheel of the wagon. "There, you'll be safe even if you aren't too comfortable."

"This is unnecessary."

"Really? I still have a lump on the back of my head that proves those words wrong. A man would be a damn fool to turn his back on you twice."

She glared at him with a look in her eyes that promised revenge, but he just smiled and reached for another blanket to place over her.

"Good night, princess. Better luck next time."

She watched him move back to the fire and sit with his back to her, quite unaware that he was having difficulty with the uncomfortable position he'd put her in.

Brad sat before the fire, deep in his own thoughts, for some time. He'd heard the rustle of movement behind him, accompanied by exasperated and angry sounds. But he refused to look at her again. Finally, he moved to his blanket, tipped his hat down over his eyes, and went to sleep.

Shelby lay very still, watching him closely, searching for signs that he truly was asleep. She waited a long time before his body relaxed and his deep breathing told her he slept.

Only then did she smile. Brad Cole was too much of a gentleman, she thought with amusement, a gentleman not used to tracking and bringing in a female. It had never occurred to him to search her.

He was a light sleeper, he had said. But tonight he slept deeply, comfortable with the thought that she was secured too well to pull any tricks. Your second mistake, Mr. Cole, she thought.

Cautiously, slowly, she sat up. Reaching down, she drew the boots she'd removed to toast her feet before the fire close to her. Carefully designed for just this purpose was a small pocket of leather that ran the length of the inside of the boot. From it she carefully drew out a slim silver-bladed knife. Not much in the way of a weapon but enough to cut her bonds, which she accomplished within minutes.

She lay very still, watching Brad closely. It would not be smart to try to move too fast. She'd surely make a sound that would wake him. She considered what she needed to do.

Inside a pocket in the wide leather belt she wore was enough money to travel comfortably. She had, with the help of Jasper and Dobbs, prepared for any extingency.

But first, she had to get away and second, she had to plan on just where she was going to go.

She couldn't try to find Jasper and Dobbs, because it would, of course, be the first place he would look. No, for a while she would be on her own, and she would need all her wits to get away.

She moved slowly, inch by inch, until she was clear of the area of the firelight. She could not saddle the horse, because that was the thing that had caught her last time. But, with silent laughter, she took both bridles. She intended to take *both* horses.

It would serve him right, she thought, to have to walk for a while. Maybe it would take some of the determination out of him to go on searching for her.

She moved into the shadows and unhobbled the wagon horses and led them away, knowing they would drift to a place where they would find sweet grass. Then she bridled his horses and hers. She swung up on the back of one, and, leading the second, she urged both horses forward at a slow pace.

She waited until she was some distance from camp before she stopped and tied the second horse to a bush. He'd find it . . . in a few hours after he woke up.

Then she rode away, heading for her new destination, Broken Bow, Nebraska, where she knew Dobbs and Jasper would eventually show up. From there they'd go on to Denver, Salt Lake City, and finally to California by rail. Of course she was reasonably certain she'd never get to California, since one very angry man would soon catch up with her. She couldn't fool his type too often, she knew. But she'd let him take her back. When the time was right.

She was quite pleased with herself when, by the time day had broken with a bright warm sun, she looked down at the town of Stockham. She would leave the horse at the livery, telling them that one Brad Cole should be along soon to collect it and pay for its care.

It would be a matter of a few short hours before she could catch the train that was leaving for Broken Bow. But even with the wait she would still be ahead of him.

She took the time to purchase her ticket, a few necessities, and a portmanteau in which to carry them. She was the first passenger to board the train. When it rolled out of town she had never felt more satisfied with herself, nor more full of pleasure at the look she could only imagine would be on Brad's face when he realized she had done it again.

Brad awoke in the wee hours of the morning only because he was being nuzzled by a horse. She had not considered that Brad's horse might pull himself loose and find his way back to the man who had cared so well for it and trained it to be a one-man animal.

When he realized what was happening he sat up abruptly. He was mentally asking himself how the horse had gotten loose in the first place when he realized it was bridled and the reins were hanging loose.

He scrambled to his feet, then gazed in total shock

t the loosened ropes he had used to bind Shelby the
ight before. He went to them and examined them.

"Cut" he muttered. "I'll be damned . . . I'll be
amned."

Rapidly, he mounted his horse bareback and
ought the other horses, which he hitched to the
vagon. Then he tied his own horse behind it and
eaded for the closest town.

He stopped before the livery stable and gave in-
truction on the care of his horses and asked if he
ould store the wagon there. But when he told the
table man his name, he was greeted with the fact that
e owed an additional amount of money for the
orse Shelby had left behind.

He was aggravated, but he reluctantly had to admire her initiative. Once he knew she had been here
efore him and left the horse behind, it did not take
im long to figure out the means of transportation
he had used, and her destination.

He smiled to himself as he crossed the street to the
elegraph office. After he sent his telegram he again
rossed the street and found a restaurant where he
te a hearty meal.

He had all the time in the world. He made arrangements for all his animals and equipment to be kept
until his return. Then he bought a ticket on the next
rain headed for Broken Bow.

Shelby was annoyed with herself because she
ouldn't get Brad out of her mind. She had possibly

cost him a lot, but she just couldn't be brought back
before the time was right.

The trip by train was not exactly comfortable, and
when they finally did arrive in Broken Bow, she felt
dirty, and extremely tired.

In addition to these discomforts she felt obligated
to smile and chat with the sweet old lady who sat
opposite her and had claimed immediately to be most
ardent fan. She informed her of her name, Hetabelle
Douglas, and the fact that she was traveling from the
East to visit her grandson. She could not have
weighed over a hundred pounds and her blue eyes
sparkled with a vigor that belied her certain age.

"Why, I saw you just a short while ago. You have
a lovely voice."

"Thank you."

"It seems to me a pretty thing like you oughtent to
be traveling alone."

"Well, I'm not really . . . I mean. It's just for this
one time. Circumstances, you know. Besides,"
Shelby smiled pleasantly, *"you're* traveling alone."

"Of course," Hetabelle replied, "but I'm an old
lady and few of the dangerous men around these
parts would be interested in me. You, on the other
hand, are a lovely creature."

"Thank you," Shelby replied, helpless to stop
Hetabelle's interest.

She listened to the lady's entire family history
while trying to keep from revealing anything about
herself.

She meant to find a good hotel, take a hot bath and

leep for several hours. She would make plans when he'd gotten some rest.

When she stepped down from the train she was approached by a very large and purposeful man accompanied by another who looked just as formidable. Both wore badges that proclaimed them the law in town. She felt a touch of nervousness and waited impatiently for her baggage.

"Miss Vale . . . Miss Shelby Vale?" the older man questioned. He wore no smile of welcome, and an alarm bell began to jangle.

Before Shelby could speak, to deny who she was, her companion spoke for her. She had no doubts in her mind why the sheriff was here. She had to admit Brad was quick.

"She sure is Shelby Vale. Have you heard her sing, too, Sheriff? She's wonderful, isn't she?"

"I'm afraid I've not had the pleasure, ma'am." He touched the brim of his hat and smiled, then turned to Shelby. "If you'll come with me peaceful like, miss, it will save us both a lot of trouble." He took hold of her arm.

Hetabelle gave a gasp of shock, then a sound of anger. "How dare you accost this sweet child! You cannot drag her to jail now that you know who she is! Why, it's almost sacreligeous."

"Now, ma'am, don't get riled up. I have to do what the law requires."

Hetabelle was incensed, and she waved her parasol at the sheriff like a broadsword.

"You cannot do this. I will . . ." she began.

"I'm not going anywhere with you until you tell me what this is all about." Shelby joined Hetabelle's protest.

"You're under arrest, miss. Now come along." Hetabelle gave another rage-filled shriek and struck the sheriff a surprisingly sturdy blow for a lady her age and size.

"I will not!" Shelby protested, struggling vainly in his hold. "Under arrest for what?"

"I'm not sure. A Ranger friend of mine is on his way here to pick you up." Sheriff McClure said as he tried to hold Shelby and dodge Hetabelle's blows at the same time. Finally, he grasped the umbrella and tossed it aside, then called out to his deputy who unceremoniously grasped Hetabelle.

"No! You have the wrong person. You don't understand—"

"Miss, don't give me any trouble or I'll have to be forced to drag you to jail. If a Ranger says to hold you, we'll hold you. If there's a mistake, you can clear it up with him."

"But I can't stay here. You can't do this. You have to let me explain!"

By now, the sheriff had, an even firmer hold of her arm in a grip that felt like iron. Despite loud and very verbal protests from Hetabelle, Shelby was taken to the jail and locked in.

She stood, holding the bars and glaring at the sheriff who silently hoped his friend Brad would be along soon to collect this bundle of fury.

Only then did he face the fury of Hetabelle Douglas, who promised him as much abuse as her mind could conjure. When he finally expelled her forcibly from the office, he breathed a sigh of relief.

Chapter 6

Anne Stapleton paced the floor with clenched fists and a brilliant glow of anger in her eyes. Jeffrey watched her from a comfortable chair nearby.

"Anne, you should calm down."

"Calm down! Do you realize how much time we have left to settle all this? By now that man should have found her and had her home. He assured us it would be no problem."

"I have a feeling little Winter is giving him a run for his money. She's always been a clever minx."

"I sense other hands in this little business."

"I don't understand?"

"Her father."

"Come now, Anne. Anyone can see he's put forth every effort to find her, plus a great deal of money."

"He's a fool when it comes to the girl. She has always been able to do just as she pleased." At that, Jeffrey laughed softly. "What's so funny?" Anne snapped.

"It strikes me that he's always pretty much tried to give you your way in most things as well."

"He has no choice when it comes to me," she replied smugly.

"You mean," his voice was slightly taunting and amused, "he believes he has no choice when it comes to you."

"Don't be obnoxious, Jeffrey."

"The Jameses have financed this little affair pretty well. I'm sure Joseph has no way of knowing it's their money keeping him solvent."

"No, and he never will."

"And there are a few things you just wouldn't want the Jameses to know, either . . . aren't there?"

"Whatever are you babbling about?"

"When all this began, you were set up to catch Joseph and then get Carl a wealthy bride. You were given a great deal of very expensive jewelry, an even larger amount of money, and trunks full of clothes to fit the situation."

"Of course. Why shouldn't they have done so? This was their plan, they should pay the price."

"Oh, I'm sure they know that. Good old Nefarious Carl has a reputation. I doubt very much if he could ever be accepted anywhere else. I do feel a little sorry for Winter once she marries him. I hear his tastes are somewhat . . . jaded."

"All the more reason it's costing them so much."

"Ah . . . the jewelry." His chuckle displayed his amusement.

"Jeffrey, you really can be tiresome."

"I have some friends in some very strange places, Anne. One of them happens to be a jeweler at the end of South Street." He looked at her innocently. "I'm sure you've heard the name . . . Benjamin Weir?"

He had to give the woman credit, she had nerves of steel. She gave every appearance of being unperturbed by what he'd just said. It might have fooled anyone else . . . anyone except Jeffrey Brenner. He saw the slight narrowing of her eyes and the rigid set of her jaw.

"It's interesting," he continued. "He and I had a long, pleasant, and very informative conversation over drinks the other night. In his cups, dear old Benjamin can be quite talkative, if one knows the kind of questions to ask."

"And you know?" Her voice was deceptively soft. "Be careful, Jeffrey. Knowing too much can be dangerous."

"Not in this case. The Jameses have no quarrel with me. Neither does Joseph. As far as you're concerned, you and I both have a great deal at stake. After all, we're partners . . . aren't we?"

"Partners? Are we?"

"Ah, Anne," Jeffrey laughed softly, then stood up and walked slowly toward her. "We came from the same gutter, you and I, and we have the same aspirations. And the same resolve. Both of us decided long ago that we were going to be very rich and on top of the social structure. We can use each other . . . or we can play the game separately. But if you become an opponent, understand this. I don't play by anyone else's rules but my own."

"You know nothing about me. Stop being foolish enough to believe I'll let you get away with blackmailing me."

"How crude," he laughed. "I know nothing about you? Let me see . . . Born Cora Strait, mother a prostitute and father unknown. Raised in a brothel until you were sixteen and realized you had to leave or end up like your mother. You ran all right, all the way to France where you found the stage the only legitimate way to expose your . . . unique charms to wealthy men. You were quite a success. You caught one Pierre Dubonette. Twice your age and with an estate and some wealth, although not as much as you wanted. When he conveniently died, you sold everything and came here.

"With the help of the Jameses, you picked out the one man who was ripe to fall for your charms: Joseph Stapleton. A man who had lost the wife he loved and was in a vulnerable enough mental state to be susceptible. He was a man with the social standing you wanted. Then you had only to wait and the opportunity came along. You and I know what a sadistic little bastard Carl James is and the scrapes his parents have bought him out of. He saw and wanted Winter . . . and you saw and wanted another opportunity."

"You're so clever. But the Jameses aren't to be played with. What if I tell them you intend to interfere in their plans? I don't think Charleston will be a safe harbor for you."

"But you won't."

"Don't underestimate me."

"I don't, not for a minute. Nor do I trust you. That's why I . . . acquired some fine pieces of jewelry from Benjamin . . . very fine jewelry, which you let Benjamin have for a nice profit and a set of perfect paste matches."

"He told me—!"

"That he would keep them safe. My dear, you should have been smarter and much more clever than to have such faith in a man to whom profit means so much."

"You have the jewels now," she stated, reading his confidence well.

"I do."

"And you're going to the Jameses with them."

"Only if you force me to."

"What do you want?" Her voice had grown cold with her demand.

"Now, Anne, don't get so upset." He walked behind her and put his arms about her, drawing her back against him. "You're a woman of strong appetites. Who knows that better than I. The situation is a fortunate one for both of us."

"I don't see what you have to gain. Once Carl is married to Winter, they'll eventually—"

"Please, don't take me for a fool. He's paid you for Winter, but you have no intention of letting all that money slip through your fingers. You like being the wife of the renowned and respected Joseph Stapleton . . . I'd say almost as much as you'd like being his widow."

There was no doubt in Anne's mind that he had all the strings well tied together. She would concede to him for now. But in time he'd make the mistake of overconfidence and she'd . . . do whatever was necessary to make sure the plans she had laid out so long ago for herself did not included him.

"Yes," she said softly, "I do look good in black."

"My dear," he chuckled, self-assurance strong in his voice, "you are a very sensible woman. There's enough for us to share, and maybe I can be helpful along the way." He tightened his arms around her and she allowed herself to revel in sensual pleasure while promising herself he'd never share what she'd taken so long to acquire.

Joseph Stapleton sat in his den, at the large mahogany desk. Across from him sat a small nondescript little man with a cherubic face that boasted a pursed mouth and twinkling blue eyes.

But his looks belied his profession, for Allen Clifford was one of the best investigators the Pinkertons had ever produced.

"Mr. Stapleton, you have my complete report before you. If there are any questions, I'd be more than pleased to answer them."

"You're sure there are no mistakes?"

Allen looked almost insulted. "No, sir, there are no mistakes. We trace our subjects very carefully and very methodically."

"I'm not doubting you, Allen, it's just that the report has been quite a surprise to me . . . to say the least."

"I suspected it might be, but when you hire a Pinkerton you get a complete and thorough job no matter what. We feel it necessary to always render the complete truth."

"I'm certainly not condemning that. You have given me more than my money's worth . . . and the tools I need to prevent a disaster, not to mention righting a wrong. Besides," he smiled at Allen, "the money you'll be saving me in the long run will be a thousand times more than this."

"Then everything is satisfactory?"

"Quite." Joseph rose and extended his hand across the desk. Allen rose, too, grasped it in a grip much stronger than Joseph would have expected. "And thank you, Allen, for your work and your discretion."

"You're quite welcome, Mr. Stapleton."

When the door closed behind Allen, Joseph sat down and again looked through the long and detailed report. He felt a touch of sadness, combined with anger. He'd been a fool, and his foolishness had nearly cost his daughter's happiness. He'd been suspicious that Anne had been having an affair for some time, and that was the reason he'd hired a Pinkerton in the first place. But the report had revealed so much more.

Allen had gone into the background not only of Anne but of the people she was associated with, now and in the past. This had revealed a side of Jeffrey Brenner he'd not known. And the James family. They'd never been any part of the elite social structure of Charleston and, reading this report, he realized how badly they wanted to be.

But it was Carl whose background brought the taste of bile to his throat and made his hands tremble in the grip of a self-recriminating anger. He'd almost let this man have his beautiful, sensitive daughter. The thought of what her life might have been was enough to almost undo him.

Well, the game he had begun had to be played out. When it was finished and he knew Winter was completely safe, he would deal with Anne. He only needed time. He'd play Anne's game no matter how she now disgusted him. But when the time came, her betrayal and her deceit would be repaid in the same coin. He only needed time.

Time, Shelby thought for the thousandth time as she paced the little cell in which she was locked. All she needed was time. Yet Brad Cole could possibly be here within another day or so and he'd take her back to Charleston before the time they needed was past.

She had to think of something, but for the life of her no solution to her present dilemma would come to her. Someone had to have the door unlocked and that someone would only be Brad.

She had to smile to herself when she considered how really angry he must be. She also felt the urge to laugh when she thought of all the misery dear Hetabelle was continuing to give Sheriff McClure.

She had brought up the reserves in the form of the temperance and suffrage league who were now crowded outside the jail shouting for her release. Before all this was over both Brad and the sheriff were going to be a lot sorrier. She had no doubts that eventually Brad would get her back to Charleston. He was too smart to be tricked by her too often.

She wondered where Dobbs and Jasper were. She knew Jasper's abilities, and was sure she and Brad were both being tracked by this time. Considering this, she wondered how to leave a more obvious trail, or whether she should try to backtrack until she found them.

Then she laughed softly to herself. She was planning as if she was already free from this cage. Sheriff McClure had proven as determined as Brad. She wondered if all lawmen had the same mental makeup. Brad must be a good friend of the sheriff, for he wouldn't listen to a word she had to say, even though she'd given what she thought was one of her best performances.

She sighed and walked again to the small, bare window and looked out. The day was bright and warm, and the street bustled with activity. The town of Broken Bow was like hundreds of other towns in the Nebraska territory. A gathering place for the homesteaders heading west and the ranchers that filled the area. It was still a wild place, and a bit farther west Indians still held the white man in a state of discomfort.

She longed to go for a brisk walk, or better still a long ride. The thought of being caged like this for any length of time could be debilitating to both mind and body.

She had no way to gauge the time except by the sunlight and the times she'd been brought food by a rather young deputy, who'd seemed awestruck by the lovely prisoner.

She'd had breakfast, and then lunch, which had been some time ago. She doubted if Brad could be here before late at night and, certain he'd not disturb the sheriff then, it would most likely be the next day before he'd have her taken out.

Trying to control the slight touch of claustrophobia and her annoyance at having nothing to do, she sat on her bunk and tried to think of methods of escape.

When the dinner meal was brought she really felt little hunger. Still, she smiled at the shy, young deputy, astutely regarding him as a possible means of escape.

"Are you on duty tonight?" She smiled at him again and spoke softly, watching him flush with surprise.

"Yes, ma'am."

"What's your name?"

"Cecil . . . Cecil Trott."

"Well, Cecil, I'm glad you're going to keep me company tonight. It will be interesting to talk with you."

"With me, ma'am?" His eyes blinked in surprise.

"Well, I come from such a small place, I've never met a real lawman before. Where I come from, there's nobody as worldly to talk to." She gazed up at him with a rapt look on her face and watched him swell with pleasure. "I'll bet you've caught so many bad men. I wish you could tell me some stories."

Within an hour he had dragged a chair close to the

bars and sat expounding on the virtues of law and order in Broken Bow . . . and creating some that put him in a shining light.

She smiled, listened intently and kept her eyes on the gun he wore that was just within her grasp.

She felt him relaxing as she encouraged him to talk, watching the last rays of sunset as she did. She needed darkness to cover her uncertain moves if she did get out, for she wasn't sure just where to go and what to do. Time ticked by while she professed deep enthusiasm for Cecil's ramblings.

Brad was amused with the idea that she must be in a state of pure rage by now.

He arrived early in the evening, but he perversely wanted to taunt Shelby just a bit that he'd spent a comfortable night in a soft hotel bed, while she spent hers in jail.

It was after nine when he arrived in town. The town was brightly lit and very active. Sam McClure was a longtime friend of Brad's and he knew exactly where to find him. He found accommodations, then walked to the small saloon that was directly across the street from the jail.

McClure had been a widower for over ten years. He had a habit of taking his evening meal at the saloon, playing cards for an hour or so, having a couple of drinks, then going home to bed.

Brad found him just where he thought he'd be, and Sam welcomed him with relief.

"Glad to see you, Brad. It's been a long time."

"It sure has, Sam. Almost eight years since I came through here."

"Sit. Have a drink."

Brad filled his glass liberally and tossed the drink down, then poured another to sip more leisurely.

"That's some little piece of work you cut out for me the other day," Sam said.

Brad chuckled, "You mean Miss Vale?"

"Yeah. Miss Vale."

"She give you some trouble?"

"I left the jail early this afternoon and I ain't goin' back until tomorrow when you take her off my hands. You're gonna have your hands full takin' her anywhere she don't want to go. For a while I was kind of glad there was bars between us . . . for my sake."

This time Brad laughed. "She's a handful all right."

"You two crossed paths before? How'd she manage to get away?"

"I made a couple of mistakes."

Sam set his glass down and grinned broadly. "You're joking me."

"Nope. You're right. It's pretty hard to take her where she doesn't want to go. I'm used to dragging in outlaws. I made the mistake of taking her the way she looked. Like a lady."

"My, my," Sam chuckled. "Here sits the man who brought in Red Markham and his gang, and one sweet little girl gets away."

" 'Sweet little girl' just doesn't fit. That was my mistake. She has more tricks than a magic show and no conscience about how she uses them, either. I've learned my lesson."

"So, what's the charge? Just what kind of a crime did this girl commit? Does she run with some gang?"

"Yeah. She's a real tough cookie who hopes her little-girl face and her sweet talk will get her anything. She runs with the Stapleton gang."

"Stapleton . . . never heard of them."

"Real tough lot. Banks, you know."

"No kidding. You never would have thought it to look at her. Dangerous?"

"Oh yeah . . . real dangerous. She's smart."

"Maybe I shouldn't have left Cecil with her. He ain't the brightest deputy I've ever had, but he's a good boy."

"You left one young deputy with her?"

"Yeah."

"Maybe I ought to take a walk over and see if everything's all right."

"Maybe."

Brad could see Sam was reluctant to see her again.

"I'll go. You stay and enjoy your drink. I'll be back as soon as I check and see there's no problems. I'll just give Cecil a little warning to keep his distance."

Cecil had never enjoyed himself so much in his life. He just couldn't imagine why someone would lock such a pretty thing up. There had to be some mistake. Surely the sheriff would find out he'd made one by morning and come in to release her.

She hung on his every word and he sympathized with her seemingly narrow world and expounded on his own much more worldly outlook on life.

When, in the course of conversation she'd reached out and touched him, he felt a moment of excitement. This happened several times, until his guard was down. But the next time she reached, it was with a purpose.

Cecil was stunned when he found himself looking down the barrel of his own gun.

"Ma'am?" he gasped in surprise.

"I'm truly sorry for this, Cecil. You're a real nice person. But I'm not too fond of this cell. Now if you'd just really be sweet and get those keys and unlock this door."

"The sheriff will kill me for this."

"He *might* be a bit angry, but I'm afraid I can't help it. Now, get the keys."

Cecil obediently unlocked the cell door. He stood aside as she moved out slowly, keeping a close watch on him.

"Now, get in."

"In the cell?" Now Cecil was really upset. To let a prisoner get away and end up locked in his own cell was not going to please the sheriff when he came in the next morning.

But when Shelby clicked back the hammer on the gun he moved quickly. He looked at her with distressed eyes while she locked the door.

After she had put Cecil's gun carefully on the desk, she walked to the door and turned again to look at him.

"I really feel bad about this, Cecil, and one day I'll come back here and try to explain it all to you and to the sheriff. In the meantime it's important that I get out of town."

"If you think you're going to get away with this you'd better think again. The sheriff is going to be awful mad when he finds you gone. He's going to set out after you, and he's a tough man to get away from."

"Great," Shelby muttered, "now I'll have two of them on my trail." She watched Cecil speculatively for a moment. "Cecil, how far are the docks from here?"

"Docks? They're quite a ways. Besides," he grinned, "there aren't any boats leaving until tomorrow. So you ought to just give up right now. You'll never get far."

She knew he was trying to make the lie sound true, as she'd wanted him to. She would plant the seed carefully and let him pass the word to the sheriff.

"Well, don't worry about it. I'm sure there's another fast way out of town. At least I have a whole night's head start."

She had her back to the door as she spoke and her hand on the door handle. In fact, now that she was out of the confining cell she felt fine.

Suddenly the door handle was gripped from outside and the door was pushed open. It took her completely by surprise when it bumped her, and forced her a few offbalanced steps away from the door.

She expected to turn and see the sheriff, and was momentarily paralyzed with surprise when she saw a familiar broad-shouldered form. She uttered a soft, disgusted groan, and Brad laughed.

"You!"

"I should have expected something like this."

"I'm sorry," Cecil said miserably. "She took me by surprise."

"Cecil, my friend," Brad's voice dripped with enough amusement to make the irate prisoner's hair stand on end and her teeth clench. "You didn't stand a chance. When I sent a message to Sam I should have sent a warning as well."

"You have no right to hold me here. I'm not a criminal," Shelby grated angrily.

"Now, now, Miss Shelby. I've just finished telling Sheriff McClure about your connection to the Stapleton gang and how dangerous you are."

"Then he'll have to hold me here until a judge comes to try me, because," she glared at him and stated the last words slowly, "I'm not going with you. Not anywhere, anytime."

"You need a night in jail to cool off," Brad said calmly. "And," his voice dripped amusement, "the judge here is a circuit judge and won't be around for," he shrugged, "three or four months." Then he started toward her. "I don't have to wait that long. The sheriff has already turned you over to me . . . in the name of speedy justice."

Shelby backed away, reaching blindly for anything she could use, to beat Brad Cole insensible.

But there was nothing, and she made a last desperate dash to try to get past him.

She gave a yelp of combined fury and impatience

as a hard arm caught her to him. She struggled wildly, and for a minute Brad found his hands full. But his strength far outmatched hers and soon she was held immobile against a chest that felt to her to be made of solid oak.

She ceased to waste her energy in a futile struggle, and, lips pressed together in an anger she could barely voice, she looked up at him.

"Now, suppose you just change places with good old Cecil here?"

"You wouldn't really leave me in this place all night! You've found me, so take me with you."

"Well, to tell the truth, I don't think I'd get a good night's sleep with you in my room. At this point, my dear girl, I don't trust you one inch. No. A cell is the best place for you tonight. I'll come collect you in the morning."

He held her tight and backed to the desk where he took the keys and tossed them to Cecil.

Cecil unlocked the door and stepped out. When Brad forced her into the cell, the heat of her gaze could have withered him where he stood.

Locked safely inside, Brad tossed the keys back on the desk. "Cecil, I won't mention this to Sam if you promise to keep your distance from the lady."

"Yes, sir . . . yes, sir. Many thanks."

"You're not going to get away with this, Brad Cole!" Brad walked to the door. "You come back and get me out of here! I promise . . ." The door cut her words off from Brad.

Cecil avoided her angry gaze and placed himself carefully behind the desk. Finally, Shelby threw herself down on the hard bunk and tried to devise ways to get revenge on Brad.

Brad's smile faded when he pulled the door closed behind him. He'd refused to lose control when he was with Shelby, but he'd found his arms full of more than he'd bargained on. She had seemed to fit to him as if she were part of him, and it began to annoy him when he couldn't wipe that memory away.

He fought giving in to the intriguing fantasy of having her share his hotel room. He crossed the street, doing battle with the idea that if he didn't have a few drinks he might not get very much sleep.

But too many drinks some hours later found him drunk and making his way to a bed that was empty and cold, and dreams that were too warm for his comfort.

Chapter 7

Brad had a fierce headache the next morning. He could hardly walk without it jarring him. In addition, his stomach was not exactly cooperating.

The last thing he looked forward to was facing an angry young woman.

He awoke to someone pounding on his door. When he yanked it open, he was not in the best humor to find the sheriff standing there. Brad was at first surprised, then a reality occurred to him.

"What time is it?" he asked.

"It's damn dear noon and you best come and take that little filly off my hands or I'm going to unlock that door and set her free!"

"Noon!" Brad groaned. "Come on in. God, I feel like hell."

"You ought to, you was drunk as a skunk last night. Now, about that pain in the rump I have locked up in my jail . . ."

"All right, Sam, all right. Let me get cleaned up, something in my stomach, and I'll come get her."

"Hurry it up," Sam finally laughed. "That girl has a mean streak and a mouth to go with it. Cecil's real shook up. I don't envy your job, not for a minute. I think the problem here is that I don't think you can get it out of your head that she's a lady. Ladies," Sam chuckled, "don't play by a gentleman's rules. They got a set all their own."

Brad laughed. "Are you trying to tell me to treat her like some of the ugly gents I've brought in?"

"No. I'm just telling you that she's got a set of rules you'd better learn or she's going to slip through your fingers again."

"Again! What the hell has she been telling you?"

"Oh, about your . . . other tries."

"You're right. I'd better get her out or she's going to have you on her side. You sound downright sympathetic."

"She told me her situation. Why do you want to drag her back to a marriage she doesn't want?"

"Not you, too? She has you believing that cock and bull story. I told you . . . she's wanted."

"Yeah," Sam grinned as he walked to the door, "I'm just wondering . . . by who?" He left before Brad could find a fitting retort.

By the time Brad reached the jail he felt he was reasonably prepared to face her . . . and he had changed his tactics. He was taking Sam's words into consideration. From now on there would be no more trust . . . and no more mistakes.

* * *

Shelby had forced herself under control after Brad left. Grimly, she struggled for sleep. She would have her time. He had to return to take her out of this cell and again try to get her back to Charleston. If she kept control she would find a way. She had before, she would again.

She had let her goal slip. She had to develop more patience and definitely another strategy. She had to get farther west before she could let him find any success in bringing her back. She was amused at the idea of the trip home with this handsome, trouble-some man. It would certainly set him off balance to find her so willing to go home. She laughed softly to herself. Brad Cole was in for a whole lot of surprises.

She had a whole night to consider a change of plans. Brad was a gentleman and susceptible to women whether he knew it or not.

It had been a game until now. Suddenly she began to wonder what made him tick. Why would a man who had his reputation . . . who claimed to be a rancher instead of a law man, now give it up to track her. Maybe, if she could find out why . . .

She had a feeling he had a softer side he didn't want to share with too many people. She considered the strange new feeling that had surfaced in a sudden brilliance when he'd held her so tight. Maybe . . . just maybe the whole situation demanded a change in plans. She smiled to herself and finally found sleep.

She awoke early to find Sam receiving a full report from Cecil about her verbal abuse of him and every-one connected to him. When Sam finally crossed the room to talk to her, she was more than ready for him.

She smiled and spoke gently, but Sam was more amused than anything. He'd seen a look in Cecil's eyes that told him more than either Cecil or she knew.

They talked for some time while she tried her best to maneuver his emotions toward sympathy for her plight.

"Miss . . . Brad is right about one thing. A person can't run from things. It's best he takes you back, and you face whatever you have to face."

"You still half believe him, that I'm a wanted person. Do I look like a criminal?"

"You'd be surprised. Criminals come in all kinds of packages. I seen Belle Star once. Pretty thing she was, too. You see, I'm not going to take any chances. I know Brad and his reputation, I don't know a thing about you."

"And I suppose our upright Ranger has never lied to you?" she snapped angrily.

"No, ma'am, he ain't."

"Oh! You men all stick together, don't you? You'll regret this mistake, Sheriff McClure. If you don't let me out of here I'll see you're sorry for this. My family wields a lot of power in Charleston."

"Yes, ma'am," Sam grinned. "But that's Charleston. Out here I don't give a tinker's damn about what your family can do."

Despite all her plans, Shelby's temper flared and she proceeded to condemn him, his deputy, and Brad Cole to unmentionable places and punishment.

"It's gettin' near noon," Sam said, "I think I'll go to the hotel and see what's keeping Brad."

He had left quickly, leaving Shelby simmering and vowing Brad was going to wish he'd never seen her. Sam had to laugh. This girl was a handful and, he thought, something his friend Brad Cole had not bargained on.

When Brad walked into the jail he spoke to Cecil but his gaze went quickly to Shelby, who stood with her back to him, arms folded across her chest and her whole body rigid. She had loosened her blond hair during the night and it shimmered in waves that spilled about her shoulders. For a minute his resolve wavered.

"I'll take the keys, Cecil," Brad said. Cecil tossed the keys to him and Brad walked to the cell door. "Oh, and Cecil . . . do you have a set of cuffs? I have a pretty dangerous person here."

At this Shelby spun about to face him.

"You wouldn't."

"No?" His laugh was soft, but she was certain she read just that intent in his gray eyes.

"You can't parade me through the street like some common—"

"Watch me."

He watched her face as she struggled for control, and was surprised when she achieved it.

"I can't get away from you now." Her voice was subdued. "I need a bath and clean clothes, and I'm hungry. Why can't we have a truce, at least for a couple of hours?"

"A truce?" he questioned, while he unlocked the

oor and walked into the cell to stand beside her. She
became instantly aware of him and it made her even
angrier. She could feel the warmth of him so potently
he wanted to scream.

He had to admit she looked like a helpless girl. Her
wide violet eyes were almost pleading, and she looked
vulnerable and scared. But he also had to remember
that this was the time when "Shelby Vale" was the
most dangerous to his plans.

"What kind of a truce do you have in mind?"

"I told you. A bath, clean clothes and a promise
that we can travel back by train."

It seemed like a reasonable request, and that was
why he became wary. Still, it made him feel a bit
guilty and ruthless to force her to travel as she was.

"All right . . . come on." He took her arm and
propelled her toward the door. Cecil stood near it
with the cuffs in his hand, two silver bracelets connected by about twelve inches of steel chain. Shelby
eyed them with dismay, but Brad took them and
hooked them in his belt.

"Just in case I need them later. Where's the key?"
Cecil handed it and Shelby's small satchel to him.
"Tell Sam thanks and I'll stop when I pass this way
again." With that he continued out the door with
Shelby held in a firm grip, and came face-to-face with
Hetabelle, whose glare brought Brad to an abrupt
halt.

"Ma'am," Brad said. "If you'll excuse me."

"Where are you taking this young lady? Don't you
know who she is?"

"Yes, ma'am, I do. She's a young lady who needs

a safe escort and I'm about to provide that. I intend to see she gets home safe and sound." Brad tightened his hold on Shelby and gave her a look filled with dire warning. She was tempted to call his words a lie to see what he would do, but Hetabelle's next words stopped her.

"I'm so relieved. I have to be on the next stage, because my grandson has made arrangements to meet me. I hated to leave before I knew this problem had been resolved. I would worry so."

Brad smiled a warm and winning smile. "You are very kind and there's no need to worry. I'll see she gets just what she deserves. I'm a friend of the family."

Brad turned his gaze on Shelby again. "We wouldn't want this kind lady to miss her stage and worry about you, would we? It might cause more a problem. You don't want to do that . . . do you?" His grip grew firmer and more threatening.

Shelby could handle Brad on her own. She was far from beaten and she didn't want Hetabelle to miss her stage.

"I'll be fine now, Hetabelle." Shelby smiled warmly at the dear lady, who beamed in response.

"Perhaps I will hear you sing again," Hetabelle said hopefully. "Until then, take care of yourself. And you, dear boy, take good care of her. She is very valuable."

"Miss Hetabelle," Brad's smile broadened, "no one has a better idea of how valuable she is. Trust me, I won't let her out of my sight until she's safely home."

Hetabelle's eyes sparkled. She hoped maybe these two would get along. Her experienced eye had assessed Brad and found him to her liking. When Hetabelle left she made Shelby promise to write to her, thrusting a piece of paper with her address on it into Shelby's hand.

As they crossed to the hotel a touch of alarm coursed through her. Few people paid much attention, with the exception of Sam, who wore an amused smile as he watched from a distance.

"We need a tub and some hot bathwater," Brad instructed the clerk. "Can you see to it?"

"Yes sir, Mr. Cole, right away."

"And how about some coffee and maybe some sandwiches."

"I'll take care of it right away."

Shelby knew the glance Brad cast her was an open challenge for her to try something. But she was not dumb enough for that. She was out of jail. She wanted the bath and the food. Then she'd concentrate on how to get out of his grasp.

Inside the room, Brad finally released her and she moved away from him, rubbing her arm where his grip had been so fierce.

"I'll be black and blue tomorrow."

"Serves you right for trying to take advantage of a nice old girl like Hetabelle, and a young boy like Cecil. Aren't you ashamed?" he taunted. "A beautiful girl like you leading an innocent boy on?"

The result he'd aimed for with his jibe was not the result he got. She didn't get angry. Instead, she smiled.

"Am I?"

"Are you what?"

"You said I was beautiful."

Brad regarded her with a dark frown. "I'm sure I'm not the first man to tell you that."

"It's just a surprise coming from you. I never expected you to say anything so nice." Her eyes lifted to his and for a minute he felt as if time had stopped as if they stood totally alone.

Then he reached for his control. She was playing a game with him he had no intention of falling for. He pretended to regard her objectively.

"Yep. I'll bet with a clean face and some nice clothes you'd be beautiful. Right now you look like a street urchin."

He saw a momentary hurt look in her eyes before she turned away from him and was angry at himself for being so aware of her feelings and her moods.

Before he could speak again there was a knock on the door. He opened it, and the tub and several buckets of hot water were carried inside. Once the tub was filled and the men had left. Brad turned to Shelby again. She was standing by the window looking out, and it took every effort he had not to go to her and . . . comfort her. He was shocked at the thought, but she looked so . . . He inhaled deeply.

"Here's your bath, you'd better take advantage of it before our food comes."

She spun around to face him, and this time it was she whose face registered shock.

"You don't actually think I'm going to take a bath with you in the room!"

"And you don't actually think I'm going to trust you out of my sight for one minute? You made the bed, now it's time to sleep in it."

"I won't. You can take your bath and your food, and go to hell!"

"Tsk, tsk, such language coming from a lady," he chuckled. Then he went to the bed and stripped off the sheets. From one he tore a piece of cloth and tied it from the top dresser drawer to the bed post. The second sheet he draped over it. Then he dragged the tub of water behind it.

"This is about all the privacy you're going to get. Take it or leave it."

With a glare that could have melted him she stepped behind the makeshift screen which shielded her from the shoulders down. She began to remove her clothes, and a few minutes later he heard the soft splash of water and a very contented sigh.

It was only minutes later when a second knock on the door heralded the arrival of a tray of sandwiches and a pot of steaming coffee and two cups.

He poured a cup of coffee, took a sandwich and found a comfortable chair. Only then did he realize he'd made a very drastic mistake. The sheet hung between him and the window, and the bright light from outside made it almost as sheer as gossamer.

He sat, momentarily frozen, the sandwich halfway to his mouth but suddenly forgotten.

The tub was small and he could see the shadowed form of her body from the waist up. That was bad enough, but when she stretched up one long, shapely leg then the other to caress them with the soapy water, his entire body responded in a way that almost drew a sound from him.

This would never do. With grim determination he turned in the chair and concentrated on the sandwich and the coffee. But even then his mind played tricks on him, because even without seeing her he was more than aware of her presence.

He cursed at himself, but he knew he couldn't just walk out. She was too smart not to realize why and he couldn't put a tool as powerful as that in her hands.

He heard her rise from the tub and the sounds of her getting dressed. Shelby was grateful to put on the clothes from her satchel and bundled the soiled clothes into it before she stepped around the sheet. Brad breathed a sigh of relief and turned again to look at her.

"There's some food. You better eat."

She didn't reply. Taking a sandwich from the tray, she went to the bed and sat cross-legged in the center of it.

They finished their food in silence. Brad relaxed in the chair and regarded her.

Whatever he was cautioned about her and whatever his own opinions had been, she was the most delicious-looking creature he'd ever seen.

Warm and flushed from the heat of the water, her skin seemed to glow. Her hair was a tangled mass of curls pinned carelessly atop her head.

Shelby was regarding him as well, only a bit surreptitiously. She didn't want him to sense both her interest and her deep attraction to him. If things had only been different, she thought.

"When are we leaving?"

"As soon as you've finished eating. I want to be on my way quickly. We have a lot of miles to cover."

"Miles? But the train . . . you promised . . ."

"No, Shelby. I promised nothing. You asked, I never answered. It can't be helped. You're too slick and too smart for me to take you on a train with so many people. No, it's far better if we travel alone."

"Just what do you have planned?"

"Another wagon, more supplies. Only this time we won't leave it behind. You're getting to be a pretty expensive project."

"Well, then it looks like you'll be out some money," she replied. "I'm sure you'll get reimbursed for all your expenses when you sell the wrong girl back."

"Now, why did you have to put it like that? I'm not 'selling' Winter Stapleton, just returning her to parents who love her."

"And a marriage to a man she doesn't love."

"She shouldn't marry him."

"It's not that simple."

"Why not? All she has to do is refuse."

"She can't."

"Why?"

"Because, if she does her father will be ruined and lose everything he's built all his life."

"Oh, come now."

He watched her eyes grow cold as she turned her face away. Had he seen tears? His good sense told him to beware, but other senses were integrating his mind. He sat down next to her on the bed. Quickly, she turned to look at him again.

There was a sheen of unshed tears mixed with a look of frightened vulnerability.

"Look, Shelby, why don't you make this easy on yourself? You're a city girl . . . a lady. You'll be helpless out here. You've no idea what kind of a victim you can be. I'm not going to let that happen. I can and will take you back home. If you want I'll even have a talk with your parents and try to make them change their mind about the marriage. But don't think that any more of your tricks are going to work. You're going home. Make it as easy, or as hard, as you choose."

"Why can't you understand? There's no way out of this right now. This marriage will take place no matter what you say. I think it's money and only money that makes you so determined to bring me back. How much were you promised . . . and why is it so important to you? You're selling me. Ask yourself if the price is worth it."

Guilt rode him like a huge monster. Why he really needed for her to understand his reasons was beyond him, but he did. He hated the look he saw in her eyes.

"Money can be an ugly necessity, and only someone with an inexhaustible supply can be so nonchalant about it. Yes, there's a price for this. But your safety is worth it."

Again she turned her head away from him. "I hope they pay you well and you enjoy wine, women, and song when it's over."

He reached out and gripped her chin in one large hand, turning her face back to him until their eyes again met.

"You're not as tough as you pretend to be. In the hands of the wrong man you could find your nice safe little life becoming a disaster such as you've never known. There are a lot of people with a lot less scruples than I have."

He could see that she was far from convinced and wondered if a lesson in fear wouldn't be worth it. Her eyes were filled with resistance and denial. Maybe he could change that.

He watched the look in her eyes change to surprise as he took her face between his hands. But she had no time to utter the sound of the shock that filled her as his mouth took possession of hers in a kiss meant to scare her.

Her mouth was soft and warm. She hadn't expected this and had not time to prepare herself for the feelings that washed over her.

But if she was the one who was supposed to feel fear, the plan was a total failure. Fear was not what was overpowering her senses and taking away her breath until she could hear the triphammer sound of her own heart beating.

Brad suddenly felt as if he had stepped over the edge of a precipice. He tumbled into an explosion of raw desire. It took every bit of control he had to put aside the vibrant thing that possessed him and enforce the subtle threat he'd tried to warn her of.

He crushed her to him roughly and forced the kiss to become domineering, almost brutal.

With satisfaction, he felt her begin to struggle, but he refused to release her. Instead, he pressed her back on the bed, lying atop her. He continued to savage her mouth, holding her easily with one arm while he caressed her body familiarly and none too gently with the other hand.

She began to fight with vigor, trying to force his demanding and ruthless mouth from hers. When he released her, she was gasping both in fury and another emotion he was pleased to see: fear.

He laughed softly and this time suggestively began to press kisses against the soft flesh of her throat.

"Stop it. Leave me alone!"

"Why? What are you afraid of? This is just a taste. We have a long and what looks like a very exciting trip ahead." His hand moved slowly from her hip to the buttons on her blouse. For the first time he saw real fear dance in her eyes, and at the same moment was stricken with self-recrimination for what he was doing. Still slowly, one by one, he unbuttoned the blouse.

Shelby felt so many new emotions that she could hardly stand it. The kiss had begun as something new and unique, and she had felt herself being immersed in a brilliant world of sensation. She had wanted to surrender to it and when she had felt herself flowing with the current of new and wildly exhilarating feelings, the whole situation seemed to suddenly change.

She felt a taste of violence, of losing what little control she had, of being tossed into a conflagration that stripped her of any hold she had on rationality.

She didn't want to plead with him. But she no

longer could control the fear that tore at her. His hand was warm against her skin and his insistent mouth was driving her to the brink of a dark chasm.

"Please!" She could hear the sob catch in her throat. "Don't . . . let me go."

Brad felt the combination taste of success and guilt. But it was for the best. He'd have very little trouble with her from now until they got back to Charleston.

Still, he could not resist one last gentle touch, and he brushed his lips across hers like a whispered kiss. Then, he stood towering over her, needing to enforce his threat verbally.

"Just keep in mind the cuffs are still very handy. You step out of line or not cooperate, and I'll use them. Cuffed like that," he added softly, "you'd find it pretty hard to defend yourself."

Shelby had prepared herself for a lot of things from whoever was sent to bring her back, but she was not prepared for this.

What had really startled her more than anything else was that one elusive moment when his touch had been gentle and the kiss sensitive. It had awakened something new and unexplainable. If it hadn't turned so rough, so . . . She paused to consider this.

Brad seemed satisfied. He turned from her, and began to gather what few things there were to take along.

He'd taken the time to get the equipment he would need before he had gone to get Shelby. One small wagon and horse, and two riding horses, in case it was necessary to ride. When Shelby saw the two horses, she was pleased and smiled at him before she could catch herself. A horse would make it easier for her.

Brad chuckled softly and her smile faded. "Don't get any ideas. From now on there will be two of us to keep an eye on you."

"Two?"

"A friend of mine."

"You need help?"

"Yep," he replied with a grin. He wasn't going to let her get to him.

Shelby remained quiet, and as they walked Brad began to wonder if he'd inadvertantly admitted something to Shelby he couldn't admit to himself. He'd feel safer with someone else along, and he wasn't too sure she wouldn't be safer, as well.

They continued on in silence. Her face was unreadable, but her eyes glowed with satisfaction.

Brad had hired a friend of long standing. A half-breed who was quite willing to bring the wagon back from St. Louis when Brad was finished with it.

Tom Littlebeaver was a slender young man in his late twenties. He loved nothing more than to be able to move about outdoors in freedom. His hair was thick and black as a raven's, and his eyes were very close to gold. He had a quick, shy smile that attracted girls like magnets, and a charm that was so subtle one very rarely knew he was using it.

He was like a silent shadow. He wanted only to do what he was paid to do. He thought Shelby Vale pretty and charming, and he wondered why Brad seemed so cold to her.

In a matter of another couple hours the small caravan left town and started its journey.

Sam and Cecil stood on the board sidewalk and watched it go.

"I don't understand this," Cecil said. "If that girl is a bank robber and runs with a gang, I'll eat my hat."

"Come to think of it," Sam said thoughtfully, "he never rightly said . . ." He stopped to consider all the words Brad had not spoken. "That boy is downright crafty. Maybe I ought to send out a couple of wires. Find out what I can . . . and just who this Stapleton gang is."

"Yeah. Maybe Brad made a mistake."

"Yeah. Or he did exactly what he wanted and let us believe what we thought he was saying and doing. Yes, sir," Sam chuckled, "that boy is crafty."

He crossed the street toward the telegraph office and Cecil watched him, still convinced that Shelby Vale was an innocent victim of circumstances.

It was nearing midday, three days later when Sam crossed the street after eating his lunch to relieve Cecil so he could do the same.

He still had the nagging memory of the beautiful young woman's face dancing before his eyes, and it angered him. He'd been a sheriff a long time and he'd never been a victim of guilt before. He just didn't like the taste of it.

Besides, he'd been more than aware of Cecil's surreptitious, and to him accusing, glances now and then.

Sam had a bitter taste in his mouth. He didn't like it. He didn't like it one little bit.

He opened the door of the office and stepped inside. Cecil was seated behind the desk, so Sam at first didn't notice another man who sat in the chair a short distance away.

"Sam," Cecil said quickly, "this here gent wants to talk to you. It's about those telegrams and that girl Brad took."

Sam turned to face the man as he rose slowly from the chair. This was the biggest man he'd ever seen in his life, he thought, and he hoped he had no reason to tangle with him.

Chapter 8

Brad and Shelby traveled in silence. Tom was cer-tain he'd never seen two people strike sparks off of each other like these two did. They were traveling slowly because the wagon could only cover so many miles in a day. Eventually they would reach a place where they could find a faster means of transporta-tion.

When they made camp that night, Tom cooked, and while he did he struck up a conversation with Shelby. Soon he found himself telling her about his life. Raised in a village not too many miles west of where they were, he'd gone to a missionary school to learn to read and write. He was content, and only walked in the white world when the need arose to get some money. He'd served as a military guide and a multitude of other things as well.

He was tall for an Indian, getting his height from his father. But his mother had gifted him with his ebony hair, and a quick smile.

Tom and Brad had been friends a long time. The

kind of friends who did not monitor each other's lives, who could pick up their friendship after years, as if there had been no interruption. Tom had even worked with Brad a time or two as a guide, when he'd been a Ranger.

"You should visit my village one day," he proclaimed enthusiastically to Shelby. "They would make you welcome. It is not customary to see light-haired people."

"I should love to, Tom," she said enthusiastically. "How far is it from here?"

"Too far," Brad broke into the conversation, "and don't get any ideas about it." He smiled. "Tom is just as susceptible as Cecil, but I'm right here to look out for any little problems."

Tom realized some kind of threat had passed between these two and he didn't want to be part of such a thing. He watched Shelby scowl darkly at Brad, rise and walk to the wagon where her blanket was spread underneath.

Tom had known Brad for a long time and had never had anything but ultimate respect for him, so he asked no questions. Brad had visited their village often and he knew a day's good ride would find them being welcomed there.

"Why don't you get some sleep, Tom. I'll stay by the fire for a while."

Certain that Brad was uncomfortable with the situation, Tom moved into the shadows and rolled in his blanket. Soon he slept.

Brad sat, watching the fire burn lower and lower. It was going to prove to be a very difficult trip and

deep within he wished he had a way to brighten it for
her a bit.

Her hatred of him was quite obvious. That thought
opened the door suddenly to a memory he wished he
could obliterate. But he couldn't. She was there in his
arms as surely as if she had risen from her bed and
came to him.

For a moment he allowed it, recapturing the taste
and the scent of her until he was immersed in pure
sensations . . . forbidden sensations that he would
never allow again.

It was a long time before he slept.

When Shelby awoke the next morning to the
sounds of breakfast preparations, she expected Tom
and was surprised to open her eyes and see Brad
kneeling before the fire.

The light of the fire in the gray of early dawn
reflected the strength of his face, and she watched his
strong, efficient hands as a warm unwelcome memory
of their touch washed over her.

He sensed her watching him, for he suddenly
looked up and smiled. "Good morning. Breakfast is
almost ready."

She was aware that he worked facing her, so that
the fire was between them . . . and that his back
wouldn't be toward her. As he had said, he didn't fall
for the same trick twice.

Only then did she realize there was no sign of Tom.
She came out from under the wagon, bringing her
blanket with her.

"There's a stream down there," he pointed, "if you want to wash up a bit."

"You trust me that far?"

"The horses are where I can see them and you aren't dumb enough to try to go anywhere on foot. I guess under those circumstances I can trust you a little." She could hear the amusement in his voice, but she had no intention of rising to the bait.

"Thank you," she replied coldly.

"You're quite welcome."

Shelby looked around carefully. "Where's Tom?"

"Oh, he'll be back in a while. Probably catch up with us by noon. He had some business to take care of."

"In his village? Is it that close?"

"Don't get your hopes up. No, not in the village, and it's certainly not close enough for a tenderfoot like you to make it alone."

She walked away from him, sure she heard the suspicious sound of a soft, muffled laugh.

After about twenty minutes, Brad went to search her out. He didn't really trust the fact that she wouldn't try to get away on foot just to be obstinate.

He found her kneeling at the edge of the stream. Obviously she'd washed her face and hands, because drops of water glistened on her skin and the strands of hair that framed her face.

Just as obviously she was caught in some daydream and didn't hear his approach. He stopped a few feet away and took the time to enjoy the picture she made.

"Penny for your thoughts," he said. His sudden

voice caused her to abruptly turn to him. He watched her eyes become shielded, and for this brief moment he hated the antagonism that was so alive between them.

"Don't waste your money. They're not worth it."

"Breakfast is getting cold."

She nodded. "I'm not really that hungry."

"You need food. You hardly ate anything yesterday."

"How did you know? Did Sheriff McClure report in to you?"

"Contrary to what you believe, I think Sam really liked you. He was worried about you."

"Then he ought to have been worried enough to believe the truth when he heard it."

"Sam's been a friend. He trusts me."

"And you lie when you choose? The Stapleton gang . . . bank robbers. Really. Couldn't you have been a bit more creative?"

"Oh, I think I did a good job on that one. After all, you *are* a Stapleton and your father *is* on the board of one of the biggest banks in Charleston. I didn't lie. I didn't say you robbed banks."

"No, you just let him believe what he thought he heard."

"You filled him in on more details."

"Which he didn't believe . . . or half believed."

"I can't be blamed for that. C'mon, it's time to eat. You need some nourishment. You're too thin now. If I let you go a few days without eating, you'll vanish. Besides," he took her arm and propelled her gently back toward the camp, "I'm a pretty good cook."

"Was the last time we camped an example?"

"Not really. It wasn't up to my usual standards."

"I have a slight headache and I'm really not very hungry. Honestly."

He turned her to face him and looked at her closely. "Are you all right?"

"I'm just fine," Shelby insisted.

"Well, you'd better try to eat something. We'll take the next few hours slow and you can rest in the wagon."

She shrugged off his hand and continued on toward the camp. After a few minutes, he followed her.

She tried to force down some food just to keep him satisfied. Tom had taken her horse, so when the wagon was loaded, Brad tied his horse behind it and they climbed up on the seat.

If she hadn't been perversely determined not to enjoy anything while with this man, she surely would have enjoyed the ride.

An undulating plain of grass shimmered before them, and far to the west rose a range of hills. She could easily see the land drained well and thought it would be excellent farm land. But in answer to one of her questions, Brad assured her the land, as far as he was concerned, was better for ranching.

"A man could graze a really large herd of cattle in this territory," he added. He would have liked to have told her that his ranch lay close by. His valley near the Platte River was the most beautiful spot in the world to him.

He'd have liked to have walked with her beneath the cottonwoods and told her about his plans to build his place into the best ranch in Nebraska. He'd have liked to have told her why he needed the money he would be paid to return her to Charleston.

They rode slowly and the only topics of conversation between them were the weather and the view around them.

It was right, it was best . . . but it annoyed the hell out of him. He'd have loved to have her tell him more about herself and to tell her more about himself. But they made preparations to stop for the midday meal with all barriers intact.

Brad took care of the horses and the building of a small fire while he kept one eye on Shelby, who walked some distance away to stretch her legs, and he suspected, to get as far away from him as she could.

Brad's close proximity and the uninvited effect he had on her was stretching her nerves. She had to find a way to get away, one that was safe and feasible. The area around her looked extremely vast, and extremely empty. She was reasonably sure Brad, especially with Tom's help, would find her in a matter of hours. It would be necessary to get closer to some town. This, of course, meant she had to be in his company for an indeterminable length of time.

For the first time Shelby felt like discarding her obligations and trying to make Brad really see the truth and look at her with no trace of distrust or disdain for what he imagined she was doing.

Despite the fact that he had tried to frighten her in the hotel room, it didn't take long for her to know his real motive . . . and to sense beneath it all something new and vital she could hardly name. And she knew he'd felt it, too.

If things had been different . . . But she had already said this to herself a million times. It did no good. She looked back at his tall form as he moved around the camp and the same breathless sensation gripped her.

Her attention was diverted by a rider approaching slowly. It was Tom. He must have left their camp in the wee hours of the morning to do whatever it was he had to do. She wondered at all the secrecy.

By the time she reached the camp, Tom was just covering something he had put into the wagon. She assumed Brad must have remembered some supply or other they had needed and sent Tom after it.

They were soon on their way again. This time Tom was guiding the wagon.

The high grass was like a rippling sea, and Shelby enjoyed riding through it. Still, she was a bit tired by the time they made camp for the night.

Tom carried a bucket of water from a nearby pond for her and heated it by the fire, then he and Brad made supper while Shelby washed away the day's grime.

When she came to sit by the fire, Brad handed her a plate of food.

"I'll help you clean up the dishes," she offered after she had finished eating.

"I'll take care of that," Brad said. "But there is something you could do that would make both Tom and I feel a lot better."

"What?"

"First, I've got something I want to give you."

"To give me?" Now she was stunned.

"Just a little gift . . . actually a gift more for us than for you."

"I don't understand."

Brad walked to the back of the wagon, where he uncovered and withdrew a guitar.

"Ohh," Shelby sighed, and smiled. and Brad had understood that music had always meant a great deal to her. She turned to look at Tom, who smiled shyly, then she looked back to Brad.

"I thought . . . I mean, I hoped you wouldn't mind a song or two. To pass the time."

"Of course." Leave it to him, she thought, not to say he'd like to hear her sing again. "To pass the time."

She found a comfortable seat on her blanket by the fire, then strummed the guitar lightly. Softly, she began to sing.

Brad still stood in the shadows by the wagon and watched her. He hadn't really understood why he had sent Tom to purchase the guitar. Maybe it was a small means of compensating for what he was forcing her to do.

The sudden thought that what she had claimed might be true, that she was somehow being forced into an unwanted marriage, became a very uncomfortable lump in the center of his chest.

He walked to the fire slowly and sat down. The song she sang was one of the first he'd heard her perform. He remembered the gown she wore and the mesmerizing effect she'd had.

When she finished the song, Tom was the first one to speak.

"That sure was pretty, miss. Reminds me of the time I first went to the mission school. It was Christmas and they tried to describe an angel to me. I guess maybe that's what they meant when they described how the angels sing."

"Thank you, Tom. That's the nicest compliment I've ever received. Would you like to hear any particular song?"

"Oh, I don't know. Anything is all right with me."

"Brad?"

"Tom's right. Any song will sound fine. You choose."

Again she strummed the guitar and sang a short lullaby. After, she laughed. "That was a song my mother used to sing to me when I was a child," she explained. As she went into the next song, Brad pictured Anne Stapleton, and for the life of him he couldn't see her singing such a lullaby to Shelby.

The next song was a vibrant tune filled with enthusiasm and laughter, and both men were so totally involved in the girl and her music that they forgot to pay attention to what was going on around them.

Shelby just finished the song when three tall, dark figures seemed to appear out of the night mist and stood just within the circle of light behind Brad and Tom. She looked up and gave a gasping squeal of shock, then froze. Brad and Tom turned to face the intruders.

Tom stood up first, and Shelby was surprised to see a smile on his face. Then Brad stood, too, and he showed no sign of alarm. Shelby was too scared to do anything but remain frozen in place.

The three visitors stepped into the light. She could tell they were Indians, and from Tom's reaction, men he knew well.

When she examined them closely, the threat vanished. They were young, not much older than herself. Dressed in buckskin, they were also quite handsome in an overpowering kind of way.

She realized their eyes were glued on her, and she tried to smile.

"You're traveling late," Brad said to the eldest of the three, who appeared to be close to Brad's age.

"We wanted to be back to our village within two days. We were preparing camp not too far from here. But we heard the woman sing and came to see."

None of the three had taken their eyes from Shelby, and she was well aware of it. Brad was even more so.

"This is Whitehawk and his two brothers," Brad said to her, "Threefeathers and Rainman. My friends this is 'Shelby Vale' . . . a *very* good friend of mine."

She was as aware of his emphasis on "very" as the three men were. It was a delicate warning, and when she realized their appraisal of her had grown a little more intense she knew why.

It was then that what she considered a very brilliant idea came to her. Brad was most definitely outnumbered, and if she could convince these men to help her, she could extradite herself from Brad and eventually from them as well.

She stood up slowly and smiled at the one who had done the speaking for the three.

"Whitehawk, it's a pleasure to meet you. If you and your friends enjoyed the music, come and sit by our fire and I'll sing a song or two for you."

The three were totally stunned. Shelby refused to look at Brad. She could sense both his surprise and his anger.

What she didn't know, or sense, was the danger she was so blindly walking into. Brad's mind began to spin with ways he could put an end to her encouraging men who were taking her actions in a drastically different way than he was sure she had even surmised.

"Would you like some food, Whitehawk?" Brad said, trying to draw his attention. But Whitehawk only gave a negative shake of his head and continued to keep his dark eyes on Shelby.

Tom was just aware, of the thoughts that were spinning through the minds of his three friends. He held his breath, sure that a calamity was about to unfold. His village was close enough to Whitehawk's that he had known them well. He knew the Indian had a very different grasp on this situation than Shelby could imagine.

Shelby, used to an audience, was the only one completely unaware of the danger. She again sat down before the fire, drew the guitar across her lap and let her fingers drift over the strings while she considered just what she would sing.

A love song, of course. A love song. Shelby smiled to herself. She meant to show Brad Cole a thing or two about being so sure of himself. She sang as she'd never sang before, directly to Whitehawk who watched her in blatant admiration.

At their insistence she sang a second song and then a third. She was tired, but she was certain she had captured a stalwart protector in Whitehawk.

After the third song was ended she invited the three to share their campfire for the night. If Brad could have put his hands around her throat and choked her until she was purple, he would have. Even Tom had begun to look a bit worried.

But once the offer was extended, neither man could withdraw it without creating even more of a problem.

When she finally went to sleep, both Brad and Tom were relieved. The men talked a while longer and then decided to sleep . . . all except Whitehawk, who lingered by the dying fire deep in thought.

The next morning he was lingering strategically near when Shelby awoke.

"I would speak with you, sun hair."

"And I would speak with you, Whitehawk. Come, let's walk for a while."

Encouraged by this, Whitehawk smiled and fell into step beside her. Brad woke just in time to see them disappearing over a grassy knoll.

"Oh, damn!" he groaned as he fairly leapt to his feet.

Tom stirred when Brad nearly stumbled over him. He sat up abruptly. "Brad?"

"I'll be back. Shelby's taking a walk with Whitehawk. See what you can do about making sure the other two don't follow us."

Tom only had time to nod. As far as he could see, the others were still asleep. He lay back down and closed his eyes in silent prayer for two things. One, that Brad could get them out of the building situation without having a confrontation with Whitehawk, and two, that he was not going to murder Shelby at the first opportunity.

When Brad crested the hill he could see Shelby and Whitehawk in conversation, standing beneath the branches of a huge oak tree. Of course, Brad thought angrily, she was doing all the talking. Digging herself a hole she couldn't foresee. He knew very well that Whitehawk was taking whatever she was offering completely the wrong way.

He had to control his anger, he had to think. He'd been friends with their village much too long to have a problem now.

Suddenly he smiled and slowed his steps to a more casual walk. After all, he could speak the Sioux language . . . and "Shelby Vale" couldn't.

When he approached the two, Shelby had such a smug, satisfied look on her face that Brad almost laughed. Whitehawk looked totally awed by the whole situation. When Brad spoke to him in his own language, he responded without considering that Shelby wouldn't understand.

"Good morning, Whitehawk."

"Good morning, Brad. I have much to say to you."

"Oh, really."

"The light-haired woman, is not your wife."

"Has she told you that?"

"What are you saying to him?" Shelby demanded belligerently. This drew a quick startled look from Whitehawk.

"She has said she wishes to go to my village with me. I look upon her with pleasure. If she is yours, then I would buy her with many gifts."

"Whitehawk is a man of great skill as a warrior," he complimented the Indian. "His courage is well known. I'm sure he will show the same courage when he takes the woman, Shelby. It is not all braves who would try to understand her . . . condition."

"Condition?" Whitehawk frowned, and his body stiffened. "What condition?"

"Damn you, Brad Cole, you tell me what he's saying and what lies you're telling him."

"Oh, it's nothing much to worry about. Most of the time she's normal," Brad went on unperturbed. But he could see Whitehawk was getting a bit upset.

"Normal?" Whitehawk repeated, but he'd cast a quick look at Shelby, then returned his gaze to Brad. "What do you mean . . . sometimes she's normal?"

"It's a little problem inside her head. That's how she came to be with me. I didn't realize it until later. You see, sometimes she doesn't know who she is or why she's there. She thinks other men are her husband at times and she tends to . . . drift. But," he shrugged, "she's just not responsible. She's never violent . . . well, not often at least."

Brad, had touched upon the one thing in the world that could bring fear to the heart of Whitehawk. He'd seen people whose minds had slipped away to a place he couldn't imagine. Insanity was a specter he couldn't face.

But Brad felt he had to take it a step further and prove a point or two. "Her name is really Winter Stapleton . . . but she gets terribly upset when someone calls her by that name. Just ask her and see."

Whitehawk did not really want a display of her condition, but Shelby was looking at them both with a dark frown. So he turned to her.

"Is your name Winter Stapleton?"

Shelby turned a furious gaze on Brad. "What have you been telling him about me!" she almost shouted. Her fists doubled at her sides, and the fury in her eyes helped Brad's cause more than she imagined.

"Nothing much. Only about your . . . little problem."

Shelby did exactly what Brad had wanted her to do. He was destroying her plans . . . and she lost her temper.

"Don't believe him!" she said to Whitehawk. "He's lying. He kidnapped me and my name is not Winter Stapleton, it's Shelby Vale. You can't believe anything he says. Take me away from here and I'll be able to prove who I am. I'm not Winter Stapleton!" Her voice ended on the high-pitched note of real fury. She glared at Brad, who only managed to look distressed and saddened.

"It's all right, 'Shelby.' Of course we won't call you Winter, if you don't want us too. We'll call you anything you choose to be called."

That the light-haired woman wanted nothing more than to attack Brad with claws and teeth, Whitehawk could plainly see. Brad had spoken the truth. The woman had a pretty face and a beautiful voice, but the gods had taken something from her when they had given her such gifts. This he could understand, but he certainly didn't want to buy a bride who was not in control of her mind.

"We must go," he stated firmly. "My brothers and I are expected home soon."

"You promised to take me to your village with you!" she cried.

"Shelby Vale," Whitehawk looked at her with a mixture of admiration and pity in his eyes, "it is best you stay with the man who understands how to care for you. My heart goes with you and I hope the gods return your reason and that you find a happy life. I'm sure Brad will take good care of you."

He turned and walked away and Shelby, her teeth grinding, turned to see Brad almost convulsed in silent laughter. By the time Whitehawk had disappeared, Brad could contain it no longer.

"You told him I was crazy! You actually told him I was crazy!" She pounded his arm with her fist until he caught her wrist. Her temper exploded into violence and the attack took Brad by surprise when several blows landed with a shocking force. Finally, he subdued her by again grasping her wrists, then pulling her arms behind her back and crushing her against him.

This was the worst thing for his peace of mind. Pressed close, he could almost feel her heartbeat. She looked up at him with a combination of emotions that he couldn't . . . or didn't want to read.

But she drew him like a magnet drew iron, and the one forbidden touch was beyond him to resist. He bent to gently touch her soft, half-parted mouth with his. The result was so electrifying he felt as if the breath was being forced from his body. He heard her soft sound of protest, at the same time he felt the momentary yielding.

Shelby was reaching in desperation for some semblance of control. She struggled and broke free of him, mostly because Brad had loosened his grip to more of a caress than a hold.

"Get away from me," she struggled again to make her words frigid.

"Don't try any more tricks, Shelby. It always ends up harder on you than anyone else." With this lie on his lips he turned and walked back toward camp.

She glared after him so furious she was speechless. But her mind churned with one thought. There *would* be a next time, and that time she would not underestimate the deviousness of Brad Cole.

Chapter 9

When the Indians had finally left their camp Shelby was still simmering. They had cast her surreptitious, nervous, yet sympathetic looks to the point that she wanted to shriek at them.

Again they were on the move and Shelby remained silent out of sheer perversity. They traveled in a decidedly strained silence until well past noon, then stopped for a quick meal for which she had no appetite.

She could feel Brad's eyes on her, and this above all things, stretched her nerves taut.

Brad knew she was angry with him. The glitter of her eyes promised retribution if an opportunity presented itself. She had her claws unsheathed, and he knew she'd lash out the moment he even suggested a desire for conversation.

Late afternoon they crested a hill and pulled to an abrupt stop. Before them, several hundred head of cattle were being hazed slowly along by eight cowboys.

Brad watched two of them separate from the group and ride toward them. He cast Shelby a quick look to see her reaction, though he knew by now, there was no way of guessing what she might do next.

"Afternoon," Brad greeted the two cowboys as they reined in beside him.

"Afternoon," the oldest of the two replied. "I'm Zeke Raymond from the Circle C. This is my son, Dave. Where you headed?"

"My name's Brad Cole, this is Shelby, and that's Tom. We're on our way to Lincoln right now, then we're going on to Charleston."

"Charleston," Dave Raymond whistled. "You got a lot of miles to go." He smiled a boyish smile. Dave was a handsome young man nearing nineteen. His eyes strayed at once to Shelby.

"Where you headed?" Brad wanted to be as friendly as he could, and he wanted to leave their company as soon as possible.

"North Platte, then on to the ranch. It's near Ogallala," Zeke replied.

"I've heard of the Circle C. Those are prime stock." Brad motioned toward the herd. He was quite aware that Dave's eyes had never left Shelby and that she was smiling a much too friendly smile to suit him.

"Yeah, I just added to my herd. Bought them from Carl Simpson. The big ranch down on the river. They're the best in this part of the country."

"We're about to stop. Don't want to run these cows too fast or too hard." Dave spoke quietly. "Why don't you all join us for supper?"

Brad wanted to groan. There was a strong social code among cattlemen, and refusing their hospitality could prove to be a problem. Yet, having Shelby Vale among this group could prove to be an ever bigger one. He was ready to try a diplomatic no when Shelby's voice, syrupy sweet, broke in.

"Oh, I'd love to." She smiled directly at Dave, and Brad grit his teeth. This lady was getting to be a large thorn in his side, and if the future of his ranch didn't hang on her return he would have happily dumped her. But the nagging vision of Dave smiling at her didn't set well, either.

"We're making camp just over there. Come on over around sundown and cook will have the grub ready," Zeke said. "It'll sure be nice to look at a pretty face for a change."

"Why, thank you." Shelby smiled the warmest, open smile she could. "I'm looking forward to joining you."

For the first time Brad noticed that Zeke was studying him closely.

"Don't I know you from somewhere? Used to know a Cole that had a ranch down by the border. Course you're pretty young to be him. You kin maybe?"

"No . . . and I don't think we've met before," Brad replied honestly.

"Sure got a familiar face. Oh, well, I got a good memory. Maybe it will come to me."

Brad was pretty certain that somewhere along the line Zeke *had* seen him, or knew of his parents' ranch. But he didn't want any of it discussed in front of

Shelby who, he was more than sure, would put two and two together.

"Yeah, maybe," he nodded. "Well, we'll see you at sundown."

Zeke and Dave touched the brim of their hats and bowed slightly toward Shelby, then turned and rode away.

Brad turned and looked at her. There was still a half-smile on her face. "Don't get any smart ideas," he warned.

"Why, Brad, whatever are you talking about?"

"You damn well know what I'm talking about. These boys play real serious and I'm not going to be forced to use my gun on any of them."

Shelby's smile widened, and Brad was certain she didn't believe him. This naive city girl was going to get him into a lot of problems if he didn't stop her. For the tenth time since he'd taken on this job, he cursed the day he'd agreed to it.

They organized their own camp, then rode the short distance to join the Raymond camp, where they were welcomed with hot coffee and sizzling steaks.

It was soon obvious that all eight of the men, excluding Zeke who seemed amused at the situation, had cleaned themselves up very carefully and were on such good behavior that Brad could have laughed if it hadn't made him so nervous.

Dave was nearly falling all over himself to make sure Shelby wanted for nothing, and Brad had to control his urge to hold on to her.

But she seemed relaxed and unperturbed. He began to feel that maybe the evening was going to nd all right . . . just a bit prematurely. The subject of horses came up, and Shelby voiced her admiration or the well-trained horses used to herd cattle.

"Why, ma'am," one cowboy said, "my horse, Mudfly, can outsmart any other critter I know."

"Oh, he's smart all right," another laughed, 'smart enough to dump you in the creek a ways back."

"I'd say Dave has the best horse in the whole remuda," Zeke said.

"Sure do," Dave agreed. "She's a mare that don't take a backseat to any other horse I've run across."

"Really?" Her voice and expression dripped wide-eyed innocence, and Brad should have known it was leading to something. "I'd love to see her." She stood up. "Could we take a walk and go look at her now?"

Brad could do nothing but watch as Dave eagerly led Shelby away from the campfire and into the darkness.

The two walked slowly toward the place where the string of horses to be ridden in the morning were tied. A long rope had been stretched between two trees and the eight horses stood there quietly.

"Here she is," Dave said proudly, as he stopped beside a chestnut mare that nickered softly as he patted her neck. It was obvious the horse knew him well and trusted him. "She's a real lady."

Shelby came to stand close beside Dave and reached to rub her hand down the glossy chestnut mane.

"She's beautiful. What's her name?"

"Sunrise. I've had her since she was a colt. Broke her myself."

"Really?" She looked up at Dave with a look that told him she truly admired such a feat.

"Too bad you aren't going our way, you could stop by our place. Not only do I have her dam there, but her sire is a real beauty."

"I would like that. Tell me, just how far is it to your place . . . I mean, the way you have to travel?"

"A few days."

"Your ranch is near North Platte, you said."

"Yes, it is. Why?"

"Is there a telegraph there?"

"Yes, but there's one in Lincoln, too. That's where you're headed, isn't it?"

"It's where we're headed, but . . ."

"But?"

Shelby turned her head, well aware that the high yellow moon touched her face.

"Is there something wrong? If there is, there's plenty of us to help."

"I . . . I can't tell you. I'm . . . I'm afraid."

"Afraid?" Dave was puzzled only for a minute, then it dawned on him just what she was afraid of. She was afraid of *someone,* not something, and that someone had to be the man she was with.

"A pretty thing like you oughtn't to have to be afraid of anything . . . or anyone," He spoke his gallantry with enthusiasm.

Again Shelby looked up at him. Tears glistened in the moonlight like silver drops. She put her hand gently on his arm.

"You're kind, but there's nothing you can do."

"Do? Do about what?" He looked at her closely. "Are you traveling with these two men willingly?"

"No," Shelby replied honestly. "No, I'm not. But I don't have . . . I mean I can't do much about it."

"I don't understand. You want to tell me what the problem is, maybe me and the others can help."

"It's so difficult. You see, he's mistaken about who I am and he won't listen to reason." She went on to explain the situation enough to convince him both of her innocence and Brad's seeming domination.

"You mean he's like a bounty hunter, and he's he's actually—"

"He's actually mistaken me for someone else and he just won't listen to me. I've . . . I've begged . . ." She let her voice break on a helpless sob.

Womanhood in tears, especially a lady, was a thing Dave couldn't bear, and when she moved closer to him, laying her hand on his arm and raising a tear-stained face, he was irretrievably lost. He put his arm around her, swelling with a protective instinct.

"If you need help, you need only say the word. There's a lot of us and only two of them."

"I don't want anyone hurt. It would be much better if I found a way to get back to your camp, maybe after they both are asleep. I know it would be a terrible imposition, but if one of you could take me to the nearest town, I'd be all right."

"I'll take you myself. I'll sneak over to your camp later tonight. There's a stand of trees between us. I'll wait on this side. Then I can just take you right on to town. I'll just tell my father I'll be gone a day or so.

There's enough men so's he won't have any problems."

"You're so kind . . . so strong and understanding."

He was actually shaking and Shelby was certain he was trying to fight the urge to kiss her. She rose on tiptoe and kissed his cheek, not wanting the situation to go beyond the boundaries.

"Thank you. I'll be very careful."

He meant to try to assure her that she would be safe and well taken care of, but a voice interrupted their rendezvous.

Brad's voice sounded cool and calm, which, if Shelby had known him better, would have told her was a dangerous sign. He had watched the kiss and was just as annoyed at his own reaction as he was with her.

"We've got to get back to camp," he said gruffly. "The men have to be up and riding before dawn."

Brad read the look in Dave's eyes, but still he smiled. He felt sympathy for the younger man. Hadn't he fallen into "Shelby Vale's" sweet-scented trap?

"Of course." Shelby smiled at Dave, then left his side and brushed past Brad, quite satisfied that he was in for a big surprise.

As Dave started to follow her, Brad held out an arm to bar his way.

"You and I have something to discuss."

When they returned to their camp, it was amid a very strained silence. Shelby was considering her timing. For sure she had to wait until Brad and Tom were sound asleep. Even then she had to be very careful. She didn't intend to underestimate Brad Cole again.

Brad remained thoughtfully silent while he watched Shelby prepare for bed. He knew she was constantly on the alert for a way out of her dilemma and that she was more than annoyed with him. Her eyes reflected the firelight, as if glowing with an inner heat.

"You'd better get some sleep, Shelby. I intend to get started as early as possible tomorrow," Brad said, ignoring her glare of condensed anger.

"I'm not sleepy," she said crossly, and was even more annoyed when Brad continued to gaze at her.

"You'll be exhausted tomorrow. I'm not asking, I'm telling you. Get some sleep!"

"You're taking me back against my will. How do you expect me to cooperate?" She could hear the tension in her own voice. Obstinately, she reached for her canteen and drank. Then she lay down just outside the ring of firelight and pulled her blanket around her, aware that Brad's eyes never left her. She wanted to release her anger verbally, but she also didn't want to force Brad to do something that would impede her escape, such as using the handcuffs he still carried.

She fought sleep, knowing she probably would not have another chance if she failed this time.

She grit her teeth, wishing away the time and hoping Brad would soon be asleep. She heard him sigh deeply and fumble about and was relieved to know that he was finally going to bed.

She watched the moon rise higher in the night sky and tried to lie still and listen. Soon his deep, regular breathing told her he slept.

Still she waited, making sure she gave Dave enough time to saddle two horses and bring them. After what felt to her like an interminable amount of time, she cautiously began to move.

First, she turned her head to look closely at the two men. Both were deep in sleep. Then, inch by inch she moved the blanket away and sat up.

While she fought the fear of the unknown, she slowly rose and drew on her boots and jacket. Now came the hardest part, slipping away from camp without waking Brad.

She edged herself, one step at a time, toward the safety of a stand of nearby trees. Only then did she breathe a ragged sigh of relief. On the other side of the trees young Dave Raymond would be waiting.

Once she felt a bit safer, she moved quickly and quietly through the darkened woods.

All the while she believed she heard someone right behind her, but she struggled for control. It was her imagination . . .

She saw the brightness that heralded the edge of the woods and breathed a sigh of relief. Her heart was pounding furiously and sweat had dampened her clothes and remained in beads on her skin.

For a second, before she stepped beyond the trees, she paused, trying to catch her breath and control the trembling weakness that gripped her.

Finally, she stepped out of the shelter of the trees and looked around the meadow before her. This was where Dave said he would be and she fought the panic that tried to rise when she could see no sign of him.

Breathlessly, she kept gazing about. Still no sign of anyone. She wondered if she could take the chance to call Dave's name softly. No, she'd wait a few minutes. Maybe he'd had trouble explaining the situation to his father.

But as the minutes ticked by, she found her courage slipping and her panic mounting.

"Dave!" she called out softly, expecting to see him slip out from the trees with his shy smile and his apology. *"Dave!"* she took the chance of raising her voice a bit.

"Don't bother, Shelby, Dave's not coming."

The voice came from so close to her that she jumped in fright and gasped.

"Brad! How . . ." She stopped speaking as the reality came to her. He'd been playing with her like a cat with a mouse. "Why isn't he coming?" she demanded, "What did you say to him?"

"I must say, you sure are stubborn."

"What did you say to him?"

"Does it matter? In a couple of hours they'll be on their way, minus the extra company."

"Why did you let me come this far? Did you enjoy playing with me?"

"No, but I thought you did need a little lesson. I warned you no tricks were going to work."

"The least you could do is tell me what you said to him to make him decide not to come."

"Oh, it was pretty easy. Zeke remembered where he'd seen me last and how good I am with this gun. He gave his son a bit of very intelligent advice."

"So what does that mean?"

"It means that he had respect for what I know . . . and a sudden blossoming respect for my 'wife.' It's a pretty serious thing to come between an angry man with a fast gun and a wayward wife he's trying to control." Brad grinned and placed his hand on his heart and looked sorrowful. "A wife he loves and who is breaking his heart."

"Oh, you liar! How can you be so sneaky!"

"Me, sneaky!" he chuckled. "You're the one to talk. First Cecil, then Whitehawk, and now poor young Dave. Why don't you pick on someone who can give you a run for your money?"

"Meaning you?" she said, challenge in her voice.

"Oh, no, not me. My job is to dump you in Daddy's lap, and that's as far as I'm going. You, my dear 'Shelby Vale,' don't play by any rules, and a man who falls for your tricks is going to pay for it by being left holding a lot of promises and a real broken heart."

"You're not fair. You see things only from one side. You've never even tried to really listen to me." Shelby walked the few steps that closed the distance between them, then looked up at him. "Brad . . ." she said softly as she placed her hand on his arm.

Lord, he thought. She was enough to turn a man's

blood to water. Any determination he had turned to putty in her small hands.

He caught her wrist, and he could feel her pulse with his fingers. Its erratic beat told him her emotions were stirred, and he wondered if she could sense the fact that his were just as wild.

In the moonlight she looked so . . . He sought the word. *Innocent* came first, before *desirable,* but *desirable* soon followed.

He hadn't even realized he'd drawn her so close until his arms were around her and she was pressed against him, her soft mouth raised to accept his.

She was sweet and soft in his arms, her lips parting and her arms reaching to encircle him.

The kiss deepened and ignited a curling flame within him. From the scent of her to the warmth of her that flowed against him, he could feel every nerve in his body as if they had been touched to an open fire.

If he was caught in the magic, it was more so for Shelby, who had not wanted to battle with him in the first place. She felt as if she were melting, as if her extremities no longer belonged to her and all the strength she had was drawn from the iron-hard arms that held her.

She surrendered to the kiss with no thought other than the heated pleasure that filled her.

The kiss deepened until the low sound she made deep in her throat told him as no words could the completeness of her surrender.

Brad tried desperately to grasp for some kind of reason, but it fled before him like a wisp of smoke.

His hands slid down the curve of her back and waist, over her buttocks until he drew her snugly against him.

When the kiss ended, both were breathing raggedly, awed by the strength of the emotion that held them in its grip.

He looked down into eyes that seemed like deep pools of warmth in which he could immerse himself.

He struggled for a ray of logic, for an answer that was realistic. Was this the truth, or was it another part of a game she was playing? He wanted an answer, needed an answer . . . but was afraid of it.

"Brad . . ." She whispered his name again, wondering if he had felt what she had . . . or was he seeking a victory of sorts that would only prove her vulnerability . . . and his point.

He took hold of her shoulders and held her away from him. All rational thought fled when she was so close.

"I think we'd better talk about this. It's too dangerous," he said, his voice still unsteady.

"Dangerous for who?"

"Both of us. You're . . . alone, away from everyone and more vulnerable than you think."

"And what's so dangerous for you?"

"That I might start believing you."

"I never thought you really listened to a word I said."

"I know I haven't listened very well, but what was I to believe? There are too many stories."

She moved away from him several steps. "You tell

me something, Brad. What are you being paid to bring me back?"

"A lot less than what it's turned out to be worth."

"I don't really believe you are so . . . so mercenary. I can't understand a man who would sell another person just for money."

"Just because you don't understand a person's motives doesn't give you the right to condemn them."

"Maybe I do understand."

"No, I don't think you do."

"Oh, I do all right. Sacrificing me is all right as long as you don't lose anything. Brad," her voice softened, "tell me the truth. Would you want to see me dragged to the bed of a man I cannot stand?"

He inhaled a deep breath as this picture came vividly to his mind, along with the knowledge that he could not let that happen.

"Shelby . . . I can't believe that any *decent* man would demand that from a woman," Brad said skeptically.

"You still don't believe my reasons. You listen all right, Brad Cole . . . you just don't hear." She spun away from him and started for the darkness of the trees and the camp.

"Shelby . . . Wait!"

She wanted to run, to be away from his powerful touch and the feelings she could not control.

Brad searched for some way to clear their problem. He still had a little time before he would get her back, and he needed that time. One way or the other he had to find the truth before it drove him crazy.

He crossed the distance between them quickly and grasped her arm to turn her to face him.

"Shelby, I hate to admit I'm as confused as a man can get. If you really are Shelby Vale . . . you can't be forced into a marriage Winter Stapleton was supposed to be forced into."

"Then what is the harm if you wait a few weeks?"

"A few weeks and the time limit will be up . . . and I can't take the chance."

"You mean I won't be worth a dime."

"That's right," Brad said grimly, "so we're at a stalemate, and neither one of us can afford to trust the other too far."

"Oh, I trust you," Shelby smiled. "It's you who doesn't trust me."

"Oh, yeah. After a couple of the tricks you've pulled, you think I *should* trust you?"

"Should I warn you that I won't give up trying?"

"You don't have to, I'm pretty sure you won't. Should I remind you that I still have those handcuffs?"

"No," she said softly, "I don't need to be handcuffed."

"Then I think we'd better get back to camp."

"Brad, I . . ."

"Let's not pretend either one of us can trust the other. You're a very beautiful woman and if I fall for another of your games, you'll turn me inside out. I can't afford that. So let's get going."

She looked up at him and knew further battle was useless. In the morning they would resume their trip and that would bring them back to Charleston in time.

She was attracted to Brad in a way she'd never known before and she desperately wanted the opportunity to find a common ground where he could accept the truth. She recognized now a sense of honor in the man that would be difficult to find a way around. He had made a bargain, and accepted a lot of money. Now he was bound to bring her back.

She wasn't sure there really was a way around that, but . . . one step, one day at a time. If she could manage to stay away the appropriate length of time, then, honor or not, Brad would have to face the truth.

"I guess you're right," she said.

She walked back toward the camp, and for a minute Brad could only stand looking after her. His confusion, and the strange need to believe what she said displeased him, as did the almost certain feeling that she was again playing him for the fool. He sighed deeply and followed. This had to be one of the most difficult jobs he had ever undertaken. Difficult . . . and interesting . . . and exciting.

When they arrived in camp neither could find any appropriate words, so they prepared for bed in silence, each to find a sleepless night filled with doubt and memories of an elusive feeling that both fought.

Chapter 10

Carl James stood beside the fireplace, one broad shoulder casually resting against it. He held the snifter of brandy in one hand, gently swirling it in the glass while he watched Anne Stapleton and Jeffrey Brenner.

He was a tall well-built man who carefully kept his body in perfect physical shape. With his thick golden-brown hair, he was heartstoppingly handsome, if one did not look deeply into hooded blue eyes to see the lack of morality or conscience.

His smile was easy, and displayed strong white teeth but never humor or enjoyment. Enjoyment came to him through more subtle and devious ways of which only a few were aware.

Anne and Jeffrey, although well aware of many of those activities, were even more aware of the James family's wealth.

"There is still over a week and a half before the wedding, Carl," Anne said. "I don't know why you feel so—"

"I don't like playing games," Carl interrupted softly, "or paying for merchandise I have yet to receive."

"It's only a matter of time. Winter's father has a very good man on her trail. He'll have her home before the wedding," Jeffrey said.

"Umm," Carl muttered, noncommittally. "Well, that could be possible. But I decided some days ago to take a few matters into my own hands."

"I don't understand," Anne frowned. "Where is the necessity to do that?"

"It is necessary because I deem it necessary." His voice was as cold as chipped ice. "I have labored too long to get this little situation arranged and I don't intend to leave a loose thread that might unravel the whole thing."

"There will be no unraveling," Jeffrey said.

"Quite right. There will not be," Carl nodded. He disliked the two people he'd been forced to work with. He considered both below his level. But they were expendable.

The James family had acquired their wealth through a number of ways that could not afford close scrutiny. But it was not wealth now that Carl desired, it was the one thing his money couldn't buy, something he desired more than anything else.

He wanted to belong to the elite who dominated the political and social structure . . . to the establishment. To the group that could open the doors his ancestors had never dreamed of breaching.

The only door that could be opened to him to

make him acceptable to this class of people he envied so deeply was marriage.

It never occurred to him that what he desired could not be forced or bought. After all, he had bought everything else he had ever wanted.

"What have you been up to, Carl?" Anne questioned.

He took a sip of his brandy, then languorously detached himself from his position beside the fireplace and eased into a comfortable chair.

"Up to?" he repeated thoughtfully. "Just doing my best to expedite matters."

"And what does that mean?" Jeffrey inquired with a puzzled frown.

"It means that I have sent several men I know I can count on to find out exactly what is causing the delay. This . . . trustworthy man that Joseph has sent to find his daughter could be, shall we say, less efficient than we had bargained on. I prefer not to depend on someone I've not personally chosen. Besides, from what I understand, he's a former lawman and might feel some ridiculous sense of honor."

"Or chivalry," Jeffrey chuckled. "You mean he might listen to, and believe, Winter's story?"

"Precisely," he sighed, and sipped the brandy again. "That could create an annoyance."

"Have you heard any news?" Anne was more than curious. His intensity and the coldness of him made her fearful. She knew Carl James stopped at nothing to get what he wanted.

"I've the name, of course. Brad Cole. I've made

sure his trail was followed closely. I expect to hear word at any time now."

"What do you plan on doing?"

"That, my dear, Anne," he smiled a frigid smile, "is none of your affair. You have your job to do. Take care of it. You've wasted enough time and money already."

"Joseph is not an easy man to do away with. He's cautious and no one's fool."

"And that's the very reason you have to do something about him. One of these days he's going to become enlightened enough to do something about you. Then it will be too late."

Anne tried to smile, to laugh Carl's words away, but the reality was as clear to her as to him. Joseph had not shared her bed since the day Winter had vanished . . . and she'd often turned suddenly to see him watching her with a strange look on his face.

She looked at Jeffrey, who had narrowed his eyes and was watching her intently. His desire to step into Joseph's place was well known to Anne, but she still chafed beneath the pressure of the hold he had over her.

She finally smiled at Jeffrey, to the amusement of Carl, who knew her thoughts as well as he knew his own. In the long run there would be nothing for Anne Stapleton and Jeffrey Brenner.

Anne walked slowly up the steps, running her hand along the polished banister. She loved the luxury that surrounded her, wanted even more of it . . . and knew just how to fight to get it.

Tonight she would not let Joseph present her with excuses. If she had to seduce him again as she had before, she meant to do it.

She remembered her conquest well. Joseph had been lonely, had missed his wife so desperately that her victory had been easy.

Anne walked down the long hall to the bedroom she had shared with him in the past. She was surprised to find not Joseph in the room, but his valet, and even more surprised to see the man busy packing two suitcases. He smiled pleasantly.

"Good evening, Mrs. Stapleton."

"Good evening, George. What are you doing?"

"Just following Mr. Stapleton's orders, ma'am. He told me to make preparations for a trip."

"A trip? But where? For how long? He never mentioned it to me."

George flushed, "I don't know where, Mrs. Stapleton. But he did say it would be for about three days."

"Where is my husband?"

"The last I spoke with him he was in his study."

Without another word, Anne turned and left the room. George sighed deeply. This house had not been the same since Martha had died, and few in it had much liking for Joseph Stapleton's second wife.

Usually Anne would have knocked at the study door, but she bypassed that courtesy now. Beneath her anger was the echo of Carl's words . . . and a touch of fear. She opened the door and walked right in.

Joseph sat behind his desk concentrating on some papers that lay before him. When he looked up and saw Anne, he took the papers, folded them, and put them in his breast pocket.

"Anne. Is something wrong?"

"I had no idea you had planned a trip, Joseph."

"Just a short one."

"But the plans for the wedding . . .?"

"I'm sure you can handle everything as efficiently as you handle everything else."

"I don't understand this. Why did you not say anything to me before?"

"It's just a business trip, Anne, for heaven's sake. Don't you realize my daughter's wedding is one affair I would never miss."

"Of course. It's just . . ." Anne had a vague feeling of unrest, yet she couldn't put her finger on any cause. "When are you leaving?"

"First thing in the morning."

"Then why don't we discuss this upstairs." Anne smiled a seductive smile.

"It's rather late, my dear, and I do have to leave very early in the morning, long before you're usually awake. I'd hate to disturb you. I'll just sleep in the guest room." He smiled as he walked toward her. "I'm sure you'll understand. Maybe we'll have more time to talk when I get back."

Anne was momentarily stunned. She had never faced such gentle and complete rejection before.

"Of . . . of course."

"Good night, Anne. Sleep well."

When Joseph closed the door softly behind him,

the slight fear Anne had felt before began to grow. Something was wrong. Joseph loved his daughter and had never let business take precedence. Why was he involved in business now when he was worried to death about Winter. Or was he so worried?

Carl had just downed a hefty glass of whiskey and started upstairs to bed when a knock on the door surprised him. Who would be here this late?

Carl had too many enemies in his past not to be cautious. He walked to the door.

"Who is it?"

"Carl. It's Anne Stapleton."

This surprised him even more, but he opened the door. Anne rushed in, and he could see at once that she was very disturbed.

"It's very late, Anne, what brings you here at such an hour?"

"I have to talk to you."

"Couldn't it wait until morning?"

"Joseph is going away."

"Away?"

"I mean, he's going on some kind of a trip."

"So? He's a businessman."

"A loving, doting father takes a casual business trip while his daughter is missing! As if he hasn't a worry in the world. A business trip, I might add, that he never mentioned before. In fact—"

"In fact, he never mentioned it to you at all."

"No," Anne said, half angrily.

"It is a bit strange."

"It most certainly is."

"I thought you had quite a hold on Joseph."

"I do. But this affair of Winter's has upset the applecart."

"Anne, I told you once today. You had better do what needs doing."

"How can I do that just before the wedding? It's going to be difficult."

"Are you afraid?"

"Afraid? No, I'm not afraid. Just too cautious to move before the time is right. I want to make sure Winter is safely in your hands, and that the will reads exactly as I want it to."

"I see. I think you'd better go back home now. Surely he might awaken and miss you."

Anne explained that he was sleeping in the guest room.

"Good heavens, Anne," Carl laughed. "Be careful or your gold mine is going to slip through your fingers . . . and out of your grasp."

"Don't believe that," she responded with a smile. "I can still handle Joseph. It's you who has to be careful."

Her look was too full of humor to suit Carl. He gripped her arm in a brutal hold until she gasped and the humor fled her eyes.

"Don't have second thoughts about me, Anne dear. What I want I get, one way or the other."

"Of . . . of course, Carl."

"I think it best you go home."

Anne nodded, drawing away from his grip.

"And Anne . . ."

"Take good care of all that I've provided. There will come a time when I'll want it back."

"It's safe."

"Good. But keep in mind who it belongs to."

Anne could only nod and struggle for a smile. Her fear of Carl was turning to a firm desire to rid herself of him as soon as she could.

Carl gave some serious consideration to the information Anne had brought.

Many questions formed in his mind. Was Joseph Stapleton going to his daughter, did he know where she was, and if so, just what kind of a charade was being performed?

He had a respect for men of Joseph's breed. They were much more intelligent than creatures like Anne and Jeffrey gave them credit for.

He put on a cloak and hat and left his home. An hour later he was seated across the table from a shabbily dressed man. The tavern in which they sat was not on the better side of town, but it was located in an area that bred the kind of men he needed to engage.

"You understand clearly what I want you to do?"

The man was a disreputable-looking figure of indeterminable age, with faded blue eyes under bushy brows, and a flat, mushroom-shaped nose that had broken many times. Several teeth were missing, but he was obviously proud of a gold tooth he flashed. He had fought a number of battles to retain it.

His voice, when he finally spoke, was a thick, rasping sound indicating alcohol had been a constant companion over the years.

"It'll cost ya."

"How much?"

"Depends on how far I got to go." He laughed a mirthless laugh. "I ain't got me own private carriage to run me around like you do now. You and yours have come up in the world, ain't ya?"

"What we've done and where we've gotten is none of your business, Mason. Do you want the job or not?"

"Yeah, yeah I want it," Mason licked dry lips, and Carl could see he had gone a long time without the drink he needed.

Carl took a small pouch from an inside pocket and bounced it a little so Mason could hear the enticing jingle of coins. When he placed it on the table between them, Mason reached for it, and Carl caught his wrist in a viselike and painful grip.

"You get into the drink tonight," Carl's voice was soft, but his eyes were filled with deadly promise, "and you don't carry out my plans, I promise there won't be a place to hide."

Mason gulped heavily. He'd known Carl, too long not to accept the threat at face value. "I'll be there. You don't need to worry about me. And I'll be on his trail no matter where he goes. You can count on me."

"I'd better be able to," Carl replied as he released Mason's arm. "I want to know every move he makes, every place he visits, and the names of every person he contacts."

"All right."

"As soon as you find out any answers, you contact me. Time is of the essence here. You understand?"

"Yeah, I understand."

"Good." Carl rose, "Make sure you're not seen. I don't want any more problems than I've already got."

Mason nodded and watched Carl walk away. His eyes glowed with a multitude of emotions he'd never have revealed to Carl—hatred and envy being high among them.

He'd been one of many of Carl's 'old friends' who had read the papers and knew of Carl's imminent marriage into the very prestigious Stapleton family.

Mason slid from his seat after Carl had gone and left the tavern. Before he went home to immerse himself in the bottle he'd just bought, he stopped to enlist the help of a companion for the next day's work. He intended not to miss a thing on this endeavor. There was no way he would face Carl's unpredictable and dangerous wrath.

Joseph left his house the next morning before dawn.

Even though he thought her still asleep, Anne stood at her bedroom window and watched the carriage depart. Carl had been right, she thought. She realized clearly that there had been strong changes in Joseph in the past weeks. He had never been cold to her, nor had he ever been less than a passionate lover. Now he had drawn away from her.

She had to find some definite answers before she

carried out all her plans. First, Winter had to be safely married to Carl, which would ensure a very large sum of money. Second, she had to find out for certain that Joseph had not changed his will. The will that stated all his possessions had to be equally divided between his wife and his daughter. Only then could she find the path clear to the completion of her plans.

She returned to her bed to consider where she would go for the next three days to find the answers she wanted.

Anne had learned long ago to fight with whatever means were possible for what she wanted. Conscience or scruples did not interfere in her thoughts as she wove her plans.

Joseph's attorney was a man, and men were objects she could handle. She would find out about Joseph's will from Herbert Magill. All it would take would be a little time.

She drifted back into sleep, assuring herself that in the end, all her plans would work.

Jeffrey knew quite well the game Anne played, and it suited him for her to be on the front line of the battle . . . the battle that would ultimately end in his own success.

In a way he admired Anne very much. She was a clever woman with steady nerves and a quick mind. The plan she had so carefully worked out couldn't have been better. He also knew quite well what her plans were for Joseph. But, he thought to himself, her guilt in that matter did not include him. He had only to wait for Anne's success to enjoy his own . . . without guilt. All it would take now was a little time.

Joseph rode relaxed within his carriage. He'd never felt more satisfied with his plans than he did right now.

When the truth about Anne had been revealed, the blow was a hard one. But he was recovering quickly from it, considering now what had truly drawn him to her in the first place.

The sweet memories of Martha had carried him past the anger and hurt to a plane of cool detachment. He'd correct all his wrongs, and would do it in his own way and in his own time.

In the past few days he had compiled more information on the three forces in his life. Information that he'd use as ruthlessly as they'd intended to use him. Him and the treasure of his life, his beautiful Winter.

As he savored memories of Winter, he didn't pay much attention to the passage of time until the carriage came to a halt.

"Your train should be leaving within the hour, sir," his driver informed him. "I shall see to your luggage."

"Thank you, Max. Be careful of the small suitcase. Its contents are fragile."

"Yes, sir."

"Max, you won't forget . . ."

"No, Mr. Stepleton, I won't forget a thing. I'll

keep my eyes open. You can rest assured I'll follow your orders completely."

Joseph looked closely at Max's open and honest face. Max had been in his employ since both were young men.

"You never really liked or trusted her, have you?"

"It's not my place to voice an opinion one way or the other, sir," Max replied, but he avoided Joseph's direct gaze.

"We are more than employer and employee, are we not? I thought we were friends. I have not asked your opinion before. I'm asking for it now."

"No, sir. If you want the truth, I'll say it to you straight. She can't hold a candle to Martha. That one was a real lady."

"Thank you, Max," Joseph said quietly. "I quite agree. Is an old man entitled to a mistake, one he intends to correct?"

"You're far from old, sir, and there's many a lady who'd take . . . her place. Of course," Max grinned, "men our age make mistakes. But that's only wrong when you make the mistake permanent."

Joseph chuckled and clapped him on the shoulder. "I'll return on the ten-fifteen three days from now. That's Tuesday. Be here to meet me."

"Yes, sir. Tuesday, ten-fifteen."

"And keep your eyes open."

"I will, sir."

Max carried the luggage inside and waited until the train pulled away. Then he headed the carriage toward home.

Joseph found a comfortable seat and unfolded his

newspaper. He was completely unaware of the two
men who'd entered the car a few minutes after him
and found seats where they could keep him in view.

The trip was long, and it was nearly sundown when
Joseph heard his station called. When the train jerked
to a halt, he made his way out, followed in a few
minutes by the two men.

They watched as he claimed his luggage, then as he
was met and heartily welcomed by a couple who
conversed with him for a few minutes then walked
with him to their waiting carriage.

Carl waited impatiently, wondering if he'd paid for
nothing and Joseph's trip really *was* a business trip.

But he pushed the thought aside with another. It
was taking this so-called expert a long time to bring
Winter home. He should have followed her himself.
He would have been successful because he would
have given her no room for disobedience.

When they were married he meant to make a lot of
changes, and the most important of these would be
taming Winter's willfulness and her obstinate inde-
pendence.

She was a beauty, and he had desired her for a long
time before he found the way to get her. He knew
quite well how to bend a woman to his will.

The first telegraph he received from Mason told
him they had arrived in Georgetown, which made the
puzzle even more profound. If Joseph was in contact
with his daughter, why had he not headed west?

But two days later he got a final report that said

only for Carl to meet Mason that night. He'd be in on the last train and had a wealth of information.

When the train rolled into the station, Mason and his companion took their time disembarking. It gave Mason a great deal of pleasure to think that Carl James had to be sitting, uncomfortable, waiting for him.

To make it even more satisfactory, after he told his partner to go on home, he walked from the station to the tavern where he was to meet Carl, stopping to have one or two drinks along the way to make sure his courage lasted through the meeting.

He could see Carl sitting at a table in a shadowed corner. As he approached, he could see the glitter of anger in his eyes.

"Sorry to keep ya waiting'. Train was a bit late," Mason said as he slid into his seat.

"Well?"

"I needs me a drink first, I'm dry as a bone." Carl waved to a girl, from whom he ordered drinks to be brought to the table. When he turned to face Mason, it was Mason who spoke first.

"I run into a wee bit of a problem. I had a lot of expenses I hadn't counted on. I'm afraid the cost is going to be a bit more than what we agreed on."

Their eyes locked. Carl knew he was being pressured just as Mason knew he'd have to pay if he wanted his report.

"Just how much added cost is there going to be?" he said coldly.

"I'd say another sack like you gave me before will do nicely."

"A bit expensive, wouldn't you say?"

"Depends," Mason added with a malicious smile, "on what you think the information I got is worth."

Carl would have liked to reach across the table and grasp Mason's throat and choke the life from him. Instead, he reached into his pocket and tossed the coins on the table, watching with scorn as Mason avidly gathered them up.

"And now tell me the news. And it had better be worth it."

"Oh, it is, it is." Mason bent toward Carl and began to talk. The words tumbling from his lips, he watched with glee as Carl's anger rose. He watched his mouth compress to a hard, thin line, his face become gray, and his eyes glitter with fury. It made Mason feel a deep sense of satisfaction. This was one time Carl James had bought more than he'd bargained on.

Chapter 11

When Joseph stepped down from the train he was welcomed by Carson and Sandra Mackentire. They had been his friends for over twenty-five years and were people he could trust completely.

Carson extended his hand to Joseph who grasped it with firm enthusiasm.

"Joseph, it's good to see you again. It's been much too long. You're looking well, my friend."

"Thanks to you and your family, I'm feeling better than I have for a long time."

Sandra smiled, then and extended her hands to Joseph who took them in his and drew her close to kiss her cheek. "Sandra. What a pleasure to see you. You needn't have come to the station." He had known Sandra even before Carson, and had been the best man at their wedding.

"I wouldn't have missed being the first to greet you, Joseph."

"You two have no idea how grateful I am for your kindness."

"Oh, please don't speak to us of gratitude. You, who have done so much for us," Sandra said. "It was our pleasure to be able to return the debt in some small way." She tucked her arm in his as they walked from the station. "We've had a marvelous time, and all the arrangements have been made. It only needed you to complete the celebration."

"Tell me, has our young man gotten over the shock?"

Sandra laughed. "When I sent Carson to get him, I can honestly say he was both stunned and elated. He had a time of it for a while, trying to digest what we'd done, and he was a bit confused as to why you didn't elicit his help."

"Because he was obviously going to be the first one under suspicion. I was forced to let him suffer a bit. But I'm sure his reward will make up for all the discomforts. Where is he, by the way?"

"I could give you three guesses, but I imagine you'll only need one."

Joseph paused and turned to look closely at Sandra. "How is she?"

"She's fine. Very worried about you and this situation, but her trust in you is so complete that there are no questions."

"This has worked exceedingly well, but I'll still be grateful when it is all over. I have a rather large debt to settle and I don't want any of my 'adversaries' to find a way to slip away."

"Well, after tomorrow you can put all your plans into action. Tomorrow will be the most wonderful day," Sandra said.

The three entered a carriage and sat back comfortbly chatting while they were taken to their destination.

As the carriage drew up before the Mackentire ome, Joseph admired the impressive structure Caron Mackentire had so lovingly built. But Joseph's dmiration was replaced by another emotion when he door was thrown open and a young woman stood n the doorway. Her face was wreathed in a smile as he paused momentarily, then raced down the steps and flung herself into his waiting arms.

He crushed her to him, enjoying the sound of her oft laughter. When he finally released her, he held her at arm's length and smiled down into her blue eyes.

"And so, my dear, it seems my little plan worked."

"Oh, Father," Winter smiled up at him. "I never really dared to dream until today. Now I know that tomorrow I'll be Gregg's wife and all of this will be over."

"Speaking of Gregg, where is that young rascal? He must be very put out with me."

"He just arrived, and he's trying hard to balance being upset with you and being so happy about everything. In fact, there he is now."

Gregg had just stepped out onto the front porch and was striding purposefully toward them. He grasped Joseph's outstretched hand with a firm grip and a wide smile.

"Mr. Stapleton, I don't know how I'll ever begin to show you how grateful I am."

"You needn't show me a thing, Gregg. Just mak‹
Winter happy. That's thanks enough for me."

"I shall spend the rest of my life trying to do that,‹
Gregg replied as he slipped an arm about Winter‹
waist and drew her close to him. "But . . . why didn‹
you tell me what your plans were?"

"Because you were the first person on whom th‹
eyes of suspicion would fall," he began his explan‹
tion. "She is an astute and clever woman and woul‹
have seen through you at once. I needed you to a‹
pear lost, bereft . . . despairing."

Winter looked up at Gregg with the warmth ‹
love in her eyes. "And were you, Gregg?" she aske‹
softly.

"I never felt so desperate in my life. I had lost th‹
one thing I really valued. She read my emotions we‹
I'm sure," he added grimly, "that it satisfied her t‹
see me suffering."

"I'm sure it did." Joseph's voice matched Gregg‹
in grimness. "But she had a great deal to account fo‹
and the accounting begins as soon as I have you tw‹
safely married."

"Then you have to explain to Gregg and me ju‹
how this little plan of yours was worked out," Wint‹
said. "I only know I had to vanish suddenly. No‹
you have to clear up the questions."

"For now," Sandra interrupted, "let's get you‹
father settled, and fetch him some food and drin‹
I'm sure that long train trip was not all that comfor‹
able."

"Well, I won't say it was comfortable," Josep‹
laughed, "but I had so much to look forward to tha‹

hardly noticed the discomfort. I *could* use a bit of ood and a glass of wine."

Joseph was pleased that the interior of the house as decorated so beautifully. It seemed his daugher's wedding would be all she had hoped it would be. Thanks to his niece Shelby and her courage.

"Wait until you see the garden, Father. Sandra has reated a masterpiece. We thought it would be nice to ave a wedding ceremony out there since the weather s so beautiful."

"Sounds enchanting." Joseph was warmed by his laughter's obvious happiness.

"Come, sit down and relax for a while. I've sent for ood," Carson said.

"And Gregg and I need to hear the story. Can't ou talk while you eat?"

"I'll satisfy your impatient questions. Carson and Sandra are probably as curious as you."

"You're right. I think this little affair took some nanipulating," Carson chuckled.

"It did. When Winter explained that she was being orced into a distasteful marriage to save me, I knew that something had to be done." He smiled fondly at Winter. "So I made arrangements with you, Carson, in that long letter I sent. Then I set about contriving a false trail for Anne and her compatriots to follow."

"A false trail? But how?" Winter questioned.

"By enlisting Shelby's help."

"Shelby! I haven't seen my cousin since Mama's funeral." Winter's eyes widened as the scene unfolded in her mind. "I'd forgotten," she said, half to herself, "that she and I look so much alike we were often mistaken for twin sisters. Dear Shelby, she wa always so smart and so much fun. The things we di when we were children!" Winter laughed. "We use to drive people crazy until they knew there were tw of us. And when we got older—"

"When you got older, you used to drive the *boy* crazy," Joseph laughed.

"Oh, really," Gregg chuckled wickedly at Winte "you'll have to fill me in on some of these stories."

"Not on your life," Winter replied with glitterin eyes. "What you learn, Mr. Phillips, you'll have t learn on your own."

"That's all right," Gregg said gently, "I hope have a lifetime to find out everything."

Their obvious love for each other justified Joseph' maneuvers to himself and made him feel good abou the whole situation. But his thoughts now were on hi niece Shelby. It seemed Winter's were, too.

"Father . . . you're sure Shelby's all right? She' safe, isn't she?"

"I sent with her two of the best bodyguards possi ble. Dobbs is an intelligent man and Jasper . . . Jaspe is someone who any aggressor would have secon thoughts about crossing." He went on to explai about Brad Cole, and Anne's insistence that he hir the best available person to bring her back.

"But she would know if you sent this man on a wild-goose chase."

"No. When I had to give Mr. Cole a picture, I gav him one of Shelby, and I did it privately. As far a Anne knows, he's still in the process of draggin Winter Stapleton home to an unwanted marriage."

"I hope Shelby doesn't have to tangle with this Cole. He sounds a little tough," Gregg said.

"With the protection she has, even Brad Cole won't be able to get too close. Shelby will know when it's time to come home. I think she sees the whole thing as an adventure," Joseph replied.

"She would," Winter said. "Even if he caught up with her, I have a feeling Shelby will give him a run for his money."

"What a family I'm marrying into!" Gregg laughed. "Life with all of you is never going to be dull."

"It won't," Joseph said wryly, "it's certainly won't." He rose. "Now suppose you show me that garden where I'm to give my daughter away."

Winter and Gregg took Joseph out to the garden, over which he proclaimed profound delight. The balance of the evening was spent enjoying one another's company.

The next morning was a day made to order for a garden wedding. The sky was blue, with white billowing clouds to decorate it as perfectly as the profusion of flowers decorated the garden itself.

The soft breeze that picked up the scent of the flowers billowed Winter's gossamer veil around her and created a picture Gregg would never forget. She walked toward him, her arm in Joseph's.

The ceremony itself seemed too long to Gregg and much too short to Joseph, who realized the finality of it. Winter was no longer his. She belonged to the tall

young man at her side. It was enough to scare him
until he thought of the day he had married Martha
If his daughter was half as happy as he had been, al
would be well.

He considered Shelby. Soon she would be home
They had arranged the time very carefully. He con
sidered, with amusement, how puzzled Brad Col
would be when the trail to the one he thought wa
Winter Stapleton led back to her home.

He would have to apologize sincerely to Brad and
try to explain as best he could. He had a feeling Brad
was not going to be amused by the whole thing, bu
he intended to make it well worth his while.

When the ceremony was ended, the festivitie
began. They had planned an afternoon garden part
because the newlyweds were to leave on the evenin
train for their honeymoon. Then it would be safe fo
the two of them to return home.

Joseph had brought gifts for the couple, but the
assured him, the most important gift he'd given them
was his help in getting them together. When he kissed
Winter good-bye and shook Gregg's hand, all three
had tears in their eyes.

Joseph and Sandra watched the train pull away
from the station. She had insisted on accompanying
them so that she could ride back to the house with
Joseph.

"You should be very pleased," she smiled. "I
seems all your plans are working out well."

"Yes."

"That doesn't sound convincing."

"I just have this nagging worry about Shelby. I

told Jasper and Dobbs to wire me as often as they could to assure me everything is all right. It's been much too long since I've gotten any word."

"They sent the messages home? What if . . ."

"No, Sandra, absolutely not. They know not to send them there. This is one of the reasons I must return home tomorrow. Winter is safe, now we must be assured of Shelby's safety."

"Of course. I, too, have not seen Shelby for quite some time. When this is all finished and you have rid yourself of . . . I'm sorry, Joseph, I have never tried to interfere."

"You, too, cared little for Anne. How everyone must have grown angry and frustrated with me."

"No, Joseph, never angry at you. You and Martha had a relationship that was . . . perhaps unique. You suffered so when she died. We all knew how very difficult it was. In such an emotional upheaval, anything can happen."

"Things that would not have happened under ordinary circumstance," Joseph added. "But now I hope to rectify the mistake that could have cost me all I really had of value . . . Winter."

"But you have won."

"I could easily have lost."

"Then . . . I have a feeling you intend for the cost of your betrayal to be high."

"High?" Joseph chuckled mirthlessly. "Yes. Higher than any of them anticipated."

"*Them.* I thought . . ."

"No, it's *them.* Carl James, my dear wife, and her lover, Jeffrey Brenner. My investigations have been more thorough than they could have imagined." He turned to look at Sandra, amusement sparkling in his blue eyes. "Sandra, my dear, please don't believe I've been devastated by this. Disappointed, maybe. But when this is over, I intend to seek out all the happiness I can find."

For a minute Sandra looked at him, her sympathetic look slowly turning to one of understanding. Joseph laughed softly, and, after a moment, Sandra's laughter joined his. They walked back to the carriage arm in arm.

Gregg stood by the large window looking out. His thoughts were on Winter, Winter who was now his wife. A possibility he'd once thought to be so remote.

He and Winter had enjoyed a late dinner together and then they had come to this beautiful suite of rooms paid for long in advance by Joseph Stapleton.

He owed every ounce of gratitude he possessed to Joseph, and he meant to repay him somehow. At this point he didn't know how but he would find a way. In the meantime he savored the fact that Winter was here, with him, and would always be with him. He could feel the happiness like a tangible thing, a brilliance that melted through him like warm honey.

"Gregg?" Her voice was soft, and he turned slowly to face her.

She was a vision in a powder-blue mist of a gown that seemed to be vague enough to vanish at a touch. Her pale-blond hair caressed her shoulders and fell

ZEBRA HOME SUBSCRIPTION SERVICE, INC.

120 BRIGHTON ROAD

P.O. BOX 5214

CLIFTON, NEW JERSEY 07015-5214

about her. The small smile and an outstretched hand was all the promise he needed.

He crossed the room and took her hand in his, feeling its smooth texture and realizing that his every sense was so tingling.

"You're so beautiful, Winter." He said it with such a touch of awe that she had to laugh softly.

"You've looked at me a million times."

"Maybe. But I don't think I ever even imagined ... You ... you," he repeated as he slowly drew her into his arms, "are far beyond what my feeble mind could imagine."

"I hope," she whispered, "you don't intend to let this end with just imagination."

He chuckled. "I'm not *that* feeble-minded. There are some things better left to the imagination and some so exquisite that they have to be experienced."

His words grew softer as he bent his head to kiss her, tasting her lips as if they were a delicacy. Again and again he kissed the corners of her mouth, her cheeks, and slowly, slowly he began to stir the flames of passion. She clung to him, her eyes closed and her warm, moist lips parted to accept his. She felt her senses spiral upward as the warmth of his love inflamed her. When his lips left hers, she stood for a moment with her eyes closed, then she felt his hands slide from her shoulders and gently tug on the belt of her gown. Her eyes opened and met his. He stood motionless waiting to see if there was any fear or doubt in her eyes. But nothing was there but warm, loving acceptance.

The nightgown she wore was thin and the neckline

low and loose. He gently drew it down from her shoulders and let it fall in a heap at her feet.

He gazed at her in profound admiration. Her slim body, kissed by the pale glow of the candle, was ivory and peach, her hair glimmered in the half-light like fine-spun gold.

"God," he said in breathless wonder, "you are everything beautiful that I've ever dreamed of."

It took him only a moment to rid himself of the barrier of cloth that stood between them. Now it was her time to admire.

He was broad-shouldered and hard-muscled. The mat of hair on his chest was as dark a brown as his hair. Slim of hip and long, lean muscles ridged his taut stomach and long legs. He was well endowed by nature, and for a moment it shocked her . . . but only for a moment.

He drew her soft, cool body close to him and tingled with the shock of her soft curves leaning against him. Her slim arms wound around him, and for a long moment they simply held each other. Then he tipped her head up and took vibrant possession of her mouth. This time there was no restraint; her complete surrender to him told of her passion.

His hands slid down the smooth curve of her slim back to her hips to press her more firmly against him, while his lips traced a heated path down her slender throat to the soft curve of her shoulder.

He needed her with an unbearable agony that cursed through him as her fingers caressed him and drew him even closer to her. He could bear no more. Swiftly, he lifted her into his arms and crossed the room to the bed that stood in the corner. He dropped against it, drawing her with him. She gasped at the suddenness of it, but the sound was silenced as he turned her to lie beneath him and sought her mouth again.

She moaned softly, yet clung to him as he caressed her hardened nipples with seeking fingers.

She called his name softly at the first invasion of her womanhood, but the pain soon turned to an intense spreading warmth that lifted her beyond all she had ever known.

They soared together to the high pinnacle of ecstasy. She could hear his harsh breath and the heavy thudding of his heart that matched the wild pounding of hers.

Deep, all-consuming fulfillment left them clinging weakly to each other as the world righted itself and reality regained control. He held her in silence, their sweat-slicked bodies quivering.

He shifted his weight from her and drew her against him. They lay in silence as he slowly caressed her hair that fell across his body. There was no need for words, for each sensed the other's feelings to perfection.

This was the fulfillment of their mutual promise, their commitment made so long ago. Each was grateful that fate had removed the barriers and given them their chance to love.

When Carl had gotten the news of the deception he'd smashed a glass of whiskey against the fireplace.

Anne and Jeffrey jumped in surprise at the sudden violence.

"Why in hell didn't you tell me that Winter Stapleton had a cousin who looked just like her!"

"Because I didn't know!" Anne replied, her anger growing to match his. "Why didn't you know about her? This . . . this Shelby Vale?"

"It seems, from what my men have found, that Joseph's sister ran away with Nolan Vale years ago, and for a while brother and sister were alienated. Joseph who finally contacted her, and the cousins became fast friends. Just before you and Joseph were married, Nolan died and his wife took Shelby to Europe. If you had been as smart as you thought, you'd have examined Joseph's entire family. You, it seems, are not as clever as Joseph. He outmaneuvered us, and it is distinctly *not* my pleasure to tell you that Winter is now the wife of Gregg Phillips."

Anne uttered a sound of fury and Jeffrey managed to hide both his surprise and his curiosity about what kind of trick she might pull to get her out of this one. He knew Anne had discovered that Joseph had changed his will the day after Winter disappeared. Jeffrey watched Anne closely. She was clever and he had confidence she'd pull this chestnut from the fire with her usual expertise.

"How . . . how do you know? How could she be married. We have a man following her? He would have stopped her if—"

"If he'd been on the trail of Winter, but it seems the girls were switched somehow. This man Joseph so conscientiously hired, was hired to follow Shelby

Vale instead. And Winter . . . Winter was in George-town. Do you realize she was within my grasp?" Carl's face was a mask of anger as he held his clenched fist before him. "Right in my grasp. All I would have had to do was reach out and take what I wanted. Because of your lack of attention, we've been following the wrong girl!"

"Oh, God," Anne groaned. Her face had gone pale. She stood up and began to pace the floor. Jeffrey remained silent, watching Carl.

Then Anne paused and looked at Carl, her eyes narrowed with thought. "Shelby . . . her parents are still living?"

"Don't you listen? I said, the father is deceased. But it seems her mother has been in fragile health."

Anne smiled. "And that means that this woman and her lookalike daughter are all that are left of Joseph's family."

"I don't grasp your point, Anne," Carl said.

"A beloved and fragile sister should really be living with her brother. I am Joseph's wife and I believe it is only charitable to invite her myself and become friends. The Stapleton name and wealth are great. I'm sure, if you check closely, you'll find that the wealth is shared . . . and the position you crave would be just as attainable."

Carl grinned. "I've already considered the best way to achieve my goal. One is just as good as the other, since they look alike."

Anne laughed. "In a dark bedroom, dear Carl, I think you could make do. Besides," she sighed dramatically, "things change. Who knows. When it's all

over, Miss Vale and I," she looked at him with
enough innocence to make him laugh, "might be the
only heirs left to the Stapleton fortune . . . and all it
benefits. There is only one flaw, and that flaw is
Shelby is not in your hands, and we have no idea
where she actually is. We simply must wait until our
huntsman brings our reluctant girl home. I'm sure
Joseph has her return planned. Just as he has Winter's and . . . her husband's."

"Well, I'm afraid your problem is not the flaw you
think it is."

"You know where she is?"

"I do . . . and I've already taken the measures
necessary to take care of the problem. I usually take
matters into my own hands. In the long run I've
found I get better results." Pressing his hand to his
heart, he said, "I simply want to reunite a family, and
what better way is there to bring happiness to Joseph
Stapleton's home than to have his daughter and his
niece return home happy and contented."

"Carl," Anne smiled, "you are so impetuous."

"Aren't I?" Carl laughed.

"I'm sure you'll make quite the happy couple."

"I must go. There are plans to be made. This marriage must be firm and consummated at once. That
way there'll be no future difficulties . . ."

"Thank you, my dear, thank you."

Carl picked up his hat and cane, bowed briefly to
Anne and a still silent Jeffrey, then left the room.

When the door closed behind him, Jeffrey stood
up, bowed in an exaggerated fashion toward her, and
applauded. "Quite a show, quite a show. Seeing you

in action, my dear Anne, can still send chills up my spine."

She threw back her head and laughed. "It doesn't pay to panic, Jeffrey. One just has to think. When one plan doesn't work, it's always wise to have an alternative."

"You never cease to amaze me. I thought for sure you were in over your head this time."

"You said nothing."

"It's not my show."

"You just want to share all the winnings, but you let everyone else do the work. Has anyone ever told you you're a parasite, Jeffrey?"

"A few times," he laughed, "but I am a charming parasite, am I not? You wouldn't want to be without me, would you, my love?"

There was no doubt in her mind about his ability to wreck everything she had so laboriously planned.

"No, Jeffrey, I wouldn't want to give up such a luxury as you."

He came to her and drew her into his arms with just enough roughness to make her gasp. Then he kissed her with a fervor that promised there would be no escape from him. She responded in a way she knew he liked, though it was, in truth, mechanical and well practiced. Her thoughts began to spin around the idea that Jeffrey was now one luxury she could no longer afford.

Carl was surprised to receive a telegraph. His attempt to catch Brad Cole and Shelby en route was

now unnecessary. He read and reread the telegra[
and found the words mysterious.

So Brad Cole was *not* on his way back. Instead, h
had made a stop, and from the report, it seemed th
ranch he stopped at was his own. To make matter
worse, Shelby was with him. Now, why would the
have stopped there if Cole had not been listening an
believing her story.

He had to consider what he intended to do abou
the situation. It was late. Tomorrow was plenty o
time to make decisions.

Chapter 12

Muttered curses from Brad brought Shelby instantly alert. She sat up, hoping some unforeseen thing had changed their plans. When she looked around Tom was nowhere in sight.

"Where's Tom?"

"His brother came for him early this morning," Brad informed her. "It seems his sister is sick and he's needed. He'll catch up in a few days."

"Then we'll be traveling alone."

"We've got another problem. While Tom and I were harnessing the horse to the wagon, the harness buckle broke and the horse bolted and snapped the trace. We can't move the wagon." He looked at her. "Don't be so happy about it, I'm not going to let it hold us up."

"What are you going to do? All our food and supplies are in there. We can't go too far without it."

"We don't have to go too far."

"I don't understand."

"I have a ranch pretty close to here. We're going to

leave the wagon and go there. I'll send someone for the wagon. It can be fixed in a couple of days. Then we'll be on our way."

"Why didn't you tell me about the ranch?"

"I didn't think it necessary. I didn't plan to stop there."

"I'd like to see it," Shelby said softly.

Brad's eyes held hers. "Just get ready to travel, don't think this is going to change things."

He didn't want to believe her, but for that brief moment she saw much more in the depths of his eyes than he intended. Wordlessly she rose and began to help.

He spoke little as they broke camp and made preparations to travel. Even while actually traveling, he kept just a few feet ahead of her. Just enough to keep conversation at a minimum.

They moved much faster than Brad had anticipated. As they drew closer to the home he loved, he felt a tingle of excitement.

But it was growing dark before Shelby questioned why they didn't stop.

"If we can keep up this pace we'll be there in another couple of hours. You game to try?"

"Yes, I'll do anything to sleep in a bed."

Brad laughed and nudged his horse on. Again they traveled in silence while Brad let his mind drift. He felt the same old sense of peace a coming home always gave him. It was nearing midnight when the two weary travelers crested a hill and looked down into the moonlit valley.

The small ranch house still glowed with light.

"I'm surprised. It looks like Abby or Jack are still up."

"Abby?"

"The housekeeper, Abigail Larson. She's a really great person. Her husband, Jack, is sort of the head honcho around here when I'm away. Come on, let's ride in. I can smell the coffee from here."

While they rode slowly down, Shelby had the time to look around. The house was low and long, and some distance behind it she could see the huge shadows of the barn, a bunkhouse, other scattered buildings, and a small cabin that sat a little farther away.

When they stopped before the house the door was flung open and a tall woman stood framed in it. Shelby thought her nearing fifty, though, she had the trim figure of a much younger woman and a mass of black hair, threaded only slightly with silver strands. Her face was tanned and smooth, and amber eyes mirrored a woman who had seen and bested most of the tricks fate offered. Her smile was open and warm, and Shelby knew this woman was an important part of Brad's life. When she finally spoke, her voice was full and resonant.

"Brad Cole! It's about time you came back. You been makin' Jack real anxious about whether or not you got what you went for."

"I smelled your coffee, Abby," Brad said, ignoring her words, "and I couldn't stop." He laughed as he stepped down from his horse and walked up on the porch to embrace Abby. But Abigail realized at once he didn't want to answer her question at the moment.

When he released her, she turned to look at Shelby,

who tensed, not comprehending why she hoped she passed muster with this woman.

"Abby, this is Shelby Vale," Brad said. Shelby could feel Abigail's eyes on her, assessing her, boring into her as if she could see through her. Shelby suddenly discovered she'd been holding her breath. There was no doubt in her mind that Abigail Larson was the force around whom all the others on the ranch moved.

"Step down, my dear, and come in. I'll fix you both something to eat. Knowing Brad can be an ornery mule, I'll bet you haven't had supper yet. You must be exhausted, too. I'll see to some hot water and a soft bed."

Shelby didn't know what she was most grateful for, the promise of creature comforts, or the tone of pleased acceptance in Abby's voice. She dismounted stiffly and walked up to stand beside her.

"I'd be grateful for the hot water. I feel as if I'm coated with an inch of dirt and dust."

"Then come in, come in." The room they walked into was large, and dominated by a huge rough stone fireplace. The walls were a cream color with large dark beams that supported the ceiling. The floors were wood, but had been polished until they glowed. The furniture was heavy, sturdy, and looked as if it had all been hand made. The room spoke welcome, comfort . . . home.

In the mellow glow of the lamplit room, Abigail turned to look at Shelby. The warmth of the room and the scent of food had struck Shelby simultaneously and she seemed to feel her weariness like a weight.

"I'm Abigail Larson," she smiled as she introduced herself formally. "What a beautiful creature you are. You'll have to tell me how this came about." Before Brad could answer, and ignoring his dark look, Abigail turned to Shelby. "Come with me. I'll show you where you can bathe and change. I have a gown and robe you can use for tonight. While you do that, I'll fix you that food."

"You're very kind."

"Nonsense. Just general hospitality. Besides," Abigail smiled, "I'm looking forward to a nice chat. We don't get many young ladies traveling out here. I'd like to catch up on all the gossip." Brad looked at Abigail, but she simply smiled pleasantly at him and continued to lead Shelby away.

Abigail guided an unprotesting Shelby to a small bedroom, and to Shelby's delight, a short time later Brad and Abigail carried in a wooden tub of very hot water. She was so grateful for it and the inviting-looking bed, she could have wept.

"You join us in the kitchen as soon as you're ready. The food will be waiting."

Shelby nodded gratefully, and Abigail left the room. She walked down the hall and joined Brad in the kitchen where he was pouring himself a cup of hot coffee.

"You scalawag, that child is exhausted. From the telegram you sent, you sounded like you was takin' in some dangerous criminal. She looks like a sweet, helpless girl."

"Please." Brad almost choked on the coffee. "I've brought in more dangerous people, but I can't remember when. Sweet, helpless girl. Boy, do you have a lot to learn."

"You're exaggerating," Abigail's eyes twinkled. "Or have you met your match?" For a minute Brad's smile wavered and Abigail gave a soft laugh. "By George, I think you've run yourself up a stump."

"Well, Abby, old girl," Brad said quietly, "you might just be right. I'm up a stump and I don't know how to get down."

Abigail sat slowly down in a chair, a surprised look on her face. "I can't say I'm sorry to see the day. I've been waitin' for some sweet thing to curb your wild ways. Want to tell me about her?"

"Abby, I'm tired and I'll probably say more than is wise. We'll talk some other time. I need to eat and get some sleep."

"Sounds cowardly to me."

At this Brad laughed outright. But he drank his coffee and didn't respond. Maybe, he thought, Abigail might just be right.

Shelby joined them in the kitchen, feeling almost drugged as Abigail placed a plate before her. She ate while Brad and Abigail spoke of things around the ranch, but she really was not listening to what they said.

When Abigail insisted Shelby go back to her room and get some sleep, she offered no arguments. Brad, cleverly evading any more of Abigail's questions, found his bed as well.

* * *

Brad had slept until dawn, then rose and left the house to find Jack.

He really didn't think any of the men would be in the bunkhouse this time of the morning, since their day started at the crack of dawn. But he had to make sure.

The bunkhouse was empty, so he saddled his horse and rode out. He had expected to find the boys scattered, and to have to look for them one at a time. But he ran across Jack first.

Brad stood well over six feet, and Jack matched him inch for inch. But Jack was as thin as he was tall. He boasted a shock of thick silver hair and the bluest of eyes. His face was lined from all the seasons he'd lived and was as brown as the earth he loved. His hands were gnarled and as tough as rawhide. Of all the men on the ranch, he'd always been the one to listen the closest to Brad's dreams and to share them.

Before Brad began explaining anything, he took a sheaf of bills from his pocket that made Jack gape in surprise.

"Today I want you to get to Sutherland's. Make the deal for the cattle and that extra piece of grazing land we need. I'm going to collect more money in a few weeks. When I do, we'll get the lake and have those water rights from the Greystokes before they move. With that, we shouldn't have any problems in the future. I also need you to send a couple of boys out to Overmann's Pass and pick up the wagon and supplies I had to leave behind. Tell them they'll have to repair it there and drive it back. Shouldn't take more than a couple of days to fix it and a couple to get there and back."

"Lordy, lordy. Whatever do you have to do to get this?"

"Don't worry about where or how I got it. I didn't rob a bank. It's all legal. Nobody's going to pay any price for this but me, and it's worth it. There won't be any more problems in the future because in a little more time I'll have a nest egg to keep us solvent."

"Brad boy, you know me and the boys would stay on here in any case. This is home for us."

"You've worked without pay. I don't plan on letting that happen again. Once I get the second half of this money, we'll be set. All I have to do is . . ." He paused, unsure of how to explain the situation to Jack.

"All you have to do is *what*, Brad?"

Brad wanted Jack on his side and he had hoped he would understand the situation completely. But he was wrong.

As he began to explain, Jack grew quieter and quieter, and as his scowl grew darker, his eyes grew brighter with angry rebellion.

"So you see, that's how it has to be. In a couple of days we'll be gone. She'll be safe at home where she belongs. It's better this way."

"Seems to me there ought to be a better way of getting hold of enough money to tide us over. I don't relish gettin' it out of . . . selling someone."

"I'm not selling her," Brad protested.

"You got another name for it? Gettin' in the middle of a problem never did work. This whole thing don't sound like you a'tall, no sir, not a'tall. 'Pears to me you're doin' more lying to yourself than to her."

"Come on, Jack."

"You really going to live peaceable with yourself . . . gettin' this money this way."

"You bet your life I am," Brad said, angry that Jack had touched a nerve. "Besides, a couple of her friends are somewhere behind me, I had to lead them offtrack. They won't know to look here."

Jack never said a word, but his eyes spoke this thoughts clearly. He didn't approve.

"Jack . . . play this out my way."

"It ain't my business. I'll take care of all the details you want me to." He stomped away, and Brad could only try to ignore the ugly feeling of guilt as he watched him go. What made it more difficult was to ignore the other feelings that refused to be smothered. He sighed. He looked forward to the day all of this was over and he could get back to working . . . and to forgetting. He mounted his horse and rode out to find the rest of the men. A couple of hours later he was again headed home.

As he approached the house he was thinking how it would be to have *her* there for all time. The thought pleased him, even though he knew it could be nothing but a wild dream.

Hearing the sound of a horse approaching, Shelby walked out onto the porch. She shaded her eyes to watch him dismount and walk toward the house.

Brad Cole was probably the handsomest man she had ever seen. His skin was a golden hue that was vital and spoke of the hours he'd spent outdoors. His gray eyes sparkled with the same vitality, and she could feel his appraising look with a penetrating warmth that shook her to her very core.

She could feel the strength of his hard-muscled arms again as she gazed at them, and a flood of other memories were released with the thought. The heat of his mouth against hers and the feel of his body close . . . She inhaled a deep breath as reality burst into her mind.

She loved him! With conviction, she realized she meant to use everything she had to get and to keep him.

He walked toward her with that forceful stride that made her want to run and meet him halfway and feel his arms close around her. She held herself back only because she knew he would interpret it as another method to deceive him.

But Brad was caught in his own dilemma. What a picture she made, standing on the steps with her pale hair blowing silky strands across her face, her blue eyes full of sunshine, and a smile on her rosy lips. He dismounted and walked toward her, but before he could speak, he heard his name being called out. He smiled as he turned to meet the girl who raced toward him.

"Brad!" Mary Beth ran to him and tossed herself unceremoniously into his arms. He hugged her fiercely, blending their laughter. "I'm so glad you're back. I've missed you. Why didn't you let me know you were here?" The daughter of Jack and Abigail was tall and slender. Her hair, twisted into a long braid, was thick and black as ebony, while her eyes were Jack's sky-blue ones. She, too, was tanned, but the sun had made her smooth skin glow like molten gold.

"You were asleep when I got here, and I've been very busy. But I'm glad to see you, too." He was talking to Mary Beth but his eyes were drifting to his blond-haired charge, who stood very still and whose face wore a look he could not read. He introduced the two of them.

"How do you do?" Mary Beth's voice was polite and controlled but her eyes held a myriad of questions.

"Hello" was the best that Shelby could manage in the face of her and Brad's obvious affection for her.

She was jealous and she knew it. She couldn't believe the fierceness of this emotion that had suddenly filled her when Brad had embraced Mary Beth with such enthusiasm. It was such a shock that for a moment she couldn't find words.

"I've broken Rainbow. Want to go for a ride . . . let you see how good I really am?" Mary Beth teased with a laugh.

"Later. I have some things to take care of first. Never thought you'd ever break that pony, though."

"Hey," she laughed as she hugged him again, "I was taught by the very best. I'll be in the coral whenever you're ready."

"Fine," he said, watching her walk away.

This did not help Shelby's equilibrium one bit.

Mary Beth seemed to be on very intimate terms with Brad.

"Good morning, Shelby," he said, looking up at her. "I didn't think I'd see you up and around already."

"Good morning. You must have gotten up before dawn."

"It's a habit," he replied.

Abigail walked out onto the porch. "I'll get your breakfast started while you clean up. Shelby, want to give me a hand?" Shelby agreed and walked up onto the porch.

"Sounds fine." Brad said. He entered the house with the two women and took the huge kettle of hot water from the stove and carried it to his room. He poured the steaming water into the bowl, adding enough cool water to adjust the temperature. Then he stripped off his clothes and washed. He walked back to the kitchen to find his plate of food on the stove, and Shelby seated at the table, waiting for him . . . alone. He had no idea where Abby had gone, but he was pretty certain she'd left them alone to talk.

He took his plate and seated himself across the table from her.

"You look like you slept well." His voice was held in iron control as was his urge to reach out and touch her.

"I did." Shelby took a sip of her coffee, glancing at him over the rim of her cup. She found it impossible to meet his eyes.

"Bad dreams?" he questioned.

"Actually, the kind you don't remember in detail.

I know they were good, though, because I woke up feeling and rested."

"It's this place. It's so peaceful, you can't help dreaming good things."

"I'd like to think those kind of dreams could come true."

"Dreams and reality are two different things, and dreams can't be trusted to come true."

"I'd like to think they can," she insisted. "They were pretty excited to see you come home." She changed the subject abruptly. "Especially Mary Beth."

"Mary Beth? She's a friend . . . no, she's pretty much like the sister I never had. We were kids together, and I was like her big brother."

"She loves you."

"I hope so," he laughed, "I love her, too, and Abigail, and the rest of the gang that runs this place. They're the only family I've known for a long, long time."

"Tell me about your family."

"It's not important."

"It is to me."

"Why?"

"Because I want to know you better."

"That's not important, either. We won't be together that much longer. I've decided to take a chance on the train. It's faster."

"Why do we have to go so fast?"

Because I have to get you home to your fiancé and your family before I do something stupid that could hurt us both, Brad thought.

"I promised . . . and I've been paid. I want the other half of my money." The words were said half angrily and meant to strike out at her. He had to keep her at a distance. He didn't trust himself.

But Shelby didn't rise to the bait this time. She looked at Brad and saw the shields. She could not tell him how she felt because she doubted very much if he would believe it. She had to find a way to make him see it for himself.

She sensed that Abigail and Mary Beth had the key to Brad, and she meant to find her answers before she left this ranch.

Shelby knew that in a few more weeks it wouldn't matter if Brad took her home at all. Winter would be safe, and all the problems would be over. But, for some strange reason, she wanted a different ending. She wanted Brad to say that he cared, that nothing was more important than her happiness . . . She wanted him to care enough to want to sacrifice the rest of the money, even though she knew Joseph meant to pay him no matter what the conclusion of the situation was. Neither she nor Joseph would let him go unrewarded, because he'd had no idea of the original plan. But it would make a difference if he knew that before he made a decision. How could she hold on for those two weeks? And how could she prove her true situation after that?

"I wish . . ."

"Wishes don't get anything done," he said with finality. She was silent. "What do you wish?" he added, puzzled at his own harshness.

"I wish you believed me, that you trusted me. I wish you'd listen to me."

"What difference would that make?"

"A lot of difference . . . to me."

Brad used the only defense he had against her wide-eyed look of sincerity.

"Is this another little game?" he laughed. "You've tried every other one you know."

He saw the flush of color on her face and the quick look of anger, followed by an even stronger look of hurt.

Shelby rose from her seat and turned from him. She never saw him hesitate and involuntarily reach a hand toward her, as if to stop her. She left the kitchen as fast as her trembling legs would carry her.

Brad sat at the table another few minutes, fighting the urge to go after her, gather her in his arms and kiss her until she forgot everything but him.

Angry with himself, he finally left the house, closing the door none too gently behind him.

Shelby stood in the middle of her room, trying to figure out a way past his stubbornness. Obviously he was just not going to believe a word she had to say and he was going to think her every move was some maneuver to outwit him.

After a while, confused and angry, she left her room. The house was quiet, and she had no idea where everyone had gone. She began to drift around.

The house was simple and plain, six rooms in all, yet it exuded a feeling of warmth and comfort.

She walked down the hall that led from the large living room and passed the door to the room she had occupied.

At the end of the hall she pushed open the door, stepped inside, and sensed at once that this room was Brad's. It looked and felt like him.

The walls were mellow from what must have been a million scrubbings. The windows were large and open to the morning breeze. The floor was the same smooth wood, and small colorful braided rugs were scattered about. She had never seen a bed quite as large, and the thick quilt on it gave it a look of inviting comfort.

When her eyes fell on the dresser she gave a start of surprise. She was *so* surprised that she had to walk closer to make sure she was really seeing what she was seeing.

It was a picture of her, braced into the edge of the mirror and its wood frame. It was the one her uncle had given him to help him recognize her. The one he had shown her the first time they met.

But why had he kept it so carefully? Why had he taken the time to put it here and why keep it? Once she was gone from his life he meant to forget her, he had told her so.

She looked at the picture while her mind spun with ideas. Ideas that made her smile. Brad Cole was not so impenetrable as he'd made everyone believe.

He had kept her picture because he felt the same way she felt. He'd kept it because he was certain he could not keep *her*.

She paused, considering the fact that she had only days to find her answers.

She replaced the picture carefully and left the room.

Chapter 13

Jasper gazed at Sheriff McClure in a kind of awestruck anger.

"You mean you actually arrested her and put her
in jail!"

"Look, Brad Cole was one of the best Rangers
ever walked. If he said to hold her, then I'd hold her.
He said she was mixed up with a gang called the
Stapletons. You have an idea what he was talking
about?"

"A gang!" Jasper snorted furiously. "There is no
gang. The girl is a victim."

"Oh, come now. Brad doesn't have that kind of
reputation. A victim of what, for God's sake? I think
you'd better settle back and tell me what's going
on."

Jasper agreed. It was the only way to get information from the sheriff. He explained the planned story
and Sam listened without interrupting. He was surprised that deep down inside he believed what Jasper
said.

"So you and this Mr. Dobbs were to be her guardians. Didn't do a hell of a good job, did you?"

"Trickery. He doesn't play by any set of rules," Jasper objected angrily. He felt guilty enough about the situation without the sheriff making it worse.

"He's tracked and brought in too many hardcases to play by rules. If he'd done that, he'd have been dead a long time ago."

"Well, he was taking her back East. Why didn't he go by train?"

"Beats me. I guess," Sam laughed, "he thought the lady too dangerous to take the chance."

"Very funny." Jasper was obviously not amused. "Was he traveling with anyone else?"

"Yeah, Tom Littlebeaver. He's been a friend of Brad's for a long time."

"How far behind them am I?"

"Three, four days maybe."

"Damn." Jasper paced the floor. "That's a pretty big head start."

"I wouldn't be surprised if they're not movin' as fast as you think. She was in no mood to be taken any place, and the two weren't hitting it off real well. She's bound to slow him down a bit."

"I've got to catch up with him," Jasper stated coldly, and the gleam in his eye was a promise of mayhem when he did.

"Mister, I hope what you've been telling me is true, but I mean to warn you. Brad Cole ain't a man to be played with."

"Yes," Jasper said dryly, "I know." He extended his hand to Sam. "I thank you for your help."

* * *

Jasper was confused. Dobbs kept saying he didn't think things were as bad as they imagined, but Jasper's anger kept getting in the way. He resented Brad's ability to outsmart them, and even more, that he had dragged Shelby away against her will like so much baggage. When, he came in contact with Cole again he was going to elicit a price from him that he'd never forget.

But when he explained the situation to Dobbs, Dobbs didn't seemed too alarmed.

"There's only a few more weeks before the time is up, Jasper. All we need to do is slow them down. We have to have more confidence in Shelby. She's done all right so far."

"You don't seem so worried about not doing the job we were hired to do. Maybe you can handle that, but I can't. I'm going to catch up with him if I have to walk, and when I do . . ."

"Jasper, don't you think we'd best leave the decisions about what happens to Brad to Shelby? She might have a different opinion by now."

"I don't understand you. He just slipped her out from under our noses. And the first time he did it, he tied her up and hauled her around like a sack of potatoes. Remember, she told us? And then . . . having her arrested like a common criminal! God knows how he's treating her now since she's outfoxed him so often. It sets my teeth on edge to think about it."

"Well, Jasper, old friend," Dobbs laughed, "since this is making you madder by the minute, I guess we'd better be on our way if we want to catch up. We've got a long journey and he has a pretty big head start."

They had their horses saddled and were on their way within the hour. They traveled slowly. It was two days later before they found Brad and Shelby's first camp. Jasper, the better tracker and sign reader of the two, read this camp and its absent occupants well . . . and their visitors.

"Three of them camped here all right, but they had a couple of friends come visiting. Indians, from what I can tell. There's a village not too far from here. Maybe we ought to go there and ask some questions."

"It will set us back a bit."

"Or make the trip a certainty. We could be guessing, you know."

"Let's go find out."

If Jasper was gritting his teeth before they reached the village, it was much worse after they arrived. Whitehawk was remarkably cooperative . . . and sympathetic. Dobbs could have laughed at the look on Jasper's face, but he didn't have that much foolish courage. Jasper heard the story of the lovely woman who was crazy and the very noble man who was taking such good care of her.

When they left, Jasper was muttering somberly to himself. Something about tearing Brad Cole limb from limb.

"Crazy! He had the nerve to tell those superstitious bastards she was crazy!"

"Kind of clever."

"Clever! I'm going to rip out his tongue and make him eat it."

"Take it easy, Jasper, we have a lot of distance to cover yet. I have a feeling there might be more surprises in store," Dobbs answered.

They traced the trail herd, which took another day, and not only was it confirmed that they had met Brad and Shelby, but more of Brad's background was filled in, along with the name and location of the ranch.

Shelby had begun to enjoy herself. She was quick to admire not only all Brad had built on the ranch but the rapport that existed between him and the people he obviously loved. They seemed to accept her completely and she warmed to them all.

Abigail had been aware of Brad's tension and hesitation, and the fact that he obviously had something more to say and didn't quite relish saying it.

"Is there something wrong, something I can do for you?"

"Yes. As a matter of fact there is. I wish you would be careful about what you say to Shelby. I don't think my financial position should be mentioned."

"Of course not. I wouldn't say anything so personal to anyone . . . unless . . ."

"There is no 'unless.' She doesn't need to hear any stories about me or this place. Trust me, her interests are elsewhere. She's easy to like, but that can be deceptive. I want you all to remember that she'll just be passing through here."

"Of course."

"You know I'm right."

"I seldom argue with you."

"You're an impossible woman and a romantic. Don't you know the world isn't the way you'd like it to be? Wealthy ladies don't have much to do with poor ranchers. She's out of her element here."

"Brad, my dear boy, sometimes I wish you just weren't so logical."

Brad laughed. "I can't argue with you, I'm always licked. And, Abby, keep your matchmaking mouth shut. As soon as we get reorganized, she's going home to Daddy before I have any more problems."

He turned and walked from the room, but Abigail only smiled. Brad was not a man to force or to preach to. She'd known and loved him like a son from the time he was nineteen and disaster had taken his parents. She and Jack had lost their home at the same time. They had all decided to rebuild together. Brad had helped them build their small house on his land so that Jack could be his foreman. They, in turn, had helped him build this house. He and Jack had worked together to start the ranch, and she and Jack had raised their daughter almost as a sister to Brad.

Abigail knew exactly how far she could push Brad. She also knew he was a man of strong emotions and even stronger commitments. She'd watched him with the girl he'd brought home and knew at once there was more between them than he'd admit to now. She wondered, as she had many times before, if Brad shied away from happiness in fear that it would be taken away from him—perhaps in violence as before.

While Abigail was in the midst of her daily cleaning and after making it clear that guests were not expected to work, Shelby walked out onto the porch.

She stood on the wide front porch for a while, enjoying the breeze that carried pleasant scents she couldn't recognize. The scene before her was so beautiful that she could understand why Brad loved this place. Lush green grass, trees that swayed gently, and a sky so blue it could be felt deep in the soul. A place to live, to grow, and to be happy.

She made a quick decision, and walked toward the small cabin that sat some distance away from the main house. She hoped Mary Beth would be there. She felt Mary Beth would understand how she felt and perhaps have some insight into Brad's feelings. She seemed to know him so well.

"I know you must be surprised to see me here," she said to Mary Beth, "but . . . I'd like to talk to you if I may."

"Of course. Come on in. What do you want to talk to me about?"

"About Brad . . . Brad and why I'm really here."

"Why you're really here? I thought Brad said he was asked to escort you back to your family in the East."

"Well, that's not exactly the truth," Shelby replied. "From what I saw before, I think you really love Brad in a very special way. If you'll listen, I'd like to tell you everything." You've heard Brad's side . . . will you listen to mine?"

Mary Beth looked at her closely. "Go on, tell me."

Shelby told Mary Beth the whole story about her taking Winter's place and Carl James. Mary Beth listened without interruption, her face so impassive Shelby couldn't tell what was going on in her mind.

When Shelby finished, there was a lengthy pause while neither spoke. Then Mary Beth's question was put quietly.

"Why are you telling me this? You don't really think any of us are going to go against Brad's wishes and help you leave alone?"

"I'm telling you because . . . because I love Brad, and not the way you love him. I love him as a woman loves a man she'd like to spend the rest of her life with."

"Have you told him this?"

"He'd never believe me."

"Then I don't know what you expect of me. I've told you, no one on this ranch will go against what Brad wants."

"You don't believe me, either."

"Not quite. Am I supposed to believe you just because you say so? I believe Brad, too, and he told us all not only to keep an eye on you but that you're pretty good at . . . arranging things to work out the way you want." Mary Beth smiled. "He told us all about the trip this far. I have to admit you're pretty smart. Brad's just faster."

Shelby had to laugh, and a second later they were laughing together. "You're right. But the tables have turned. I don't want to get away, I want to stay. But in a day or two he'll be ready to travel and he'll drag me home . . . too soon."

"Shelby, you're confusing me, and I need a little time to digest all this."

"And to talk to Brad?"

"Yes."

"Mary Beth . . . don't tell him I love him. He'll think I'm using you to play some kind of trick on him."

"Are you?"

"No. I need to tell him myself. I have to find a way he'll accept and believe. I need time."

"Just what he doesn't want to give."

"Yes."

"You don't make things easy. No wonder Brad is confused."

"Is he?" Shelby asked hopefully.

"I can tell the signs. He walks away to get things straight in his mind."

"Mary Beth, if he takes me back too soon he'll not only ruin my happiness, he'll ruin Winter's as well."

"Then try and take your time. If you make him want you to stay . . . then I'll help every way I can. But I won't trick Brad."

"That's enough. I'll find a way . . . I have to."

"Good luck, Shelby. I hope this is no game, because if it is . . ."

Shelby smiled at Mary Beth, and left the cabin, closing the door quietly behind her. She was overjoyed to be assured by Mary Beth herself that she and Brad loved each other . . . but like brother and sister.

Shelby considered the plan that was slowly forming in her mind. She knew Brad was working hard to get the wagon back into shape and to move on again. She had to put her plan into action before he did that, and she had to prove to him that it was him she wanted.

Shelby was on her way back to the house where she saw Brad approaching. As he dismounted and came to her side, she realized that despite the fact she had known him for some time, she still couldn't read his thoughts.

"What are you doing roaming around?"

"The sunshine feels so good. I decided to take a little walk. I guess we'll be riding a lot."

"You're right. In a few more of days we'll be ready to travel."

"Is it really that necessary to be in such a hurry? You can't seem to wait to be rid of me."

"I think it would be best all around," Brad admitted.

"You make me sound like some sort of outlaw. Dangerous and troublesome."

"I didn't say it. You did," Brad laughed.

Shelby frowned and bit back the anger she felt. She would have enjoyed striking him soundly, just to take the arrogant smile from his eyes.

"It's so beautiful here. I'd like to see the ranch, to walk, and maybe just to talk. I thought you might share that much at least. We don't have to be enemies for these few days. Is that so much to ask?"

Suspicion danced in his eyes, but he could read nothing in her face but sincerity.

"You asking for a truce?" he grinned, "I believe we did that once before. Just before you clouted me on the head and skipped."

"But I mean it this time. I'm outnumbered and I don't really have the ability to run far."

Her words created a sense of unrest, an impending *something*. But somewhere in the recesses of his mind . . . or his heart, he wanted to believe her.

"Well . . . a couple of days won't hurt. But you try anything," he grinned, "and those handcuffs are still handy."

Shelby's smile was quick, warm, and hit Brad right between the eyes. He returned it, and walked the rest of the way to stand beside her.

"Where's Abby?"

"I don't know. She was cleaning, so I walked over to the cabin and spoke with Mary Beth."

"Oh?" Brad looked at her closely. "About what?"

"Oh, just girl talk. You know how women are when they get together."

"Knowing you . . . and knowing Mary Beth, I'm not too sure. She's never too shy or too busy to get into someone else's business."

"Brad . . ."

"Yeah?"

"Show me the ranch? If we rode out tomorrow I could make us some food and we could spend the day."

"You'll never see all this place in a day."

"Then you choose what we see."

"All right. You go on in, I'm going to see what's become of Abby."

As Shelby turned from Brad and started toward the house, Brad watched her. He found it hard to believe he might be falling for another of her tricks. Shaking his head, he walked to Abby's cabin and rapped on the door. As he walked in, Mary Beth was quick to smile.

"Brad, I was just going to ride out and see where you were."

"Where's your mother?"

"She's planted that small garden down by the riverbank and is collecting some things for supper."

"What have you been up to?"

"Actually, having a nice conversation with your friend."

"Oh?" Brad said suspiciously.

"She had a lot of questions about you. Sounds to me like she's interested."

"Don't get carried away."

"No?"

"No," Brad smiled, "and it's not interest in me, it's interest in . . ." He paused. It didn't pay to reveal too much to Mary Beth. But he did see the glitter in her eyes and now it was his turn to laugh. "Actually, it's none of your business."

"Okay, I'll mind my business."

"Knowing you as well as I do, I doubt it," he said dryly. "But try to control yourself for a few days."

Mary Beth nodded and watched Brad walk to the door.

* * *

Shelby had been surprised to see how many people gathered about the supper table. Mary Beth and Abigail she already knew. Brad had introduced her to the foreman Jack, and the hands who just smiled shyly and remained silent through most of the meal.

But just before the meal ended, another situation Brad had not expected arose. Mary Beth asked Shelby about herself and Shelby was pleased at the opportunity to reveal some details, and eventually talk about her singing. That stirred everyone's enthusiasm, and they *prematurely* sympathized that there was no guitar around or Shelby could entertain them.

"I've heard her sing and she really does have a beautiful voice," Brad felt safe expressing his enthusiasm. But he was pleased a minute too soon.

"Ah . . . Miss Shelby," Clyde Baker, the youngest of Brad's hands, flushed a brick red, but spoke anyway. He was not quite used to a beautiful woman looking at him with such a warm and interested smile. He was so engrossed in her, he never noticed Brad's frown. "I got a guitar. It used to be my mother's."

"That's wonderful, Clyde. Would you mind if I played it? I'd be very careful, knowing it's such a valuable family treasure."

"Oh, no, ma'am. I'd be right honored if you would. You see, I can't sing a lick and it ain't been played for a real long time. I bet it's really out of tune." This was probably the longest speech Clyde had ever made in his life to a woman as close to his

ge as Shelby was. "I'll go right on out to the bunk-
ouse and get it." He rose quickly and left.

Brad could happily have wrung his neck, and he
vas aware that Jack, Mary Beth, and Abby knew it
nd were amused.

Clyde returned with a well-beaten guitar in his
and, and Shelby took it from him with a warm smile
hat again turned him brick red. While she tuned the
uitar, the rest gathered around and found comfort-
ble places.

The firelight danced in her hair making it halo her
ike gossamer. Brad was sitting opposite her and
vhen the guitar was tuned to her satisfaction, she
ooked up at him from her low stool. For a moment
heir eyes held. He felt something deep inside him stir
o life. It angered him that he seemed to be losing
ontrol.

"You've heard many of my songs, Brad," Shelby
aid softly. "Is there any particular one that you'd
ike to hear again?"

"No," he replied, "they were all beautiful." He
vas surprised that his voice was a bit hoarse, and
ie'd have done anything rather than tell her that
:very song he had heard her sing still lingered in his
nind like unwanted phantoms.

Shelby strummed the guitar lightly and then chose
he most destructive song she could have chosen. The
'ery first one he had ever heard her sing. As she sang,
he memory of that night and Shelby in the center of
he light on the stage curled through him. He felt
igain the same feeling, as if he were not quite able to
;et his next breath.

"When love is proven by adversity
And stands the test of time
When passion gives way to deeper truth
Then, true love survives."

When she finished there was a long moment o
silence. Then finally Abby spoke.

"Shelby, that was beautiful. You have a lovel
voice."

"Would you mind singing another?" Jack ques
tioned.

"No," Shelby laughed. "Of course not." Bot]
Abby and Mary Beth were quite aware that Brad said
nothing at all.

She sang two more songs, and there was no one in
the room who wouldn't have enjoyed hearing he
sing on and on.

"Well, that was beautiful. But," Abigail said, "al
of us have to get up early." Good nights were said
and when the door finally closed behind them, the
house was pregnant with a thick vibrant silence.

Chapter 14

Again Brad and Shelby were going to be left together for the rest of the evening. This was a situation that Brad did not relish. To keep himself on an even keel, he was quick to search for excuses.

"You ought to get some sleep. The trip ahead of us won't be easy and we'll be traveling in about five or six days."

"I'm really not tired. Could we take a walk? It's a really beautiful evening."

"Fine." Brad was certain walking would be much better than being confined in this small house, which suddenly seemed to be growing smaller by the minute. "Here, take a coat. After dark it gets cool." He reached out to a hook behind the door and took down two jackets. "It'll be a little big, but at least it will be warm."

When they stepped out on the porch, the huge full moon was already climbing into the night sky.

They walked down the area between the main house and the bunkhouse, until they stood just outside the barn. Finally there was nothing more than a path, and the night enfolded them. They walked in silence, just enjoying the beauty about them.

Shelby inhaled the cool night air. "This is a beautiful place. You are a lucky man."

"It doesn't take just luck to build a place. It takes hard work."

"Yes, I suppose. But loving work, too. Tell me. How did it happen that you and Mary Beth grew up together?"

Brad couldn't completely kill his suspicions. He had been tricked by her sweet, relaxed manner before. Her interest most have an ulterior motive.

He explained the events leading up to their present living situation as briefly as possible. "A man couldn't ask for a better family," he ended with a smile.

"What about . . ."

"That's enough questions about me. Tell me about you."

"I thought you knew everything there was to know about me?"

"I discovered a long time ago that I don't know you at all. You're really two people. I'd like to know one of you."

Shelby stopped walking and turned to face him. When she stopped, so did he.

"Which one of us would you like to know?" she asked with a soft laugh.

He looked at her for a while in silence. The moonlight had turned her hair to spun silver and washed across her skin with a golden glow. Even though she was wrapped in his jacket, he was well aware of every inch of her. He'd caressed that soft skin in his mind a hundred times. He couldn't convince the memory to go away.

"Shelby Vale," he said softly. "Even if she is a figment of someone's imagination, I think she's . . ."

"What?"

"The more real of the two. Does that make any sense?"

"Yes it does. Shelby Vale is real, whether you want to believe in her or not. She'd never promise anyone she would marry him, and she doesn't lie."

"Does that mean I do?"

"Well . . . maybe just a few small white ones," she smiled.

"Like what?"

"Like . . . part of your protection of me is not all connected with whatever money you're being paid to bring me back. That you're not the tough man you want everyone to see, and that you're not as heartless as you want me to believe. Your ranch is the most important thing in your life. I can understand that. I can even understand what lengths you'll go to to keep it."

"You've got all the answers, don't you," he laughed. "Or you think you do."

"Maybe. What makes you think I can't understand loving your home?"

"I'd rather not talk about me or my motives. You said you were going to tell me about Shelby."

"Shelby? She's no one special really. She likes home, family, laughter." She put a hand on his arm and drew closer to him. "I suppose what every woman likes. Warmth . . . affection . . . love . . ."

Brad smiled, and to Shelby's surprise he gripped the lapels of her jacket and almost lifted her from her feet as he drew her face within inches of his.

"Let's clear something up. Don't try playing any games with me. Invite the wrong things, for the wrong reasons, Shelby, and you might find you're biting off more than you can chew. When I play, I play for keeps, not to break hearts. This is a kind of truce. Keep your side of it and I'll keep mine. You behave, and we won't have any problems."

Brad was wise to her plan from almost the first second she had become so soft, sweet, and gentle. What had shaken him was . . . at this moment he wanted to make love to her more than he wanted his next breath.

But he was sure she was planning to do the same to him as she had Cecil, and lock him in a barless jail for which there was no key. It was time to prove a point to the not so innocent, innocent Shelby Vale.

"I hadn't intended to break your so-called truce," Shelby denied, half angry and half hurt. She was surprised at just how much his amused and mistrusting words affected her. "Do you see some kind of devious motive in everything I say and do? Don't you believe I can have one honest feeling?"

"Yes, you honestly want to put as much distance between you, me, and everyone back East that you can. You've tried every trick in the book and been pretty good at it, I guess. But I'm not going to go for any of your games anymore. Why don't you just make it easy on yourself and everyone else concerned and let me take you back without any more problems?"

"You are the most insufferable, stubborn, mule-headed man I've ever come across. Are you always this one-track-minded?"

"Only when I meet up with someone as one-track-minded as I am. This was self-defense, you know. You have so many tricks up your sleeve, a man has to be careful. Trust you an inch and I'll find myself holding thin air."

"I'm not running!"

"You bet your life you're not."

"Brad . . ." She calmed her voice, but her hands were still balled into fists and jammed in her jacket pocket to keep from striking him. She tried to smile but it was aborted by his laugh.

"Shelby, why don't you just give it up? Tomorrow, if you like, we can go for that ride. We can make your stay here as comfortable as you want. Everything depends on you, because if you try one more of your little tricks, so help me God, no matter's who's around I'm going to cuff you, hog-tie you, toss you over my saddle, and drag you home. I hope I've made myself real clear."

"Yes," she grated through clenched teeth, "very clear. You haven't got one shred of decent feelings. If I didn't hate you so much at this moment, I'd feel sorry for you. You're a blind fool!"

Shelby spun away from him and walked rapidly toward the house. She refused to let him see the tears in her eyes. But once in her room she flung herself across the bed and wept the angry, frustrated tears.

After a while she sat up and dried her eyes. She was not going to give in. There was still time, and still hope that Brad would soon wake up to the fact that he was not as hard as he would like her and the rest of the world to believe.

Brad watched Shelby walk away from him, her back rigid with her anger. He'd hurt her and he knew it, but he had little choice. He was too close, and was afraid of the fire she had the ability to build in him.

How badly he wanted to kiss her, to taste the sweet warmth of her soft mouth. He had no doubt he'd be totally lost if he did. Still, his unleashed imagination played his emotions. He could literally feel her in his arms.

There was no way he could go back in the house, not until he knew she slept and there was a closed door between them. If he walked in now and was met by those melting violet eyes, he wouldn't be responsible for what might happen.

He muttered a curse and walked to the barn. He could find something to keep his mind . . . and his hands busy.

When Brad finally did enter the house, it was quiet and seemed empty. But that devious devil in his mind whispered that she was only a few steps away. Grimly determined, he walked slowly to his own room, closed the door behind him, took off his clothes and got into bed.

Sleep was not easy for either Brad or Shelby. Both

lay, wondering if the other slept. It seemed a century before they finally succumbed.

Shelby awakened to the sound of voices. By the time she had made herself presentable, most everyone had gathered for breakfast.

She walked into the kitchen amid a laughing conversation. Brad was the first to see her.

"Good morning." His smile was clear and open, and aggravated her to the point of wanting to pour his cup of coffee over his head.

"Good morning," she replied sweetly, her smile matching his in sincerity.

"Come join us for breakfast. Time's wasting."

"Time's wasting?"

"I already had Abby pack us a lunch. If you want to see as much of this place as you can, we'd better get started."

"I . . . I thought maybe you'd changed your mind."

"Any reason why I should?"

Shelby bit back a rigid retort. She had no intention of airing last night's, or any other, argument in front of everyone.

But she didn't have to. There was no one at the table who couldn't sense the electrical current between these two.

"If you'd like to wait a while," Mary Beth said wickedly, "I'll help Mom with the dishes and go along with you."

"Why, Mary Beth," Brad's voice carried just as much wicked amusement, "I'm sure there's a whole lot you have to do around here. But," he added before she could protest, "if you don't, I can find a few things."

"Don't let her get away with anything, Brad," Jack laughed. "You know what a little troublemaker she can be when she puts her mind to it."

"Dad!"

"Well, girl, it's the truth," Jack answered mildly. "Never did learn not to mind everyone else's business. You need a nice young fella to lasso you and tame you down a bit."

At this Brad laughed. "Well, well, Jack. That's the first time I've seen Mary Beth speechless."

"I'm not speechless," she smiled, "I'm just thinking of all the ways to plan revenge."

"Will you all stop it?" Abby said sternly. "You'll have Shelby thinking you all mean your tormenting. Shelby, I've packed a real nice lunch. You're in for a treat. This ranch is one of the prettiest in the state."

"I'm sure it is, Abby," she said, "and I'm looking forward to seeing it."

"Come on to the house," Mary Beth said. "I have a clean pair of breeches that'll fit you, and a shirt. You're welcome to them. Your riding clothes still need to be washed."

"Thanks, I appreciate it."

"Follow me." Mary Beth walked to the door and Shelby followed.

Brad finished his breakfast and waited while Shelby ate. He was very proud of what he had built and wanted her to see it through his eyes. He refused to question himself about why.

When Shelby walked back into the kitchen, Brad found it hard to believe the picture she made. She must have been one size larger than Mary Beth, for the jeans fit every curve and line of her as if she had been poured into them. The plaid shirt was snug enough to end any doubts about her femininity. Mary Beth had even given her a wide-brimmed hat.

"Well, I guess I'm as ready as I'll ever be." She smiled brightly and spun around. "Is this all right for riding?"

"Missy," Jack laughed, "that outfit is all right for anything you care to do. You look like a spring morning."

"Thank you." She spoke to Jack, but her eyes were on Brad, who seemed temporarily out of words. It took him a minute or two to tear his gaze from Shelby.

"Well, give me that basket of food, Abby. We'd better get a move on."

Abby handed him the basket and he opened the door to let Shelby precede him out. Only then did Mary Beth laugh softly and wink at her father.

Brad had ordered two horses saddled, and they rode away from the ranch side by side. Brad always took the time to absorb the beauty of it. Now he was even more aware of it as he pointed out special places to Shelby: a grassy, wild flower-strewn meadow . . . a tall stand of trees that rose against the background of shadowed blue green hills.

They rode along a stream of crystal-clear water

that rippled over a pebbled bottom. Small fish darted within it from place to place.

"Abby's young niece and nephew came out here last summer and I taught them how to catch minnows in that stream."

"Minnows?"

"You've never caught minnows! Lady, your education is sadly lacking. Let's stop while I give you a lesson on the hand being quicker than the eye."

"Are you bragging?"

"Are you doubting?"

"Yep."

"I'm crushed. Come on. Let's see what you can do." He dismounted and set the basket of food aside. Then he came to her, put his hands around her waist and lifted her down. He made sure the horses were carefully hobbled, then they walked to the grassy bank that rose a foot or so from the water.

"First you have to lie down on your stomach."

"You're joking." She looked up at him doubtfully.

"No, I'm not joking. Come on, try it." He took her hand and drew her down beside him. They lay on their stomachs on the grass with their heads over the water. "Now, look close, and pretty soon you'll see one and then another. They're little and they're fast."

"What do we do with them when we catch them?"

"Put them back."

"Then why . . ."

"Sometimes," he chuckled, "you don't do something for any other reason than to prove that you can."

"I don't see anything."

"You're talking too much and you're not concentrating."

Brad edged closer to her until they were shoulder to shoulder. "Look," he whispered. In the depths of the water she saw them and laughed softly.

"What do I do?"

"Cup your hands together. Like this." He demonstrated. "Then put them in the water gently and then, when you think you're ready . . . snatch one."

"They're so little."

"They're fast as lightning. I'll bet you can't catch one."

"What do you want to bet?"

"What have you got to offer?"

She turned to look at him, and the smile on her lips faded. They were only inches apart. So close that the gray of his eyes seemed to reach within her to strum senses already taut.

Both felt as if something brilliantly vital swirled around them. Brad grasped almost desperately for a thread of sanity. This was a well-played game and he had no intention of falling into a scented trap that would cost him more than he could afford.

"You're not going to catch a thing if you don't pay attention."

She turned her attention back to the stream, well aware that he had deliberately pushed her and any emotions away. She concentrated on what she was doing. But Brad continued to look at her. Every instinct told him to reach out and touch her, to feel the texture of her hair and the smoothness of her skin.

He watched, fascinated, as her brow furrowed with concentration. She nibbled at her bottom lip, and her whole body tensed with anticipation. She had dipped her hands just beneath the surface of the water, and suddenly she gave a soft shriek of delight as she pulled her hands up holding a few ounces of water and a wiggling silver-gray fish, about a quarter of an inch long.

Brad had to laugh at the excitement in her eyes and the satisfaction when she turned to look at him again. "You win. I didn't think you could do it first time around."

Gently, Shelby returned the small creature to the water, than sat up, rubbing her hands dry on her jeans. "So, I won. What do I collect?"

"You never said what the wager was."

"Why don't you let me consider it and we'll talk about it later?"

"Done," Brad said. He stood up and reached a hand down to draw her up beside him. "Let's get going. I have a perfect place picked out to have lunch and it's over an hour away."

They rode for some time before they came across the first of Brad's herds. The healthy-looking cattle grazed contentedly.

"These are all yours?"

"Every last dog-eared one of them. I've delivered a lot of them personally."

"How many do you have?"

"I won't have a new count until round-up, but I can make an educated guess. About . . . close to a thousand. That's where my problem is. I wanted to buy the smaller herd and water rights from a rancher next to me who's selling out. I have everything . . . except enough water."

"And," she said softly, "it takes money to buy water."

"Yes," he said, refusing to look at her. He suddenly felt as if he was selling a lamb to slaughter.

She said nothing more, and that didn't make him feel any better.

Shelby watched the beauty unfold around her. The spaciousness, the blendings of green from grass to trees and the blue sky. She could be more than happy here.

She was tired of riding by the time they reached the place Brad had chosen for lunch. But not tired enough not to enjoy it.

She had never seen a tree as large as the one Brad spread a blanket beneath. Its branches unfolded a huge green canopy over them and the shade was cool and very refreshing.

They ate fried chicken, boiled eggs, and a huge slab of chocolate cake. Then Brad lay back with a sigh and folded his hands behind his head.

Shelby watched him for a minute, comparing him to other men she had met. He was unique. A man contented with what he could build with his own hands.

"You can see so far," she said as she leaned comfortably against the trunk of the tree.

"Yeah. You see that ridge of hills on the horizon?"

"Yes."

"My place goes to those hills, and just as far on the

other side. I could run maybe fifteen, twenty thousand head with no problem."

"I know . . . if you had the money to buy them."

"I can build it that high in time, money or no. I need the water."

"Why have you never married, Brad?" she asked abruptly.

"Haven't had the time to consider it, nor the means to make it work."

"It isn't money that makes a marriage work."

"There speaks a lady who's never been without it. There aren't too many women want to make a future the hard way."

"And so you judge me again," Shelby said softly.

"No, I'm not judging you. I'm not getting close enough to do that."

"You still don't trust me an inch."

"Let's don't spoil a nice day." Brad sat up and began to gather the remains of the meal. "If you want to see the river and get back to the ranch in time for supper, we'd better get moving."

It was, as Brad had said, a long ride to the river. But it was worth it.

Shelby insisted they rest for a while, then promptly took off her boots and socks, rolled up her pantlegs, and sat on the bank dangling her feet in the water.

Brad hated to acknowledge the fact that she looked quite at home, and he wondered if he'd see her over and over again in all these special places once she was gone forever.

They lingered by the river for a long time, while Shelby asked a million questions about his life and ranch. She could hear the enthusiasm in his voice and enjoyed the interlude. Even though she knew the seed of distrust hadn't died, she realized he was trying to make this as pleasant for her as he could. Of course, if she moved a bit closer, reached to touch that well-protected area, she could sense him mentally reinforcing his barriers.

He was half kneeling a foot or so from her, and Shelby smiled to herself as she bent forward, dipped her hand in the cool water and flicked it at him. He laughed, so she did it again, this time cupping a bit more water.

"Hey!"

Again she splashed, then she began a serious attempt to wet him down. Amid their mingled laughter, he bent forward to grab her wrists. But this put him off balance, and when she reflexively jerked backward to keep from being caught, the force of it pulled him toward her and they tumbled backward on the grass together laughing.

Her wrists held in an iron grip and her body tucked half beneath his, Brad could feel her pressed intimately to him. Laughter danced in her eyes and her mouth looked too soft and inviting to resist any longer. He bent his head and caught her half-parted lips with his. For this moment all other thoughts but the sheer pleasure of the kiss was pushed aside. He didn't exactly remember when her lips parted to accept his, or when he released her arms and gathered her to him, or even when her arms came about him to hold him closer.

Only a soft sound from her brought him back to

reality. It was too easy to relax with her, to lower his defenses to her quick smile, her soft laugh and the sensuous beauty that had totally captivated him.

He released her and sat up, trying to get hold of his breathing and his equilibrium. Then he rose and reached down to help her up. Neither spoke. Brad wanted to say he was sorry, but the lie died on his lips. He wasn't sorry. He wanted her and was completely sure she knew it.

"I think we'd better get back. Abby will have to hold up supper."

"Brad . . . I . . ."

"Shelby. Let's just get going. It's a long ride."

Shelby followed him to their horses, and they rode back in silence. She had no way of knowing of the immense battle Brad was waging with himself.

He'd kissed her before. In anger, in jest, but this had been different. Before, he had not had her participation. He had laughed it off, knowing she would find any vulnerable spot. But this time . . . this time he could not wipe it from his mind.

When they arrived home, Mary Beth was just setting the table.

"You two just made it in time."

"If you wait until I get cleaned up, I'll help," Shelby offered.

"You just go ahead. Everything's under control here."

Shelby escaped to her room, and both Abby and Mary Beth gazed after her, sensing at once something was wrong. Brad had seen to the horses, then crossed to the front porch where a bucket of water and a large basin was waiting for anyone who wanted to clean up before entering the house.

There he stripped off his shirt and washed himself in the very welcome cold water. His hair still damp and shirt in hand, he entered the house.

"Brad . . . what's . . ."

"I'll be dressed and back in a couple of minutes." He neatly evaded Mary Beth's questions. Right now he couldn't find an answer for himself let alone for her.

"My, my," Abby chuckled, "seems Brad has a lot on his mind."

"Yes, doesn't it," Mary Beth agreed.

"You think he'd going to be fool enough to let that girl go? From what I see, I think she's in love with him."

"Brad's no fool," Mary Beth said. "Maybe he just feels he's made a bargain and has to carry it through."

"Well, right now I'm sure our interference wouldn't be welcomed by either of them."

Before Mary Beth could answer, the door opened and Jack and the hands trooped in, noisy and laughing. Brad was next to appear, and a few minutes later Shelby came to the table.

Supper was the usual boisterous affair, though Brad seemed more quiet and thoughtful than usual.

When supper was over, Brad quickly decided there were things he had to do, so he left with Jack and the men. Shelby helped with the cleaning of the kitchen. Mary Beth and Abby left an hour or so later, Shelby was again left alone.

She sat before the fireplace deep in thought. She wished fervently things were different, but she had to face the fact that Brad did not believe anything she said or did. Even the magic of the moment they had shared was, in his mind, another form of deception.

She rose slowly. There was no use in waiting for him. She was certain he didn't mean to take one step into the house until he knew she was in bed and safely out of his way. To him she was a nuisance, a job he had to complete to get what he really loved and wanted.

She undressed and put on her nightgown. Then she sat on the bed to brush her hair.

She heard him come into the house, heard him move around for a while then walk to his room. When his door closed, silence enclosed the house.

But Shelby couldn't face the bed and sleeplessness. Quietly she left her room and went back to sit before the red-embered fire. She had no idea what the sound was that drew her attention, but she raised her head slowly.

Brad had been so deep in his own thoughts during supper, he hardly heard what was said. He watched Shelby and again was struck with how well she fit here.

He wanted to say many things to her and was afraid if he spent any time alone with her, he'd reveal everything that was bottled up inside him. That was why, he left the house as soon after supper as he could.

He found work to keep himself busy, but he was aware of the moment everyone left . . . and when the lamp in the house was put out.

Inside, the house was still. The last of the evening fire was a mass of glowing embers. He moved around the familiar room and, for a minute, was angry that he couldn't put Shelby out of it or out of his mind.

Finally, he went to his bedroom. He started to remove his clothes, then paused as he heard a sound.

He opened his door, but there was no other sound. Then he listened at Shelby's door but heard nothing. She must be asleep. Carefully, he walked down the short hallway and was several steps into the room before he realized Shelby was kneeling before the fireplace.

He stood frozen. The fire glowed a soft red, lighting the room in a rose like glow. Her hair was kissed by it, falling about her in profusion.

As Shelby slowly stood up, the filmy nightgown she wore revealed the shadowed form beneath it.

Brad could feel his heart begin to pound with a fierce beat. She had always been breathtakingly beautiful to him, but this sight was beyond anything he had experienced before.

Shelby stood very still. He had to come to her. He had to. There was no other way he would believe.

Slowly Brad walked across the room. He stopped so close that she had to look up at him. Gently he put his hand against her cheek.

But Shelby could not surrender to this, not before he knew and believed how she felt . . . and felt the same. The force she felt within her now, urging her into his arms, would be a destructive one if he did not share it.

Quietly, hopefully, she rested one hand against his chest. "I love you, Brad Cole, and if you have believed in anything in your life, believe in that. If you can't," she inhaled a ragged breath, "then please . . . don't touch me . . . please just don't pretend."

Chapter 15

"I'd like to tell you that I don't believe you, that this is some game you're playing. But I keep imagining you walking out of my life, and I can't stand the thought of it." He caught her face between his hands, "Shelby Vale, you've turned my life inside out and upside down, and I want you more than I've wanted anything in my life. I think I've felt it from the moment I was handed your picture. Now . . . you're right," he added softly, "I don't think there's any room to pretend anymore."

Shelby closed her eyes as she felt the touch of his lips. His mouth searched hers until she felt as if every bone within her had melted and flowed around him, until every nerve tingled. Until her body awakened to the heat of desire with a vibrancy that made her tremble like a leaf before a hurricane.

When she responded to his kiss, when the hunger for more of her exploded within him, he was suddenly swept into dark waters whose force was beyond his. He lost his grip on well-laid plans, on the reality of his own caution. He was washed away on a tide so powerful that all the logic and wariness flowed away with it.

He lifted her in his arms and took the few steps to his room. Her arms wound around his neck as he pushed the door closed behind him and let her feet slide to the floor. He still held her pressed intimately to him.

"I've never really pretended with you, Brad. What I feel for you is so real and wonderful that I can hardly believe it."

"You're certain, Shelby?"

"I couldn't be more certain. And you?"

"You've had me uncertain and off balance since the day we met," he laughed softly. "And excited and filled with confusion."

"You're still confused?"

"Not about what I want," he said softly, "not about how you make me feel. Not about wanting you." His voice was a whisper now, and she could hear the depth of a desire that matched her own.

Brad saw the look in her eyes and knew it was only an echo of the fire that licked through him. He reached out with one hand and gently caressed her cheek, then slid his fingers into the thick mass of her hair and drew her to him.

As his embrace tightened, he bent his head to let his mouth fuse with hers again, and his tongue slipped between her parted lips to taste and savor the warmth of her mouth.

He was a man accustomed to controlling himself, and it amazed him that with her there was no control.

It was as if he had no power at all except the magnificent emotion that surged through him at her touch.

Shelby felt the warmth wash through her followed by a calm assurance, as if the world and its troubles were far away. She wanted the touch of his hands and the feel of his hard body. Her heart began to pound and her breathing became labored.

With hands infinitely gentle, they undressed each other, wanting to touch, to absorb, to learn. Touching his warm skin caused her to tingle with excitement. Contact with him set her on fire.

He kissed her forehead, her cheeks, and then her mouth as his hands began to move over her making her body quiver in sensual pleasure. They stroked her back and arms, then captured her breasts, savoring the texture of her skin beneath his fingertips. He inhaled the sweet scent of her hair and felt the pulse of desire grow to a throbbing demand.

She moved against him wanting, no, *needing* more of the fiery touch than his hands elicited.

He took her hands in his, kissing each finger, her wrists, the curve of her elbow, then drawing her arms around him again he molded her body to his.

She could feel the hardening of his manhood against her and the iron sinew of his body as he cupped her buttocks with one hand to press her even closer, and finally, draw her down with him to the soft bed. They lay together, twining around each other, hands searching, caressing mouths heated by a flame growing higher and higher.

He tangled his hands in her hair and his mouth attacked now with surging possessiveness. Her hands moved over his body with the same tantalizing heat. Finding his manhood, she stroked with slow, taunting moves until he groaned aloud.

He sought with gentle hands and found the wet hot center and began a movement meant to drive her beyond her control, guiding her to release before he began again the agony of lifting her to the summit.

With control far beyond what he had thought his capabilities to be, he slowly lifted her again and again until she sobbed raggedly, and he knew her body was caught in a force beyond reality.

Only then did he let himself find the sheer pleasure of thrusting into the depths of her. He raised himself on his elbows to watch the glory of the moonlight dancing across her tear-streaked, passion-filled face.

Her eyes were closed, her lower lip caught between her teeth to keep the cry of ecstasy from bubbling aloud. Her hair fanned about her as her head rolled from side to side.

At first he moved slowly, glorying in the feel of her moist depth closing around him. But he could not bear this wild pleasure much longer. The long, driving thrusts increased in force, and her body arched rhythmically to meet each demanding drive.

No part of Shelby was free of his touch. Her hands spread against the heavy muscle of his back, sliding lower, holding him closer, caressing him in a way that left him unable to stop until the climax of their lovemaking left them both gasping for breath and lying still and silent in each other's arms.

Bright moonlight made the room glow with mellow light, and Shelby could look up into Brad's eyes without shadows veiling what she saw. Brad bent to kiss her lips lightly.

"Remarkable," he whispered.

"Us?"

"No, you. You're remarkable."

Shelby laughed softly and raised one hand to brush his hair from his brow, then rest against his cheek. "You've called me many things before, but remarkable wasn't one of them."

"Funny, but right now I can't seem to remember. The only word that comes to mind is . . . remarkable." His laugh matched hers in warmth. "Of course, now that I think about it, I get a glimmer of other words."

"You do? Like what?"

"Like . . . beautiful, exceptional . . . Lord, right now I can think of a myriad of choices."

"It's about time."

"I guess I was rough on you," he admitted, "but to be honest, you played hell with my feelings, too. If I were going to be an outlaw I'd definitely want you in my gang. You ran me seven ways for Sunday."

"Me?" she questioned innocently.

"Oh, brother. Now I suppose I have to tell you how jealous I was when you flirted with Whitehawk and Dave."

"Actually, it would do me a lot of good to hear that."

"Well, I was. I don't suppose I would have been able to admit it to myself then. But it's true. Shelby?"

"Yes?"

"Did you mean it when you said you loved me?"

"I couldn't have meant anything more."

She curled closer to him, and Brad lay back against the pillows, drawing her with him. Her head against his chest and one arm circling her, Brad felt a peace and contentment he hadn't known for a long time.

They didn't speak for a while, finding pleasure in simply holding each other.

"Brad?"

"Hmm?"

"I wish we never had to make the rest of the trip back. I'd be just as happy staying here."

"Maybe we ought to see what can be done about that," Brad chuckled. "The only problem is, one day soon your two diligent bodyguards are bound to catch up with us."

"Well," Shelby teased, "I'll be right here to protect you. And, by the way," she asked with a nonchalant shrug of a shoulder. "What do you do about weddings way out here?"

"Are you proposing?"

"Looks like I'll have to. You're pretty slow about getting around to it."

"I just wanted to give you plenty of time to think about it. Life out here is not always an easy one."

"Life can get complicated wherever you are. I'm not a weak woman."

"I can attest to that. I didn't say you couldn't handle it," he turned so he could look down into her eyes. "Don't you see, Shelby, I just want to give you the chance to be sure."

"I am sure," she said softly, "but if you're not . . ."

She reached up to draw his head down to hers and kissed him deeply.

Brad was effectively silenced. The feel of her warm, soft body in his arms and the touch of her lips on his were enough to convince a stone.

"You know so much about me, Brad, and I know so little about you."

"What do you want to know?"

"Everything. From the day you were born until this minute, especially details of all the women you've known."

"Shelby!" Brad laughed.

"Well, you were jealous of me. How did you think I felt when Mary Beth threw herself into your arms?"

"I didn't think you cared for a minute."

"Shows what you know. I cared all right. Tell me everything."

"Fine," Brad grinned, "I was a good little boy, a good young man, and a good grown man, so I have you as a reward to prove it. That can sum up a lifetime."

"Brad Cole, I doubt very much if you were *ever* a good little boy. Now, if you don't come clean," Shelby replied threateningly, "I'll just have to ask Mary Beth."

"Okay, you win. God only knows what kind of stories she'd tell you. Let's see. I was born in Philadelphia. My parents bought a ranch when I was about twelve and I loved it. My father and I worked twelve-hour days, but it was a labor of love. Then . . ." he paused, unsure he could bring up the past without tearing open old wounds. But this was

Shelby, the woman he wanted to share the rest of his life with. "When I was nineteen, everything was wiped out in a couple of hours. The ranch was destroyed and both my parents were killed."

"Oh, Brad," Shelby said softly, "how terrible."

"I guess my parents didn't really realize the danger the Indians presented."

"What did you do?"

"Got stubborn and stupidly decided I'd try to rebuild and run it myself. For a while I really thought I was going to make it. Then some renegades just passing through caught me alone and unprepared. Didn't succeed in killing me, but they *did* burn out everything I had."

"Is that how you got the scars?" Her finger lightly traced the rough-knit scars along his ribs and upper chest.

"Yeah. They were pretty sure I was dead. But I guess I was just too obstinate to oblige them. I needed to fight back. It took me a long time to heal up, but all that time I concentrated on remembering their faces. When I was well enough to ride again . . ."

"You went out for revenge."

"No, I joined the Rangers. When I got them I wanted it to be all neat and legal."

"And you got them?"

"Every last deadly one of them. The only problem was, I got myself shot up pretty bad. It was my second near-brush with death and I began to get the idea that if I stayed in that profession, I just might not get a chance to see old age. Only I was at loose ends for a while afterward. In fact I ran pretty wild. It was Jack and Abby who grabbed hold of me and stopped me from sliding. Like I told you, we all started this ranch together and they've been my family ever since."

"It's going to be wonderful."

"Going to be," Brad replied. "But it's far from that yet. It's going to take a lot of hard work and sweat, and even more luck."

Shelby smiled to herself. "Perhaps we've found our luck in each other. There might be better things ahead. We have each other and that makes us stronger than you think. You never can second guess fate, and I'm a believer."

"And you plan on making me one, too."

"That I do, Mr. Cole, that I do. I happen to love you very, very much." She drew her head down and the kiss pushed all other thoughts away.

It was not dawn yet when, from habit, Brad awoke. But it was not a habit to find someone curled against him. He lay still, enjoying a sense of peace and rightness in Shelby's softness. They had made love last night to the point of exhaustion and she slept soundly.

The mornings were very cool, so Brad decided to restart the fire so the house would be warm when Shelby finally awoke.

He got out of bed slowly, put on his pants and tiptoed from the room. He knelt before the fireplace and built a new fire.

After the room was brightened by the glow of the flames, he relaxed in a nearby chair and gave himself over to the pleasing thoughts of what the subsequent days would bring. A home, a wife, and someday children. He would build his ranch into something they would be proud of.

Engrossed in his thoughts, he didn't hear footsteps on the porch and was shocked from his contemplation when Jack spoke.

"You're up early. I was just coming to build the fire."

Brad told Jack he had gotten up awhile ago. "I've got a few things to tell you," he announced.

Jack crossed the room and sat on a stool near the warmth of the fire.

"I've decided to ask Shelby to marry me and stay here. Of course we'd have to go back to Charleston, but just to settle things up. I'm in love with her, and that seems to be the most important thing on my mind right now."

"Well, it's about time," Jack said calmly.

"You're not surprised?"

"There ain't none of us here that don't know how you two feel about each other. It's sure been obvious. We all just been wondering how long it was going to take you to see the light and get to it."

"I'm sure Abby's going to be pleased, too. She's been wanting me married and settled for a long time."

"Shelby's a nice girl. Abby took to her right away. I think it's real important to Abby for you to be happy. She's been mothering you long enough to know you haven't had an easy time of it. Well, I guess I can take my time with that wagon now?"

"You can take a month of Sundays if you like."

Neither men was aware that Shelby had awakened and found Brad gone. She got up and walked to the door and started to open it. The sound of voices came to her. What she heard struck her so hard that for a minute her heart froze . . . before it broke.

"I'm going to do what I should have done long ago," Brad was saying. "I can't stand things the way they are now. Jack. You can drag that wagon back. I have this ranch to concentrate on. There are water rights and cattle, and a few other problems I have to tie up."

Water rights! Cattle! Shelby bit her lip to keep control, but tears flooded her eyes. He meant to take her back, he hadn't believed a word she had said. He had thought it still a game.

She thought of what she had felt had been a wonderful love-filled night. But memories came clear. He had said he *wanted* her, but he had never said he *loved* her . . . not once.

He was laughing at her surrender, thinking to keep her in control while he carried out his mission and collected the money he needed to protect himself.

Slowly and quietly she closed the door and returned to the bed to think.

Chapter 16

There was a great deal of work to be done the next day, and, Shelby saw little of Brad. She *did* see that the wagon had been repaired. She had never felt so miserable in her life. He still meant to take her back.

Well, if he meant to stick by the original plan, then she had to stick to hers. She knew there was a town nearby, she just didn't know in which direction it lay. But she would find it.

At supper she was quiet and withdrawn. Brad was puzzled. When she claimed fatigue and went to her bedroom. Brad intended to follow her and ask what was bothering her, but Jack summoned him to the barn, saying there was a problem with one of the horses.

By the time the problem was solved, it was very late. Reluctantly Brad decided he would force an explanation from Shelby the next day. He wasn't about to let her slip out of his life . . . not now when he'd just found her.

The night that had begun with soft breezes and a

starlit sky, began to subtly change. Beyond the high ridge of hills, deep slate-gray clouds began to gather. Even the animals sensed the change in the night air. The breeze shifted its direction and cooled.

Jack was the first to leave his house. He moved through the semidarkness toward the stable, sniffing the air like one of the animals. He knew the kind of storm that was coming.

Inside the stable he hung his lantern on the hook and began his daily work. It was over an hour later before he noticed one of the horses was missing.

He left the stable and started toward the house, which was already well lit by now.

Abigail was preparing breakfast when Jack entered.

"Breakfast isn't ready yet, Jack," Abigail said, surprised to see him. "You can't have all your chores done already."

"No, I don't. I just came to tell Brad that one of the horses is gone."

Brad grew pale. The cup of steaming coffee he was sipping almost spilled as he almost leapt from the kitchen table and raced to Shelby's room . . . to find it empty. He returned to the kitchen to face Jack and Abigail's stunned looks and then Jack's solemn voice.

"There's a hell of big blow coming," he said quietly, "a hell of a big one."

"Damn!" Brad muttered. "Jack, saddle me a horse."

"That girl can't find her way around out there, Brad," Abigail said.

"Just saddle my horse," Brad replied. "I've got to find her." He grabbed the jacket he'd hung again behind the door, hating himself for believing . . . and for not believing. A truce, she'd said. A truce long enough for him to drop his guard again. And he had dropped it . . . he had begun to believe her. How could he have been so foolish?

He was angry, but more than angry, he was scared. He was damn sure this huge territory could swallow her up. A million things could happen to her before he found her. He knew she was no novice at traveling, but he also knew she could misjudge the vastness of the territory they were in, and that would be a fatal mistake.

When he stepped out on the porch, Jack was leading his horse toward him and Abigail was following him out.

All three viewed the sky and the darkened horizon with misgivings. The storm that was about to hit would be bad. They had seen them before. But Shelby had no idea what she might be in for.

"Lord, Brad," Abigail said worriedly, "you've got to find her before this thing hits."

"I know, Abby, I know. I'll find her," he said grimly, not sure if the words were true.

"You want me and the boys to start searching, too?" Jack asked.

"No. When that storm hits there's going to be enough to do here. If I need help I'll come back for it."

Abigail's worry increased. "Brad, be careful. The wind is picking up already."

He mounted his horse. "I've got to get on her trail before the rain starts or I'll never find her." There was nothing more to be said.

Carefully he searched until he found the direction in which Shelby had gone. Then, as Jack and Abigail watched, he vanished over a grade and was gone from sight. At the same moment a brilliant gleam of lightning brightened the sky and a low rumble of thunder sounded in the distance.

Brad rode with desperation following. "Be safe, Shelby. . . . God, please be safe."

Shelby had tried to sleep . . . but couldn't. All she could think of was that she couldn't stay with Brad, knowing he thought she was lying to him.

She had to go someplace where she could think, and figure out just what to do. Confident that she could find her way to town, she hardened her determination. Once there, she could send for help. This time she would make sure he couldn't find her again.

In fear of lighting a lantern and exposing herself, it took her some time to find the right tack and get the horse properly saddled. She finally led him out of the stable, and walked him for a while so finally there would be little sound. After a while, she kicked the animal into a trot.

She'd been moving at a slow steady pace. Her mind had been so engrossed in escape that she hadn't noticed the weather change until the chilling air made her shiver.

She had no time to consider comfort. She had to be

free of this problem. Maybe there would come a day when she could face Brad with proof of the truth. Maybe he would believe in her then.

Shelby tried to use the stars to make sure she was keeping her path straight, but only an hour or two after she left the house they seemed to vanish along with the moon. She soon found herself totally lost.

Still she pressed on, hoping any landmark she could find would keep her moving in one direction. Surely there had to be a town somewhere!

She sensed the horse's weariness. It was cold and the wind had begun to build. She brought the animal to a stop and dismounted so she could lead him for a while to give him rest.

The horse himself seemed skittish. Several times Shelby had to stop, caress it, and speak soothingly. But the thunder began to grow closer, and she felt she'd have more control if she mounted again.

By early dawn she was more than aware of the building storm. With any luck, she'd find her way to some sort of civilization before it struck.

It was late morning and the promise of the storm looked more than fierce. Again, the horse was dancing uncomfortably . . .

The sound came in a sudden burst of thunder and bolt of lightning. The horse reared in fright, and with one cry of shock Shelby was dumped unceremoniously in the dirt.

Despite Shelby's ability to hide her trail, Brad concentrated and found the vague reminders of her passage. She was good, damn good, he noted with a touch of admiration, but not good enough. She had left a trail a man with his experience could follow. The coming storm worried him. She would never be able to protect herself from it. He had to find her.

He pressed on, going as rapidly as he could and still follow the signs. Occasionally he looked up, seeing the blackness above and trying to consider if he could find Shelby before it broke. For some reason he couldn't fathom, she thought staying with him was more dangerous than the coming storm. She was running right into it and that alone scared him to death.

Lightning flashed more often now, followed by the ever-growing rumbles of thunder. He prayed even harder that he would find Shelby safe.

It seemed as if he'd ridden for hours. He crested a hill and then drew his horse to a halt. There were two directions from here that she could have taken: down into the lower part of the ravine, or up to the narrow pathway that led along the ridge. He looked for a sign to see which way she had chosen, but there was nothing. He dismounted to examine the ground closer.

Finally, he found it, and it brought another frightened curse. She'd gone down. Down into the ravine that could become a flowing river if the rain came with the force he knew it could.

He mounted and rode down. Now he bent close to his horse's neck, searching for any minute sign.

When he heard the sound of an approaching horse he almost stopped breathing. She'd had enough sense to start back the way she'd come. Relief turned to doubt, then to stark fear as the horse approached him . . . riderless.

He felt as if a huge fist had gripped his heart and squeezed. Expertly, he captured the reins of the fleeing horse and brought it to a stop. He had no idea how far it had run since it had left Shelby. Leading it behind, he again moved in the direction from which it had come. When he'd first discovered Shelby gone he'd been angry. But the anger had fled before his fear for her and the truth that had struck him as fiercely as the lightning that brightened the sky. He loved her and he couldn't stand the thought of losing her.

Shelby was more angry than physically hurt as she got up from the ground and gazed after the retreating horse. She was aggravated at her own self. She should have had better control. She'd always been an excellent rider. With grim determination, she set off at a brisk walk. Surely there was a ranch or a town somewhere close. She was not going to be defeated by Brad Cole . . . and she was not going to be defeated by this country!

Lightning was coming more often now, and the thunder seemed to roll across the sky. The little daylight left was darkened by black and heavy clouds. Still, she pressed on. Her only alternative was to turn back, and that she would never do.

The walls of the ravine grew about her, black against the dark gray sky. If worse came to worse she would find an outcropping of rock and wait out the storm under it. After all, it was just a storm. She'd never been afraid of storms before, and she wasn't going to be afraid now.

Shelby might not have been wise enough about the rugged country to be afraid, but Brad was becoming more worried by the minute.

Since she was now on foot he'd expected to find her easily. But then the rain came, and it fell in a sheet of water so thick it was hard to see two feet before him. And the wind whipped it about like froth.

Nature shrieked about him. The rising wind, torrent of water, and thunder and lightning now seemed as if it would go on forever.

Shelby was drenched to the skin within minutes. She sought some kind of shelter, quickly discovering that any storm at home could not hold a candle to this.

Finally, she saw a huge triangle-shaped rock protruding from the canyon wall about twelve feet above the ground. She raced to it, and even though it gave inadequate protection, it was still better than being out in the midst of the fierce elements.

She wrapped her arms about herself, but the air, which seemed to be growing colder by the minute, penetrated the jacket she wore as if it were paper. She moved back against the wall and hunched down to try for more protection as the storm seemed to increase in fury. Finally, she had to admit to herself she was scared to death.

Brad moved on, his pace slowed by the burden of the second horse and the rain. He gazed intently at every crevice or rock formation he saw, hoping to spot her.

He knew she had to be near, he sensed it. How far could she have gone on foot? He began calling out her name, trying to make himself heard over the storm.

"Shelby! Shelby!" His voice was strong, but the wind seemed to tear the sound away as soon as he would utter it. "Shelby!"

Shelby sat with her back to the wall, her knees bent and her arms wrapped around them.

Admitting to weakness and fear was not her way, and this was the first time ever she had let those two emotions take control. Resting her forehead on her knees, she wept, and knew with anger they were tears of self-pity. Still, she couldn't stop them.

In her misery she thought she could actually hear Brad calling her. But it had to be a combination of wild imagination and wishful thinking. Neither Brad nor anyone else could find her here. She would just have to wait out the storm and continue on as best she could.

Again she thought she heard Brad's voice. She lifted her head, gazing out into the heavy rain.

"Shelby! Shelby!"

It *was* Brad's voice! He was somewhere near. She rose to her feet and concentrated on listening intently. The voice came again . . . maybe . . . just a bit closer.

"Brad! Brad!" She tried to shout above the surrounding fury. Then she listened again, but there was only silence. Had he heard her, or had he passed her by? She called out again and again until her throat seemed raw.

As the unwelcome tears came once more, he seemed to suddenly loom before her, appearing out of the mist and rain and the thunderous upheaval like an answer to a prayer. She ran to him and threw herself into the welcome refuge of his strength.

She felt his arms close about her, and for a brief moment she looked up into warm gray eyes that searched hers. His expression revealed the combination of great anguish and relief that he had found her.

She felt the power of him as he crushed her to him and rocked her in his arms. She heard the whisper of her name and forgot all else but the joy she felt.

Wordlessly, he held her from him for a minute and studied her face, then he kissed her with a passion the intensity of which rivaled the storm around them.

She surrendered to the hardness of his mouth on hers with abandon. When he again held her from him she could hear his voice indistinctly above the wind.

"Are you all right!"

"Yes."

"Come. We've got to get out of this!" As he led her

to her horse, she was still filled with wonder that he had found her.

When they came to the entrance of the cave it amazed her further that he obviously knew a place of shelter. And she'd only been a few hundred feet from it.

She stood shivering in the entranceway to the cave while Brad unsaddled the horses and led them to the back of the cave. She heard him moving around before there was a flicker of light . . . and a flame. She realized that there must have been broken logs and branches scattered about the cave and that he had gathered some to build a small fire.

"What the hell did you think you were doing!" he burst out with what she heard as anger.

"Getting as far away from you, and your sweet lies as I could possibly get!" she cried, furious at him. He was more guilty of deception than she was.

"Where did you think you were going?"

"To California, where else?"

"You and this horse, all the way to California!" His voice was a harsh bark of disbelief.

"I would have gone to town first and found a better way. I'm not exactly stupid."

"Well, for your information you were going the wrong way. There's a hell of a lot of rough miles between you and anything, going in this direction." He glared at her for a minute before her first words sank in. "What do you mean, *my* lies? You're the one who played the whole game out. Were you laughing at me for being a fool to believe you meant what you said?"

"Me!" she almost shrieked, "I'm the one who lied! What about you?"

"I never lied to you."

"You are right now."

"That's not true."

"No? Didn't you stand in your own house and tell Jack to hurry and get the wagon fixed? Don't you think I can see how anxious you are to get me back? God, the money means so much to you that you'd pretend . . . pretend that . . ." Her voice broke against and anger so virulent she could hardly stand it. "I told you, but you thought it was all a game. Well, I'm tired of your games."

It took only moments for Brad to understand what had happened. She'd heard his conversation with Jack. . . . But only part of it.

She was shaking so hard her teeth chattered. He was barely in control of his own anger, but at least he knew the answer. He'd convince her of the truth later. She had to get out of her wet clothes before she got sick. He knew she'd fight with him until hell froze over before she complied with any of his wishes.

"God, you're the most stubborn woman I've ever run across," he muttered as he started for her.

When he got to her side he gripped her arm and forced her toward the fire. Then, to her alarm, he began to pull the clothes from her body.

"What are you doing?" she gasped as she struggled wildly.

Brad gripped her shoulders and shook her. "You damn little fool! Don't you realize you could get sick. You've got to get out of those wet clothes."

She was shaking now, and it was not with fear of the elements surrounding them. Despite the cold, his hands felt not only warm but much too strong for her to do battle with.

He stripped her wet shirt from her and bent to pull off her boots. The breeches soon joined the shirt by the fire and she stood only in pantalettes and chemise, quite unaware the wet garments molded to her like a second skin.

Brad hastily stripped to his underwear and draped a blanket around himself, then took the other blanket and put it around her, clutching it closed in front so her arms were useless. It was safer that way while he explained, he reasoned. He could see the bubbling anger in her eyes and he needed time to tell her the truth.

"What you heard was half a conversation."

"That was enough."

"The wrong half," he continued. "Not the part where I told Jack to take his time, that I didn't care if it took a month of Sundays to get it fixed. I wasn't going to take you back right away. You didn't hear me tell him that I loved you. That I wanted you to be part of my life for good. That I was going to ask you to marry me."

"More lies," she said, but her words were weak in the face of the warmth and the truth she saw in his eyes.

They stood, inches apart, looking at each other.

Shelby's hair had come loose in the scuffle, and it poured around her like a stream of pale satin. It clung to her cheeks and bare shoulders in wet tendrils.

Her skin picked up the glow of the fire and the same glow echoed in her violet eyes.

Brad never even realized when he reached out a hesitant hand to brush the damp strands of hair from her cheek, then let his fingers linger to caress the softness of her skin.

Neither would ever know who moved first, but suddenly she was in his arms, returning his kiss with every sense she possessed. When it ended, both were shaken and breathing deeply.

"God, Shelby, I thought I'd never find you."

"I should have known you would. But I couldn't stay, I just . . . . I couldn't stand it."

"And I couldn't stand to lose you. Come back with me, Shelby. This time I'll make you understand how much I love and need you."

"And you'll believe me."

"Yes."

"When I say I love you?" she added softly.

"It's nothing compared with how I feel for *you*. I think I've loved you from the day I saw that picture. I love you now, and I'll go on loving you no matter what." He wrapped one arm around her, drawing her down with him beside the warmth of the fire. Both were shivering and not only from the cold or the rain. He pulled her onto his lap and held her close to him. She could feel the pervading warmth of the blanket, of the fire, and of Brad's body intimately snug against her.

"Maybe now is the time for you to tell me the whole story, Shelby. Not that anything else matters but you and me, but I don't want any barriers between us."

Shelby found it very difficult to pour out her story when he began to slide his hands over the blanket. His touch was creating havoc, as was the clean scent of him and the warmth of his eyes.

She finished amidst words that stumbled one over the other, and he reached up to tangle a hand in her hair and draw her head to his. When his mouth took possession of hers all lies were forgotten. She wanted him with a fervor that matched his, and she surrendered to the kiss, opening to him, accepting him, her arms around his neck and her body soft against his.

She closed her eyes and savored the sensation of his heated kisses against her skin as he pushed both the blanket and the thin lacy straps of her chemise aside.

Brad could feel her mouth soft against his, tasting warm and sweet. He drowned in that sweetness.

When the kiss ended, both were so immersed in the magic of it that for a time neither could say anything.

"I know it's the wrong time and the wrong place, Shelby," Brad said as he brushed a light kiss against her throat where he could feel the pulse of her heart beat, "but I want to make love to you."

She put one hand on each side of his face and bent to kiss him. "I know," she breathed the words softly, "and I want you, too."

The elation he felt was tempered by caution. She had just offered him all, and he was going to make certain she never regretted it.

He stood, drawing her up with him and kissed her

again, leisurely, deeply, and so thoroughly that he felt her melt against him.

He spread the blanket near the fire, then, taking her hand in his, led her to it.

She could feel the warmth emanating from him as he stood close. Again she felt the now welcome touch of his hands against her skin as he slowly pulled away the barriers that separated them. They stood just a breath from each other.

He gently brushed his lips across hers, then kissed her forehead, her closed eyes, her cheeks. When his mouth returned to hers, it was to drink deeply of the sweetness he had dreamed of.

The dam within her burst and released the floodgates of desire that flowed through her like molten lava. Slowly, her lips parted under his searching mouth as his tongue explored the sweet recesses within. She responded with a heated need that blinded her senses to everything but Brad.

They knelt, then reclined on the blanket. His hands reached again to caress her with a feather-light touch. His fingers touched her lips, then drifted down her slender throat to a soft shoulder, down to caress one passion-hardened breast, then the slim curve of her waist. He rested his hand gently on her hip, then slowly drew her toward him and again bent to taste her upturned mouth.

Tenderly and with exquisite patience, he teased her mouth with soft kisses, then, knelt before her, pressing his lips to the valley between her breasts. His hands slid around her and held her tightly to him.

She gasped with the delicious pain as he nibbled

her sensitive skin, and her hands turned in his thick hair to press him closer.

He heard her muffled sob as her body trembled in expectant agony. He felt her body quiver beneath his hands, and heard her passionate words call to him.

His mouth on hers was hard and seeking now, finding a response as demanding as his own. The smoldering fires of love burst into an explosive blinding need that consumed them both.

They came together, fused into one like molten metal. Their bodies blended, each possessing, each surrendering all.

They lay very still, holding each other, aware of the rare and intensely beautiful emotion they shared so completely.

He had doubted Shelby's word many times, but this experience he couldn't doubt. He knew that there was no pretense about what they had shared.

He rolled to his side and looked down into her eyes.

"I've wanted to ask you something."

"What?"

"Your aunt Anne . . ."

"She's not my aunt, she's Uncle Joe's wife."

"But didn't she miss you? Wasn't she suspicious?"

"Actually, she never met me. Everything about her I know was from Winter's letters. Frankly, I'm glad we never met. I hope now that Winter will be safe from her clutches, and that Uncle Joe will be wise enough to see she causes no more problems."

"Remember the night at the campfire, when you sang that lullaby?"

"Um hum."

"You said your mother used to sing it to you. I just couldn't picture Anne Stapleton as your mother, or singing you lullabies."

"Wait until you meet my mother. She's so much like Uncle Joe, generous and kind. She'll love you."

"You're sure about that? I'm taking you away a long distance."

"You'd be surprised. My mother eloped with my father, and they were blissfully happy. Besides, it gives us all some places to visit. Trust me, Brad, she'll love you."

"So . . . Shelby it is."

"Yes," she smiled, "and I truly hope Winter is as happy as I am right now. If my calculations are correct, she should be marrying Gregg Phillips about now. I'm sure Uncle Joe had no idea it would all end like this. He thought I was so well protected that nothing could happen. I think he overestimated the three of us. And underestimated you."

"And Uncle Joe is the one who hired me, then sent you a telegram to warn you about me coming."

"Telegram?"

"Yes," Brad grinned. "You were sent a telegram in Kansas City. It came after you left on the wagon train. I was asked if I'd be so kind as to bring it to you."

"And you," Shelby laughed, "were kind enough to get rid of it."

"Kind enough and clever enough. It was the best piece of timing I've ever fallen into, thanks to your uncle."

"He was doing what was best."

"I'm not angry," Brad laughed, "I want to thank him. He was doing a good job of protecting you. But I think *I'm* the one who will need protection when we meet up with your friend again."

"You mean Jasper? He's as sweet as a kitten."

"Well, that pussycat has every intention of tearing my head off."

"By the time we meet the two of them again, I'll explain everything. Brad . . . you believe me now?"

"I believe *us*. That's all I need to worry about. I guess . . . maybe I'll have to return the money."

"Your ranch . . ."

"I'll think of a way."

"You earned that money, Brad. You did exactly what Uncle Joseph wanted. Besides . . . I think I made your life unbearable for a while."

"You sure gave me a chase," he chuckled. "I've chased some pretty hard cases that weren't as difficult to catch."

She twined her arms around his neck and smiled up at him seductively. "But you've caught me. The real question is, what are you going to do about it?"

"I intend to do a lot about it. I only need one promise from you"

"Promise? What kind of promise?"

"Time. I need time. How does a lifetime sound? Maybe then I could manage to show you how I really feel."

"A lifetime," she murmured. "Sounds about right to me." He heard her soft and very satisfied laugh as he bent to kiss her again.

Chapter 17

Curled against Brad under the warmth of the blanket he had drawn over them, Shelby sighed contentedly. The storm raged outside like a howling monster. Still, she had never felt so safe and so comfortable.

"I should put something on the fire," Brad said softly as he cradled her against him, savoring the pleasure of her soft skin. "Are you cold?"

Shelby laughed and hugged him fiercely. "No, I'm not cold. Actually," she said devilishly, "I never felt warmer in my life." She nipped his ear lightly and felt his arms tighten about her. He growled deep in his throat and kissed her until she could barely breathe.

The only light came as a vague gray glow from the cave entrance, punctuated by flashes of lightning and the glow of the red-embered fire. Still, Brad turned to rest on his side so he could attempt to see her face. In the faint glow, her eyes seemed luminous.

"You know if I had any sense I'd bundle you up

and take you home where you belong. You're giving me much more than I'll ever be able to give you."

"I've had all the best things in the world. I know that. I've been blessed. But don't you understand that I'd gladly trade all of them to stay with you?"

"I wonder if your uncle is going to feel the same way."

"Yes, he will. We'll have succeeded in freeing Winter so she could marry the man of her choice. We will have thwarted 'Aunt' Anne's plans for us all. Uncle Joe will be happy for me . . . for us. We have to make sure enough time has passed, then we can explain to my family, and come home . . . home, here, where we can forget everything and go on with our lives."

She could hear his deep chuckle and felt very pleased with herself.

"You have everything all neatly tied up, don't you, my love?"

"I do. I've just been waiting for you to come to your senses."

Shelby sighed seductively. "Well, since this rain shows very little sign of stopping . . . it looks to me like we'll be here for a long while."

Brad gazed down into her eyes and was stricken with the sudden crazy idea that somehow Shelby had managed to maneuver this situation. He tried to push it aside, but it lingered on the fringes of his mind even as he gathered her to him again and kissed her deeply. But as the kiss progressed to much more satisfying thoughts, the idea vanished completely.

The first time they had made love it had been an explosion of passions reined in too long. But this time was encompassed in magic. It was as if they could not touch each other enough, kiss each other enough, or explore each other enough. Each wanted to know every inch of the other, every perfect part, every flaw. They moved toward the pinnacle of completion and crested the summit with words and sounds neither heard.

After a while Shelby slept in his arms. Brad enjoyed the sheer pleasure of holding her warm body close to him and thinking about the past few weeks with amusement over how they had met and awe at the miracle they had shared and would, he hoped, share for a long time to come.

"I love you, Shelby Vale," he whispered as he kissed the fine silk of her hair. "I guess I've known that since the first minute I looked at you. I'm going to spend the rest of my life making sure you don't regret this."

As if she heard him in her sleep, Shelby snuggled closer. This made him smile and wrap her tighter to him. Only then did he drift into sleep.

In the middle of the night Shelby awoke. She blinked her eyes open, then closed them against the throbbing ache that had begun behind them. She was dreadfully thirsty and she felt oppressively hot. She rose slowly so she wouldn't disturb Brad, and went to find his canteen. She drank deeply, and still felt unsatisfied. Walking to the mouth of the cave, she reached out her hands to cup the cool rain. It felt so good that she extended her arms, then her body a little so the coolness of the water could ease the warmth of her skin.

The rain was icy cold and soon she felt better. She returned to the blanket and crept under to snuggle closer to Brad. She felt his arms come about her even in the depths of his sleep, with a half-smile of satisfaction she again slept.

It was just nearing dawn when Brad and Shelby dressed, then stood together at the mouth of the cave watching the falling rain. Nothing could be seen beyond the curtain of rain and Shelby felt as if they stood in their own private little world. The headache persisted, but she attributed it to the fact that she was ravenously hungry.

"I've never seen such a storm," Shelby commented, leaning against Brad, who stood with his back against the arch of the cave wall.

"You're a city girl," Brad laughed.

"Now, I gave you quite a race. I'm not *exactly* a city girl. I was born on a farm and I've ridden since I was a child. Besides, I like it out here. Storms have their compensations." She turned into his arms. "But Brad, I need to know what your plans are. Eventually, I must go back. I have to tell my mother and Uncle Joe I'm safe."

"Then . . . you stay with me until you tell me the time is right and we'll go back, together. We'll congratulate your cousin Winter and wish her happiness. We'll give your uncle back the money and tell them you're coming home with me."

"But I've told you about the money . . ."

"Shelby, I don't want the money. There's not

enough money in the world to buy you. I'm sorry I put you through what I did. Of course," he grinned, "you didn't give me an easy time."

"Uncle Joe will be amazed that you caught me at all. As far as Jasper and Dobbs are concerned," she laughed, "well, I think at least Jasper is going to be disappointed. I wonder where they are?"

"A few hundred miles away, I hope." Brad put one arm around her and they turned to walk back to the fire.

"I wish I'd brought something better to eat than just biscuits," Shelby sighed. "I'm starved."

"The rain will be over soon and Abby will be delighted to feed you. I'll bet she's worried to death."

"I'm sorry for that. She's been very kind."

They sat down on the blanket again and Brad put a few more twigs on the fire to encourage it.

"How much longer will this rain last?"

"Truthfully I've seen it last for days," he laughed at her quick look. "But I don't think this storm will last much longer." He propped himself up on one elbow, reaching to catch strands of her hair in his hand. "Still I can't honestly say I'm that anxious to leave. This cave has more charm than I'd ever imagined."

"I'm looking forward to seeing all your ranch, now that we can stay for a while."

"I'm going to enjoy showing it to you."

"What will you do for the money you need to go on with it?"

"First I have to end the deal for cattle and water

rights, and get the money back. Then . . . I'll just have to tighten my belt some more."

"You're so stubborn."

"Not really. The money was never earned. I agreed to bring you home, and I'm not going to do that. Don't worry. I've made my own way since I was a kid."

Shelby lay down beside him, then reached up to brush his thick hair away from his brow. "Tell me more about you."

"Maybe, a bit. Actually I was a pretty ordinary, happy kid before . . ."

"Before your parents were killed," she answered for him.

"Yes," he said simply. He went on to talk of his childhood. Shelby listened closely. She knew why he needed the money so badly. She also knew his stubborn pride and she began to wonder what she was going to do when he found out she would soon have a great deal of money of her own. She would cross that bridge when she came to it.

"Your life hasn't been easy."

"Oh it's had its good times, too. And," he chuckled, "things seem to be looking up." Shelby smiled at him, and for the first time he noticed the way her eyes seemed to glitter. At the very same moment, the heat of her body seemed to envelop him. He was about to examine these two perceptions when Shelby spoke excitedly.

"Look, the rain has stopped and the sun's coming out." She got to her feet at once and raced to the cave entrance. Brad was right behind her.

As she reached the entrance the sudden brilliance only made Shelby's nagging headache expand. She paused with her hand against the cave wall and looked out at the trees that still glistened with silvered drops of rain.

But a wave of vertigo struck her and her whole body seemed weighted with lead. The trees bowed and swirled around her, and the headache suddenly burst into a million stars . . . and then things began to grow dark.

She heard Brad's voice echo in her mind, drifting farther and farther away until oblivion claimed her.

Brad watched her pause, stagger, then sag to her knees. He called out her name and ran to her side just as she collapsed completely.

He tasted a new kind of fear. He bent above her, lifting her slightly, condemning himself for being so caught up in his own feelings he hadn't realized the heat of her body hadn't been normal.

He cradled her in his arms and carried her to the blanket and laid her down, drawing a second one over her. Then he tossed more sticks on the fire.

He grabbed for his canteen and tore off his neck scarf. Soaking it, he placed the cool cloth across her forehead.

He could feel her body trembling and knew he had to get her back to the ranch as quickly as possible. There was no doctor close by, but Abby was very efficient in medical matters.

He left Shelby only to take the horses outside and saddle them, trying to figure out how he was going to get her safely back to the ranch. Suddenly, he heard his name shouted in the distance. In the distance he saw a lone rider approaching. There was only one man who could ride with that smooth ease, and who would have the ability to find him. Tom Littlebeaver.

Tom drew his horse to a halt and dismounted beside Brad.

"Tom, am I glad to see you! How did you know . . ."

"I stopped at the ranch to join up with you, and Jack told me what happened. I had an idea you'd hole up somewhere. Then I remembered these caves. Did you find Shelby?"

"She's here. We were caught in the storm, and now she's gotten sick. I'll need your help to get her home."

Tom went back into the cave with him and he, too, was alarmed at Shelby's appearance. They wrapped her in a blanket, and when Brad mounted his horse Tom handed her up to him. They started for home.

It seemed to Brad the miles were endless and the hours slower than molasses. As they traveled, he kept wetting a cloth with his canteen, trying to soothe the blazing heat of Shelby's fever. He knew it would do very little good, and had never felt so powerless in his life.

When they drew their horses to a stop in front of the house, Tom leapt from his and took Shelby from Brad, who then dismounted and took her trembling body in his arms. At the door, one well-placed kick slammed it open and drew a shriek from Mary Beth.

"Brad?"

"No time to explain," he said. "Get some cool water and fetch your mother."

Mary Beth ran, and Brad placed Shelby gently on her bed and bent above her smoothing her damp hair away from her face. It was the first time in a long time he'd prayed.

Brad couldn't remember when he'd been so tired, or so scared. For two days, Shelby had tossed and turned, burning with fever and mumbling incoherently.

He had not slept at all. Instead, he'd cared for her, gently washing away perspiration, forcing sips of water down her. Abigail tried several times to get him to go to bed, saying she would take care of Shelby. He refused all her offers.

Brad stood up from the edge of the bed where he had been sitting. He stretched his tired muscles and looked down at Shelby.

She seemed so helpless that the ache that had begun deep within him when she collapsed had grown into a deep and throbbing pain.

Abigail watched him closely. She knew without a word why Brad worried so. Several hours later she came quietly into the room to light a lamp and saw him there still beside Shelby.

"Brad, I have a hot meal for you."

"I'm not hungry. Damnit, it's been so long." He turned to look up at her and she could read the fear and misery in his eyes.

"So, all the things she told Mary Beth are true."

"She told her the whole story?"

"Yes, and the fact that she was in love with you."

"Why didn't . . ."

"Mary Beth wouldn't jump the gun and Shelby didn't want her to. She thought you might think it another trick." Abigail smiled. "I think I knew you were in love with her from the first. But you insist on being a stubborn ox."

"Abby, go away."

"Of course. I'd be glad to. I don't have to say any more. You aren't lying to yourself any longer? You and I both know what ails you."

"Yes," Brad said quietly. "But I have to think about it."

"Think about it? Why? You want her here and you know it. So what's bothering you?"

"Yes, I want her here," he said firmly.

"Then, what's the problem? Ask her to stay."

"I did. But . . . maybe it's just me I'm thinking about. What about her?"

"What *about* her?"

"She comes from a whole different life. It's going to be a sacrifice . . ."

"Sacrifice!" Abby said sharply. "I don't think she'd think of it that way. You love her, Brad?"

"Yes."

"And the money . . ."

"Has nothing to do with it. I guess you're right, Abby. *Knowing her like I do, and knowing how much I'd be giving up,* it would hurt like hell to let her go. We'll have to talk about it when she gets well."

Abigail walked to the door. But she'd been Brad's friend much too long not to have the last word. She paused in the doorway.

"If you're in love with her, and if you let her get away, it will be the biggest mistake you ever made in your life."

She closed the door quickly before he could voice any resistance and chuckled to herself all the way to the kitchen.

Brad dragged a chair beside the bed and sat down. He reached out and took Shelby's hand in his, still feeling the heat of fever. He closed his hand about her wrist, feeling how small and delicate it was, and feeling the soft pulse of her heartbeat.

"Shelby," he whispered, his voice ragged and hoarse from hours without sleep. "Shelby, come on. Come out of it. You're scaring the hell out of me and I don't think I can take it much longer." He sighed a deep weariness, then, lifting her hand to his lips, he kissed her fingers gently, tenderly. Again he stood and paced the small room. The silence hung in the air like a heavy weight, broken only by Shelby's deep breathing. He was angry at his own helplessness. What really shocked him was that he'd never felt the urge to weep before, and the weakness left him a bit stunned. He crossed the room again and looked out at a view that had always been a consolation. Now it left him empty.

Shelby battled the heavy darkness that seemed to be pressing her down until she could hardly breathe. A frantic panic surged through her and she felt as if she were drifting . . . alone. Searching for something she couldn't name.

She wanted to call out but there didn't seem to be enough breath to do that, and the well of fear began to grow and grow.

The heat of blackness that enveloped her was so intense that she felt as if she were on fire and the fire was sucking the life from her.

Once she dreamed someone was with her, but she couldn't see or hear. Then it came again and again. A gentle voice, a cool touch that seemed only breath. She wanted to reach for it, but her bones felt like water.

It came again, the gentle voice, calling to her, drawing her back from the blackness.

She couldn't open her eyes, they seemed weighted, but she wanted the soothing comfort of that familiar voice . . . that familiar touch. Then suddenly it was gone.

She felt bereft, frightened. With all her will; she struggled to open her eyes. She felt as if her entire body was weighted, and she was much too weak to move.

It took her a minute or two to realize she not only didn't know where she was, but that she was in someone's bed and her clothes had been removed. Along with this came the realization that she was not alone. She turned her head and saw him. She needed no time to recognize that tall form and broad back.

Trying to speak was another surprise. First, she opened her mouth and nothing came out. When she finally did make a sound, it was a hoarse rasping whisper.

"Brad?" It was so weak that he didn't recognize it

...s anything more than the babbling she'd been doing
...or the past two days. She struggled with it again.

"Brad."

Brad spun around, his eyes piercing to see if he'd
...eally heard. When he saw her eyes were open and
...he was looking at him without the glaze of fever, the
...urge of relief was almost painful.

"Well, you've finally decided to rejoin us."

"How did I get here . . . I don't remember . . ."

"Shelby, calm yourself. You've been really sick. It
...ill come back to you. Why didn't you tell me you
were sick? This just didn't come on that fast."

Shelby licked her dry lips and tried to smile. "I
...idn't think you were in much in a mood before for
me to tell you anything, and then," she smiled,
..."other things got in the way. Besides, I didn't really
...think I was that sick."

"Well, you were. Good thing the storm broke
before you collapsed. I don't know what I'd have
done in that cave without water or food . . . and
Abby's invaluable help."

"I must thank her for being so kind."

Shelby looked more closely at Brad. He hadn't
shaved . . . he looked at if he hadn't slept either.

"You look exhausted."

"Don't worry about me, I'm fine. You're the one
who needs to get your strength back. Are you hungry?" he asked. "You ought to be, you haven't had
anything but water for almost three days."

"I am hungry . . . but water or no water, I'm really
thirsty."

"I'll go see if something can be rustled up for you."

He reached out and took her hand in his. "You'll b‌
up and around in no time." He kissed her finger‌
lightly and she could easily read the profound relie‌
in his eyes.

"Thank you," she said softly.

Brad had to struggle to defuse the need to hold he‌
and reassure himself. She needed care now.

"When you're well enough we'll talk about plans‌
There won't be any more games." He rose abruptl‌
walked to the door. When it closed behind him‌
Shelby stared at it for a long while unsure of what h‌
had said. She hoped he had not changed his min‌
when he'd had time to think it over.

In the kitchen Abigail looked at Brad closely‌
"How is she?"

"She's awake and it looks like the fever has bro‌
ken. She's hungry and thirsty. Can you get somethin‌
together?"

"Sure can," Abigail answered. "What about you?‌"

"I could eat a horse," Brad admitted. "But see t‌
Shelby first. I'm going to get a couple hours sleep‌
then I'll eat."

Abigail began to heat water, and to prepare a tra‌
of light food. A little soup and some tea would b‌
more than enough for a stomach deprived of food fo‌
so long.

While the water heated, she carried the tray t‌
Shelby's room.

"It's good to see you awake. You had us all prett‌
frightened for a while," she said setting the tray on ‌
small table near the bed.

"Where is Brad?"

"He went to bed. I wish he would have eaten first, but he was so exhausted he just wanted to sleep." Abigail sat on the edge of the bed and began to feed Shelby. "Now, don't try too much at one time, your stomach won't handle it. Once you've gotten some of this soup in you, I'll scat out and get that water you wanted and bring you one of Mary Beth's clean nightgowns. You'll feel a lot better when I get you cleaned up and change that bed for you."

Shelby had raised herself up on the bed. She was surprised at just how weak she was. She managed a few sips of soup, then sighed a grateful sigh.

"The soup is delicious."

"Thank you." Abigail watched her closely. "Shelby, tell me something, will you? Why did you run away? Didn't you see the storm brewing?"

"I had an idea, but storms out here are apparently very different than the ones I know. I needed to put a great deal of distance between Brad and me . . . or to have him ask me to stay." She went on to explain hearing Brad and Jack talking and how she had misinterpreted what they were saying. "I felt he was going to go on with his plan, I had to go. I had to."

"I don't know what happened between you two out there. All I know is that he has been beside himself with fear all the time you were sick. And I know he loves you . . . very much."

"It cannot be any stronger than the love I feel for him," Shelby replied softly.

"Then your differences are over?"

"As far as I can see. We can go home and finish this affair. Winter is married by now, and I'm sure the cat's out of the bag and Uncle Joe is happy. So we can come back here . . . together.''

"I'm glad you've both decided that. If I asked a nosy question, it's because I've loved that boy a long time. I wanted to be sure.''

Shelby reached out and placed her hand on Abigail's. "Be sure, Abby. I love him, and I want to make him happy. But I'm afraid about the money. He needs it to keep this ranch solvent. I can see how he loves this place.''

"I know he needs it.''

"But he won't take it. He insists he's going to return all the money to my uncle. If he does . . .''

"It will cost him more than you know.''

"Abby, I have money. But . . .''

"But his damn pride will get in the way,'' she finished with a laugh. "Want some advice?''

"Absolutely.''

"Marry him first, then tell him about the money.''

"He'll be furious.''

"I know. He'll rant and rave for a while. But,'' her eyes twinkled, "I've a feeling you'll find a way to put an end to that.''

Shelby had to laugh, but she knew the advice was sound. She would do anything to ensure she and Brad had a future together. Abby was also right that she knew how to put an end to Brad's anger . . . and she meant to use the power he had given her that night in the cave to help build that future.

She lay back against the pillows and smiled contentedly at a very pleased Abigail.

Chapter 18

Shelby's young, healthy body was recuperating quickly and she wanted out of bed, out into the sunshine, and to be with Brad. He pampered her, constantly hovering as if she were so fragile she'd break at the slightest touch, like porcelain.

From the amber glow through her window she could see the sun was beginning to set. Brad came in carrying a tray of food.

"Brad, I could have come to the table to eat," she protested.

"You just stay put until you get your strength back," Brad said firmly. He set the tray on a nearby table and came to sit beside her. His look was so intense she almost laughed, but she was certain he wasn't going to find it amusing. She saw the lingering fear in the depths of his eyes.

"Brad," she said softly, "I'm fine."

"I know, and I want you to stay that way." He bent close and kissed her lightly, but when he started to back away, she looped her arms around his neck and drew him closer for a deep and hungry kiss. For a second she could feel him hesitate, but she clung to him, her lips parting to deepen the kiss. With satisfaction she felt his arms come about her and lift her against his chest. His mouth searched hers and the kiss grew deeper. When he finally released her lips, she looked up into his eyes.

"I love you very much, Brad Cole," she said softly, "and if you don't let me out of this bed," her smile was now decidedly wicked, "you might find yourself in a very compromising position."

"For two cents I'd call your bluff," Brad grinned. "I couldn't think of anything I'd rather do right now than make love to you for the rest of the night. But you be a good patient, eat your dinner and rest, and in the morning we'll go out and take another look at my ranch if you feel up to it."

Brad brought his coffee and stayed while she ate, and when Abigail paused outside the door sometime later she was pleased to hear the sound of soft laughter from inside.

The supper dishes were done and there was no need for her to linger. She extinguished the lamps and left the house and walked slowly toward her own. She considered, with a smile, that those two needed this time together. She felt relaxed and pleased.

Abigail sat on her rocker on her own front porch and looked across the clearing at the main house. Only one window glowed with light. After a while, she rose slowly, and as she started to turn toward her door she saw the light in the main house dim, then go out. She smiled. The future of those she cared for looked promising and bright.

The next morning Abigail made as much noise in the kitchen as she logically could. She prepared breakfast singing, "Amazing Grace," but abruptly stopped in midsong when she turned to see Brad standing in the doorway.

"Good morning," she said as if she had no other concern in the world. "Shall I make a tray for Shelby?"

"No, she insisted last night that she was going to get up today."

"She's a strong girl. She'll bounce back easy. I expect she's as fit as a fiddle today."

As if to concur with her last words, Shelby appeared behind Brad, fully dressed and wearing a smile that to Abigail looked completely contented.

"I *am* as fit as a fiddle, and I'm famished. Brad has promised to take me around to see more of the ranch today."

"I'll pack you some food for lunch," Abigail replied. "If you're going to see this place you'll be gone most of the day and then some."

"Thanks, Abby," Brad said, "but I'm not pushing it. We'll ride out as far as Miller Creek and eat lunch there. We should be back before suppertime."

Brad and Shelby moved to the breakfast table, and Abigail smiled to herself. A six-foot table and they sat side by side, as if inches were too much distance to put between them! Mary Beth and Jack came in and found their seats at the table, and they were soon followed by the hired hands. When Abigail put the food on the table and joined them, the gathering seemed to merge and blend. Laughter and teasing remarks filled the room. There was not a person at the table who could not see the potent magic that existed between the boss and his lady.

Their hands would touch, their glance meet and unspoken words exchanged. When they left there was a few amusing remarks passed around the table, but everyone was more than pleased. They liked Shelby . . . but they *loved* Brad, and were united in the thought that he deserved the happiness.

Brad and Shelby rode slowly while he pointed out places they had skipped on the last tour. Again it pleased him to see how caught up she was in the beauty around them.

By the time they reached the creek, Shelby was tired. They dismounted, tied their horses, and walked along the bank.

"I can see why you would have done most anything to keep this place, Brad. It would break my heart to give it up if it were mine."

Brad stopped walking and turned her to face him. "Shelby, I'd give a lot for this place, yes. But it wouldn't be enough if you weren't going to share it with me."

"Why Brad Cole," she said softly, "are you proposing to me?"

"You bet I am. I don't think it really comes as

much of a surprise, does it? After all, you proposed first and I don't want you to forget. I'm not taking a chance of you walking out of my life."

"And it shouldn't come as much of a surprise to know that I had full intentions of doing whatever it took to catch you . . . even if I had to do the proposing," Shelby laughed as she slid her arms around his waist and pressed close to him. "Oh, Brad, I'm so happy I could burst. I'm so glad we met. What would have happened if I'd said no to Uncle Joe?"

"It wouldn't have mattered," Brad said with a confident smile. "I believe fate had a hand in it all. Some great power up there finally decided I'd been lonely long enough and rewarded me with the most beautiful creature in the world."

"You could spoil me very easily," Shelby laughed. "After all the nasty things you've said to me, those are very sweet words."

Brad cupped her face in his hands and looked intently into her eyes. "I'd like to spoil you, Shelby. I'd like to give you everything you're used to, everything you deserve. But God knows it will be a long way before I can do that. You're getting yourself into more than you know."

"Are you by any chance trying to wiggle out of this?" she teased. "If you are, it won't work."

"I'm serious, Shelby."

"So am I. Stop treating me like a hothouse flower. I'm strong, and I'm ready to help you build. I want to be with you, I want to have your children and watch them grow up to be the kind of person you are. I love you, and that's the end of it."

"I've said it from the beginning: you are the most stubborn, most persevering woman I've ever met."

"That's how I caught you, mister," her eyes glittered with laughter, "and that's how I'm going to keep you caught. You might as well just give in gracefully."

"You sound like a woman who knows exactly what she wants," he said quietly. Then he kissed her deeply. "I love you, Shelby, you know that."

"I don't doubt it," she said with a soft and wicked laugh. "Right now, I think there's something I really want."

"Oh?" he said with a hopeful grin. "What?"

"Food."

He lifted his head abruptly and blinked in surprise. "Food?"

"You won't deny Abby's the best cook in the state. And we've been riding all morning, so I'm starved." She tried to move out of his arms but he wouldn't let her.

"You're heartless. But I know you too well to try and fight," he chuckled, "so I'll get the food if you spread a blanket." She started to turn from him but he caught her hand and lifted it to kiss her fingers. "But I'm not making any promises."

"It's every man for himself," Shelby laughed. In a moment Brad was laughing with her.

They spread the blanket and enjoyed a meal punctuated with laughter and occasional kisses.

The afternoon seemed perfect to them. They shared details of their past and their hopes for the future. They laughed and played in the sun. Brad led her to a shady place where the stream eddied into a pool. They swam there, then lay side by side on the grass and soaked up the sun, comfortable and satisfied that there would be more days ahead like this. Their passion could not be ignored, but it built slowly, with a gentle culmination that left them sated. For a while they slept in each other's arms.

Reluctantly Brad said they would have to start back soon not to miss Abby's supper. They gathered their things and walked to the horses.

Neither was aware that some distance away a collapsible telescope was slowly being lowered. The man who had been looking through it had a broad smile on his face.

Carl James's men had picked up on Brad and Shelby's trail, and had followed it, staying ahead of Jasper and Dobbs. They found the Cole ranch with little difficulty, and for over a week they'd been watching, searching for an opportunity to find Shelby in a vulnerable position. They had arrived two days before the storm struck, had made sure Shelby was there, then wired Carl, who had responded with definite and precise instructions.

But the instructions proved difficult, since no opportunity had presented itself to find Shelby alone.

Shelby had slipped away so stealthily the night of the storm they had not seen her leave or they would have grabbed her. Now they could see that both Brad and Shelby's guard was relaxing. The moment would come soon . . . and they would take it.

"That them?" A second man questioned.

"Sure is. She's one beautiful woman."

"Don't get no stupid ideas. He wants her back safe and sound. Besides, we have to make some careful plans. I don't think getting her away from him is going to be so easy."

"Yeah," the first man licked his lips, "looks like he's right fond of her. Too bad."

"He's no man to play with."

"I got no intention of playing games with him. We're after the girl. When the right time comes we'll take her. He gets in our way . . . well, that'll be just too bad."

"All right, all right. Let's go."

The next three days were so perfect that both Brad and Shelby began to forget they had to be cautious. They were planning the trip home, confident that all was well there. Shelby had never been so happy. Her one nagging worry was the uncertainty of Jasper and Dobbs's whereabouts, and the certainty that they were worried about her. She knew they were thinking thoughts about Brad that would bode him no good if they caught him somewhere alone . . . which was exactly what happened the day before they were to leave.

Jasper rode beside Dobbs in grim silence. He was angry and he was worried. From the tracks he read, it looked as if there were others following Brad and Shelby as well as the two of them.

"Why would someone else be following them,"

Dobbs asked pensively, when Jasper drew his attention to it.

"I'd say our Ranger friend has made a lot of enemies over a lifetime."

"That's too easy. I don't like it."

"To tell you the truth, neither do I. We'll just have to keep our eyes open."

"What if it's Shelby?" Dobbs asked suddenly.

"No reason for anyone to be looking for her," Jasper replied. But now his brow creased with worry. "I don't trust that Carl James. We'd better keep our eyes open."

Dobbs knew Jasper's anger at Brad was getting more explosive every hour. And he felt sorry for anyone else who got in his way or had any designs on Shelby.

Within another day they'd be riding across the range that belonged to Brad. Even this seemed to stoke Jasper's anger. It worried Dobbs that he might not be able to stop Jasper from doing Brad bodily harm before they had an opportunity to talk to him.

Despite what Jasper thought, it was Dobbs's opinion that Brad was innocent, and that a friendly conversation might enlighten all four of them. He wasn't too sure his very clever friend, Shelby Vale, was in any real danger at all.

"If we camp tonight and get an early start in the morning we should be there before noon," Dobbs announced.

"We can ride a few more hours yet," Jasper answered gruffly.

"Jasper, I don't know about you, but I'm more

used to the stage than I am a horse's back. My bones are complaining mightily. Besides, I'm hungry and very thirsty."

"All right, we'll stop. But every minute we waste just gives him another chance to get away. I have to know why he brought her here instead of taking her home. I have a feeling something's wrong. She could be hurt—worse. I don't like it, and I won't be satisfied until I see for myself she's all right. She's worth a lot of money, you know."

"Good Lord. You don't think he intends to ransom her back to Mr. Stapleton?"

"It's possible."

"He was paid and paid well."

"How does that compare with what he could get?"

Dobbs was silent. This was something he had not considered.

They rode on for almost another hour before Dobbs insisted they come to a halt. They made a camp and ate. All the while Dobbs was contemplating what Jasper had said.

"You've got to give the man a chance to explain his motives," he stated emphatically.

"The hell I do. He's got too much to answer for. I don't like the way he's lied about her and dragged her all over the place."

When they finished eating, Dobbs, curled in his blanket near the fire and slept. But Jasper sat, contemplating his own private visions.

The next morning Jasper urged Dobbs awake when dawn was a thin gray line on the horizon. They had eaten a very swift breakfast and were prepared to travel as the sun was just coming up.

Again they rode in the same strained silence. The sun rose higher, and Jasper's face grew grimmer. Finally, they crested a hill and looked down on the Cole ranch—just in time to see the door of the ranch house burst open and a man race across the clearing to the barn. They immediately recognized Brad. Jasper kicked his horse into motion and rode toward the barn, coming up on the blind side so no one in the house could see them.

Brad, too, had awakened very early that morning. He was concerned that for most of the day neither Abby nor Mary Beth would be home, having planned an excursion to the nearest town for supplies. He had to be gone most of the morning also. This would leave Shelby alone for several hours.

"Brad," Shelby had laughed, "what could possibly happen? If Jasper and Dobbs should by chance happen to catch up with us, it would give me a chance to explain things to dear Jasper before there was any problem. There's no one else for miles who wants to cause me any harm."

"I suppose you're right," he admitted, "but right or not, I'm coming back home for lunch."

"That's all right with me, but I think you're in for a nasty surprise."

"Oh?"

"I can't cook worth a nickel, so you'll just have to make do with whatever we can find."

Brad laughed and took her in his arms. "Don't worry about me, what appetite I've got, you can satisfy very well."

Shelby laughed with him and willingly surrendered to his kiss, but when he began to take it further, she wiggled free. "If you want to be back for lunch you'd better get a move on."

"All right, all right, I'm going. But I'll see you at noon."

"I'll be here."

Brad left, as did Abby and Mary Beth an hour or so later.

"Are you sure you don't want to go along with us, Shelby?" Abby asked.

"No, not really. I like being here. Besides, Brad is coming back for lunch and I really ought to fix him something."

"Lunch . . . Brad is coming back for lunch? But . . ." Mary Beth began, but a quick look from Abigail silenced her.

Shelby walked through the empty house, considering with pleasure that one day soon it would be hers. The house was plain and simple, yet she felt the kind of warmth here she had found in her own home.

She thought of Brad coming back for lunch. It might be fun to at least try to prepare something. Surely there would be something she was capable of putting together. Abby was the best cook Shelby had ever come across. When she went to the kitchen and searched, it surprised her that there was no sign of a recipe anywhere.

She sat down in a chair in disgust. No recipe, no

meal. She was considering this annoying dilemma again when a sound from outside drew her attention.

At first the possibility that Brad was back drew her to her feet. But it hadn't been that long since he'd left. Then it occurred to her that luck just might have brought Jasper and Dobbs to her door.

She smiled as she walked quickly to the door and opened it. The man who stood on the porch was a stranger, and danger signaled her instincts quickly. As he stepped forward and reached for her, she closed the door and slid the lock home. Then she raced to the front door. But she was a second too late. The door opened and a man stepped inside with a smile on his face that shook her nerves. She backed away from him.

"What do you want?"

"You, Miss Vale," he said softly. "You're going for a nice little ride with us." He drew a gun from his holster. "Go and unlock the door, and don't try anything stupid. We've watched this place and you long enough to know that there's no one around to help you. Don't be dumb."

Shelby unlocked the door, fear whipping her pulse to a throbbing beat. She had no idea who they were or what they might want.

It dawned on her then that the man at the front door had called her Miss Vale.

"Who are you? How did you know my name? What do you want?"

"Like I said, you're going for a little ride with us. Now, don't give us any problems. There's a couple of people who want to talk to you."

"I'm not going anywhere with you. I'd suggest you both get out of here before—"

"Don't tell us anyone's coming. We been watchin' this place and know there won't be anyone here for a long while. You going to come along without a struggle or do we have to take you?"

"You must have me mixed up with someone else, why would anyone—"

"I don't have time to explain. You can relax, we don't want to hurt you."

"Someone's paying you to . . ." It came clear to her just what they were doing. They had called her Miss Vale, but were they being humorous? Could they, too, believe she was Winter? But why would they send Brad and then . . . Suddenly she thought of Winter's step mother. Of course. Brad had been gone too long and "Auntie" Anne was impatient.

Her mind began to click. Despite the lascivious looks from the one man, the other looked as if he was in control. They did not mean to hurt her, just return her. She wondered if she could delay them long enough for Brad to catch up.

She had too much confidence in Brad not to know he would be on her trail immediately after he found she was gone. Then another thought shook her. Would Brad believe she had been lying and had run at the first opportunity?

No! . . . No, he wouldn't believe that! Not after what they had shared. She had only to give him time. He'd said he would be back sometime around noon. She looked at the clock. Six-thirty. Five and a half hours before he'd be back.

"Well?"

"Where are we going?"

"Our friend back East is real impatient. We don't have that far to go to meet him."

"Him?" she said blankly. "What do you mean we don't have far to go?"

"That's enough talk. I know you're playing for time. You going to come along or do I have to have Hank here hog-tie you?"

To Shelby, the one called Hank looked quite eager to do just that.

"All right," Shelby said helplessly. "I'm going."

"Smart girl. Let's go out and get your horse saddled."

Between the gun in Hank's hand and being outnumbered two to one, she reluctantly moved.

She was sure a five-and-a-half-hour lead would prove no obstacle to Brad. He would catch up to them, she thought with certainty, riding between them as they left the ranch.

She was confident until she realized just how adept those two were at destroying any sign of their passage.

Two hours later they rode into a relay station for the stagecoach. It was clear that the man who ran it was a friend of theirs.

"Stage will be here in maybe twenty minutes," he said gruffly, without looking at her.

"You remember, Dice, you ain't seen us and you ain't seen her."

"Yeah, sure, I'll remember."

That was the moment Shelby began to panic.

* * *

It was past ten-thirty when Abigail and Mary Beth were piling the bundles of supplies in the back of the wagon. Mary Beth laughed. "If we get on our way we could be back at the ranch in time for lunch."

"Mary Beth," Abigail's chuckle was as mischievous, "you really are a troublemaker."

"Me make trouble for dear Brad, the man who tossed me in the river to teach me to swim. Who dipped the ends of my braids in the inkwells at school, who . . ."

"Never mind, I get your point. But this is one time you're not going to be up to any deviltry. Brad and Shelby are walking on eggs anyway. Let them have some peace."

"You really like Shelby, don't you?"

"I sure do. When have you ever seen Brad's eyes light up like they do when she's around. I think she wants to make him happy and I know he loves her. That's enough for me. Brad's had a lot of trouble. It's about time he got a good hand for a change. Now, let's give them all the time they need. We'll get something to eat and then do some shopping."

"For a wedding present?"

"Right," Abigail said firmly. She linked her arm in Mary Beth's and they laughed together as they started down the street.

Brad struggled to keep his mind on his work, but humorous remarks flew between the men as to how long he was going to be able to do it. He gave the men orders to carry out and informed them he was leaving, then turned his horse and rode toward the ranch . . . and Shelby. He took the teasing with a smile, chalking it up to the fact that there wasn't a man present who didn't envy him.

He rode easily, enjoying the thoughts that would culminate in Shelby's arms and hoping Abby and Mary Beth weren't back from their shopping yet.

He almost expected to see Shelby on the porch waiting for him as he rode up, and was surprised at how quiet everything was. Something tugged at his consciousness, but he ignored it, cared for his horse, then walked across the distance between barn and house and up onto the porch. Only then did the first ripple of alarm go through him. The door was standing partway open. He pushed it open the rest of the way and a silence met him that set off every sense he had.

"Shelby!" He started through the house. "Shelby!"

But there was no sign of her, nor was there a sign of any kind of struggle. For one second doubt raised its head. Had Jasper and Dobbs come? Had all the things Shelby said to him been a lie?

"No," he muttered to himself. "It wasn't a lie. Something is wrong."

When he stepped back outside, he examined the area around the house. He soon realized strangers had been there. He circled the house only to find the back door ajar, too. Whoever they were, they did not expect Shelby to go along with them peacefully. They had come at her from two directions. He realized then it couldn't be Jasper or Dobbs, because Shelby would have welcomed them with open arms, and they wouldn't have had to split up to approach her. Besides, if only to satisfy Jasper's vengeance against him, they would still be here.

There was no way to tell how long ago they had left. Brad found paper and pencil and hastily scribbled a note for Abby and left it on the kitchen table.

Then he left the house and raced to the stable. One quick look told him Shelby's horse was gone.

He gathered his equipment, then led his horse out of its stall.

So intent was he on saddling the animal as rapidly as he could that he didn't hear anyone approach. Nor was he aware when the huge broad-shouldered form came to stand in the open doorway.

"No point in saddling that horse, you ain't goin' anywhere."

Brad spun around. Even with the sun behind him and his body no more than a black shadow, Brad knew exactly who it was.

"You ain't leavin this barn until you tell me Shelby's all right and where she's at."

Brad took a backward step and Jasper started toward him like an avenging angel . . . a huge and powerful avenging angel.

Chapter 19

The stagecoach held only the three travelers as it lurched along the rutted roads. It moved at a speed Shelby had hardly thought possible, but she soon realized it was not a scheduled stage on a prearranged route, but part of a well-laid plan. Brad would be trailing riders. If he stopped at this out-of-the-way stage station by chance, he would be misled. She faced the fact that she might just have to deal with the mysterious man she was to meet on her own. It was not a comfortable thought.

It felt to Shelby as if they bumped along the rough-rutted roads for hours. She was hungry and tired. It was well into the afternoon before they stopped, and when they did, it was in front of a shack she instinctively knew could not be a regular stop for the stage.

The stop was short and unenlightening. The couple who had prepared a meal for them were quiet. Still, the meal was reasonably good and Shelby knew enough to eat her fill. Stubbornness could only hurt her. She had no idea when they would stop to eat again.

They were on their way again as soon as the meal was over and Shelby was allowed to refresh herself. She had to admit that the two men who were her captors had caused her no problems. Although Hank continued to watch her as if the thought was in the back of his mind, he also appeared to be controlled by John, the second man who paid her little attention.

She was curled into a corner of the coach and trying to find a comfortable position. The ride felt bumpier and more uncomfortable by the minute.

From the window she had watched the sun set, the last light of day fade, and the mellow light of the moon bathed the scenery beyond the coach window. She had no idea of the time, but from her exhausted state it must have been late at night.

Finally, the coach came to a halt. The door was opened from outside, and a shadowed form appeared in the doorway. "Get out," he said to her in a voice devoid of any emotion.

Every bone and muscle complained as Shelby moved stiffly to comply. She wasn't too sure her legs were going to hold her once she was standing, but when Hank reached out and touched her in the guise of aid, she jerked her arm away. This was met by a threatening sound from Hank and a soft chuckle from the third man.

"Hank, keep your hands to yourself."

Shelby was surprised when a few soft words from the third man seemed to squelch any desire Hank had to come near her again. In a way she was relieved and in another way she realized she quite possibly should be more afraid of this man than the other two.

"Come in, miss. There's some food and you can rest for a while."

"Where are you taking me?"

"In good time you'll have your answers." His hand was like an iron band around her arm as he propelled her toward the house. "For now I must warn you not to try anything."

"You could at least tell me what this is all about! You come in my house and . . ."

His chuckle was almost warm. "Please, Miss Vale. There's no need for us to play games. I know quite well who you are, just as you know quite well why you're going with us."

"If you know I'm Shelby Vale, then why are you taking me back? I'm not the woman you want."

"Oh, but you are."

"Why! Why me? You're after Winter Stapleton."

"Whatever gave you that idea?" His voice dripped amusement. Shelby blinked in surprise. She had no idea who this man was, but she did have a sudden sinking feeling that without her knowing it, the rules in the game she'd been playing had suddenly changed. "You'd better see if you can get some sleep. We'll be moving at dawn," he added, and pushed her gently inside. She heard the door lock click behind her.

Shelby was surprised to find the small house looked not only lived in, but reasonably comfortable as well. She lay down on the hand-hewn bunk positioned against one wall. After a few moments she realized just how tired she really was.

It was still dark when she was awakened by the sound of the door being unlocked and then opened. She sat up, still groggy from sleep.

It was Hank, carrying a bucket of water which he placed a few feet from the door without even looking at her.

"The boss says to go ahead and get cleaned up. Then come out, there's some breakfast ready. We have to be on our way."

Shelby nodded, but before she could speak he left, closing the door solidly behind him. It seemed pretty clear "the boss" had had a few words with Hank. She wondered about this quiet-spoken man who seemed almost a gentleman.

Outside, the three men were standing close to a small fire, and the scent of bacon and coffee made Shelby realize how hungry she was. She watched as the new leader bent to pick up a tin plate of food that had been placed on a rock near the fire to keep it warm. He carried it to her.

"You'd best eat well," he suggested firmly. "We have quite a ways to go and we won't be stopping for any meals."

"Why can't you tell me what this is all about?"

"Because it's not my affair. I was hired to bring you to a meeting place, not to explain anything to you."

Shelby watched as he returned to the fire and knelt on one knee to pour a tin cup full of coffee. He was a rather handsome man, somewhere in his late thirties or early forties. His face was expressionless, closed to the world. He was lean and strong-looking, as if he were well used to hard work. He was a puzzle, one piece that didn't fit in this charade they were playing.

As soon as Shelby was finished eating the three men made hasty preparations to leave. She realized she must have slept deeply, for sometime during the night the coach had gone and horses were being readied. Within half an hour they were mounted and on their way. The two men led the party, followed by Shelby, then Hank. She imagined the mysterious leader was pretty certain she wouldn't try anything foolish with Hank right behind her.

They rode at a steady pace. Occasionally the leader would look back over his shoulder and seemed satisfied with Shelby's ability to travel at such a pace.

Despite his satisfaction, Shelby was tired. By noon she was beginning to ache all over and was developing a fierce headache. Still, the group showed no sign of stopping. She clenched her teeth with grim determination. None of them would hear her beg or complain if she had to collapse first!

By midafternoon Shelby could have wept with exhaustion. In fact, she hardly realized they had stopped until the leader had spoken to her for the second time.

With surprisingly gentle hands he helped her down, and she stood unsteadily for a minute.

"Go sit under that tree while we scrape up some food."

Shelby was in no mood or condition to argue. It

was obvious he wouldn't tell her anything anyway, and she needed to retain all the strength of will and body she had. Wordlessly she obeyed.

He came to her a short time later carrying two tin plates in his hand. He gave her one, then, to her surprise, eased himself down on the ground a short distance from her and began to eat.

Brad backed up several steps while his mind grasped desperately for the right words . . . hell, for *any* words that would stop the massive bulk of furious humanity that was bearing down on him. The first words were definitely the wrong words.

"She's not here. You have to let me explain. It's not the way you seem to think it is."

Dobbs appeared behind Jasper. He'd heard Brad's words and they weren't what he wanted to hear, either.

"Dobbs! For God's sake!" Brad was looking at Jasper's advancing form. But Jasper was too close now, and Brad knew he was going to have to consider a way to defend himself. He'd never run across a time when he couldn't defend himself . . . until now.

He felt Jasper's hamlike fist explode against his jaw. Lights sparkled before his eyes and he felt his body rebound with a merciless force. The next thing he knew he was on his hands and knees, his head spinning and the taste of blood in his mouth. He had a feeling half the vertebra in his back were either cracked or broken, and taking a deep breath wasn't the easiest thing he'd ever done.

"Wait a minute . . ." he began.

"There ain't no need to wait. I been trailing you long enough. I know the games you been playin'. Now I want some answers." Jasper reached down and gathered the front of Brad's shirt in his fist and dragged him to his feet. When he put his face close to Brad's, Brad could not see an ounce of mercy in his angry, blazing eyes.

"Jasper," Dobbs said, "maybe you ought to let me try first to bring Mr. Cole to his senses."

Brad was all for this idea. At least Dobbs sounded like he might listen.

"Maybe if the two of you would listen to reason," Brad began. "I told you the truth. Shelby isn't here and you're wasting valuable time. We'll lose the trail if we wait much longer."

"What trail?" Jasper growled. "You ain't following no one."

"Damnit!" Brad returned his glare. "Someone came here while I was gone. Shelby didn't leave because she wanted to, she was dragged away from here against her will!" He could read the disbelief in Jasper's eyes. "Dobbs," he said, desperate to get free, knowing the miles separating him and Shelby were growing by the minute. "Leash this animal and let me explain . . ." This brought another growl from Jasper and a rough shake that rattled Brad's teeth and lifted his own anger another notch. He was about to engage in what he knew would be a one-sided affair with Jasper when Dobbs spoke.

"Shelby," he said in a soft, thoughtful voice. With intense relief, Brad knew what he was thinking.

"Yes . . . not Winter Stapleton, Shelby Vale . . . Shelby Vale," Brad watched Dobbs's eyes. "She told me the truth a long time ago. For God's sake, I would never hurt her." Brad could see Dobbs was assessing his words very carefully. "Dobbs, listen to me. Every second we waste is going to make it harder to get to her. I don't know who took her or why, but I've got to find her!"

"Jasper, let him go," Dobbs ordered. "I think we'd better listen to what he has to say." Jasper started to protest, but Dobbs put a restraining but gentle hand on his arm. "He's not going to do anything foolish, and for Shelby's sake I think we'd better listen. I have a feeling he's telling the truth." Brad breathed a ragged sigh of relief as he felt the huge hands slacken.

"I *am* telling the truth." As rapidly as he could, Brad explained how they came to be at his ranch. "We've got to leave now if I'm going to find any trail to follow."

"I don't believe a word of it," Jasper said angrily. He didn't want to believe it. "Let me force him to tell us the truth." His angry eyes held Brad's. "Tell me what you've done with her or I'll . . ." Brad realized suddenly that Jasper loved Shelby, was deathly afraid for her, and this was what fueled the anger.

"Jasper," he said quietly, his gaze locked with the angry gaze above him. "I'm not lying. I love her, too. I know how you feel. But if Shelby is going to be helped, she needs us both. While we fight each other, the men who've taken her are putting miles between us. We've got to work together or we'll lose her."

"I do believe he's right," Dobbs said quietly. "We have to work together."

For a breathless moment Brad didn't think Jasper intended to listen to a word either one of them had to say. Then slowly, reluctantly, he seemed to relax, and met Brad straight in the eye. "All right, go on and saddle your horse. But I'll be keeping a close watch on you. You'd better not try any of your fancy tricks."

Dobbs spoke thoughtfully. "I think it would be best, Jasper, if you and Mr. Cole went on ahead and followed the trail. Leave a good trail for me. I'm going to go back and wire Mr. Stapleton. We'll see what he has to say. I should be able to catch up with you in a few hours."

Neither Brad nor Jasper were much in favor of this. Brad didn't trust Jasper's anger that far. Still, he was overcome by the urgent need to get on the trail the abductors had taken and find Shelby as fast as he could.

Jasper waited while Brad rapidly saddled his horse. Brad could feel his gaze burning holes in his back.

"I'll make it as fast as I can, Jasper," Dobbs was saying.

"Maybe we should wait here until you get back. Neither of us has looked through the house yet. For all we know she could be tied up in there. He's done that before."

"I doubt if he's lying, but if it makes you feel better, go and look. I'll keep an eye on him."

"Yeah, maybe I'd better." He cast Brad a cold look and left the barn to walk toward the house.

Dobbs chuckled softly at Brad's obvious relief to have Jasper out of his vicinity for a while.

"You'll have to forgive him, he gets a little carried away when there's a threat to those he cares for."

"A little!" Brad replied. He spat out the taste of blood that still lingered and touched the cracked lip Jasper had provided. "I'd hate to see him really angry if you call that a little."

"You can't blame him, my friend. His job was to protect Shelby. He cares a great deal for her. You made his job a bit difficult. He became somewhat annoyed with you because he was so worried about Shelby."

Brad laughed at Dobbs's way of understanding things. "I think he was more than 'somewhat annoyed.' But I guess I can't blame him. It's pretty much what I'm feeling right now for whoever is responsible for this."

Jasper was struggling with his anger. He'd found the house empty, but he had also found the note Brad had left for Abigail. Its short message was proof Brad was telling the truth. Still, Jasper didn't want to let go so easily. Brad never should have taken Shelby in the first place and subjected her to the conditions he had. No, Jasper was not ready to forgive Brad Cole yet, not by a long shot.

As Jasper and Brad rode away, Dobbs refrained from any sign of laughter. It was, he was certain, not going to be a comfortable ride.

*   *   *

The moon was high by the time they camped again that night. Shelby had no idea of the time, but she knew they had pushed remorselessly to put a great deal of distance between them and whoever might follow.

She was extremely tired, but she refused to complain and never noticed the look of admiration in the eyes of the leader of the group.

The ride seemed to go on and on until Shelby lost track of everything but how miserable she felt. For the third time they had traveled long into the night.

It had to be well after midnight when the ground they were on eased down into a small valley. The lights of a small town nestled between the hills came into view.

Shelby watched the three men closely and soon realized this town was a place they meant to stop. The leader took a watch from his pocket and consulted it. Then he turned to the other two.

"Make camp. I'll be back in hour or so." The two men nodded. "And, Hank," the leader's voice had a chill that made the hair on the back of Shelby's neck prickle. "You touch her and you'll answer to me. You understand?"

"Sure . . . sure, Dakota. Sure."

So his name was Dakota, Shelby thought. She heard him give a dry mirthless chuckle.

Shelby watched him ride away, puzzled by the unique man. A man who would kidnap a woman, who talked like a cultured gentleman, and who had the power to instill fear and respect in the men who worked with him. She had a million questions she would have liked to ask, and knew he wouldn't answer any of them.

The two men made camp, ignoring her to the best of their ability and still seeing that she didn't get away. They prepared supper, gave her a tin plate of food, and again left her alone.

They sat far away from her so that their low-spoken words didn't carry, and Shelby wasn't too sure she cared to hear what they were discussing, anyway.

Shelby was very tired. She relaxed against her saddle and drew her blanket over her. She wondered how far behind her Brad could be. There was no doubt in her mind that in time he would find her. It was up to her to see that he had that time. She would find a way . . . Her eyes grew heavy and her exhausted body relaxed. She drifted into a deep deep, dreamless sleep.

It was well past three in the morning when Dakota returned. Hank and John sat before a low-burning fire.

"She's asleep?" he questioned quietly.

"Yeah," Hank replied, "been asleep for a couple of hours. What are we going to do now?"

"The train's coming in in the morning. You two get some sleep yourselves. In a few hours our job will be over."

Gratefully the two men rolled in their blankets. Dakota remained by the fire. After a while he turned and looked at Shelby. Then, in a slow, quiet movement he stood, walked the short distance between them without making a sound, and knelt on one knee beside her. In the light of the full moon Shelby looked very vulnerable.

She did not awaken. If she had she would not have understood the expression that fleeted across his face. He had made a decision. He rose and went back to the fire.

True to Dobbs' prediction, Jasper and Brad rode together in tension-filled silence. Brad knew Jasper was not only still angry with him for taking Shelby the way he did, but he was even more angry over the fact that he believed Brad was to blame for wherever Shelby was right now.

What made it worse was that Brad blamed himself, too. He had relaxed his usual vigil, and he had made it easy for her abductors.

Jasper had watched Brad closely and realized within an hour that he was very adept at what he was doing. The slightest evidence was seen with sharp eyes. Still, the shadows of early evening were falling and there was no sign of Shelby or her abductors. It was then they spotted the shack. Brad drew his horse to a halt and Jasper did the same, looking at him curiously.

"What?" Jasper said. "What's so special about that decrepit-looking place?"

"It's the old stage relay station."

"You think she's there."

"No. But some very wise man might just have tried to pull a fancy little trick on us."

"Like what?"

"Like taking a stage."

"Hell, this place ain't been used for a long time. Just look at it."

"You're right. But old Dice Macklin still lives there. He had nowhere to go when the line changed. They felt sorry for him, and he stays and takes care of the place. If a stage needs to come this way, he's here to see it's taken care of."

"You think maybe . . ."

"Yeah," Brad said quietly, "just maybe. Come on."

Before they drew their horses to a halt, the door to the shack opened and Dice stepped out onto the porch. He hoped the fear he felt didn't show on his face or in his eyes. He knew Brad, and he didn't like the looks of the man who rode with him. Hank's threat echoed in his mind. He had a pretty good idea why Brad was here.

"Hey, Brad, what're you doin' round these parts? I ain't seen you for a month of Sundays."

"Dice," Brad replied as he stepped down and walked toward him. "There been a stage through here lately?"

"A stage through here," Dice laughed nervously. "Hell, they ain't been one for over three months."

"You're sure about that?"

"Yeah . . . real sure."

"What kind of animal you think makes tracks like that?" Brad questioned as he pointed. Dice's face went pale. He'd thought all signs had been taken care of, but about twenty feet from them ran two lines deeply imbedded in the dirt, obviously made by a wagon . . . or a stage.

"Jasper," Brad said in a voice softly full of threat, "I think you'd better step down and come over here. Old Dice needs a bit of convincing."

Dice licked his dry lips and backed up a step as the mountain of a man slowly dismounted. He felt his courage draining out like the sand in an hourglass.

"Look . . . ah . . . Brad. Maybe I was mistaken."

"I think you were. There was a stage and a girl."

"Yeah."

"How many?"

"Just the girl . . . and two men. They put her on the stage and took off. I don't know nothin' else."

"You knew them, didn't you?"

"Look, Brad . . . they'll—"

"I wouldn't worry about them. I'd worry about my friend here. He has a real short temper. As far as those two are concerned, we plan on making sure they don't cause anyone any problems."

Dice could hear in Brad's voice that the biggest threat of his life stood before him. "You know that girl? She did seem a bit skittish . . . like maybe she was scared."

"She happens to be the girl I plan to marry."

"She wasn't hurt!"

"She was scared," Brad said coldly, "that's bad enough. Where were they headed?"

Dice cast Jasper another stricken look. "I swear to God, Brad, I don't know." Jasper's face looked fierce. "I don't! Honest to God! I'd tell you if I did.

I don't think they was takin' the stage that far. It was . . ."

"To throw any followers off their trail," Brad added.

"Yeah." Dice cast another pleading look from Brad to Jasper, who continued to approach. "Brad?"

"Forget it, Jasper. He's telling the truth. We'd better get a move on. Once they leave the coach they'll probably have fresh horses. We'd need to move as fast as we can now."

Dice breathed a ragged sigh of relief when both Jasper and Brad remounted. He'd thought Hank was a threat, but he'd never tasted real fear until he'd looked into Jasper's eyes and saw the fire there.

Brad and Jasper rode on, again in an explosive silence. Both were engrossed in their troubled thoughts: worry that they might not be able to catch up with Shelby's abductors . . . and fear that if and when they did . . . what they would find.

It was barely light enough to see when Shelby awoke. The fire had burned down to gray embers, and Hank lay curled in his blanket, close to it. Shelby sat up and looked around, wondering if she had an opportunity to try to slip away.

It was then she saw her captor, sitting some distance away.

Again her curiosity was aroused. He was not a man cut from the same cloth as Hank, and she was certain his shadowed background included an education and a gentile upbringing.

She could hear culture in his voice, and see it in his eyes when he looked at her. Shelby rose slowly and walked toward him. He was the first to speak.

"You're awake early." His voice was low and deep.

"So are you."

When he turned to look at her, she could see a quick smile that died almost at birth.

"Shelby Vale," he said quietly, "you're not what I expected."

"Obviously you've been told some untruths."

"Maybe. Don't believe that it makes a difference, though. I've been hired to do a job and I'll do it."

"That is pretty mercenary when lives are at stake."

"You have a sharp tongue."

"It's what I see as the truth."

He turned his face from her again, as if he was giving her words a great deal of thought.

"You're right, it *is* the truth. A mercenary is what I am. I'm paid very well for what I do and I'm good at it."

"Tell me," her voice was chilled, "what is a life worth today?"

"A life?" he laughed dryly. "No one intends to kill you or even to harm you. My job is to take you back to the man you left behind. The man you seem to owe a great deal to."

"There is only one man I owe any debt to, and he would be the first to wish me well. In fact, he is the reason I am here."

"Do all women lie when it is convenient for them?"

"I don't lie!"

"And of course you have no idea who Mr. Carl James is, do you?" He saw her stiffen and surmised it was because he had caught her in a lie. This he understood, he thought. Who knew better than he what a woman's lies could do to a man. "Go back and get as much rest as you can. Sometime before noon tomorrow his train will arrive here. You can settle your disagreements with him then."

"If you would only listen! This is a mistake. I know that if we could just wait a while I could prove to you what you're doing is wrong."

"I can't do that. I don't betray a man who hires me."

"You just take his word that what he says is true."

Again his mirthless laugh touched her. "I've found out that it's not very wise to believe a woman when she sets out to have her way."

"But . . ."

"Don't waste your time. You'd better get some more sleep. It will be morning soon, then you can be rid of us. I don't expect you'll be crying over the lack of Hank's company."

"Why do you work with him?"

"He's fast with a gun and stupid enough to follow orders without giving me too much grief. Besides, who else would I travel with, if not an outlaw?"

"You and Hank are so completely different. He's an animal."

"And me?"

"You . . . you're an enigma. You were not born to this life. Tell me," she said softly, "who was she?"

"She? What are you talking about?" His voice was brittle and defensive.

"The woman who drove you to this."

For the first time since she'd been kidnapped she heard anger in his voice. He rose and walked to stand inches from her. "Don't pry into what's none of your business, and don't try playing any of your sweet games with me. They won't work. Go back to your blanket, Miss Vale, or do I have to tie you up and gag you?"

She could hear, beneath the anger, a pain too intense for him to handle. "I feel sorry for you. It's a shame to give your life to someone who wasn't worth it. You're dying and you don't have enough compassion to have pity on yourself and begin again. All women are not alike."

She left him standing there and went back to her blanket. Minutes later she saw him sit down again and turn his gaze to the distance.

Chapter 20

Brad was beside himself with angry frustration when they finally had to stop. There simply was no way to see the trail closely enough to follow it. Jasper was no happier than he was.

When they had eaten, they settled down to get some rest. Still, both knew neither of them would find sleep very easy.

"I guess you've known Shelby a long time," Brad began a bit hesitantly.

"I was a good friend of her father's before he died. I've known Shelby since she was a little girl."

"You must have cared a great deal for the Stapleton family, too."

"They were nice people. Until Winter's mother died and her father remarried. He made a mistake that could have cost him everything. It was a good thing he recognized the danger before it was too late."

"So he set up this little game."

"It wasn't a game and we all had a little more

confidence than we should have had. I guess none of us counted on you."

"I can't say I'm sorry for it. I would never have met Shelby any other way. We were half a world apart." The pain of possibly losing her made his voice waver. "Do you think they're dragging her back to force 'Winter' into the wedding, The people who have Shelby *can't* know they have the wrong girl."

"Hmm. Winter should be married by now. If that's the truth, surely Mr. Stapleton would have let the word out. I'm beginning to worry that Shelby might have fallen into the hands of someone who has something bigger in mind."

"Like what?"

"I don't know. Now that he's got his control back, Joseph Stapleton is wealthy and Shelby is even wealthier."

"What?"

"Shelby has a trust from her grandfather that will make her a rich girl. I think she'll be old enough to step into it in another year or so. She told us all about it on the way out."

Brad was silent long enough for Jasper to realize he'd said something that had quite a potent effect on him. He was about to question it when a sound drew their attention.

"Someone's coming," Jasper said.

Brad drew his gun and held it ready. Both breathed sigh of relief when Dobbs rode into camp.

"You two have moved pretty fast," he commented

by way of greeting. "I didn't know I'd have to travel half the night to catch up. What have you found?"

Brad filled him in.

"What about you, Dobbs? What did you find out?"

"Joseph said to track Shelby as fast as you can. Winter is married and he is planning a showdown. He's scared for her."

"Then Shelby is in more danger than we realized," Brad spoke angrily.

"Let's don't let anger control us," Dobbs said. "Let's just put every effort into finding her. We'll get our answers when we do."

"You have your own suspicions, don't you?" Brad asked.

"I suppose I do. Suspicions, not proof."

"Who?"

"Winter's stepmother . . . and Carl James, they have the most to gain from this . . . and the most to lose when they find out Winter's married and they've been after the wrong girl."

"Dobbs . . ."

"There's nothing more I can say. We have to find out who, why . . . and where they're taking her before we can do much. If you remember, Mr. Cole," Dobbs said, "Shelby has always been very resourceful."

Brad paused, hope in his eyes again. "Shelby *is* pretty clever. But she's dealing with different men now."

"Still, if they're connected to Anne, they'll have come to take her back, with us hot on their trail. You are also a very resourceful person, but do you recall how difficult Shelby was?"

"Do I remember . . ." Brad had to smile reluctantly. "What is it you're saying, Dobbs?"

"I'm saying keep faith in the fact that she'll not only give them a run for their money, but that she'll have hope as well. Hope and faith in the fact that we won't give up until we find her."

Brad's gaze held Dobbs's eyes for a long moment, then he smiled grimly. "We'll find her, Dobbs, that I can promise you."

"I know," Dobbs smiled, "I know. Now it's time to rest a bit. I believe we have a long hard trail before us. We," he paused for dramatic effect, "are going to the first town that has a railroad and a theater."

"A theater," Brad repeated.

"Of course," Dobbs grinned, "we'll trace Shelby the same way you did. We know it and so does she, but I'm sure they don't. I predict Shelby Vale will perform again, and our dear kidnappers will regret the day she does."

Shelby hadn't been able to sleep again, and when Hank awoke, the four of them ate breakfast and silently waited for the time to pass. Shelby was quite aware of Dakota's efforts not to look at her any more than he had to. He seemed to be worrying something over in his mind.

The sun rose higher and still they waited. Shelby began to wonder just who she was going to have to face. She knew that somewhere behind them, Brad, and Jasper and Dobbs as well, she hoped, were searching for her. She had only to slow the situation down until one of them found her. The only problem was she hadn't the faintest notion how she was going to do that.

By the time the sun was overhead, Shelby's nerves were stretched. She stood, paced for a minute, then walked a few feet away to look down into the valley. She sensed Dakota coming to stand behind her.

"I think I'd better make one thing very clear to you before you get a lot of ideas about what you might do when we get into town. I don't want anything to happen to you, and it won't if you behave. Keep your head and be quiet until we get this over with. Do you understand me?"

"Yes, I understand you," Shelby said. It surprised her that he seemed more the protector than the abductor.

"I'm not a fool. I won't do anything stupid."

Before he could say anything more the distant sound of a train whistle came to them. "Come on, it's time to go."

"Dakota?"

"What?"

"I'm not like the woman who hurt you so badly," she said softly. "Give another thought to what you're doing."

"I've given it all the thought I need. *You* think about it. Go back and settle your problems instead of running out on them."

She could see her battle was useless. This man had

a shell about him that she would never penetrate. She sighed deeply and walked toward her horse.

Carl James stepped down onto the train platform and looked around him with a sense of satisfaction. He'd been very smart to choose the men he had. Hank and John had been no problem, he knew them for what they were. Dakota had been a different matter. He'd had to . . . elaborate on the truth to get his cooperation and he had known his weak point and played upon it expertly.

And he'd succeeded. Shelby Vale would be in his hands in a short while. He'd thought about her all the way out on the train, making a decision on the most profitable way to handle the situation.

At first he had decided that one wealthy Stapleton was as good as another. But he soon realized his position would be an even better one with Shelby than as Winter's husband. He had time, he would consider what was the best route to take.

He quickly acquired a hotel, room where he, dropped his suitcase, removed his jacket, and sat down comfortably to wait. A half hour later he consulted his watch, but he was not impatient. His fortune was coming to him.

It was another half hour before he heard someone stop before his door and knock. When he opened the door he smiled.

"Hello, Shelby. My, you have given everyone a merry chase, haven't you? You've been missed terribly. Everyone was worried sick."

"Please, don't continue with this act. I know you must be Carl James. Now, what is going on?"

"I only have the pleasure of taking you home, where you belong." He took Shelby's arm in a grip that was iron hard and far from gentle. He drew her inside, and the others followed. But he didn't shut the door. Instead, he took his leather wallet from his breast pocket.

"Dakota, I'm grateful for all you've done to reunite a family. Here's the money I promised." He handed Dakota a sheaf of bills. Dakota was a bit surprised at himself that he was reluctant to take them. "I guess that will satisfy the agreement," Carl asked pleasantly.

"Yes, yes it does," Dakota replied. He knew he was expected to leave. He looked at Shelby and saw the coldness in her eyes and the proud lift of her chin. Without another word, he turned and left the room.

Carl turned to look at Hank and John, and smiled, "I think I will need both your services for just a bit longer. We have tickets on the late train tonight. Until then, we will just have to make ourselves comfortable." Again Carl turned to Shelby. "I trust you're not going to make me any trouble."

"Don't count on it," she smiled back at him. "I'll make you every ounce of trouble that I can. Tell me, what do you plan to do?"

"I don't know yet. You spoiled some very important plans Winter's mother and I had."

"She's not Winter's mother, and spoiling her plans was exactly what we meant to do. Since Winter is married, it seems we were quite a success."

The smile never left Carl's face, but he reached out so quickly that Shelby was unprepared. The slap sounded like a rifle crack, and Shelby was flung backward onto the bed. For a minute pain held her breathless and tears filled her eyes. Still she struggled to her feet, pressing her hand against the throbbing cheek that would soon show a bruise.

"Don't get clever with me. You're not going to cause me any trouble unless you want to see a lot of others pay for it. My friends here aren't too fussy who gets gunned down. If you don't behave, you'll be responsible for a lot of grief."

Shelby knew he meant every word, and looking at Hank made her realize the sobering fact that Dakota was no longer around to give her any protection at all.

"What do you want from me?"

"We're going back to Charleston. You either behave . . . or pay the price for whatever difficulties you cause."

"And in Charleston?"

"That's my affair for now. You just keep in mind that if you cause me any real trouble along the way I'll allow Hank to take care of it . . . and you. Trust me, my dear, you won't enjoy it."

"Why do you want me? Winter's wealth . . . position . . . everything, are out of your hands and I hope, by now, her precious stepmother's as well."

"You must allow me some credit, I know what you'll be worth. You see, I don't have all my eggs in one basket. A marriage would be a most satisfactory conclusion."

"I'd do away with myself first," Shelby snapped.

"Ah," Carl laughed. "Taming you might prove very interesting. I have not considered all points yet. Once we get back to Charleston we shall just find which way would be the most advantageous for me."

Shelby returned his look with cold disdain. She knew she would never surrender to him. Deep inside she knew that Brad was following her. She had only to stall for time, to slow them down until Brad could find her.

"You may was well get settled. We'll be taking the next train out."

Shelby sagged into a chair, her mind spinning. She had no doubt that Hank would carry out any threats and she could visualize the destruction he could wield. No, she would not do anything foolish, but she *would* take advantage of any situation that came up that offered her a glimpse of freedom.

Later that afternoon, she walked between Carl, Hank, and John to a nearby restaurant where she forced down food. She needed all her strength if she meant to outwit Carl.

They were just leaving the restaurant when she noticed the little man bustling toward them, his bald head agleam with perspiration and a wide smile on his face. It took a minute for Shelby to recognize him. She smiled. Fate was dealing her a new hand. She felt Carl's hand tighten on her arm as the man greeted her delighted chatter.

"Miss Vale! Miss Vale! How wonderful to see you again. Had you told me you were coming I would have made arrangements. The entire town would have swarmed out to hear you sing again!" He clasped one of her hands in his and fairly beamed at her. Shelby was quick to grasp the opportunity.

"Why, Mr. Charles. How delightful. I'm sorry I didn't get a chance to wire you, but I didn't know I would be visiting again so soon. Since you were so charming and so gallant, I would be delighted to sing in your theater again." She almost gasped and cried out as Carl's hand tightened painfully.

"I'm afraid we have a train to catch," he said. "What is the gentleman saying, my dear? You are not . . ."

"But I am," Shelby smiled despite Carl's brutal hold. "I have sung in Mr. Charles's theaters before . . . all the way from Charleston. He would be very . . . upset if I didn't sing again. Heaven knows who he would—"

"All right. But our train prohibits—"

"Oh, the next train is not until ten-thirty. There is plenty of time and we would be so grateful. We'll see you get to the station on time," Mr. Charles said anxiously.

"I'd be delighted to sing for your lovely town again." Shelby smiled sweetly at Carl as she spoke and saw the rage that lit his eyes. "But I'm afraid I have no costumes with me."

"Oh, not to worry, dear lady. The theater is full of costumes, you can just take your choice. I shall go and make preparations at once so we can spread the word. Why, I believe we still have the posters we put out the last time you entertained here."

"Excellent," Shelby smiled, even though Carl's fingers were leaving marks on her arms.

"I'm afraid we will have to supply some makeup as well. Whatever happened to your face, dear lady?"

"Oh just a little accident," she smiled at Carl. "I ran across a snake and had to escape being bitten."

"Good heavens, how terrible. It was killed, I hope."

"I'm afraid I couldn't do that myself, but I have hopes it will be taken care of in due time."

Carl inhaled deeply and Shelby could read easily the desire to strangle her.

"I'll be at the theater by seven if that is all right with you."

"Fine! Fine. Oh, I'm so excited. I shall look forward to hearing you sing again. I must go and make preparations."

Shelby watched with a smile as he scuttled off to go about his business.

"You think you're very clever," Carl snarled. "But your excitable little friend might just be the first victim of your cleverness. At the theater tonight Hank and I will remain very close to him . . . should you try any other tricks. He's my insurance, you might say, that you'll finish up this little charade you've begun and be prepared to leave on the train tonight. I'd hate to see him pay for your trickery."

"Oh, I intend no trickery. I shall sing and leave with you peacefully," Shelby replied. Just being seen was enough for her. It was a trail Brad could follow, had followed before. He would find out what train they had left on and where the stops would be. It would certainly not surprise her to find him waiting at one of the stops when they arrived.

They continued on to the hotel, Shelby with a secret smile, Carl with a seething rage, and Hank and his companion with the shaky sensation filling them that maybe they had caught a tiger by the tail. Hank began to wish he'd never seen Shelby Vale.

That night Shelby stood between Carl, Hank, and John in the wings at the theater, which was filled to overflowing. Mr. Charles, the still abundantly excited owner, was on the stage calming the audience and expounding on Shelby's voice and charm.

"Just remember," Carl said quietly to Shelby, "he'll be standing right here with us. One little trick and that little rooster will have crowed his last."

"I'll remember. But don't hurt him. He's harmless."

"Hank isn't. Just keep that in mind."

The roar of applause silenced anything Shelby might have answered.

The applause grew as Mr. Charles came off the stage and Shelby walked on. She could feel the warmth of the audience as it surrounded her. Grateful tears welled in her eyes and she finally raised her hands to bring the applause under control.

She didn't know that Dakota was sitting in the audience. After he'd left Carl's room he was more than uncomfortable with the situation. Something he couldn't name ate at him like a sickness. At first, when he saw a poster being nailed up he was surprised. Then he was curious. Something about Shelby had touched him in a mysterious way. He'd bought a ticket, and now he sat, watching the stage.

When Shelby began to sing, she reached out and touched the deepest well of memories inside him. She opened the doors so gently that he had no time to close the defenses he'd built for so many years. He sat through the next two songs, then, to the aggravation of the people sitting next to him, he rose and left the theater. He needed time alone to consider what had just happened.

He walked across the street to the saloon, ordered a bottle, and carried it to a table in the corner of the room.

Shelby sang four songs. The applause filled the theater, and to her pleasure she saw that Hank, John, and Carl were, to say the least, impatient. This only made her more obstinate and she decided to sing until the people were satisfied.

It was past nine o'clock when she walked from the stage. She was gloriously tired and definitely pleased with the looks on Carl and Hank's faces. Her mind was spinning the whole time of the performance, and now she intended to throw another block at Carl.

Mr. Charles greeted her when she came off stage by taking both her hands in his.

"Miss Vale, you were exquisite. I cannot say how grateful I am. This has been a night I shall always remembered. How I wish . . ."

"What, Mr. Charles?" Shelby urged him hope-

fully, sure she knew what he was going to say. She
knew Mr. Charles owned a string of small theaters
from here nearly back to St. Louis.

Mr. Charles licked his lips. "I know the train will
stop for several hours in the next town."

"Yes?" she continued to urge him. Hoping he
would ask before Carl could figure it out and halt
him.

"I . . . well, you know I also . . ."

"Say no more, Mr. Charles. I should be happy to
stop and sing a few more songs."

"Yes." Carl's cold voice seemed to emerge from
nowhere. "In fact, it would please us if you were to
travel with us."

Shelby cast him a surprised look. She hadn't
counted on this. She'd hoped to leave the defenseless
and mild-mannered Mr. Charles safely behind. "I'm
sure Shelby will enjoy your company."

"Oh! Oh! This is wonderful. Thank you so much.
I shall dash right out and purchase my ticket at once.
What a delight. I shall meet you at the station." He
pressed a cold, damp kiss to her hand and raced away
as if he was afraid she would change her mind.

Shelby could hear Carl's chuckle. She had given
him a hostage and she knew that he was certain
Shelby would do nothing to endanger his life.

"Sometimes," Carl said softly, "it doesn't pay to
get too clever. We can trip over our own little tricks,
can't we, my dear Shelby? I do believe our Mr.
Charles will make a fine guard against you doing
anything more to disrupt this trip."

Shelby remained silent. Let his mind remain on

Mr. Charles. Her mind and her heart were with Brad. One more town, one more stop, would add to Brad's precious time. Surely he would come soon.

They met Mr. Charles at the station after they had gathered their belongings at the hotel. At precisely ten-thirty the train chugged away from the station.

Shelby was so exhausted that she felt her body sagging and her eyes growing heavy. She settled herself as comfortably as she could and drifted into sleep. Hank regarded her with annoyance, Mr. Charles with a look close to adoration, and Carl with a regard that, had she been awake, would have truly frightened her.

Carl had watched her performance on stage very closely. At first he felt a strong anger, but as she sang, a new emotion developed.

A woman with a future inheritance, and a talent and beauty such as Shelby's would be a considerable asset to Carl. He could see himself controlling her future, her career, and her money. Controlling them as her husband, with the right to control and possess all her obvious charms as well. Yes, the thought intrigued him. Anne and Jeffrey could land in hell for all he cared. They could fend for themselves. He would have Shelby, her money, and her future. He'd end up on top as he always did.

It was nearly three in the morning when they arrived in the next town. Carl sent Hank to the hotel to get two rooms. Mr. Charles bustled off to make plans. Shelby rose stiffly from her seat and refused to protest Carl's merciless grip as he took her from the train.

When they arrived at the hotel, Carl told Hank and John to get some rest. They would take turns watching Shelby. Carl would take the first watch. Hank was too tired to care, but Shelby was alarmed. Spending the rest of the night in a hotel room with Carl James was more than dangerous. She reached mentally for her courage.

Carl closed the door, then locked it and put the key in his pocket. He turned to Shelby who was watching him warily. In the morning he would send a wire. After her final performance in this town they would go on . . . to the next town . . . and to Shelby's wedding.

"I have no intention of harming you in any way, Shelby. You might as well get some rest. I shall be quite comfortable in this chair for a few hours." He could see the doubt in her eyes and he smiled. "I promise you, you will be unharmed. You must sing soon, and . . . my plans begin only when I get you back to Charleston," he lied glibly.

Still unsure that she could believe a word he said, Shelby sat on the bed and wrapped a blanket around her, then lay back against the pillows. Despite her struggle, she fell asleep.

He watched her as she slept. Her pale hair became undone and fell about her in glorious profusion. The hand holding the blanket relaxed and rested just below her breasts. A delicate hand with long, tapered, and sensitive fingers. Her breathing was steady and even, and he felt his body respond to the rise and fall of the soft flesh beneath the dress.

He could almost feel how her skin would be, soft

and warm. The parted mouth looked lush and inviting, and as he watched her, he made himself a lot of promises. Yes, he would enjoy Shelby and all she could offer to the fullest.

Brad hadn't been able to sleep. A million visions danced through his head. All of the past weeks flowed like a series of pictures. Shelby, the first time he'd seen her, standing in that circle of light in the center of a dark stage. Shelby, angry and storming after he'd carried her away the first time. The laughter in her eyes and the teasing kiss she'd given him when she'd tied him up and left him. The tricks she had tried her best to play on him with Whitehawk and Dave Raymond. The helplessness he'd felt when she had become ill, followed by the realization of how he had grown to love her. And then the glorious magic of making love to her. He had tasted a love so giving, so warm, and so gentle it had twined tendrils around his heart that could never be released.

Other visions crowded his mind, visions he wanted to ignore but couldn't. Shelby, needing him, caught in a trap from which she could not escape. It set his mind on fire and he sat up abruptly, uttering an oath.

He put more wood on the fire, resenting the fact that Jasper slept like a proverbial log, his snore renting the air. Brad fought the urge to kick him. He was jolted when Dobbs's voice came to him.

"Can't you sleep?"

"Seems you can't, either," Brad responded.

"No. I'm afraid not." Dobbs sat up, too, and he

and Brad contemplated each other across the fire. Finally, Dobbs smiled. "We all love her, Brad."

"I know."

"To Jasper she's a sister. To me a daughter. To you . . ."

"She's every breath I take, every beat of my heart. I can't lose her, Dobbs, I can't."

"The trail and the knowledge of the train station leads us to a town we performed in before. I have a feeling we'll get word of Shelby when we arrive."

They talked a while, then Dobbs drifted into sleep and Brad was left with his dreams.

When dawn finally came, all three were already mounted and on their way. Brad was an excellent tracker, but after some time he had to admit grudgingly that Jasper was better. Places where the trail had been vague or, to Brad, nonexistent seemed to pose little difficulty to Jasper. Brad admired and resented this in the same breath. and it didn't pass Jasper's notice. In fact, it pleased him a great deal. Jasper just wasn't quite ready to forgive and forget that. Brad had taken Shelby from under his nose.

He hadn't spoken very much to Brad during the trip. Maybe Shelby could heal the breech in time, Brad thought.

The three crested a hill and looked with satisfaction at the town below. The silver ribbons of track that ran past the town offered hope that they were on the right trail.

Chapter 21

Joseph stepped down from his carriage with a look of satisfaction on his face. His daughter was safely married to the man she loved, the man who was right for her. Now, he had other arrangements to see to before he went home.

Despite the plans he had made, he had been enticed to stay in Georgetown a few days longer. On an evening two days later, he had shared a drink with Carson. They were the best of friends, and Joseph confided in him. He fully intended to sever the ties to the past and to set his house in order. He could not live with the way things had been in the past year.

If nothing else, Carson's words of support and consolation were a comfort. His decisions were made, now he had only to match his actions to them.

His banker was first, and when he began to explain what he wanted, the man was not only speechless, his eyes grew wider with each word.

"You mean . . . everything?"

"Yes, everything. It's time I began to accept what has happened and rearrange my life."

"Joseph . . ." the banker's eyes were sympathetic.

"I know, William. You needn't say it. The old adage is true. There is no fool like an old fool. But I'm not too late, thank God."

"You needn't worry. I'll do everything I can to help you."

"I appreciate it. Handle everything as expeditiously as you can."

"I'll do that. What is your next step?"

"I'm going to see Herbert Magill."

"Your attorney."

"My attorney," Joseph smiled, then rose and extended his hand to William. "It's time a few other very necessary changes were made."

"I wish you luck, Joseph, and if I can be of any more help please let me know. I'll see that all your accounts are taken care of at once."

"Very good. Thank you again. I'll be talking to you soon. I intend to have a huge celebration one day soon. My daughter will be home with her new husband. I'd like all my friends there to help us celebrate."

"That's wonderful. Let us know. My wife and I will be delighted to join you."

"Again, thank you."

William followed Joseph to the door, and when he closed it behind him he smiled. For the first time in a long while he had his old friend back and that made him feel very good.

Joseph, too, felt good as he again got back into his carriage and made his way to the office of the attorney who had also been his friend for over thirty years.

He was welcomed effusively.

"Joseph, my friend, I haven't seen you for a long time. I was just telling Anne when she came to see me a few days ago that we hadn't seen you for some time. Is this visit pleasure or business? If it's pleasure I'll take you to lunch at a fine little restaurant not far from here."

Joseph realized he wasn't surprised that Anne had been to visit Herbert. As clever as she had been, she wouldn't have let this stone go unturned. It only made his determination firmer. Anne had a lot of surprises coming.

"It's a combination, Herbert. I'll take you up on the lunch, but there's some business we have to transact first."

"Business?"

"Yes. I want to change my will."

Herbert looked at Joseph in a combination of surprise and curiosity.

"I have a lot of changes to make and I want them to be made as rapidly as possible."

Herbert sat down behind his desk and slid a note pad toward him, picked up a pen and dipped it in a nearby inkwell. "All right, just what changes do you want?"

Joseph began to talk, and for a minute Herbert's hand hovered over the pad and his face registered an even deeper surprise. But as Joseph continued to talk, Herbert began to smile. Then he began to write.

It took some time before a satisfied Joseph stopped talking and Herbert sat back in his seat. "You certainly did make changes."

"I take it you agree?"

"I hesitated to say anything to you before, but . . . yes, I agree. I'm sorry. You and I have been friends a long time, Joseph, and I'd like to see you at peace and have some of the happiness you richly deserve."

"Well, I have taken the first step. Now . . . there is one more step I want to take."

It was midafternoon when Joseph's carriage deposited him in front of his home. Inside, he questioned the butler and as Roberts took his coat.

"Is my . . . wife at home?"

"Yes sir. She's in the library . . . with Mr. Brenner."

"Excellent," Joseph smiled at Roberts's puzzled look. "I want you to get my wife's maid. Tell her to please pack all . . . all," he emphasized, "Anne's belongings. Every stitch of clothing. She will take more than she came with, but none of her jewerly is to be packed. It belonged to Martha. Tell her to deposit her luggage in the hall."

This only confused Roberts more.

"The hall, sir?"

"Yes. Tell her to do it right away. She has a lot of work to do, and I want her to get started at once. My . . . Mrs. Stapleton will be leaving today on an extended trip."

Joseph did not miss the smile on Roberts's face as he walked away. He began to wonder how many more servants would be pleased to hear the news he was about to impart on his beloved . . . and very unfaithful wife.

He walked with determined steps toward the library. He paused and listened at the closed door to the sound of laughter from inside. Anne and Jeffrey. He knew now the real relationship between the two, in fact had enough evidence to push them both from his life once and for all. He opened the door and stepped inside so abruptly that the two of them, who had been standing so close together, leapt apart guiltily. But Anne, consummate actress that she was, recovered quickly, smiled, and walked toward him.

He watched her, realizing for perhaps the first time that it was only his extreme loneliness and the loss of Martha that had allowed him to be blinded by Anne. She exuded raw sensuality, but her eyes were as cold and calculating as those of any wanton whore. Still, he no longer hated her as he had before. Instead, he felt sorry for her. She would never know love as he had known it, and when her beauty faded he had a feeling she would taste the loneliness in a way he never had.

"Joseph, my dear, how was your trip? Where did you go?" She attempted to kiss his cheek, but he grasped her shoulders and held her away. She blinked in surprise, but still the coldness in his eyes did not penetrate her mind. Then his eyes met Jeffrey's over Anne's head. Suddenly Jeffrey stiffened and became alert. Something had gone dreadfully wrong.

"I shan't interrupt your reunion," Jeffrey said quickly. "I must be on my way." He started toward the door, but Joseph remained motionless, blocking the way. Jeffrey paused.

"No, no, Jeffrey." Joseph said so quietly it sounded like velvet-covered steel, "you stay for a while. We have some things to discuss, and I know they will interest you."

"I . . ." Jeffrey began, but any weak excuses fled his mind when Joseph's eyes hardened. "Yes . . . yes, of course."

"Sit down, Anne. I think I have some very unhappy news for you."

"Joseph, what in heaven's name is the matter with you? You seem so . . . so ominous," Anne had finally realized his gaze was not warm at all.

"Anne, for God's sake shut up," Jeffrey hissed softly.

"Yes, Anne," Joseph smiled for the first time, "do shut up. I have a number of things to tell you." He walked back toward Jeffrey, one hand gripping her arm as he drew her with him. "I have had a very busy day so far, and I think what I have done will be of deep interest to you both."

"I don't understand," Anne said.

"You will, my dear. As I said, I've had a very busy day. I have been to see William. As of this minute you have been cut off from any credit. You cannot use my name or my money in any of the very expensive shops you frequent." Anne gasped. "Also, at this moment, your maid is packing your clothes. You've carried on your affair with your lover here so long, I think it's time he had the pleasure of your company permanently. That is," Joseph smiled grimly, "if he wants it."

"You can't do this!" Anne shrieked. Jeffrey had turned pale and silent.

"Can I not? I have filed for divorce. And it will be your job to explain to the Jameses why you failed to coerce my daughter into the marriage you and they had planned for her."

"You . . ."

"Know? Yes, I know all the sordid details. That is why I want you out of my house as fast as you can go."

"I'll fight you!" Anne nearly shrieked. "You can't throw me out!"

"No?" Joseph came close to her, so close she shrank from the overwhelming anger she saw in his eyes. "Go ahead and fight me. I have my finances under control. Fight me if you choose. But now that Winter is married, I don't think the Jameses are going to support you any longer. It looks like you will have only your lover to take care of you."

"I'm afraid," Jeffrey said coldly, "that Anne is a bit beyond my means."

"I thought perhaps you'd feel that way," Joseph replied in bitter amusement.

Anne glared at Jeffrey in furious disbelief. She felt like a trapped animal, and she lashed out like one. She realized Joseph must be aware of everything, and she knew the Jameses were too dangerous to play with. Besides, now she no longer had the money to redeem the jewels that belonged to the Jameses.

"You are as deep in this as I am," she snarled at Jeffrey. "You had your own profit in mind!"

Jeffrey gave a cold, mirthless chuckle. It was a bit of a pleasure to see Anne caught in her own web.

"But the Jameses are your own cup of tea, my dear. I never dealt with them. Why not be philosophical about the whole thing. The jig is up."

"No! No!" she screamed at Joseph. "You cannot throw me out like this. Where will I go, what will I do?"

"Frankly, Anne, I no longer care." His voice was cold. "If you'd had your way, my daughter would have lived a life of hell. You would have sacrificed her to Carl James, the way you sacrificed me to your happiness. Jeffrey is your lover. See if he has enough pity on you to help you, though I think such is not the case." Anne saw her defeat. "Go ahead, fight me. Bring this into open court. But remember, you have no force, no money behind you. Who will be the loser, Anne, who will be the fool?" He inhaled deeply, "I'm giving you a chance to go in peace, with all you have accumulated from me. Fight me and I'll destroy you so completely you will not survive. That I promise."

Her face had gone stark and pale as the reality that Joseph meant every word he said came to her. All her plans crumbled around her. She looked at Jeffrey, who shook his head negatively and shrugged his shoulders. There was no way he could or would help her.

"I guess you are right, Joseph," he said coolly, "one has to learn how to cut one's losses and retreat. I'm sorry, Anne. Perhaps you will have better luck next time."

"There will be no next time in this city. Not for her," Joseph smiled, "and not for you, either. I have many friends. The word is being spread at this moment. You will not be accepted in any household by this time tomorrow. I suggest you try traveling, Jeffrey, and seeking a way to repair your useless, wasted life."

Jeffrey's face paled, but he remained silent as he walked to the door, closing it softly behind him.

Anne and Joseph faced each other. He saw the tears in her eyes, but they were tears of self-pity.

"Joseph, you can't . . ." she sobbed, and came toward him with outstretched arms. But all he could see was her in Jeffrey's arms, betraying his love. All he could remember was Winter's grief-stricken face and the knowledge that she had been driven from her home by this woman. Any residue of fascination he had ever had for her died.

"Your baggage will be in the hall. The carriage will take you any place you choose to go. Be gone from my home within the hour. I'd hope you have enough sense to take the first means of transportation out of the city. I don't believe the James family is very forgiving."

"Please. I . . ."

"Don't waste your acting ability. Use it on someone else. I seem to have acquired an immunity to it. Good-bye, Anne."

Pleading was replaced by fear. She, as well as Joseph, knew how unforgiving the Jameses could be. Joseph knew nothing about her sale of the jewels. Of course she could not get them back. Her mind began to spin. Like a cat, Anne intended to land on her feet. She drew herself up proudly, gave him a look of contempt, spun around and left.

Joseph breathed a sigh of relief. All the loose ends were tied neatly together. He had only to hear from Dobbs now that Shelby was safe and that they would be home soon, and all would be well.

He intended to have a huge celebration. For many reasons: his freedom from Anne, his daughter's marriage, and the safe return of his friends and his beloved niece Shelby.

He stood at the window of the library and watched Anne enter the carriage and leave without a backward look.

When he sat down again behind his desk it was to begin preparation of a list of names he would send invitations to. He intended to make this the celebration of the century.

He was well into the project when Roberts rapped lightly and entered. "Sir, there is a telegraph message for you."

"Bring it here."

Joseph opened it quickly, frowning at the message within. Dobbs was not easily alarmed, and if he was upset, Joseph felt he had every right to be as well.

Mr. Stapleton,
    Shelby has been taken by two men. Brad

Cole, Jasper, and I are on their trail. Did you send others to bring Shelby home? If not, we have a problem. Please reply to above address at once since we are anxious for her welfare.

                                                    Dobbs

Joseph crumpled the message and tossed it on his desk. Anne was still causing problems for the people he cared for. He sent for Roberts and prepared an answer, instructing him to see it was sent at once.

Dobbs,
    No, I have sent no one else. Do all in your power to find and bring Shelby back to us at once. Spare no expense. Please guard her with every effort.

                                                    Joseph

Joseph eased himself back down into his chair, frightened that he might have sacrificed a very lovely and generous person for his own gain.

Brad, Jasper, and Dobbs rode into town slowly, watching every face they saw. When Brad reined in sharply, both Dobbs and Jasper looked at him expectantly.

"Well, Dobbs," Brad said, "you were right. If I'm not mistaken there's a poster that says Shelby sang here . . . last night."

"Well I'll be . . ." Jasper began.

"So will I," Dobbs added with a laugh. "Let's find

our theater and see what's going on. No one will forget Shelby and someone will surely know where she is."

Brad could feel his heart pounding with excitement. Shelby might be just minutes away. He wanted to have her safe in his arms so badly that his breath seemed caught in his throat.

But the theater was locked up tight. Brad stopped the first passerby. It was obvious the man knew nothing and Brad was intimidating him to the point where he was nearly inarticulate.

"Brad," Dobbs said in a soothing voice, "let's find someone else to ask."

Brad realized what he was doing and apologized to the man. They went on their way. But it was some time and several people later before they got an answer.

"Yes, sir," the young couple agreed. "She sang here last night. We had tickets ourselves. She sure was something. Why, me and my missus haven't enjoyed nothing like that before. She had a voice like—"

"I know about her voice. I've heard her sing and I agree she's wonderful. But I have to know where she is now? Where is the theater owner? Where—"

"Well, if you let me get a word in edgewise, I'd be able to tell you."

"I'm sorry. I didn't mean . . . Look just tell me what you know."

"I know she's not here no more."

"In the theater?"

"No. In town. She left on the evening train. Her and her friends and—"

"Friends?"

"Yes. The three men she's traveling with, and Mr. Charles. He's the theater owner."

"Where did they go?"

"I don't know."

"The next town?"

"I don't know. Could be any town in the next five hundred miles. Maybe that other fella knows."

"What other fella?"

"The one that came into town with her," the man answered patiently. "He didn't go on the train with them. Fact is, he's still over at the saloon."

"Thanks . . . thanks a lot," Brad was already walking away as he spoke, and Dobbs and Jasper were only a step behind him.

They crossed the street at a half run and all three paused to exchange a hopeful look before they swung the saloon doors open and entered.

A few men were scattered here at random tables and several were standing at the bar. Brad looked at the faces. Which one . . . which man.

Brad's gaze fell on one lone man seated at a table looking as if he didn't want any company. Brad walked across the room and stood before the table, motionless, until the man looked up.

"I'd like to talk to you for a minute," Brad said, trying to contain both his anger and the urge to kill the man.

"And just who might you be, friend, and why would I want to talk to you?"

"Because a woman's life hangs in the balance, and if I have to beat the truth out of you I'll get it. You're one of the bastards who dragged Shelby Vale away from my ranch. I want to know where she is."

"Shelby." Dakota half whispered her name. He'd been fighting the battle of his conscience for hour after hour. A conscience he had thought he'd killed a long time ago. He had certainly not expected this man to tear away his shields so abruptly.

But Brad had heard the whispered name and his anger burst beyond his control. He reached across the table, grasped two large handfuls of Dakota's shirt and dragged him across the table.

"Shelby. Yes, Shelby. You came on my land and took a girl who didn't have a chance against you. Now, you damn well better tell me where she is or by God, I'll tear you apart."

"Let go of me," Dakota said calmly, "I don't intend to give you any trouble."

"Where is she?"

"You're running up against some pretty hard men. That girl seems to mean a lot to him."

There were three protesting sounds of fury. Dobbs gave an exclamation of anger, Brad uttered a curse, and Jasper growled deep in his throat like a wounded animal and started for Dakota and Brad. But Brad's anger was enough.

"Wait a minute! Hold it!" Dakota urged. "Don't do something stupid. I have no intention of protecting them. I made a hell of a mistake. Give me a chance to rectify it."

Brad realized almost from the first words Dakota uttered that this was a different breed of man.

"I'm a bounty hunter by profession," Dakota began his explanation. "I was hired to do a job just like you."

"By who?"

"By a man named Carl James. I've done some work for him before. He pays well."

"Where are they now?"

"On their way back East, I suppose."

"What do you mean, you suppose?"

"Well, if you'll let go of me, I'll tell you what you want to know. One thing is certain, you can't follow them on horseback. The train will be through in a couple of hours."

Brad released him and sat slowly down in a chair. Jasper and Dobbs dragged chairs up to the table. "I think you'd better talk," Brad said quietly, "and you damn well better make it real good, or I think Jasper here and I are ready to make sure you don't do any more bounty hunting in the near future."

Dakota talked, but Dobbs and Jasper couldn't understand why they would want Shelby when the problems with Winter was already settled.

"So Carl James came out here?" Dobbs questioned.

"Yes. In fact, as I said, we met him here with . . . her. Carl . . . he seems to have a lot of definite plans of his own. They have something to do with Shelby. How the hell she got him to let her sing last night is beyond me. She's a clever one. That bastard lied to me. He said she was going to be his wife. I didn't doubt it until I saw her, and . . ."

"Heard her sing?" Brad said softly.

"Yeah. I guess that's kind of what made me change my mind about what I'd done. I was sitting here deciding how to take her away from them and let her go where she wanted. Come to think of it . . ."

"What?"

"That theater man, he went with them."

"Hell and damnation!" Brad said. He smiled for the first time. "Shelby has made a plan! She's going to sing somewhere else. I'll say she's waiting for me and is leaving a sign as big as that theater. She'll get them to stop in every town from here to Christmas."

Dakota spoke quietly, "You're one damn lucky man. That girl's got a lot of backbone. You should have seen her sass Carl."

"I don't doubt it. I have a couple of stories myself that would curl your hair. How much time before that train leaves?"

"About another hour or so."

"The stationmaster should know some kind of schedule. Perhaps I can second-guess Shelby. I think I'll go down to the train station," Dobbs offered. "She and I sort of knew how each other thought. Come along with me, Jasper."

Jasper rose reluctantly to his feet, his cold eyes still intent on Dakota.

"Make it a good guess, Dobbs. I don't want to take the chance of overshooting and miss her completely. This James fellow sounds pretty rough, and from what our friend here says, his companions aren't very savory. We can't afford to waste any time."

"I'll do my best," Dobbs replied quietly. "She's pretty important to me as well."

Brad felt immediately contrite. His worry over Shelby drove every other thought from his mind. But before he could apologize, Dobbs clapped him on the shoulder and smiled. Though he left without another word; Brad knew his careless words were forgiven. He turned his attention back to Dakota.

"Now, suppose you tell me everything."

As Dakota talked, Brad became aware of a lot of things. One, that he did not fit the mold his profession generally called for. Two, he was educated and, Brad thought, well bred . . . and three, he had been captured completely by Shelby. Brad guessed he'd fallen in love with her. He did not fault the man's taste, but Shelby was his and no one was ever going to come between them again.

". . . so we brought her to James. I guess, at first it was just another job, and I needed the money. But after a while, after I knew her better, I began to get the idea James had been telling a pack of lies."

"Why didn't you let her go then?"

"It was too late. It's been eating at me ever since. In fact, as I said, I was sitting here considering going after her myself."

"And," Brad said with a dangerously quiet voice, "what would you have done with her?"

Dakota's gaze met Brad's and held it for a long and very honest moment. "To tell you the truth, I don't know. But I'm not sure I wouldn't have tried to keep her as long as I could."

"It's an opportunity you'll never have again, my friend."

"That's the story of my life," Dakota laughed bitterly, "not grabbing the right opportunities when I could."

Before Brad could answer him Dobbs and Jasper returned. Both Brad and Dakota looked at the two men expectantly.

"I found out a great deal," Dobbs smiled. "The train makes three stops within the next five days. I checked with a couple of people here in town. It seems our theater owner has a string of them, about six to be exact. And two of the train's stops are in the same towns as these theaters. Our Shelby is clever enough to remember that we've already played at one of these theaters. If I don't miss my guess and if I estimate Shelby right, I have a feeling we'll find her in Bennet, singing like a lark and hoping we're smart enough to see the truth."

"Bennet," Brad said with a half smile of remembrance. "That was the first time I saw her. If we cut cross country we'd be able to get there before they get a chance to move on. It means Shelby has to be with them through one more stop, but the hours they eat up there, will give us a chance. We could get to Bennet at least by the time she's performing."

"She's going to be worried . . . maybe scared if she thinks we're not catching up with her," Jasper protested.

"This is our best chance, Jasper," Brad said evenly,

"and Shelby knows I'll be there. She knows I'd never let her go."

"Mr. Cole," Dakota said, "I'd like to go along with you. You might need some help, and . . . I'd at least like one more opportunity to apologize to the lady. If nothing else, it might help me soothe my conscience."

Brad was silent for a moment, and both Jasper and Dobbs realized more had passed between these two men than they knew. Neither intended to interfere in Brad's decision.

"All right, come along."

Dakota stood and extended his hand to Brad, who refused to take it.

"Maybe," Brad said softly, "if we find Shelby safe, if we get her back without harm, I will shake your hand. Until then . . . I don't shake the hand of a man I might one day kill."

"Fair enough," Dakota said softly, "fair enough."

Chapter 22

When they reached the next engagement there was no sign of Brad, Jasper, or Dobbs anywhere. If Shelby's faith sagged momentarily, it was only a brief second. Brad would come for her, she had only to continue her little charade and give him as much time as possible.

Mr. Charles was beside himself with pleasure. Shelby watched Carl's face and was surprised that he did not display the same anger. It sent a tingling sense of alarm through her. She had a reasonably good idea he had some plan she knew nothing about.

Carl actually was quite satisfied. When they reached the next town he would let his clever little prisoner believe she was thwarting him. He would let her perform. Then he would make her take part in another performance, a wedding ceremony. That would effectively put an end to any more games she had up her sleeve. Now he was only amused at her plotting. He not only meant to marry her, he meant to make sure he enjoyed her many physical charms thoroughly. He knew many ways to subdue a woman and bend her will to his.

Now he walked from the bar, across the street to the hotel. From there he would escort Shelby to the theater. He was suspicious of her quiet mood, but he had her so heavily guarded there was no way she could get away with anything.

He used his key and let himself into her room. She sat in a chair near the window, while the two men he had left there to guard her played cards at a small oval table nearby.

Shelby refused to turn and look at him, and this made him smile. She could be as cold as she wanted for now. She would change eventually, she had little choice.

"It will be time to go to the theater soon." Carl spoke to the two men. "You two go get Mr. Charles and take him over there. I'll be there in a while. As soon as Shelby is dressed and ready."

This brought Shelby's head around, and despite her efforts a touch of fear surfaced. Both men grinned and left the room.

"It's time you prepared for your performance," Carl ordered.

She stood, her face paling slightly, but her jaw clenched in determination. "If you think . . ."

"I don't think, I know," Carl smiled cruelly. "Your gown is there in the wardrobe. I'm an impatient man. You get ready . . . or shall I do it for you?" He took a step toward her, and Shelby knew he would take great pleasure in doing what he said.

"I'll change," she said coldly. She was just as determined that he was not going to intimidate or control her. She went to the wardrobe and removed the deep-bronze-colored gown. Laying it across the bed, Shelby never took her eyes from Carl as she reached for the buttons of her dress.

Shrugging it from her shoulders, she let it drop to the floor, then stepped out of the circle of material and bent to pick it up and put it on the bed.

The thin lace straps of her chemise revealed the creamy texture of her shoulders and the gentle swell of her breasts. She watched Carl's eyes darken and felt a shiver as his eyes raked over her. But she refused to surrender to the emotions he stirred. Brad would come . . . Brad would come.

To Shelby's surprise, Carl continued to just watch as she slipped the shimmering gown over her head. Her hands fumbled with the laces at the back, and despite the fact that she wanted to fight him, she did nothing as he came to stand behind her and slowly do them up.

She stood immobile as he brushed his lips over one bare shoulder. She wouldn't give him the satisfaction of showing fear . . . or any reaction at all. Again, to her surprise, he simply chuckled softly, walked to a nearby chair and picked up her cloak and draped it gently about her shoulder.

"It's time to go."

Shelby turned to look at Carl and saw the burning desire in the depths of his eyes. When he smiled, she felt a real tingle of fear.

Backstage at the theater she found Mr. Charles with the men who were his jailers, though he didn't have the slightest idea that was the case. He could only see Shelby.

"How lovely you look tonight. I know the audience is impatient. I shall announce you immediately."

Before Shelby could say another word he had already gone out onto the stage, separated the curtains and stepped out.

Amid thunderous applause Shelby gave what she felt was one of her best performances. She treated the audience to song after song, wanting to leave them with a memory they would be talking about if Brad came here.

When the show was over, Mr. Charles mourned the fact that they could not stay for one more night's performance.

"After all, my dear," he said, "the next stop will be the last, and I am sorely distressed I shall not have your company any longer. If you could just agree to—"

"I'm afraid, Mr. Charles," Carl interrupted, "that this little tour will end at the next theater. Miss Vale needs some rest. We must be on our way."

Shelby wanted to scream at him, but what she didn't want a tragedy before Brad had a chance to find her. She had played the game this far; she could do it as long as she had to.

"I am sorry, Mr. Charles," she said, "but perhaps when I've been home a while I shall decide on another tour. I may be out this way before you know it."

"We can't make promises, my dear," Carl smiled,

and his eyes were full of humor as he looked at Shelby. "We have no idea right now what the future might hold. Perhaps more than you expect."

"Perhaps." Shelby looked at Carl, her eyes filled with stormy defiance. "Or perhaps more than *you* expect."

Carl looked at her for a long moment, as if he could read her thoughts. But her face revealed nothing. Annoyed that he felt a momentary sense of insecurity, Carl gripped Shelby's arm in an iron hold. "Come, my dear, I've ordered supper to be brought to your room tonight. I know how tired you are and we have to be up quite early in the morning. You did say a stage leaves very early, didn't you, Mr. Charles?"

"Yes. But why do you not use the comfort of the train?"

"Because it doesn't arrive until early morning and doesn't leave until noon. By that time we will be well on our way, perhaps over half way there."

If Mr. Charles suspected any other reason, Shelby saw no sign of it.

She refused to eat a late meal with Carl, who only smiled condescendingly. "All right, Shelby. I suspect you are very tired and we are going to get a much earlier start than you had planned on. Hank and John will take you back to the hotel. Eat and then get some sleep."

Shelby's look was cold, but she continued to contain her anger. She would not give him a moment of satisfaction. Silently she returned to her room with her two guards watching her closely.

When she found she couldn't sleep, she concentrated all her thoughts on Brad and prayed he would come soon.

It was close to two o'clock in the morning when she sat on the edge of her bed, fighting the thought that Brad just might not reach her in time, and trying to decide what Carl's real plans were.

She lay back on the bed, still fully dressed. After a while she drifted into sleep. She was wakened later by her door opening. Her senses had been attuned to that fear for days. She glanced at the window. It was still dark outside.

Carl stood framed in the doorway, and Shelby rose from the bed, determined not to give an inch to this man.

"It's almost dawn, and the stage will be leaving in an hour. It's time to get ready."

Shelby breathed a soft sigh of relief. She had been certain she'd would be in for a battle. Carl recognized her relief but only smiled.

She gathered her things and made preparations quickly, but it was still some time before dawn that their baggage was being placed atop the stage. The sun was just beginning to rise as the stage moved out of town.

The morning train was precisely on time and when Brad, Dakota, Jasper, and Dobbs disembarked they were more than pleased. If they had planned right, this very train was the one Shelby and Carl had to use to leave town.

"Now, we just have to find them before they have a chance to board," Dakota said.

"She would have performed here. Let's ask a few questions," Dobbs replied.

They went first to the theater, which was empty and closed. Then they went to the hotel, where they were presented with the news. At first Brad was stunned, then he grew helplessly angry.

"You mean we've missed them just by a few hours!"

"Yes, sir. Stage left just before day light."

"Damn!" Brad growled.

"And the train doesn't leave again for another four hours," Jasper said, his anger matching Brad's.

"Let's get horses here and cut cross country," Brad suggested. "It might be a pretty nasty ride and we'll have to really push it, but we ought to be able to get there not too long after they do. Want to give it a try?"

"You know we'll all go along with whatever you think best," Dobbs smiled.

"Then let's get started. This is going to be one hell of a ride."

Brad's anger was at the point where he would not take much more. He carefully chose the horses, with an eye to endurance. He meant to find Shelby at the next town if it killed him . . . or them and the horses as well.

Shelby stepped down from the stage after a dusty and very bumpy ride. She felt exhausted and desperately in need of a hot bath, clean clothes, and something to eat.

This was the last town in which she could perform. The last chance she would have to leave any further trail for Brad to follow. If he didn't find her soon . . . he might never find her. The thought left her breathless and shaky.

Carl took Shelby to the hotel and made arrangements, cautioning her not to try to leave the room until he returned. He made sure he locked the door behind him. Then, when he had hot water brought, he unlocked it for the tub to be brought to her room for her. He stayed only briefly, telling her he would be back to take her to a restaurant.

"Right now I have to have a conversation with your little friend. We want this performance to be your very best, don't we? After all, he owes his life to you, so he'll have to make all the arrangements perfect, won't he?"

"You are a miserable wretch," Shelby replied.

"Now, my dear, I know you're very tired so I'll excuse that little outburst." His smile was amiable, but he reached out and gripped her arm roughly and pulled her close to him. "But be careful how far you push my patience. You're the one who caused all this difficulty. If you hadn't tried to be clever and promised that little nuisance of a man you'd sing, this situation—"

"Would be what? Winter is safe from you. Kidnapping me is stupid."

"You'll be worth a great deal to me. Even if I can't collect it all now, I have plans. Besides, your mother or your uncle is executor, arrangements can be made. He'll be guilt-stricken if anything should happen to you. And it could if you're not careful. Now, take your bath . . . before I decide to do it for you." He pushed her roughly from him, locking the door behind him.

Shelby stared at the closed door. She felt as if she were missing something. Ransom was all he could expect, and that was a dangerous game to play. Still . . . ?

She removed her clothes and sank gratefully into the warm water. She tried to cling to her common sense and place all her thoughts on Brad again. It would do her no good to try to fight Carl now. If Brad didn't come soon and they left Mr. Charles behind . . . then would be her time to concoct a plan to get free.

It was almost two hours before Carl knocked on the door. She had no way of knowing how he had spent the time or she might have tried her escape then.

Actually, Carl had made good use of the time to make arrangements for their wedding. He'd found a judge to whom gold coins meant more than the virtue or agreement on the woman in mind.

Carl was satisfied, he need only play Shelby's game a little longer. Her mamby-pamby theater owner friend would be safe . . . providing the "I do" came willingly from her lips. He had taken care of every thread. The marriage would be consummated that night, and that was one part of the situation he was looking forward to.

Now he was knocking on her door with all his plans well laid.

"Shelby, are you ready?"

"Yes."

Good, he said to himself. When he opened the door he was struck again by Shelby's unique beauty. It was a pleasant thought that he would one day own her and all that she possessed. Another pleasant thought was the vision of Joseph's face when he found out the coup Carl had pulled off.

"How lovely you look."

"Don't bother with flattery, Carl. I'm not going to pretend this is a welcome social affair. I'm hungry. Where is Mr. Charles?"

"My men are taking good care of the delicate Mr. Charles. You needn't worry, as long as you behave yourself."

"Mr. Charles is a fine, sensitive, and considerate man. If he knew—"

"He would do nothing, so don't alarm him. It will only cause him distress."

He took her arm and they left the hotel together. Although Carl tried to keep up a conversation during dinner, Shelby merely answered his questions with desultory one-word answers until she saw his anger growing. She wanted his anger, it was much easier to cope with than what she had seen in his eyes before.

"We'll be catching the midnight train later, but after the show tonight we're going to visit an old friend of mine for an hour or two. It will help pass the time . . . unless you would rather go back to the hotel. I'm sure we could while away the hours constructively."

"I'd be delighted to visit your friend. I didn't know you had any."

"You're amusing, my dear. Be careful. Your sharp tongue can cause you more problems than you can imagine."

They finished the meal in silence and then walked to the theater.

Brad, Dakota, Jasper, and Dobbs rode as if demons were pursuing them. But they had to rest the horses a time or two or they might have collapsed before they got to their destinations.

During one of these pauses, Brad brought something up that had been bothering him.

"None of this is like Shelby, Dobbs."

"What do you mean?"

"She's so damn clever. Look how many times she got away from me. I know the performances are meant to leave a trail, but she couldn't trust that alone. He has some means to hold her."

"Means to hold her? What do you mean?" Jasper questioned.

"I mean, he's keeping her in line by using something or someone that's making her afraid of leaving."

"I've got a pretty good idea he's still got hold of that little man from the theater. He seems so helpless that a threat to him might just convince Shelby to do what James wants her to do," Dakota said.

"We're going to have to be careful. Once we get to town we'd better check things closely before we move. We don't want Shelby hurt and we also don't want her feeling guilty if someone else gets hurt."

"You're right. Now, let's get a move on. We have a lot of miles to cover yet."

The train had chugged along at a steady speed, but it was forced to take a more circuitous route than Brad and his friends were.

When the riders arrived in town the horses had reached the point of exhaustion. Dobbs consulted his watch. "Shelby should be in the middle of a performance."

"I'm sure she's well guarded and someone's probably holding Mr. Charles," Brad said grimly. "If they see any sign of Dakota or me they'll recognize us at once and the whole game will be over. They might hurt Shelby, and for certain they'll hurt Mr. Charles."

"What are we going to do?"

"I have an idea," Brad said. "Dobbs, you go over to the theater. I don't believe the men who have Shelby would recognize you, and most people already know you as a performer. Play it for all your worth, give them a performance they'll never forget. And in the process get word to Shelby that we're here. Keep her on stage as long as you possibly can. In the meantime, I'm going to find out if any of his friends are lingering around. Maybe they'd know who they might have gotten hold of that would keep Shelby in line."

"In line," Jasper snorted angrily. "You think her putting on all these performances and stopping all these times is letting them force her into line? She's been fighting as hard as she always did when she was running from you."

"I know, Jasper," Brad said quietly. "But she's only been leaving a trail for us. Her hands have been tied, and now we know how. We have to find out where he is and get him free."

"I don't like wasting time."

"Neither do I." Brad knew he and Jasper were still far from friends, but he also understood how Jasper felt about Shelby. He just had to convince him of what he felt.

"Jasper, Shelby's important to you. I know how she feels about you and Dobbs. I need you to trust me, Jasper. I love Shelby, more than any human being can imagine. I want to share the rest of her life if she'll have me. I know she loves me, too, she's told me. I want her free, I want her safe, and I desperately want to get my hands on the person behind this They'll pay, believe me, they'll pay. But we mustn't be careless. If we charge in there, they might do something real foolish . . . like killing someone. Maybe Shelby. You have to trust me."

Brad kept his gaze directly on Jasper, who stood immobile and silent. Dobbs was pretty sure Jasper was digesting this slowly and would come to the right decision.

"All right," Jasper said quietly, "what do you want me to do?"

"We'll have to separate. Move through town as quietly as possible and try to find out where they are. While Dobbs keeps Shelby and her abductor busy, we have to break the hold he has over her. The four of us will split up now and meet behind the theater . . . say," he looked at Dobbs, "forty-five minutes? Can you keep them busy that long?"

"My dear boy, give me a stage and Shelby to occupy it with me and I'll keep their attention just as long as you need me to."

"Good man. Get going, we'll come just as fast as we can find our answers."

"I'm on my way." Dobbs paused by Jasper. "Don't worry, Jasper. We'll take care of this, and I'll let Shelby know you're here."

"Thanks, Dobbs."

"We all care," Dobbs replied.

"Yes," Dakota said softly, "we all care. And we all have to make sure this works out." He turned to look at Brad. "I don't suppose you'd let me have first chance at Carl James?"

"You don't stand a snowball's chance in hell for that unless I'm dead. I want my hands on him so bad I can taste it. Now let's get going. Dobbs, behind the theater, forty-five minutes. We'll be ready to come in. You just keep Shelby as close as you can . . . if you can."

Dobbs left them and started the walk to the theater. He entered the darkened building and the first and most welcome sound he heard was Shelby's voice.

Jasper headed for the stagecoach office to check on the people who had arrived on it.

Brad and Dakota went to the hotel. Brad paused outside the door. "If we go charging in there, we're going to scare the hell out of that clerk and it might just warn someone. You go around and come in the back door," he instructed Dakota. "I'll see what information I can get peacefully."

"And if that doesn't work?"

"Then," Brad grinned, "we'll just stop being peaceful and do whatever we need to do."

"I'll see you inside," Dakota responded.

Brad walked inside and up to the desk where a bored young clerk was reading the evening paper. He looked up, and put aside the paper on his chair.

"Yes, sir, may I help you?"

"Yes. I'm looking for some friends of mine."

"Are they guests of our hotel?"

"I'm not sure. I hoped you'd be able to tell me."

"Who are you inquiring about?"

"Well, first off, you have a young woman here . . . an entertainer. I believe she's performing at the local theater now."

"Ah, Miss Vale."

"Yes. I believe she arrived with several friends."

"Yes, she did. Mr. Charles, the owner of the theater. I believe he has been traveling with the group for a while. He owns several theaters, you know."

"Ah . . . yeah, I know," Brad replied. He had a hard time keeping control, knowing Shelby would not let this innocent man pay for her freedom.

"They have rooms here now?"

"I'm certain, sir, that Mr. James said something about checking out tonight. Catching the late train, I think."

"What room are they in? In case I miss them elsewhere, I could catch them here before they leave."

"Thirty-six and thirty-nine. Top of the stairs at the far end of the hall."

"Thank you. Thank you very much."

"My pleasure. And, your name, sir?" the clerk asked as Brad turned to leave.

"My name?"

"In case you miss your friends I can tell them you were here."

"Oh . . . yes. The name's Smith . . . John Smith."

"Have a nice evening, Mr. Smith."

Brad circled around to the hotel, and entered through the back door into a semidarkened hallway. There he found Dakota waiting.

"Smith?" He questioned with a grin, "You sure are original."

"Right now that's as original as I can get. We have to check two rooms. Thirty-six and thirty-nine. Maybe we'll be lucky, and find Mr. Charles and our friends in one of them."

"Wouldn't they put guards? They wouldn't just—"

"No, they wouldn't just leave him unguarded. After all, his usefulness to him is over. He's expendable. Most likely there's someone with him. Could be just Hank and John. If that's all, we can take the two of them easily."

"You've got a lot of confidence."

"No, I'm just twice as fast as Hank and three times faster than John. Besides," Dakota chuckled "you're a very angry man and I'm counting on that. When it comes down to it, Hank can be a bit of a coward."

"Let's go up and see if they're there. Then, we'll just have to see how brave Hank really is."

Chapter 23

Dobbs had walked directly to the theater. There was no way for Carl James to recognize him, and even if someone in the theater did, it would be as one of the past performers.

Shelby would, of course, know him at once, but he trusted her to be actress enough to display no recognition. And once Shelby saw him she might understand that at least Jasper, and perhaps Brad, were somewhere near.

He wrestled with several different plans of approaching the situation. He didn't want to do anything until he could judge the safest approach. It had to be smooth enough not to raise an alarm in Carl James until Dakota, Jasper, and Brad got to the theater.

He entered the semidark building by the front door and stood in the back, watching Shelby and trying to think.

Shelby's song was just coming to an end when Dobbs began to get a little frantic. He had to make sure she didn't leave the stage until Brad found out what hold Carl had over her and eliminated it.

The applause was resounding, and Dobbs smiled as Shelby raised her hands to quiet everyone. She thanked them for their enthusiasm and said she intended to sing several more songs.

Dobbs thought that was clever of her. What Shelby had really said was she was going to hold Carl James and any of his friends here as long as she could.

Just as she finished speaking, Dobbs decided he had to let her know they were there, that she was not alone.

As Shelby quieted the audience and they began to settle expectantly back in their seats, Dobbs walked down the center aisle toward the stage.

He was only halfway there when Shelby spotted him. He watched as she fought revealing her reaction and won.

"Ladies and gentleman." Shelby smiled a brilliant and relieved smile. "We are so fortunate to have a gentleman here whom you and I have heard perform many times. I would like you to help me entice him onto the stage." Shelby began to clap, and the audience, who was just beginning to recognize him, began to follow. "Mr. Robert Dobbs, one of the best Shakespearean actors on the stage today," Shelby continued.

Carl stiffened and his eyes glowed with wary shock. He debated dragging Shelby off the stage, but that could cause a scene he was not prepared to handle. No, let Shelby play her little games. She was stalling for time and he knew it, but all the time in the world wasn't going to stop his plans. By midnight Shelby Vale would be Mrs. Carl James and nothing, no law in the world, would be able to do anything about it . . . especially once the marriage was consummated.

No, he would watch and enjoy the show along with all the others. Shelby would not endanger the hostage. She would play, but in the end she would do exactly what he wanted her to do.

As Dobbs crossed the stage to Shelby's side she extended her hand to him. By the fierce grip of her hand he could tell she was panic stricken.

"Dobbs!" she hissed through a clenched teeth smile. "Where's Jasper . . . and Brad?" she added hopefully.

Dobbs smiled and bowed to the audience while he spoke softly under his breath.

"Jasper's here . . . Brad, too."

"Oh." She breathed a sigh of relief so intense she almost cried aloud.

"Hold steady, my dear. In a short while your friend in the wings will have lost his hostage and Brad will remove him from your life."

"Hostage. You knew?"

"Brad figured it out."

By this time, the audience had again settled back in their seats. They were getting twice what they paid for and this satisfied all of them. Now Dobbs had to think of a way to keep Shelby next to him on the stage.

"Do you remember the Shakespeare I taught you?"

She turned distressed eyes to him. She scared and it was affecting her memories. "No . . . no, I . . ."

"Yes, you do," Dobbs said firmly. "Don't think, just react. I trust you to remember."

Though she was nervous, she had to smile when Dobbs chose *The Taming of the Shrew* to perform. Dobbs raised his hand and the theater grew silent. They paused to let the suspense build and to capture the mood of the actors.

" 'Good-morrow, Kate; for that's your name, I hear.' "

Dobbs lowered toward her with elaborate gesture.

" 'Well have you heard, but something hard of hearing: They call me Katharine that do talk of me,' " Shelby replied saucily, her hands on her hips and a taunting smile on her lips. She picked up Kate's character quickly, as Dobbs knew she would.

" 'You lie, in faith; for you are call'd plain Kate, And bonny Kate, and sometimes Kate the curst; But, Kate, the prettiest Kate in Christendom, Kate of Kate-Hall, my super-dainty Kate, For Dainties are all cates; and therefore, Kate, Take this of me, Kate of my consolation;—Hearing thy mildness prais'd in every town, Thy virtues spoke of, and they beauty sounded—

And so they continued their performance with a confidence and smoothness that was their undoing. It was that very expertise that made Carl's suspicions blossom into surety. These two knew each other. Much too well.

While the audience was still applauding, Carl ordered the stage manager to close the curtains.

"But, sir, I don't believe Miss Vale—"

"I said close the curtain," Carl said coldly.

"I can't do that, sir. I . . ." His voice faltered and his eyes widened in shock when Carl roughly pushed him aside and drew the curtains closed himself.

Shelby and Dobbs were in the middle of a bow when the curtain swirled closed in front of them. They could hear the murmur of surprise and disappointment that rippled through the audience.

Carl had followed the curtain out and was beside them by the time they realized his presence.

"I say, sir," Dobbs bluffed expertly, "it's not good showmanship to interrupt a performance. The audience sounds a bit put out as well."

There was a rhythmic clapping and several masculine voices called out Shelby's name.

"Let's don't play games," Carl smiled coldly. "It seems you know Shelby well. That's too bad."

"I didn't mean to intrude. I know Miss Vale is a marvelous performer in her own right. Since we had performed together once or twice, I didn't think she would object too strenuously to my appearance. Of course if it upsets anything I shall be glad to step aside." He turned to Shelby and raised her hand to kiss it. "I am truly sorry, my dear. Perhaps I can apologize a bit more effectively over dinner."

Carl laughed softly and removed a small derringer from his pocket.

"Don't do something very foolish," Carl said quietly. "You're clever, but maybe not as clever as you think. Quite obviously you are very friendly with each other."

Shelby and Dobbs both knew there was little use in arguing with a gun in the hand of a merciless man. Dobbs only prayed he could still keep Carl here until Brad came.

"I'm taking Shelby out of here," Dobbs said.

"Are you now? I hate to disillusion you. You are an admirable actor, but the performance is over."

Dobbs expected to do some battle with Carl. But he was no real match for Carl.

Carl had no boundaries of honor as he reached out with lightning speed and grasped Shelby's wrist, jerking her close to him. As swift as the strike of a snake he raised the gun and struck Dobbs a blow that dropped him to his knees.

Carl was dragging a strenuously resisting Shelby along, but she was so forceful in her resistance that he came to an abrupt stop.

"Shelby," he hissed furiously, "if we don't return in the time I told Hank and John we'd be back, your little friend is going to be the one who pays."

Shelby had little choice. Dobbs was all right and Brad was near. That was the important thing. Obviously Dobbs had been sent here both to comfort her and to assess the situation. She was confident Brad was at this moment freeing Mr. Charles. She knew he would be here soon. But . . .

She moved along, with a relentless Carl beside her, and they left the theater through a back door that led to an alley. She was surprised to see a horse and buggy were waiting. He had something planned that did not include going back to the hotel.

Once he forced her into the buggy he took the reins expertly in one hand, while he held the derringer against her side. She had no doubt he was vicious enough to hurt her, she had seen it in his eyes.

"Where are we going?"

"You'll know in due time."

"There's not much use in running, I have friends on my trail that won't give up."

"You mean Brad Cole?" he sneered.

"You know . . ."

"I know much more than you can imagine. The game you and Winter played is over. Now we will see just who the final winner will be."

"Brad will kill you."

"No, I think not. We have one stop to make and then we'll be on our way."

"On our way where?"

"As I said, in due time."

"Carl, let me go and I'll see no one will stop you. You can just go."

"I've no intention of doing that. The people who succeed in life are the ones who have enough courage to see their plans carried through to the end. I always win, Shelby. Now, be quiet. We're almost there."

Shelby tried to discern just where "there" was. They had ridden at a rapid speed and were some distance from town. All she could see was a large white frame house that stood some distance from the road.

Shelby was almost overcome with anxiety. What did Carl plan to do here?

He drew the buggy to a halt and forced her to disembark in front of the house, which had a slightly run-down look to it. Then, taking hold of her arm in a brutal grip, he propelled her toward the porch.

The door was opened before they reached it by a small, rotund woman who smiled at them.

"Come in, come in. We've been expecting you for over an hour. Everything is prepared."

Shelby's heart began to pound. What was "prepared" and who was "we"? She licked dry lips and gathered her courage. She would not lose her faith in Brad. He would get to her before whatever plans Carl and his friends had for her came to pass.

She didn't want to save herself at the expense of others, especially the harmless Mr. Charles. Once Brad had him free there would be nothing standing between him and Carl.

Carl did not let go of her arm as he forced Shelby into a large and comfortable living room.

The rotund woman joined a tall man who must have, in his younger years, been quite handsome. But his face and body revealed disillusionment, and his red-rimmed eyes gave testament to an overindulgence in alcohol.

It soon became clear to Shelby that the man was a judge and the woman his wife.

The judge's eyes evaded hers, and in that instant she knew exactly what Carl had planned. If he could force her into a wedding ceremony here and be able to escape Brad long enough to . . . She could not face the rest of the plan.

She looked at Carl and he could read the obstinacy in her eyes. He grasped her arm and pulled her aside. "Don't cause me any trouble. The judge will do as I say, but his wife . . . and your friend at the hotel are expendable. Are two lives worth it to you?"

He saw the defeat flit momentarily in her eyes and he smiled. "Be smart, Shelby. Make it easy on yourself, on them, and on your dear old friend at the hotel. All that's required of you are two little words: I do."

"And then what?"

"We get out of here, your friend will be safe. We'll go back East and settle down into comfortable married life."

"You may succeed here. I won't have an innocent person suffer for me. But don't even give a remote thought to the idea of a 'comfortable married life.' You'll wish you'd died and gone to hell."

"Will I now?" Carl smiled a cold, grim smile. "We will see. My wife will never be disobedient. There are ways."

"No matter what words are said, no matter what I am forced to say, I will never be your wife. That I guarantee you," Shelby said furiously. "Besides," she struggled for a smile, "Brad will be on your trail. He may not find us right now, but you'll have to keep looking back over your shoulder because you'll never know when he'll be behind you."

Carl's smile wavered a bit before he turned to the judge, and inclined his head.

"All right. We're ready to begin when you are."

Carl forced Shelby to move beside him, her mind struggling for a way to slow the procedure. Suddenly, she smiled. She stood beside Carl quietly, which should have been warning enough.

The judge began the ceremony, while his wife beamed at the couple, certain that this was the beginning of a long and beautiful marriage.

Carl repeated the necessary words and the judge turned toward Shelby. She uttered a soft sound, placed the back of her hand against her forehead, and sagged forward in a faint. Straight into the judge's arms. He promptly dropped his book to try to catch her. Half inebriated as he was, the weight of Shelby's relaxed body staggered him and he stumbled backward.

They fell to the floor in a profusion of arms, legs, and ruffled petticoats. The judge's wife gave a squeak and rushed to their side. For a minute Carl was stunned into immobility. Then his face reddened in fury. He aided the woman to her feet while the judge got unsteadily to his. When Carl knelt beside Shelby and looked down at her serene face, he wanted to throttle her.

He reached down and gripped her arm so hard he could feel her stiffen in response. He slid his other hand to the back of her head and grasped her hair. He used his grip on her hair to jerk her upward.

"This game won't work with me," he snarled. "Now, get up. Any more little tricks like that and I'll see to it you pay a price you won't enjoy."

He drew Shelby roughly to her feet. His grip on her

arm was so brutal now that she had to clench her teeth to keep from crying out. She had no intention of giving him the satisfaction.

The judge intoned words she didn't even hear. Now she could only face the fear that Jasper—Brad—didn't know where Carl had taken her and they would not find her in time. Once Carl got away from here the possibility of him eluding them until . . .

Suddenly she realized everyone was quiet and looking at her. "Uh . . . what?"

"You need only say 'I do,' my dear," the judge's wife smiled, still believing Shelby's reticence was caused by shyness.

"I . . ." Shelby's voice caught on the words. She just couldn't say them. Carl's grip on her upper arm tightened until she nearly cried out.

Brad and Dakota had stood outside the rooms thirty-six and thirty-nine, trying to figure out which door to choose. If they broke in the wrong one, the noise would warn the kidnappers.

The doors were opposite each other and Dakota looked at Brad, silently telling him the choice of doors was his. Brad knew time could be running out, so he inhaled deeply, prayed, and rapped lightly on one door. No response. He rapped lightly again, then smiled at Dakota. There was no doubt this room was empty. They crossed the hall and stood on either side of the door.

They were just preparing to take action when they

heard a footstep on the back stairs. They didn't want an innocent bystander caught in a crossfire.

But the bulk of the shadow that preceded the person up the steps could only belong to one human being. Jasper.

When he reached the head of the steps, he spotted Brad and Dakota who cautioned him to silence. Half motion and half mouthing words they explained the situation. Jasper nodded understanding, and again the three men faced the door. This time their strategy was planned.

Brad and Dakota had their guns in their hands, and they stood on either side of the door. Jasper poised himself, then with one mighty kick he nearly tore the door from its hinges.

The two men guarding Mr. Charles were momentarily frozen. Frozen long enough for Brad and Dakota to take the advantage. The theater owner was white with shock and fear.

Hank had given the impression he was going for his gun, but Dakota's soft words stopped him in his tracks.

"I wouldn't if I were you, Hank. I'm in the mood to fill somebody with holes and it might just as well be you." Hank remained still. He had seen Dakota in action too often to try him.

"Mr. Charles," Brad said to the nearly apoplectic little man who seemed to shrink at the sound of a voice. "You'd better come with us."

"Oh, dear. Oh, dear me. Whatever for? Just let me go and . . ." Mr. Charles was near panic.

"Calm down, Mr. Charles," Brad laughed, "we're going to the theater to see that Shelby is safe."

Mr. Charles breathed a sigh of relief when he saw Jasper. His relief was so intense he trembled, fluttered his hands, and began to explain the situation. Carl and the others had treated him well until this night. Then, after he had introduced Shelby at the theater, he had been whisked here and treated abominably. Abominably!, he shrilled. A virtual prisoner, not to mention his worry about Shelby.

What amused Brad was that it was only Jasper who seemed able to soothe the little man's ruffled feathers.

"I think you two boys ought to come along. I have a feeling Mr. Charles here would like to press charges of kidnapping. Besides, I know Shelby might have a few plans for you," Brad said to Hank and John.

Jasper's huge presence and malevolent glare was making any strategy Hank and John might have drain away. They led the way from the hotel and started toward the theater.

Brad was surprised to see the last of the audience leaving the building. The performance couldn't be over yet, it was too early. Alarm streaked through him. Where was Dobbs?

"Bring these two along, Jasper," Brad ordered. "Dakota, come on. Something's going wrong."

They raced on ahead and entered the theater. It was empty, the curtain closed. The two exchanged a quick glance and Brad continued toward the stage.

There was no sound as they climbed the three steps to the stage. Then Brad reached out to push the heavy curtain aside so he and Dakota could get through.

Dobbs still sat on the floor with the stage manager kneeling beside him. He looked dazed and the hand that had been gently touching his head came away bloody.

Brad and Dakota went to his side and knelt beside him. "Dobbs, what happened? Where's Shelby?"

Dobbs looked up at Brad, his face pale from shock. "Shelby," he mumbled.

"That man just struck Mr. Dobbs down and dragged Miss Vale away." The stage manager was indignant that such a thing could happen here.

"Where?" Brad demanded. "Where did he take her?"

"Good heavens, sir, I've no idea. It all happened so suddenly."

"Damn! Which way did they go?"

"Out the back door."

"He could have had someone waiting," Dakota said. "If he had horses, we're going to have a hell of a time trying to track them when there's hundreds of them coming and going in town."

Brad stood slowly. Which way? Where would Carl take her? He was still trying to assess the situation when Jasper entered the theater with Hank and John.

Brad watched them approach. He could see Jasper's look turn murderous when he didn't see Shelby among those on stage.

Brad was smiling grimly. He had a pretty good idea who could illuminate them about Carl's destination.

"Jasper, Carl has taken Shelby somewhere," he said immediately. "He must have gotten wise to Dobbs." Jasper became more explosive by the minute. "I have a feeling," Brad continued, "that these two boys have a good idea where they went. Now, if they don't want to tell us, do you think you could persuade them?"

Hank's face went white at the low growl of fury that came from Jasper, and John was just as shaken. They began to talk, one over the other and rapidly, trying to assure the volcanic Jasper that they had no secrets they wouldn't share with him.

"He's taken her over to Judge Morgan's house," Hank said.

"A judge's house? Where is it?" Brad demanded, "and why take her there?"

"Judge Morgan is an old drunk," the stage manager said. "But he's still a judge. There's not too many things he wouldn't do for money."

"Hank?" Brad said threateningly.

"He's going to have the judge marry them. He has a plan to escape. By the time you find them—"

"It would be too late." Dakota added, "That bastard."

"He's outside of town about three miles east. Big white house. You can't miss it." The stage manager continued. "But you might already be too late. It don't take the judge long to marry someone."

"Take these guns," Brad ordered the stage manager, "and see they get safely to the jail." The man nodded vigorously.

"Dobbs?" Brad questioned.

"I'll be all right," he replied. "You just find Shelby. I can take care of myself. For God's sake, don't lose her, Brad. I know how brave she is, but—"

"Don't worry. Dakota, come on. Let's get going."

The three men raced for the stable and their horses. The ride to the judge's house seemed to take forever. But Brad was overjoyed to see the horse and buggy in the yard. They weren't too late. Shelby was just a short way from them.

They dismounted and walked up onto the porch quietly. They had to find out just where Shelby was before they made a move.

Brad went to a lighted window and looked inside. The scene that met his eyes made the rage in him bubble up.

Shelby was lying on the floor. Carl suddenly jerked her to her feet viciously and forced her to stand before the black-clad man Brad assumed was the judge.

Brad turned from the window, motioned Jasper and Dakota to follow him, and went inside. Just in time to hear Carl trying to force Shelby to say the final word.

" 'I do,' Shelby," Carl's voice was merciless and cold.

"I . . . I . . ." Shelby struggled.

"No, she doesn't," Brad said firmly.

Shelby spun around, a smile lighting her face. "Brad."

"Damn you," Carl snarled, "you're too late. The judge has already signed the paper. Shelby and I are legally married."

Jasper moved forward, but Brad put out a hand to stop him.

"She may be a wife now," Brad smiled, but his eyes were like shards of steel, "but she can soon become a widow."

"Let me have that pleasure," Dakota said pleasantly.

"Sorry. It's all mine," Brad advanced toward Carl. Shelby stepped between them, facing Brad.

"Don't waste your time on him. You're here and that's all that matters." Her eyes sparkled. "What took you so long?"

Brad couldn't contain his emotions any longer. He grabbed Shelby in his arms and crushed her to him so hard she half laughed and half gasped.

But Dakota was still looking at Carl. He had a feeling Brad was not quite through with this man and didn't want him making a dash for freedom. Jasper was looking at Carl as if he wanted to separate parts of his body.

After Brad kissed Shelby thoroughly, he gently pushed her away from him. "I have some unfinished business," he explained, smiling at her. Then he turned to face Carl, who suddenly realized there was no escaping the vengeance of the man who walked toward him slowly. He made his last drastic mistake.

"Look! For Christ's sake, she wasn't worth it. I can offer you a lot of money. Just forget this. I—"

Brad leapt upon him before the last words could leave his mouth. He felt a great sense of satisfaction as his fist exploded against Carl's jaw. The judge, pale-faced and shaken, stood by his equally frightened wife while they watched Brad proceed to beat Carl into a whimpering mass.

When he stood over him finally, he was panting from the exertion, but pleased. "Wasn't worth it? My friend, you are a fool. You're not worth the laces in her shoes. I think we can provide the law with a good reason to see you put behind bars for a long, long time."

Jasper came to stand beside Brad. For the first time ever he smiled at Brad. "Not a bad job."

"Felt good," Brad chuckled. He extended his hand to Jasper, who took it in a grip that made Brad wince.

Shelby came to Brad and again he took her in his arms. "I haven't felt so good in a long, long time. What do you say we take you home."

"Home?"

"Temporarily. Until I can settle things and get you back to my place. Then . . . how about a real, proper wedding?"

"Since I proposed to you once and you proposed to me once, I think it's time we considered the matter settled."

"Shelby," Brad laughed, "this time we'll make it permanent."

"Shelby?" Dakota stood beside them. Shelby turned to look at him.

"Dakota. I'm glad you're here," she said softly, understanding at once what he'd done.

"You have to let me say I'm sorry."

"You needn't. You're here and that's what matters. I hope you'll go back with us and be a guest at our wedding. Perhaps," she added gently, "it will give you some ideas."

"Perhaps I will. Thank you, Shelby."

"I think it's time we all go home."

"Let's go back and collect Dobbs. The sooner we go, the sooner I get you tied up tight. I want to get started building our home and I have to find the means."

Shelby tucked her arm in Brad's and they walked to the door. "Speaking of means . . ." she began, and neither of them heard Jasper's soft chuckle as he followed them out . . . dragging the still inert Carl like a sack of spoiled grain.

Epilogue

Winter was Shelby's maid of honor at one of the grandest weddings Charleston had ever seen. Joseph had spared no expense.

Dobbs was more than proud to escort Shelby down the aisle. She was a vision in white, and Brad could feel the beat of his heart as she walked toward him. He could also feel the towering presence of Jasper, who took his position as best man very seriously.

When the pastor had intoned the proper words and it was time to place the ring on Shelby's finger, Brad turned to Jasper, who was fishing in his breast pocket. When he handed the ring to Brad, their eyes met. Jasper, the self-imposed guardian of Shelby's happiness, was giving Brad his final warning. He handed the ring to Brad and watched as Brad slipped it on Shelby's finger.

The reception was large and well attended. Shelby whirled around the dance floor in Brad's arms never feeling happier in her life.

Brad, could not get his concentration on anything

else but Shelby and the need to get her away from the boisterous crowd as soon as he possibly could.

Dakota and Jasper tried to get Brad to match them drink for drink, but Brad only laughed at their efforts. This was one time he had no intention of being out of control. This night was the beginning of his life with Shelby, and it had to be no less than perfect.

They made their escape just before the nearby town bells chimed midnight. Shelby's first surprise was that Brad had booked them passage in a luxurious stateroom on the *River Queen* for a slow, upriver journey to Lake Moultrie where the Stapletons owned a cottage. They would spend a week or two before going home.

They had a late but exquisite candlelit dinner in their stateroom, and made love in the huge four-poster bed.

Later, they lay together in totally contented silence. Through the open, shuttered windows the warm breeze carried the sounds of the paddle wheel as it shushed through the water and the strains of music from the ballroom.

"Happy?" Brad questioned as he brushed a kiss against her hair and drew her tighter to him.

"Deliriously so. But Brad, do you know what will *really* make me happy?"

"What?"

"When you carry me over the threshold of our home. I can't wait to get back."

"To put all your plans to work?" Brad chuckled.

"All *our* plans," Shelby replied firmly.

"You know, I still don't know when or how I lost

that discussion." Brad's voice was tinged with humor. With his arms full of Shelby and all the battles over, the situation was one that he could now look at with amusement.

Shelby looped her arms about his neck and drew his head down for a long, lingering kiss. "It's because you didn't lose," she replied softly. "It's because we both won. What's yours is mine and what's mine is yours. We will make our future together, Mr. Brad Cole, and don't you ever forget it."

"Mrs. Cole, I wouldn't have it any other way. I happen to love you more than anything or anyone else in this world. I have a feeling you and I are going to work things out just fine."

"And I wouldn't have it any other way," she repeated his words. "We land tomorrow. Why don't we catch the first train home from there?"

"Abby, Mary Beth, and Jack won't be back by then. They're staying in Charleston for a while until Mary Beth gets the last of the shopping out of her system."

"I know that," Shelby smiled seductively. "It means we have all those beautiful days and all those starry nights all to ourselves."

"Now that you put it that way, it sounds like a pretty good idea to me."

"Then we'll go tomorrow after the boat docks?"

"Yes. As soon as the boat docks. Shelby . . . you are something pretty special. It's going to take a lifetime to show you how much I love you."

"Then take a lifetime, Brad," Shelby said softly. "And we'll start tonight."

Brad gathered Shelby to him, and the warmth of the kiss grew into a night of brilliant passion.

Just a few days later, Brad swung a laughing Shelby up in his arms, crossed the threshold of their home and closed the door between them and the rest of the world.